BY J. KENNER

THE STARK TRILOGY

Release Me

Claim Me

Complete Me

STARK EVER AFTER NOVELLAS

Take Me

Have Me

Play My Game

Seduce Me

Unwrap Me

STARK INTERNATIONAL NOVELS

Say My Name

On My Knees

Under My Skin

MOST WANTED SERIES

Wanted

Heated

Ignited

stark after dark

stark after dark

A STARK EVER AFTER ANTHOLOGY

J. KENNER

BANTAM BOOKS NEW YORK

2016 Bantam Books Trade Paperback Edition

Take Me copyright © 2013 by Julie Kenner
Have Me copyright © 2014 by Julie Kenner
Play My Game copyright © 2015 by Julie Kenner
Seduce Me copyright © 2015 by Julie Kenner

Published in the United States by Bantam Books, an imprint of Random House, a division of Penguin Random House LLC, New York.

BANTAM BOOKS and the HOUSE colophon are registered trademarks of Penguin Random House LLC.

The novellas contained in this anthology, *Take Me, Have Me, Play My Game,* and *Seduce Me,* were each published separately by Bantam Books, an imprint of Random House, a division of Penguin Random House LLC, in 2013, 2014, 2015, and 2015, respectively.

ISBN 978-0-399-59415-1
eBook ISBN 978-0-399-59416-8

Printed in the United States of America on acid-free paper

randomhousebooks.com

9 8 7 6 5 4 3 2 1

stark after dark

take me

Chapter 1

White.

It is all around me. Soft and billowing. Gentle and soothing.

I am standing in a room, though I can see neither walls nor windows. There is only the endless flow of material. The sensual caress of silk against my body as I move through the drapes that fill the space before me. Hundreds, maybe thousands. They are beautiful. They are perfect. And I am not afraid.

On the contrary, I am perfectly calm. And as I move forward, my bare feet padding softly on the cool floor, I realize that I am heading toward a light. It shines through the diaphanous panels that flutter as I pass, as if struck by an ocean breeze.

I know that I am traveling toward something—*someone*— and I can feel the wellspring of joy rising up inside me. *He* is there. Somewhere beyond this forest of sensuality. Somewhere in the light.

Damien.

I quicken my step, my pulse increasing as I move faster and faster.

I am desperate to see him. To feel his fingertips upon my skin, as gentle as the brush of these curtains against my body. But though I hurry forward, I don't seem to be getting anywhere, and now the soft flutter of the drapes has taken on a menacing quality. As if they are reaching out, clutching me, holding me back.

Panic bubbles inside me; I have to get to him. I have to see him, touch him, and yet no matter how hard I try, I do not seem to be moving forward at all. I'm stuck, and what had only a moment ago seemed like the welcoming beauty of a curtain into heaven now seems like a trap, a trick, a horrible nightmare.

A nightmare.

My pulse quickens as the truth settles over me. I am not in a room; I am in a bed.

I'm not running; I'm sleeping.

This is a dream, a dream, and only a dream. But it is one from which I cannot seem to wake, even though I am moving faster now, clawing my way through these damnable drapes because I am certain—with the kind of certainty that comes only in the world of dreams—that if I can just get through them then I will be free. I will be awake. And I will once again be safe in Damien's arms.

But I cannot get through.

Though I push and shove and beat my way through the gauzy silk—though I run and run until I am certain that my lungs will burst with the exertion—I can get nowhere other than where I already am, and I collapse, defeated, onto the cool ground, my skirt billowing out around me like the petals of a flower.

I tentatively stroke the material. I had not realized when I was running that I was wearing a dress, but this is a dream and

I know better than to think too deeply about the odd parameters of this version of reality. Instead, I focus on gathering myself. On staying calm. On breathing deep. I am no longer moving forward, and that is good, because now that I have come to a stop, the curtains are falling away, drifting gently to the ground only to disappear like cotton candy touching water until there is nothing left but me and this room with white walls that seem to press in around me, moving closer and closer with each breath that I take.

My chest is tight, and when I look down, I realize that my hand is fisted in the silk skirt. There are small yellow and gold flowers embroidered against the white silk at the hem, and the flowers are inset with shimmering white pearls that now feel hard beneath my palm. I glance down at the fitted bodice, the perfection of the silk, the gentle pressure of the stays.

I am in my wedding gown, and for a moment, that reality soothes me. *Damien,* I think again. He is not beside me, but I know that he is with me. This man—this incredible man who will soon be my husband.

Just the thought of him calms me, and I am able to breathe more easily. I can continue, I can move. I can stand and go forward and leave this room.

I can go into Damien's arms.

I start to do exactly that, shifting my weight so that I can rise to my feet.

That's when I see the stain.

A blur of pink rising up from the pure white silk of the skirt. It is so faint that at first I think it must be a trick of the light. But then the hue deepens, shifting from pink to red as it spreads out, tainting the purity of my beautiful dress.

Blood.

Frantic now, I scramble backward, as if I can somehow escape the stain despite the fact that I am wearing it. But of course there is no escape, and I claw at the skirt, trying to yank it up, trying to see beneath it. Trying desperately to find the source of the blood.

I can't. My hands are too slippery. Red and wet and stained. I rub them on the skirt, trying to clean them. My breath is coming in gasps, my pulse pounding so loudly in my ears I can hear nothing but my own blood flowing through my veins. That same blood that is coating me, escaping me.

No, no, oh, god, no.

But it is true—I am certain of it. The blood on the skirt is mine, and with one final, desperate jerk, I draw the material up, tugging at the silk and satin and lace until it is gathered around my waist and I can see my legs, bare and slick with blood.

I hear a noise—a gasp. It came from me, and I'm rubbing at the blood, searching for the source. I'm on my knees, my thighs pressed together, but now I separate them, and I see the scars that have for so many years marred the soft flesh of my inner thighs. Self-inflicted wounds made by the pressure of a blade held tight in my hands.

I remember the sweet intensity of that first slice. The glorious heat when steel penetrates flesh. The relief that comes with the pain, like the screech of a boiling kettle when it finally releases steam.

I remember the pain, but I no longer need it. That is what I tell myself. I don't need the wounds; I don't want the pain.

I don't need to cut anymore.

I'm better now. I have Damien to hold me tight. To keep me centered and safe and whole.

But there is no denying the blood. And as I look down at the open wound—at the raw and mangled flesh, and at the blood that pools around me, so sticky and pungent—I feel the tightness building in my chest and the rawness in my throat.

Then, finally, I hear myself scream.

Chapter 2

I come awake in Damien's arms, my throat raw from the violent sound that had been wrenched from it. My face is pressed to his bare chest, and I sob, my breath coming now in gasps and gulps.

His hands stroke my shoulders, the movement both strong and soothing, possessive and protective. He is saying my name, "Nikki, Nikki, shhh, it's okay, baby, it's okay," but what I hear is that I am safe. That I am loved.

That I am his.

My tears slow and I breathe deep. I concentrate on his touch. On his voice. On his scent, sexy and familiar and desperately male.

I focus on all the little things that make up the bits and pieces of this man I love. All the things that make him who he is, that give him the power to calm me. To look my demons in the face and send them scurrying. He is a miracle, and the biggest miracle of all is that he is mine.

I open my eyes, then lean back as I tilt my head up. Even thrust out of sleep as he was, he is exceptional, and I drink in the vision of him, letting the beauty of this man soothe my parched soul. My breath hitches as I look into his eyes, those magical dual-colored eyes that show so much—passion, concern, determination. And most of all, love.

"Damien," I whisper, and am rewarded with the ghost of a smile upon his lips.

"There she is." Gently he strokes my cheek, brushing my hair back from my face. "Do you want to tell me about it?"

I shake my head in the negative, but even as I do, I hear myself say a single word, "Blood."

Immediately, I see the worry prick in his eyes.

"It was just a dream," I say, but I don't completely believe it.

"Not a dream," he corrects. "A nightmare. And this isn't the first."

"No," I admit. When the nightmares started, they weren't even truly nightmares. Just a vague sense of unease upon waking. More recently, I've jerked awake during the night with my heart pounding in my chest and my hair damp with sweat. This, however, was the first dream with blood.

I pull back more and sit up straighter, clutching the sheet around me, as if it offers protection from the nightmares, too. I twine my fingers with his and our legs are still touching. I do not want to think about the dreams, but if I must, then I need Damien's touch to anchor me.

"Did you cut?"

I shake my head. "No. Except—except I must have. Because it wasn't scars on my legs, but wounds. And they were open. And there was blood everywhere and—"

He silences me with a kiss, so deep and firm and demanding that I cannot hold on to my fear. Instead, he fills my mind with a raging heat so intense that it destroys everything except Nikki and Damien and the passion that is constantly smoldering between us, ready to ignite at the slightest provocation. Ready to burn away anything that threatens this life that we are building together, be it the ghosts of our pasts or my fears of the future.

My fears of the future?

I turn the words over in my head, and realize with a violent shock that they hold the weight of truth. The realization baffles me, because I am not afraid of being Mrs. Damien Stark. On the contrary, I think that being Damien's wife is the thing in this world that scares me the least. It is what and who I am meant to be, and I am never more certain of that than when I am in his arms.

Is that it, then? Am I afraid of the span between now and "Do you take this man"?

His thumb gently brushes my lower lip, and I see the knowing glint in his eyes. "Tell me," he says, in the kind of voice that allows no refusal.

"Maybe they're portents," I whisper. "The dreams, I mean." The words feel foolish on my lips, but I must say them. I can't hold the fear inside. Not when I'm certain that Damien can turn it around.

"Portents?" he repeats. "Like a bad omen?"

I nod.

"Of what?" His brow rises. "That we shouldn't get married?"

I hear the tease in his voice, but even so, my response is both violent and firm. "God no!"

"That I will hurt you?"

"You could never hurt me," I say. "Not the way you mean." We both know that there have been times when I have needed the pain—when I would have once again taken a blade to my flesh if Damien had not been there. But he is here, and he is all that I need now.

"Then what?" he asks as he gently lifts our joined hands to his lips. Softly, he dots kisses along my knuckles, and the sweet sensation distracts me.

"I don't know."

"I do," he says, and there is such certainty in his voice that I feel calmer. "You're a bride, Nikki. You're nervous." He presses a playful kiss to the end of my nose. "I think you're supposed to be."

"No." I shake my head. "No, that's not—" But I go no further. Because the truth is that he may be right. Bridal jitters? Could it really be as simple as that?

"But there's nothing to be nervous about," he says, even as his hands go to my shoulders, even as he gently slides his palms down my arms, making the thin sheet drop away.

I am naked, and I shiver. Not from the slight chill in the air, but from the longing in Damien's eyes. A longing to which I so willingly surrender.

"What is it they say about marriage? That the bride and the groom are becoming one?" He trails a fingertip lightly over my collarbone, then down slowly, the touch butterfly soft, until he reaches my breast. "That isn't true for us, baby. It's not true because we already are one, you and I, and this wedding is just a formality."

"Yes," I say, my voice little more than breath.

His hand cups my breast as his thumb rubs idly over my hard, tight nipple. The touch is so soft, and yet I feel its echo throughout the whole of my body. Just one simple brush of flesh against flesh, but it is not simple at all, because it holds the power to destroy me. To rip me apart and put me back together.

I close my eyes in surrender and in welcome, then lie back as Damien guides me down onto the bed. He pulls the sheet away, leaving me exposed, and then I feel the bed shift as he moves to straddle me. He is naked and the hard steel of his erection presses against my thighs, hot and needy. I reach for him and cup my hands on his tight, firm ass. He is not inside me—he is not even stroking my sex—and yet I am awash in awareness, my muscles clenching with desire for him, my hips writhing in wanton, unashamed need.

"Damien," I murmur, then open my eyes to see him above me, his eyes soft as he gazes upon my face.

"No," he says. "Close your eyes. Let me give this to you. Let me show you just how well I know you. How intimately I know your body. Because it's not just yours—it's mine, too. And I intend to show you how very well—and how very thoroughly—I take care of what is mine."

"Do you think I don't already know that?"

He doesn't answer with words, but the soft brush of his lips over mine is all the response I need. Slowly, he trails gentle kisses down the arch of my neck, then lower still until his mouth closes roughly over my breast. My nipple is already tight and hard and so very sensitive, and he drags his teeth over it.

I arch up as little shock waves shoot through me to pool like warm liquid in my womb. The muscles of my sex clench with longing. I want him inside me—I want it desperately. But he is not even touching me there. He's not touching me anywhere except on my breast, where he is suckling and biting, tasting and teasing. He is erasing everything—thought, worries, fears—until I am reduced to that one point of pleasure that seems to fill me, dazzling me from the inside, sparking and singing until I am certain that I am going to come simply from the sensation of his mouth upon my breast.

Slowly—so painfully slowly—he moves his mouth away from my breast and then kisses his way down my midline. He pauses at my navel, his tongue teasing me, the touch almost a tickle, but far more sensual. He slides a hand under my lower back, and I arch up as he nips at me, tiny bites and the scrape of teeth against the soft skin of my belly.

He has moved down the bed, and my legs are spread wide. He is between them, but he is not touching my sex. He's not even stroking my thighs. He has one hand beneath my back and the other on the mattress beside my hip for balance. But there is heat coming off of him, and the triangle made up of my thighs and sex seems on fire. I am alive with need, with desire, with want.

And yet Damien makes no move to satisfy me. He is content to tease and torment, and as he slowly traces the shape of my navel with the tip of his tongue, I moan in both pleasure and frustration.

"You like that?" he asks.

"Yes," I murmur.

"So do I." His voice is low and reverent. "You taste like candy."

"Candy is bad for you," I tease.

"In that case," he says with a low growl, "I like being bad."

"Me, too," I whisper, even as my hips rise in unspoken demand. "But, Damien—"

"You want more," he says, finishing my thought. He kisses the top of my pubic bone, then trails his lips over the bone of my hip, following it down to the juncture of my thigh.

"Yes, oh, god, yes."

"And if I'm not done tasting you? If I want to kiss and suck and tease every inch of your body? If I want to have my fill of you before I thrust myself deep inside of you? Before we get lost together? Before I let you come?"

He lifts himself up, then bends over me, so close that I am certain he will kiss me, so near that we are breathing the same air.

Then he shifts away, moving his mouth to my temple. His lips brush lightly over my skin before he whispers, "I will always give you more, baby, but first I want you ready, I want you hot, I want you desperate."

"I am." The words are wrenched from me, and as Damien pulls away, I see the smug smile pull at his mouth.

"You are," he says. "But you also asked for more. And that, my darling Nikki, is a demand I'm always happy to satisfy. The question is, more what?" His mouth closes over my breast, and I cry out as he bites my nipple. "More pain?"

I cannot answer; my body is reeling from the erotic storm he is conjuring inside me.

"More pleasure?" he asks. He slides farther down my body, and this time skin does touch skin, the contact making the embers within me burst into raging flames. His lips move down between my breasts, then lower and lower until he reaches my clit. He blows gently on my sex even as he places his palms firmly on my inner thighs, spreading me wide. He takes one hand away, then strokes his finger gently over my slick, hot sex.

I tremble, so close I think that if he breathes on my clit, I will come.

"More anticipation?" And then his mouth is moving again, tracing down my leg, over the scars on my inner thigh, to that sensitive spot behind my knee. I am lost, melting. I am his to control, to command, and I can do nothing but absorb the pleasure with which he is bombarding me.

He continues on, lower still, until he reaches my ankle, then the sole of my foot. He drags the tip of his finger from heel to toe, and my foot arches in response, along with my back. My sex clenches greedily, and I am astounded at the reaction from a simple touch upon my foot. Then again, how can I be astounded by my reaction to any touch rendered by Damien? I can't. I can only surrender, which was of course Damien's plan all along. To take me away from myself and bring me to this place that we share, a place where there is only Nikki and Damien and the pleasure we find in each other.

He is not done with me, and he slowly trails kisses up my leg until I am squirming, my hips gyrating in both pleasure and need. I want more. I want it all. And, miracle of miracles, Damien finally gives it to me. His tongue flicks gently over my clit, just the tiniest of touches, but he has primed me so thoroughly that I explode, shock waves shooting out to my fingers and toes, pleasure spiraling through me.

A tiny touch, yes, but also just the beginning. He closes his mouth over my sex, sucking and teasing. He holds my legs wide so that I cannot shift or move. He doesn't relent, making my orgasm grow and grow until there is torment behind the pleasure, until I am ripped open and needy, desperate for him to come to this place with me, to find me in the stars.

"Now, Damien. I need you inside me now."

This time, thank god, he doesn't hesitate, but neither is he gentle. He is on his knees, and he turns me onto my side. He straddles one of my legs, but hooks my other over his opposite hip, then holds me steady with his palm on my outer thigh. His other hand is cupped on my ass, but he slips down so that he teases the rim of my anus even as he thrusts deep inside my cunt.

This is not a position he's taken me in before, and the sensation of my legs being scissored, of his hand and cock so intimately on me, of the way he is kneeling against me, his body as erect as his cock while I lie prone like a vestal offering, is astoundingly exciting, and as he moves inside me, I feel the orgasm rise within me again.

I close my eyes, letting the sensations flow through and around me. It is magical, this feeling. Being so open to Damien. Being so joined with Damien. *Joined.* In sex, in life, in marriage.

A shiver runs through me, and I hear Damien moan as the muscles of my vagina tighten around him, drawing him deeper and deeper into me.

"That's it, baby. Open your eyes."

I do, and see him looking not at me, but at the juncture of our bodies. I am watching his face—watching the passion build—and when he moves his gaze and meets my eyes, the storm I see building there nearly does me in. I am breathing hard in time with the waves of pleasure that crash through me. The same pleasure I see on his face, driven by the same heat I see burning in his eyes.

A heat that is melting me.

That is ripping me apart.

That is going to shatter us both, I think, as the climax breaks over me and I arch back, held in place by Damien's body and hand as my sex clenches tighter and tighter around him, milking him to his own fantastical release.

Reality returns slowly, like stars appearing in a newly dark sky.

For a moment I have to wonder if I have melted, but it is

only the limbless feeling that comes with a release born of pure pleasure.

Damien pulls out, and I mourn the loss of our connection, at least until he lies beside me, our arms and legs a tangle, our faces close. "Thank you," I murmur.

"For what?"

"For distracting me. From my nightmare."

He laughs. "I didn't realize I was that transparent."

"Only to me. Like you said, we know each other."

He kisses the tip of my nose. "You have nothing to be nervous about."

I nod, but the truth is that he is wrong. I realize it now. I want this wedding to be a reflection to the world. An outward manifestation of what he and I are together. Beauty and grace and something special and unique. I want it for him. For us. And for the whole damn world.

And so yes, I am nervous.

"I want the wedding to be perfect," I confess.

"It will be," he assures me. "How can it be anything else? Because no matter what happens, the wedding will end with you being my wife. And that, my darling Nikki, is the only thing that matters."

I brush a kiss over his lips, because he's right. I mean, I know that he's right.

But I also know that he's forgetting about the cake and the dress and the band and the photographer and the tents and the tables and the champagne and on and on and on.

Men, I think, and then snuggle close, reluctantly acknowledging that for tonight, at least, he's distracted me.

For tonight, I care only about this man who will soon be my husband—and who already is my life.

Chapter 3

I awake to an empty bed and the smell of frying bacon. I roll over to find my phone on the bedside table, then glance at the time. Not yet six.

I groan and fall back among the pillows, but I don't really want to go back to sleep. What I want is Damien.

I slide out of bed, then grab the tank top and yoga pants I'd left draped across a nearby armchair. I head barefoot out of the bedroom and move the short distance down the hall to the third-floor kitchen.

We're in Damien's Malibu house, and the wall of windows that faces the ocean is wide open, the glass panels having been thrust aside to let in the breeze. The smell of the ocean mingles with the scent of breakfast and I breathe deep, realizing that I am content. Whatever demons had poked at me during the night, Damien effectively banished them.

I glance toward the windows and out at the darkened Pacific. Waves glow white in the fading moonlight as they break upon the shore. There is beauty there, and part of me wants to walk to the balcony and stare out at the roiling, frothing water. But the siren call of the ocean is nothing compared with my desire to see Damien, and so I turn away from the windows and head straight to the kitchen. It is larger than the one in the condo I used to share with my best friend, Jamie, and it is not even the primary kitchen for this house. That is on the first floor, and could easily service a one-hundred-table restaurant. But this—the "small" kitchen—was installed as an adjunct to the open area that serves as a venue for entertaining, and since it is just down the hall from our bedroom, Damien and I have gotten into the habit of cooking our meals and eating in this cozier, more informal area. Usually we're joined by Lady Meow-Meow, the fluffy white cat I took custody of when

Jamie moved out. I know Lady M misses Jamie, but she's also enjoying having the run of this huge house, and Gregory—the valet, butler, and all around house-running guy—spoils her rotten.

Now I lean against the half wall that marks the break from hallway to kitchen. Damien is standing at the stove cooking an omelette as if he were nothing more than an ordinary guy. Except there is nothing ordinary about Damien Stark. He is grace and power, beauty and heat. He is exceptional, and he has captured me completely.

At the moment, he is shirtless, and I cannot help the way my breath stutters as my eyes skim over the defined muscles of his back and his taut, strong arms. Damien's first fortune came not from business, but from his original career as a champion tennis player. Even now, years later, he has both the look and the power of an elite athlete.

I let my gaze drift down appreciatively. He is wearing simple gray sweatpants that sit low on his narrow hips and cling to the curves of his perfectly toned ass. Like me, he is barefoot. He looks young and sexy and completely delicious. Yet despite his casual appearance, I can still see the executive. The powerful businessman who harnessed the world, who shifted it to his own liking and made a fortune in the process. He is strength and control. And I am humbled by the knowledge that I am what he values most of all, and that I will spend the rest of my life at his side.

"You're staring," he says, his eyes still on the stove.

I grin happily, like a child. "I enjoy looking at pretty things."

He turns now, and his eyes rake over me, starting at my toes. "So do I," he says when his gaze reaches my face, and there is so much heat in his voice that my legs go weak and my body quivers with want. His mouth curves into a slow, sexy smile, and I am absolutely certain in that moment that I am going to melt. "You spoiled my surprise," he says, then nods toward the breakfast table where a tray sits with a glass bud vase displaying a single red rose. "Breakfast in bed."

"How about we share breakfast at the table?" I move to him, then stand behind him with my arms around his waist. I gently kiss his shoulder and breathe in the clean, soapy scent. "Early meeting?" Damien is hardly a slacker, but he usually doesn't go into his office until after nine. Instead, he works from home, then showers after a brief workout before heading downtown. Today, apparently, we're operating on a compressed timeline.

"Not early," he says. "But also not here. I've got a meeting in Palm Springs. The helicopter's coming in twenty."

"I've got an appointment in Switzerland," I counter airily as I step back so he can finish putting our breakfast together. "The jet's coming in an hour."

His mouth twitches with amusement. The omelette is already on a plate, and now he adds the bacon. I follow him to the table, pour us both orange juice and coffee, then sit across from him. Putting a napkin in my lap, I realize I'm smiling like an idiot. And the best part? Damien's smile matches mine.

"I love this," I say. "Breakfast together. Domesticity. It feels nice."

He sips his coffee, his eyes never leaving my face, and for a moment there is nothing between us but contentment. Then he tilts his head, and I see the question rising in his eyes. I should have expected it. Damien wouldn't leave for a meeting without being absolutely certain that I am okay. "No more shadows this morning?" he asks.

"No," I say truthfully. "I feel good." I take a bite of the omelette we're sharing, and sag a bit in my chair in ecstasy. I'm a lucky girl in so many ways, not the least of which being that my fiancé can cook. "How could I not with you taking such good care of me?"

As I hoped, my words bring a smile to his lips. But worry still lingers in his eyes, and I reach across the table to squeeze his hand. "Really," I say firmly. "I'm fine. It's like I told you—I want this wedding to be perfect, which is ironic considering that I've spent my whole life trying to escape from my mother's plan to mold me into Perfectly Plastic Nikki." I immediately regret mentioning my mother. After years of playing the good and dutiful daughter, I've finally come to terms with the fact that my mother is a raging bitch—one who also happens to despise my boyfriend. She made my childhood miserable, and while I am fully prepared to accept the responsibility for my cutting, there's not a shrink in the world who wouldn't agree that the causative threads of that particular vice lead back to Elizabeth Fairchild and her various quirks and neuroses.

"You're not your mother," Damien says firmly. "And there isn't a bride in the world who doesn't want her wedding to be everything she's dreamed of."

"And the groom?" I ask.

"The groom will be happy if the bride is. And so long as she says 'I do.' And when he can call her Mrs. Damien Stark. And once we get to the honeymoon."

I'm laughing by the time he finishes. "Thank you."

"For putting up with your wedding jitters?"

"For everything."

He stands and refills my coffee before clearing the table. "Is there anything you need my help with today?"

"Nope."

"We're getting married on Saturday," he says, as if this was news to me, but the words make my supposedly nonexistent jitters start jittering again. "If you need Sylvia's help, just ask," he adds, referring to his supremely efficient assistant.

I shake my head and flash him my picture-perfect smile. "Thanks, but I'm good. Everything is on track."

"You've taken on a lot," he says. "More than you had to."

I tilt my head, but stay silent. This is a conversation we've had before, and I don't intend to have it again.

We'd traveled across Europe for a month after he proposed, and while we were there, he'd suggested we simply do it. Get married on a mountaintop or on the sands of the Côte d'Azur. Return to the States as Mr. and Mrs. Damien Stark.

I'd said no.

I want nothing more than to be Damien's wife, but the truth is that I also want the fairy-tale wedding. I want to be the princess in white walking down the aisle in my beautiful gown on my special day. I may not agree with my mother about much, but I remember the care that she and my sister put into Ashley's wedding. I'd envied my sister a lot of things, not really understanding that she'd had her own demons to battle, and when she walked down the aisle on a pathway of rose petals, my eyes filled with tears and my one thought had been, *Someday. Someday I will find the man who will be waiting for me at the end of that aisle with love in his eyes.*

And it wasn't just my own desire for the fantasy wedding that made me insist we wait. Like it or not, Damien is a public figure, and I knew that the press would be covering our wedding. It didn't need to be the fanciest affair—in fact, I wanted it outside on the beach—but I did want it to be a beautiful celebration. And since I knew the paparazzi would be pulling out all the stops to get tacky pictures, I wanted a collection of portraits and candid shots that we controlled. Fabulous pictures that we could give to the legitimate press, outshining—I hoped—whatever ended up in the tabloids.

More than anything, though, I wanted the story and photographs to overshadow the horrible things printed just a few months ago, when Damien had been on trial for murder. I wanted to see the best day of our lives on those pages in sharp counterpoint to and in triumph over the worst days.

I have said all of this to Damien, and while I know he doesn't fully agree with my reasons for needing this wedding, I also know he understands them.

As for me, I understand his fear that I've taken on too much. But this is my wedding we're talking about. The nightmares are only my fears; they are not my reality. I can handle it; I can handle anything if the end result is walking down that aisle toward Damien.

"Everything is going great," I say to reassure us both. "I've got it all under control. Really."

"You found a photographer?"

"Are you kidding? Of course." It is a lie. And that's a risk, because Damien can read me better than anyone. I force myself not to hold my breath as I wait for him to ask me details—name, studio, credentials. Those are questions I can't answer because the truth is, I *haven't* found a photographer to replace the one Damien fired last week after we learned the man had made an under-the-table agreement to sell unapproved candid photos of the wedding and reception to TMZ.

And that's not even our only problem. I found out yesterday that the lead singer for the band I'd lined up had decided to drop everything and move back home to Canada, which means we are now entirely without entertainment.

I need to get off my ass and find someone—and I need to do it fast. As Damien had so kindly reminded me, the wedding is just a few days away.

But, hey, it's not like I'm feeling stressed or anything.

I frown, realizing that maybe there is a solid explanation for my nightmares, after all.

"What is it?" Damien asks, and I fear that despite all my efforts to keep these minor ripples in the wedding planning out of his hair, it's about to get gnarly.

"Nothing," I say. "Just thinking about my massive to-do list."

I can tell by his expression that he doesn't buy it. But I am a bride, and like most grooms, he knows innately that "handle with care" is standard operating procedure. "In case it escaped your notice, we have the cash to pay someone to help you. Use it if you need it."

"What? Like a wedding planner?" I shake my head. "For one thing, the wedding's too close for that. For another, as I keep telling you, I want to do this myself. I want it to reflect us, not the latest fad in weddings."

"I get that," he says, "but you've taken on a hell of a lot."

"You've helped," I respond.

He chuckles. "As much as you've let me."

I lift a shoulder. "You have a universe to run."

It's a simple fact that I have more time than Damien. I'm juggling only one small business, which has exactly one employee—me. He's running Stark International, which has about as many people as an emerging country. Maybe more. And, yes, I have been busy, but that's partly because Damien didn't want a long engagement. And since I didn't think I could stand waiting, either, I was happy to agree.

It's been three months since he proposed, two months and twenty-nine days since I started diving into planning and prep, balancing my software development business against the business of my wedding. I'm proud of what's come together, and I'm even more proud that I've done so much of it on my own. Hell, I've actually been getting some use out of all those etiquette classes my mother forced me to sit through. Imagine that.

I aim an impish smile at him. "Maybe you're right. I mean, it is a bit stressful doing everything so fast, but I'm actually having a lot of fun working out the details of decorating the beach and organizing the caterer and pulling all the pieces together. I suppose we could push the wedding back a few months to make things even easier on me."

His eyes narrow dangerously. "Don't even joke about that. Not unless you want me to scoop you up, toss you on the helicopter, and elope to Mexico. Which, for the record, I still think is a fantastic idea."

"Vegas would be easier," I tease.

"There's no beach in Vegas," he says, his expression going soft. "Even if I'm kidnapping you, I won't deny you the surf or the sunset."

I sigh and fold myself into his arms. "Do you have any idea how much I love you?"

"Enough to marry me," he says.

"And then some."

He hooks his arm around my waist and tugs me close, then brushes his lips over mine. The kiss starts softly, a feather-touch, a tease. But there's no denying the heat between us, and soon I am moaning, my mouth open to him, his lips hard against mine, taking and tasting. He pulls me closer to him, my name like a whisper on his lips, and the embers that are always burning between us burst into white-hot flames.

His hand slides along my back, then under my tank top at its base. The sensation of skin upon skin is delicious, and I sigh with pleasure, then gasp with longing as those clever fingers slip beneath the waistband of my yoga pants and curve over my rear. He tugs me closer, his erection hot and hard between us, as his fingers slip inside me. I'm liquid heat, and I want nothing more than to strip us both bare and let him take me right here, on the hardwood floor.

Passion thrums through me, and I swear I can feel the house vibrating around us.

It takes me a moment to realize that the thrum isn't entirely the result of my lust for my fiancé—it's the arrival of his ride, the helicopter approaching from the north to settle on the helipad that Damien installed on the property.

I pull away, breathless. "You're going to be late, Mr. Stark."

"Sadly, you have a point." He kisses the corner of my mouth, and the pressure of his tongue at that sensitive juncture is almost as enticing as the feel of his erection hard against me. "Are you sure you don't want to come with me today?" he asks. "I don't think I've ever fucked you in the helicopter."

I laugh. "It's on my bucket list," I assure him. "But today's not the day. I'm meeting with the cake lady." Rather than a regular wedding cake, I'd decided to go with tiers of cupcakes, with only the top layer being the traditional cake with fondant icing. The baker, a celebrity chef named Sally Love, came up with an exceptional design for the icing on each individual cake, and she's going to incorporate real flowers on the tiers, making the overall design both elegant and fun. Not to mention tasty. Damien and I went together to pick out the flavor for the top layer, and also selected ten possible flavors for the cupcakes. Today, I'm going back to narrow the ten finalists to the final five.

"Do you need me?" he asks.

"Always," I say. "But not at the bakery. You did your part, I'm just finalizing the cupcake choices."

"Don't ditch my tiny cheesecakes," he says.

"I wouldn't dare."

"Is Jamie going with you?"

"Not today," I say. My best friend and former roommate recently moved back home to Texas for the express purpose of getting her shit together. She'd come back three days ago determined to be the best maid of honor ever—which meant that I'd had to field a full hour of apology when she explained to me why she might not make it to the bakery today. "She drove up to Oxnard last night, and she's not sure when she'll get back today. She did a play there a few years ago, and the director's a friend who now does commercials, and . . ." I trail off with a shrug, but I'm sure Damien understands. Jamie's still trying to land a gig.

"And if she gets a job?" he asks.

I shrug again. I'm torn between wanting her to be cast and wanting her to take as much time as she needs to get her head back on straight. I miss Jamie, but Hollywood pretty much ate her up and spat her out, and although my best friend likes to pretend like she's tough enough to take it, underneath the care-less sex kitten veneer is the heart of a fragile woman. And it's a heart I don't want to see broken.

Damien kisses my forehead. "Whatever happens, she has you. That makes her one step ahead of the game already."

I smile up at him. "Will you be back tonight?"

"Late," he says, then trails a fingertip over my bare shoulder. "If you're sleeping, I'll wake you."

"I look forward to it," I say, then tilt my head up for a quick kiss on my lips. "You better go get dressed, Mr. Stark," I say, then push him off toward the bedroom. He's back remarkably fast, securing his cuffs as he walks toward me, then taking my hand as he tugs me onto the balcony with him. I follow him down the staircase and along the path toward the helipad.

We pause at the edge, and he kisses me gently one last time. "Soon, Ms. Fairchild," he says, but what I hear is *I love you.*

I watch as he bends over and hurries under the spinning blades to board the helicopter, which has *SI* emblazoned on the side. Stark International. I grin, thinking that *SU* would be more appropriate—Stark Universe. Or Stark World. Damien is, after all, my whole world.

I shield my face from the wind, then watch as the bird rises, taking Damien away from me. I know he'll be back tonight, but already I feel hollow.

I consider going inside to get dressed, but instead I follow the flagstone path that cuts through the property until it reaches the beach. I walk along the sandy shore, imagining my wedding. We've planned it for sunset, with a party to follow. Considering who Damien is, the guest list is relatively small. We've invited our mutual friends as well as a number of key employees of Stark International, Stark Applied Technology, and the rest of Damien's subsidiaries. Also, some of the recipients of grants from Damien's various charitable organizations.

The ceremony itself is going to be short and simple, with Damien and I having only a best man and a maid of honor, respectively. Since my father ran off ages ago, I don't have a man to walk me down the aisle. I considered asking one of my best friends, Ollie, but even though he and Damien have negotiated a truce, I didn't want to risk marring my wedding day with drama.

And there's no way I'm having my mother do it. How could I stand to have her give me away when I've spent the last few years running from her? I have not, in fact, even invited her to the wedding. Which means I have no parent to give me away. So I'm going to walk myself down the aisle, a journey on a pathway of rose petals, with Damien Stark standing tall and elegant at the end of it.

We've written vows—short and sweet—and we both agree that what is important is getting to the meat of the ceremony: *Do you take this man? Do you take this woman? I do, I do, dear god, I do.*

The reception is a different story—*that* we expect to go on all night. Maybe even into the next day. After Damien and I head out on our honeymoon after the appropriate socializing and cake-eating interval, Jamie is taking charge of the Malibu house and she, with the help of Ryan Hunter and the rest of the Stark International security team, will make sure that anyone who needs a place to crash has one, and anyone who needs a lift home gets one.

Even though we'll be off on our honeymoon for most of it, it is the details of the reception that have been occupying most of my time. I've arranged for tents, dance floors, lanterns, and heaters. There will be a buffet, three bars, and a chocolate fondue station provided by Damien's best man, his childhood friend Alaine Beauchene. I'm a little flummoxed by my music conundrum, but I'm revved up and eager to solve it, and I tell myself that by the end of the day I will have arranged both the music and the photographer. I am nothing if not optimistic.

Other than that, the only major things still needing to be wrapped up are finalizing the cake—which I'll do in a few hours—and then the final dress fitting. The dress is a Phillipe Favreau original that we purchased in Paris after hours of conversation with Phillipe himself. It is insanely expensive, but as Damien reminded me, there's very little point in having gazillions of dollars if you don't enjoy them. And I really did fall in love with the design.

Phillipe is custom-making it for me, and it is being shipped from his Paris studio. There were some nerve-racking delays, but I've been assured that all is on schedule now, and it is set to arrive at his Rodeo Drive boutique tomorrow morning. His most trusted associate will make any final alterations tomorrow afternoon and deliver it the next morning—Friday—so that it will be locked up safe in the Malibu house, all ready to transform me into a bride on Saturday.

All in all, things are going reasonably smoothly, and I can't help but smile. So what if I've had a few nightmares? For the most part, I'm kicking serious wedding butt, and I don't intend to stop.

I breathe deep, content, then fling my feet through the surf, sending the water sparkling. *Mrs. Damien Stark.*

Honestly, I can't wait.

"Ms. Fairchild!"

I look up to see Tony, one of Damien's security guys, hurrying down the beach toward me.

"What's wrong?"

"I'm sorry, Ms. Fairchild, I tried your phone but there was no answer."

My phone, I remember, is by the bed. "What is it?" I ask, alarmed. "Is it Damien?"

"No, no, nothing like that. But there is a woman at the gate," he says, referring to the gate that Damien had installed at the property entrance after the paparazzi got all crazy during his murder trial. "Ordinarily, I would simply send her away and insist that she make an appointment, but under the circumstances . . ."

"What circumstances?"

"Ms. Fairchild," he says, "the lady says that she's your mother."

Chapter 4

My mother.

My mother.

Holy shit, my mother?

My knees go watery and I have to force my arms to stay at my sides so I don't reach out automatically for Tony. There's nothing on the beach that I can use to steady myself, and right now I really need steadying, so I stand perfectly still and smile and hope Tony doesn't yet know me well enough to pick up on the fact that I'm totally and completely freaking out.

"I wasn't expecting my mother," I manage to say. "She lives in Texas."

"I knew she was from out of state, Ms. Fairchild. I checked the lady's ID. Elizabeth Regina Fairchild, address in Dallas. I assume she's here for the wedding."

"Right. I just—she's not supposed to be here until Friday," I lie. I conjure what I hope is a bright smile, but I fear it looks like something out of a low-budget Halloween thriller. "So, right. I guess tell her to drive on up to the house. If you could buzz Gregory and ask him to settle her in the first-floor parlor, I'll run in and get dressed," I add.

"Of course, Ms. Fairchild." If he has picked up on my nerves, he is either kind enough or well trained enough not to say anything.

I hurry back up the path and take the stairs to the third floor. I want to ensure that I don't see my mother until I'm dressed and made-up and looking polished and pretty enough that maybe—*maybe*—she'll wait an hour or two before she starts in on me.

Once I'm in the bedroom, the first thing I do is grab my phone off the table and dial Damien. The second thing I do is end the call before it has the chance to connect.

I sit on the edge of the bed and suck in air. My heart is pounding so hard, my chest hurts, and I am holding my phone so tightly in my right hand that it is making indentations into my palm. My left hand is curled in on itself, and I concentrate on the sensation of my fingernails digging into my palm. I imagine my nails cutting through skin, drawing blood. I focus on the pain—and then, disgusted with myself, I hurl my other arm back and toss my phone across the room. It shatters from the impact, an explosion of plastic and glass, a smorgasbord of sharp edges now glittering on the floor, tempting and teasing me.

I rise, but I am not heading toward those shards. I will not touch them, not even to sweep them away. They are too tempting, and despite the fact that I've grown stronger in my months with Damien, I do not trust myself. Not now. Not with Elizabeth Fairchild just two floors below, waiting like a spider to draw me in, wrap me up, and suck the life right out of me.

Shit.

My mother.

The woman who locked me in a dark, windowless room as

a child so that I had no choice but to get my beauty sleep. Who controlled what I ate so meticulously that I didn't make the acquaintance of a carb until college.

The woman whose image of feminine perfection was so expertly pounded into her daughters' heads that my sister committed suicide when her husband left her, because she'd clearly failed at being a wife.

The woman who said that I was a fool to stay with Damien. That once you passed the ten-million-dollar mark one man is pretty much like another, and I should move on to one who came with less baggage.

The woman who said that I'd ruined the family name by posing for a nude portrait.

The woman who'd called me a whore.

I didn't want to see her. More than that, I wasn't sure I *could* see her and manage to stay centered.

I needed Damien—I *wanted* Damien. He was my strength, my anchor.

But he wasn't in town and my mother was downstairs. And while I knew that one phone call would have him returning within the hour, I couldn't bring myself to go to the kitchen, pick up the house phone, and make that call.

I could do this on my own—I had to.

And with Damien's voice in my head, I knew that I'd survive.

At least, I hoped I would.

"Well, look at you!" My mother rises from the white sofa, then smoothes her linen skirt before coming toward me, her arms out to enfold me in a hug that is capped off by her trademark air kiss. "I was beginning to think you were going to leave me down here all alone." She speaks lightly, but I can hear the indictment in her words—I left her unattended, and broke one of the cardinal rules from the Elizabeth Fairchild Guide to Playing Hostess.

I say nothing, just stand stiffly in her embrace. A moment passes, and I decide to make an effort. I awkwardly put my arms around her and give her a small squeeze. "Mother," I say, and then stop. Honestly, what more is there to say?

"Married," she says, and there is actually a wistful tone in her voice. For a moment, I wonder about her motive for coming. Is she here because she honestly wants to celebrate my marriage? I'm not quite able to wrap my head around the possibility, and yet I can't help the tiny flame of hope that flickers inside me.

She steps back and looks me up and down. I've taken the time to shower and change and put on my makeup, and I know exactly what she sees as she looks at me. My blond hair is still short, though it has grown out since I took scissors to it and violently whacked off large chunks after the last time I saw her. I like this new shoulder-length style. Not only is it nice not to have the weight of all that hair, but the curls are bouncier and frame my face in a way that I like.

I'm wearing a simple linen skirt that hits just above my knees and a peach sweater over a white button-down. My feet are in my favorite pair of strappy sandals. The three-inch heels are wildly impractical for an afternoon of running wedding errands, but these are the shoes I was wearing the night I met Damien at Evelyn's party so many months ago, and as I stood in my closet a few moments before, I was certain I'd need the extra bit of magical shoe confidence they impart if I was going to survive my mother.

The truth is, I know that I look good. It's not possible to have entered and won as many pageants as I have and still hem and haw and pretend not to know how you look. Objectively, I'm pretty. Not movie star gorgeous—that's Jamie—but I'm pretty, maybe even beautiful, and I know how to hold myself well. Under other circumstances, I'd be standing tall, knowing that I passed the inspection of anyone who took the time to look me over. But these are not ordinary circumstances, and I am suddenly feeling like an awkward teen, desperate for my mother's approval. And the thing I hate the most? That soft look in her eyes only moments before. She'd knocked me off kilter, and now I don't know what to expect. My defenses are down, and I'm left hoping for affection, like some lost puppy that followed her home looking for a handout.

It's not a feeling I like.

"Well," she finally says, "I suppose if you're going to wear your hair short, that style is as good as it's going to get."

My rigid posture slumps ever so slightly, and I look down so that she can't see the tears pricking my eyes. I really am that puppy, and she's just kicked the shit out of me. I can either cower, or I can bare my teeth and fight back. And damn me all to hell, but the cowering almost wins out.

Then I remember that I'm not Elizabeth Fairchild's pretty little dress-up doll anymore. I'm Nikki Fairchild, the owner of her own software company, and I'm more than capable of defending my own damn haircut. I suck in a breath, lift my head, and almost look my mother in the eyes. "It's shoulder-length, Mother. It's not like I've been shaved for the Marines. I think it's flattering." I flash my perfect pageant smile. "Damien likes it, too."

She sniffs. "Darling, I wasn't criticizing. I'm your mother. I'm on your side. I just want you to look your best."

What I want is to tell her to turn around and go home. But the words don't come. "I wasn't expecting you," I say instead.

"Why would you be?" she asks airily. "After all, it's not as if you invited me to your wedding."

Um, hello? Did you really think I would after the things you said? After you made it clear that you don't like Damien?

That you don't respect me? That you think I'm a slut who's only interested in his money?

That's what I want to say, but the words don't come. Instead, I shrug, feeling all of ten, and say simply, "I didn't think you'd want to be here."

I watch, astonished, as my mother's ramrod straight posture sags a bit. She reaches a hand back, then takes hold of the armrest and lowers herself onto the couch. I peer at her and am astonished at an emotion on her face, one I'm not sure I've ever seen there before—my mother actually looks sad.

I move to the chair opposite her and sit, watching and waiting.

"Oh, Nichole, sugar, I just—" She cuts herself off, then digs into her purse for a monogrammed handkerchief, which she uses to dab her eyes. Her Texas twang is more pronounced than usual, and I recognize that as a sign of high drama to follow. But there are no tears, no histrionics. Instead, she says very softly and very simply, "I just wanted to spend some time with you. My baby girl's getting married. It's bittersweet."

She reaches out, as if she intends to take my hand, but draws hers back into her lap. She clasps her hands together and straightens her posture, then takes a deep breath as if steeling herself. "I think about your wedding, and I can't help but remember your sister's. I want . . ."

But she doesn't finish the sentence, and so I do not know what she wants. As for me, I don't know when, but I've risen to my feet, and have turned away so that she can't see the heavy tears now streaming down my cheeks.

I squeeze my eyes shut, determined not to think of Ashley, and even more determined not to think of the hand that my mother had in her suicide. But these thoughts are hard ones to banish, because they have lived inside me for so long. And now—well, now I can't help but wonder if this is my mother's way of showing remorse.

Or am I simply being a fool and wishing, perhaps futilely, that there is a detente to be had between my mother and me.

Chapter 5

"Cupcakes." My mother's voice is flat, but her smile is perky and falsely polite. She's speaking to Sally Love, the owner of Love Bites. It's one of the most popular bakeries in Beverly Hills. Sally has catered dozens of celebrity functions, has been featured in every food and dessert magazine known to man, and is a longtime friend of Damien's. She's also an artist with icing and a pleasure to work with.

I am terrified my mother is going to offend her.

Mother's smile stretches wider. "What a perfectly charming idea. And was that your suggestion?" she asks Sally.

"I believe in working with my clients to figure out exactly what they want, to make their event not only special but uniquely theirs."

"In other words, you don't feel bound by tradition or societal expectations?" Her words are venomous, but her tone and manner are so polite that it's hard to tell if she's being deliberately offensive or making genuine conversation. I know the answer because I know my mother, and I step in and flash my own perky smile.

"I'm completely in love with the cupcake idea. I saw it in a magazine and it seemed like the perfect way to combine tradition and whimsy." I turn to Sally, purposefully excluding my mother. "So we're good to go on the top tier, right?"

Sally grins, displaying rosy cheeks that make me think of Mrs. Claus and Christmas cookies. She's probably only ten years older than me, but there's something maternal and soothing about her. I can understand why she does so many wedding cakes. She can calm a nervous bride with nothing more than a look.

"We're all set," she assures me. "But we do need to narrow down the choices for the cupcakes." The plan is to have five different flavors of cupcakes—one for each of the tiers—so the guests can pick their favorite. Additional cupcakes—in case anyone wants seconds—will be scattered artfully on the table, mixed with the fresh wildflowers I have on order from the florist. Daisies and sunflowers and Indian paintbrushes that remind me of the incredible arrangement Damien sent me after the night we first met.

Sally nods to the table set up at the back of the storefront, elegantly draped in white linen. It's topped with a row of ten tiny cakes. "I thought you might want to refresh your memory."

I laugh. "Even if I'd already decided, you know I'd have to sit down and taste those." I glance at my mother as I head toward the table. "Do you want to try, too? They're all amazing."

Mother's brows lift sky high, and I wonder when my mother last had a carb that didn't come from a lettuce leaf or a glass of wine. "I don't think so."

I shrug. "Suit yourself," I say, and see my mother's lips purse as I settle behind the table. "More for me."

The first cake is a tiny cheesecake. It's Damien's favorite, and I restrain myself from taking a bite because I'm going to ask Sally if I can take it home for him. I can think of all sorts of interesting negotiations we could have if he's bargaining for cheesecake.

I smile as I taste the next cake, not because I'm a fan of red velvet, but because I'm imagining all those possibilities. The next is a deep, delicious chocolate that I savor with a moan that is almost sexual. Sally laughs. "That cake gets that a lot."

"It totally stays," I say, then grin wickedly at her. "In fact, let's have a dozen packed up to take with us on the honeymoon."

We're laughing, and Sally's asking me about the honeymoon, and I'm telling her that it's a secret even from me—a Damien Stark surprise—when my mother clicks her way over on her nail-point heels. She stops in front of me, effectively ending my moment of bridal bonding with Sally.

"Chocolate, yellow, white," she says. "A pound cake. A cheesecake. If you insist on doing cupcakes at least stick with traditional flavors."

"I don't know," I say, taking a second bite of the cupcake I'm working on. "This one—butternut?—is to die for."

"It's very popular," Sally says. "But try the strawberry."

My mother reaches over and snatches the fork out of my hand. For a moment, I'm fool enough to think that she's going to get in the spirit and try the cake. But all she does is point the tines at me. "Honestly, Nichole," she says, in a tone that leaves no doubt that I have committed some heinous sin. "Are you trying to ruin your wedding? Have you thought about your waist? Your hips? Not to mention your skin!"

She turns to Sally, who is clearly struggling to wipe the expression of appalled shock off her face. "Bless her little heart," my mother says, in a tone that practically drips sugar, "but my Nichole isn't a girl who can eat cake and then get into something as form-fitting as a wedding gown."

"Nikki is a lovely young woman," Sally says firmly. "And I'm sure she's going to look stunning at her wedding."

"Of course she will," my mother says, her voice sounding farther and farther from me. It's as if I'm sliding back, moving down some tunnel, away from her, away from Sally, away from everything.

"That's why I'm here," Mother adds, her tone entirely reasonable. "My daughter knows she has no self-control about things that are bad for her—*cakes, candy, men,*" she adds in a stage whisper. "I've always been there to help her keep her eye on the prize."

"I see," Sally says, and I have a feeling she sees more than my mother wants.

As for me, even from the depths of this well into which I've fallen, I am seething. I want to leap out of my chair and tell my mother that she's never helped me, she's only manipulated me. That she's not interested in what I want, but only what I look like and how I act and if I'm presenting an image that stands up to the Fairchild name—a name that's not worth what it used to be since she took over—and decimated—the oil business that she inherited when my grandfather passed away.

I want to say all of that, but I don't. I just sit there, my plastic smile on my face, hating myself for not moving. For not telling her to get the hell back to Texas.

But what I hate even more is the fact that I'm now clutching the second fork in my hand, and it's under the table, and the tines are pressing hard into my leg through the thin material of my skirt. I don't want to—I know I need to stop, to stand up, to simply get the hell out of there if that's what it takes—but whatever strength has been building in me over the last few months has scattered like dandelion fluff under the assault of a ferocious wind.

"Nikki," Sally begins, and I can't tell if the concern in her voice is because of my mother's speech or if she sees some hint of my struggle on my face. It doesn't matter, though, because her words are cut off by the electronic door chime.

I look up, then draw in a breath. The tunnel disappears and my vision returns. The fork tumbles from my hand to the floor, and I realize I've stood up.

It's Damien—and he is moving like a bullet toward me.

I head around the table, unconcerned about anything else.

He stops in front of me, his face hard, his eyes warm but worried. "Turns out I could work the cake thing into my schedule, after all."

I try not to smile, but the corners of my mouth twitch, and I feel tears of relief prick my eyes. "I'm glad."

He reaches out and strokes my cheek. "You okay?"

"I'm perfect," I say. "At least, I am now."

The worry fades from his eyes, and I know that he believes me. He takes my hand, then turns to face my mother. "Mrs. Fairchild. What a pleasant surprise," he says, in the kind of overly polite voice that suggests there's nothing remotely pleasant about this particular surprise.

"Mr. Stark—Damien—I—" She stops abruptly, and I am amused. My mother is very rarely rendered speechless, but the last time she and Damien met he sent her away, effectively getting rid of her by flying her back to Texas on one of his jets. And that was before she'd said the variety of nasty things she's since uttered about the two of us. I have to wonder if she doesn't now fear that her ride out of California this go-round will be significantly less pleasant.

Damien, however, is the picture of cultured politeness. "It was so kind of you to come with Nikki today. I think we both know how valuable your opinion is to her." My mother's eyes widen almost imperceptibly. I can tell that she wants to reply, to lash out with the sweet sting of words that she'd want to cut him as deeply as a blade has cut me, but they clearly don't come. I'm not surprised. My mother is formidable, but Damien is more so.

Her expression shifts from consternation to surprise when Jamie bursts into the bakery like a tornado. "I'm here! I'm here! Big ticky mark for the maid of honor!"

For a moment I think that she really is here simply because she promised me she'd try to make it to Love Bites on time. But when I see that it is not me she looks to first, but Damien, I realize that he called her—and that she is part of the cavalry, too.

A moment later, Ryan Hunter, Damien's head of security, hurries inside as well, only to stop short when he sees Damien, then fall back toward the door, his eyes on my mother, as if she is a bomb about to go off. Laughter bubbles in my throat. I never felt loved by my mother. Damien not only makes me feel loved, but also cherished and protected and safe.

I understand what has happened, of course. Tony called Damien. Since Damien was in Palm Springs, he called both Jamie and Ryan in order to ensure there was someone with me to run interference. I squeeze his hand, then mouth, *Thank you*. The words are simple; the emotion is not.

He squeezes back, but his attention is focused on my mother. I look toward her, too, and as I do I realize that Sally has gracefully exited, leaving the drama of the showroom for the relative calm of the kitchen.

Damien's voice is firm as he addresses my mother. "Between Jamie and me, I think we have it covered. I'm sure you have unpacking to do. Why don't you let my security chief drive you to the hotel?"

"Don't be silly," my mother says. "I'm happy to stay." She smiles at me, and my stomach curls. "I want to spend time with my daughter."

"Awesome," Jamie says. "Today's her bachelorette party." She glances at her watch. "In fact we're supposed to meet the other girls at Raven in about half an hour. It's a strip club," she adds in a stage whisper. "It's going to be awesome. Wanna come?"

My mother goggles at her, and it takes all my power not to laugh. I know Jamie is joking—I specifically told her I didn't want to do the bachelorette thing—but in this moment it would almost be worth going through with it.

"Um, no. Thank you. I—" Her eyes cut to Damien. "I suppose I should get settled."

"I keep a suite at the Century Plaza hotel," Damien says. "I insist you stay there."

"Oh, no. I wouldn't want to be any trouble."

He doesn't say what I know he is thinking—*You've already been that.* Instead, he graces her with his most formal corporate smile. "No trouble at all. In fact, your car is already there. You're all checked in."

I see the confusion on Jamie's face—*she's* been staying at the Century Plaza suite.

"Oh. I see. Well, then." My mother turns her attention to me. "I'll go with you tomorrow to the dress fitting," she says, and I remember with regret that I'd nervously prattled off my schedule for the week as I drove us from Malibu to Beverly Hills.

"Sure," I say, though what I really want is to scream that there is no way in hell I want her in my head as I try on my wedding dress. "That would be great."

Damien is looking at me questioningly, and I shrug in reply. Part of me wants him to step in and send her packing. But she *is* my mother, and another part of me—the secret, buried part that I don't like to take out and examine too closely—wants to have her at my wedding. Wants to have her hold me and tell me she's sorry for all the years of horror and drama.

I want it, but I do not expect it. Yet still that flame of hope is alive, and I feel it flickering inside me.

"Ryan will take you," Damien says to my mother. I glance at Ryan and watch as he turns his attention away from Jamie to this new assignment. I turn to look at my best friend. Her expression suggests that she's oblivious to Ryan's attention, but there's an unfamiliar color to her cheeks, and as she watches him lead my mother out the door, I can't help but wonder.

Jamie crosses the room to join me at the table, then picks up the red velvet cake with her fingers and takes a huge bite. "You realize that there's no way I'm sharing a suite with your mother."

I laugh. "Neither of you would survive."

"I had Tony pack your things when he delivered Mrs. Fairchild's car," Damien says. "You're staying in Malibu with us."

Jamie does a fist pump. "Score!"

My smile is so wide it almost hurts. "Thanks for having my back," I say to Damien.

"Always." The softness in his eyes hardens a bit. "Do you want me to send her back to Texas?"

I almost say yes, but then shake my head. "No. I'm getting married, and she is my mother. I'm strong enough to handle it," I say, in response to his reproachful look.

"You are," he agrees.

"And there was a moment—" I shake my head, thinking about the way she'd talked about Ashley's wedding, and the vulnerability that I'd seen in her eyes.

"What?" Damien is looking at me intently.

"I just think that, despite all the Elizabeth Fairchild nonsense, part of her really does want to be here for me on my wedding day."

For a moment, Damien only looks at me, his hands on my shoulders. Then he leans forward and captures my mouth with the sweetest of kisses. When he pulls away, I expect an argument. I expect him to recite an itemized list of every horrible thing my mother has done to me, to us. I expect him to point to his own father, whom neither of us want at this wedding. Hell, I expect him to talk some sense into me.

Instead, he says simply, "Be careful."

I swallow and nod, because I know that he's right to be concerned.

Once again, the door chimes, but this time I do not know the man who enters. He is drop-dead gorgeous, with dark hair highlighted by gold and red. He carries himself with a Damien Stark kind of confidence, and when his gaze sweeps the room, I see both calculation and intelligence in his sharp, gray eyes.

"We should finish up with Sally and get going," I say to Damien. "She's got other customers to deal with."

"I'm sure she does," he replies, "but Evan isn't one of them. He's with me."

"Holy crap," Jamie says, "do you travel in packs?"

Damien frowns, and I almost laugh. There aren't many people who can knock him off kilter. "What are you talking about?" he asks.

"Never mind," Jamie says, waving her hand as if wiping the words away. But she turns her attention to me, and I nod slightly. I have understood her perfectly, because this guy is hot. Maybe not Damien Stark hot, I think loyally, but he's got some serious sizzle going on.

"Evan Black, let me introduce you to my fiancée, Nikki Fairchild, and her best friend, Jamie Archer."

Evan strides across the room to join us. He shakes my hand, then Jamie's. I can't help but notice that she holds on a moment longer than is necessary.

"Congratulations," Evan says to me. "I knew the first time he talked about you that one day you two would be married. I wish you all the best."

"Thank you," I say, looking curiously at Damien. He's never mentioned this man before.

"I've known Evan for years," Damien says. "He lives in Chicago—we had a drink when I flew out there a few months ago," he adds.

"We met when we were both looking to acquire a failing business," Evan adds.

"Who got it?" I ask.

"Damien," Evan says, without regret. "But today it's my turn."

That I don't know what he means must be obvious by my expression. "Evan's acquiring the galleries," Damien says, referring to the art galleries that Giselle Reynard recently transferred over to him. "We were in Palm Springs examining the items in storage, and Evan's going to come to Malibu tomorrow to take a look at the main property."

"I have a few other things to take care of while I'm here," Evan says, "but I'm honored to have been invited to the wedding. I'm very happy for both of you."

"Thank you," I say, noticing that Jamie is still peering at him with interest. This is something that needs to be nipped in the bud. Not only is Jamie supposed to be backing away from men, but considering Evan is Chicago-bound, he could be nothing more than a fast fuck. And that is *so* not what my best friend needs.

Jamie pulls out her phone and makes a face, then looks at me. "We need to hurry," she says. "We're going to be late."

"Late? For what?"

She rolls her eyes. "I told you. We're meeting the girls at Raven," she says, referring to a male strip club in Hollywood.

"Raven," Damien says, his brows lifting.

"Um, hello?" Jamie says. "Bachelorette party. Alcohol. Mostly naked gorgeous men." She looks him up and down. "Not that she doesn't already have that in her life, but still. This is the night to be naughty."

"It's only barely past lunchtime," I say stupidly.

"I know," Jamie says. "That's when there's less of a crowd. More attention for us."

Oh my.

I glance toward Damien, but this is one of the few times when I cannot read his expression. My gaze shifts toward Evan. He is easier to read, as he's not even trying to hide his amusement.

"I told you I didn't want a bachelorette party," I say. "And I have stuff to do today. The music. The photographer," I remind her, then grimace when I see Damien's brows rise again. *Damn.* My little lie earlier has been soundly caught out.

"And I need to make sure the flowers are confirmed," I add, rushing on. "I need—"

"To chill with your friends," Jamie says. "Come on, Nick. Music or not, pictures or not, come Saturday night you're going to be married. You'll never, ever, ever get to go out as a hot single girl again. So we're doing this. I'm your maid of honor and I'm insisting." She glances at Damien. "Sorry, dude. It's in the best friends rule book."

"I'm certain it is." He turns to me, his expression implacable. "I need to speak with you alone."

I shoot Jamie the kind of look that could bring down an army, then follow Damien to the far corner of the showroom. We're standing beside a case filled with gorgeous, decorative wedding cakes. I glance at them, then wish that I hadn't, because all they do is remind me of how quickly Saturday night is barreling down on us. And while Damien's entry only moments ago might have felt like the cavalry, now those prickles of stress and nerves are starting up again. Because Jamie is right—this is my last chance to cut loose with my girlfriends.

But I don't want to irritate Damien, and though it has never actually come up between us, I feel confident he is not going to graciously accept the idea of another guy getting up close and personal. And we both know that even if we insist on ground rules, Jamie will make sure that they are soundly ignored.

"It's not my idea," I say.

"But you want to go." His voice is low, sensual—and it's making me nervous, because I can't figure out his angle.

"I didn't even know about it," I say.

He twines a strand of my hair through his fingers, then releases it as he brushes his thumb over the curve of my jaw, then over my lower lip.

My mouth parts, and I feel my body go soft and needy. There is no one in the world who has ever had the effect on me that Damien does, and right then I want nothing more than to fold myself into his embrace and lose myself in his kisses.

That, however, isn't where the moment is going.

"Go," he says. "Have fun with your friends."

I blink. "Really?"

He chuckles. "Would I deny you the full wedding experience?"

"I—well, no, but Raven . . ." I trail off, because really, what is there to say about buff men dancing in thongs?

"Mmm, yes, about that." He moves closer, his heat so palpable I feel the sizzle. "You go. You have fun. And you come back and tell me all about it."

I lick my lips. "All about it?"

He leans forward so that his lips brush my ear. "Every last thing, baby. Have as good a time as you want. And when you get home," he adds, his hand sliding down to cup my ass, "I'll decide whether I need to simply spank this beautiful ass, or whether you need a more thorough punishment so that you remember just how much—how thoroughly, completely, and irrevocably—you belong to me." He pulls back so that he is looking straight into my eyes, and the desire I see there almost makes me come on the spot.

"Do we understand each other?"

I nod.

"What's that?"

"Yes," I say, and then meet his eyes defiantly. "Yes, sir."

The corner of his mouth twitches. He takes my hand and pulls me close, then brushes a gentle kiss over my lips. "Just so you know, Ms. Fairchild," he whispers, "I'm secretly hoping you spend this afternoon with your friends being very, very naughty."

Chapter 6

Jamie lets out a laugh as a guy in nothing but a thong and a cowboy hat gets up close and personal in her face. I'm sitting right beside her and am listing toward the left—away from him—but Jamie is eating it up, gleefully tucking ones and fives into the elastic band of his thong. Elastic that, from the stretched out look of it, is going to snap at any moment.

Which probably wouldn't bother Jamie at all.

But even though the guy's not bad-looking, the only naked man I'm interested in anymore is Damien. And this guy is no Damien.

Jamie pulls out a fifty, and I roll my eyes, thinking that I'm about to witness a new level of hip-gyrating entertainment. That's when Jamie hooks her thumb toward me, nods, and very deliberately sticks the fifty right over the guy's package.

"Jamie!" I squeal, but I'm laughing now, because she's laughing and so are Lisa and Evelyn and Sylvia. I try to squirm away, but Jamie holds me in place, grinning wickedly.

Beside me, Evelyn takes a shot of straight Scotch. "Honey, you know I love your boy—and I am quite fond of my own man's attributes, too—but you need to relax and appreciate this from an artistic perspective." As if in illustration, she leans back, takes another drink, attaches her eyes firmly on the cowboy, and sighs.

Evelyn Dodge is brassy, opinionated, and often inappropriate. She says what she thinks, takes no shit off anyone, and has conquered Hollywood and then some. A former-actress-turned-agent-turned-patron-of-the-arts, Evelyn has been friends with Damien since his early days on the tennis circuit. She's known his secrets for longer than I have, and she loves him as much as I do. Damien lost his mom when he was just a kid, and I've always been grateful that Evelyn was in his life. Now I'm grateful that she's in mine.

But this isn't the time to be sappy, and I flash her the kind of smile that would make my mother proud. "Evelyn," I say sweetly, "you are so full of shit."

"It's the years in Hollywood, Texas." She cocks her head at Jamie. "At least this one already has the mouth for it."

"Fuck, yeah," Jamie says. Then she waves another bill and points at me. "Come on, John Wayne," she says. "Don't stop now."

The dancer obviously knows which of us is shoving bills down his pants, because he does as she says, gyrating closer and closer, and I'm squirming out of reach and laughing so hard that I almost pee my pants.

And all the while I'm wearing a fake diamond tiara that says *Virgin Bride* in equally fake red gemstones.

"It's no use," Jamie finally announces, then waves the dancer away, but not before giving him one more fifty. "She only has eyes for Damien."

"Can you blame her?" Sylvia says. I turn to her, eyebrows raised. Sylvia is Damien's assistant, and we've spent so much time together as I've planned the wedding that we've become pretty good friends. "What?" she says, holding her hands up in a sign of innocence. "Just because I work for him doesn't mean I'm blind to him."

"What happens in Raven stays in Raven," Jamie says wisely, then points a finger at me. "And don't even pretend to be jealous of her. You'd have to be jealous of the whole world, because every straight female out there thinks he's the most fuckalicious thing on two legs. Besides, you know Damien's only got eyes for you."

"I do," I say happily. At the moment, I'm very happy. It may not even be five yet, but I've had a Happy Hour buzz going for the last couple of hours, and have imbibed more than my fair share of Manhattans, because Jamie says that the little cherry garnish is appropriate for a bachelorette party, even though my cherry was popped long ago.

My best friend has a way with words.

The waiter comes with another round of drinks, but before I can snag a fresh Manhattan, Lisa snatches it off the tray. "I think it's about time we get you home to Damien," she says. "You're getting glassy-eyed."

I squint at her. "No way."

She laughs. "He will be so mad at all of us if we send you back tonight only to pass out. Especially since you're going home with a goodie bag."

"I am?" I'm beginning to think that Lisa's right and I'm a little wasted, because even if she's talking in euphemisms, I have no idea what she means by a goodie bag.

"Instead of each of us buying you a present, we went in together and got you a Bag O' Fun from Come Again," Jamie explains, referencing a local sex toy shop.

"You didn't," I say, not sure if I should be amused or mortified. "What's in it?"

"You're just going to have to wait and see," Jamie says, while the rest of them grin.

"I promise it's good," Lisa says. "I may have to re-create a bag for Preston and me." Lisa is a business consultant who has done some work with me, and her fiancé, Preston, is one of the top executives at Stark Applied Technology.

"You're supposed to save it for your wedding night," Sylvia adds.

"But we won't think less of you if you dig in tonight," Jamie says. She shares a mischievous grin with Evelyn. "She's going home to Damien, after all, so how could we blame her?"

*   *   *

The limo parked outside of Raven is one of Damien's insane stretch numbers that the company keeps primarily for impressing competitors and rewarding employees. Since this isn't the greatest neighborhood in the world, a crowd of gawkers have gathered. I think some of them are drooling. A few must recognize me, because about ten feet from the car I start to hear my name called out. I see phones being thrust into the air, and a flurry of shouts and camera flashes surround me.

I walk faster, flanked by my friends.

I'm surprised that Edward isn't on the sidewalk holding the door open for me, but it doesn't matter, because Jamie and Evelyn have taken the lead, and they bundle me into the limo, tell me that they hope I had a great time with them and that I have an even greater one with Damien—wink, wink—and then slam the door, effectively blocking the paparazzi and tourists who are determined to get in my face.

I lean back against the soft leather and take deep breaths. Dealing with the paparazzi is part and parcel of dating and marrying a multi-bazillionaire who owns half the world, and I know that. But once the press got hold of the fact that Damien had paid me a million dollars to pose for a nude portrait—and once Damien was indicted for murder—the press went a little nuts. Now it's a good day if we go out in public with only a small swarm.

I've learned to live with it, but I don't like it. It makes me tense and uncomfortable, and if there was a way to avoid it, I would.

What I hate the most is that I know they will be out in full force for the wedding. Although all of the Stark International security force will be at the house to make sure we don't have party crashers on the perimeter, the beach itself is public—and I'm certain that it will be crowded with paparazzi with long lenses and lots of determination.

Since I can't do anything about that except move the wedding inside or to another location altogether, neither of which are options that appeal to me, I have come to terms with the fact that I'm going to have to simply deal with the paparazzi and all the pictures that will surface afterward.

Yay.

That realization was one of the reasons we fired the photographer that we'd hired to do our wedding day portraits. I really didn't need one more underhanded person trying to snap a picture of someone who is having just a little bit too good a time at the champagne fountain after the wedding.

I frown, remembering that I still have to find a photographer, and it's already Thursday and the wedding is Saturday. *Shit*. If it weren't my own wedding, I could take the pictures myself. For that matter, I suppose I could take my Leica to the ceremony . . .

I shake off the ridiculous thought. Honestly, the black camera strap would totally clash with my dress.

Still, I should use this time in the limo to be productive. Maybe call some of the folks on my initial list of maybes and see if they're booked for the day. But my head is too light from my Manhattan indulgence, and all I want to do is sit back, enjoy the ride, and think about seeing Damien again in just a few minutes.

The fact that I tossed my phone across the bedroom and broke it also puts a crimp in my plan to manage a little work.

Frustrated at being without Damien, and irritated about my own foolish temper, I glance out the window and frown, because this isn't the way that we usually go home. I am about to hit the button for the intercom when a phone rings, which is odd because there is no permanent phone in the back of the limo, and, as I have just reminded myself, my iPhone is toast.

The ring comes again.

I lean forward, cock my head, and decide the sound is coming from the bar. I get off the leather bench and move carefully in that direction. Another ring, and I narrow the source down to the ice bucket. I pull off the lid, glance down, and find a phone in the otherwise empty container.

With a grin, I answer the call. "Hello?"

"Ms. Fairchild," he says—his voice is low and enticing and flows over me like warm chocolate.

"Mr. Stark," I say, unable to hide my amusement. "Funny you were able to call me, since I have no phone."

"I told you—I will always take care of your needs."

I smile, feeling warm and satisfied. "Where are you?"

"I'm not with you," he says. "Other than that, does it matter?"

My mouth curves into a smile. "No, but you're wrong. You are with me. You're always with me."

There is a pause before he answers. "Yes," he finally says, and I don't think I have ever heard that simple word spoken with so much meaning and complexity before.

I sigh with satisfaction, then close my eyes. He may not be beside me, but for the moment, I am content.

"We've done this before," he says. "You, alone in the back of my limo. Me, somewhere else, thinking of you. Imagining you. Wanting you."

I swallow, my body already tightening in anticipation of where these words are going. Because we *have* done this before—and the caress of his voice upon me that night is one of my most treasured memories.

"Tell me what you did," he says.

"That night in the limo?" I ask, though I know that is not what he means.

"Tonight. At Raven."

"I watched the dancers."

"What did they do?" His voice has a hard edge, and I shiver a little, remembering his promise to punish me.

"They danced," I say. And then, because I'm feeling reckless, I add, "They stripped down to thongs. They were slick with oil. They got close."

"How close?"

I think of the way the cowboy was gyrating right in front of my face. I remember the way that Jamie laughed and Lisa and Evelyn egged him on. "Pretty close," I whisper.

"I see."

There is a pause, and I squirm on the seat. My legs feel prickly, my sex clenches greedily. I'm thinking of Damien's promise to punish me, and I yearn to be home. To feel his hands upon me.

"Did it turn you on?" he asks, with that low, dangerous tone.

I almost lie, but I can't do that. "Yes," I whisper. "But only because it made me think of you. Your body hard and naked in front of me. Your chest close to me. That thin strip of hair that leads down to your cock, so near I could lick it. And those amazing muscles that form a V as if arrowing down to heaven."

"Christ, Nikki."

I smile, pleased I can bring that ragged tone to his voice.

"Mostly, though, it turned me on because I was watching other men. Because they were nearly naked, and I knew that when I got home to you—" I cut myself off, my bravado suddenly evaporating.

"What?" he asks. "What will happen when you get home?"

"You said you'd punish me," I say, so softly I'm not sure that he can hear me.

"Did I?" There is a note of triumph in his voice, and it makes me weak. "How should I punish you?"

I lick my lips. "You should probably spank me."

"I probably should," he agrees. "Would you like that?"

"Yes." My voice is nothing more than a whisper of air.

"Why?"

I close my eyes. It's a question that I expect whenever I ask for the pain, and I know that after my dreams he will be even more careful with me. I love that he understands me so well, but it means that I have to say aloud what I want from him, and that voicing of my desires is both awkward and undeniably exciting.

"Why, Nikki? I want to hear why you want the sting of my palm."

I lick my lips, forcing them to wrap around my words. "Because of the way it feels."

"Tell me."

"Tiny pinpricks of pleasure," I say, my soft words becoming bolder even as they sizzle through my body, sparking like currents of electricity that fire my senses. "They melt into heat, into liquid desire. It makes me wet, Damien, you make me wet." I pause, knowing that my words have captured him. "Pleasure and pain, Damien, and you're the only one I trust to give me both."

For a long moment he is silent. Almost too long. And then I hear his intake of breath, followed by his slow, clear words. "There is no one else who has the power to tear me apart the way you do, Nikki. No one else who can reach in and squeeze my heart. You are my world, Ms. Fairchild, and I love you desperately."

"I know," I whisper.

"But, baby," he adds, with a lightness now coloring his words, "that doesn't change the fact that you were naughty."

"Was I?" I am breathing hard now, anticipating what is to come.

"Have you seen the internet?"

I frown. That wasn't a question I was expecting. "Um, no."

"Your party is all over Twitter," he says, and I cringe. *That*

I should have expected. "I imagine it'll be on TMZ by morning. The gentleman who was, shall we say, in your face looked quite energetic."

"I think he probably works out," I say dryly.

"You realize this puts me in a bit of a predicament."

I'm trying very hard not to smile. "Does it?"

"I'm just not sure how to punish you now. Considering your . . . eagerness . . . I'm beginning to think that spanking isn't quite the punishment it ought to be."

"Damien!" I'm laughing—but I'm also a little worried. Damien is nothing if not creative.

He chuckles, and it's obvious the bastard is enjoying himself.

"Maybe I should just hang up?" he says.

"No."

"No, what?" he asks, and I hear the tightening in his voice. Whatever playfulness has been between us, it's fading under the slow burn of something else. Something hot. Something dangerous.

"No, sir," I say. My breath stutters in my chest, and I know that I am already wet. I've been wet since the moment I heard his voice. "Please, sir. Please don't hang up."

"I'll stay on the line, but only if you obey. Bend my rules, and I hang up."

"Yes, sir."

"Take your skirt off. And your panties."

I unbutton the skirt and shimmy out of it. I toss it onto the floor of the limo and drop my panties on top.

"Okay."

"Are you sitting back down?"

"Yes."

"Are you wet?"

"Yes."

"I'm going to punish you, Nikki, just like you want. I'm going to make you come. I'm going to make you explode."

I close my eyes and lean my head back, lost in the power of his words.

"But it won't be fast." He pauses, then, "Tell me how wet you are."

"Very."

"No, not like that. I want you to touch yourself. Just one finger. Imagine it's mine."

"I am."

"Now slide it down the juncture of your thigh," he orders. "Let me feel how silky your skin is. How soft. How tempting."

I do what he says, trembling as much from the gentle touch as from the fantasy that it's Damien's.

"Don't touch your clit," he says, and though I desperately want to, I obey. "Now tell me."

"Like I said, I'm very wet."

He chuckles. "I'm very glad to hear it. Tell me, what's in the goodie bag?"

"I don't know. Hang on."

I tug the bag over and peek inside. "A mask, a vibrator, some sort of oil, handcuffs, a video."

"Oil?"

"Yeah." I pull out the small bottle and read the label. "Arousal oil."

"Interesting. Open it."

"I—okay." I break the seal and unscrew the cap. Immediately, I can smell the spices. "It's a bit minty. There aren't instructions."

"Dab a little on your finger," he says. "Then stroke it onto your clit."

"Are you kidding?"

"Should I hang up?"

"Right. Okay. No problem." I'm not at all sure what this stuff is, but I figure if it's in a bag from Jamie, it must be fun. I put a drop on my finger and ease my finger over my clit. I'm so sensitive that even that tiny sensation makes me shiver.

"Well?" Damien asks.

I cock my head, expecting some sort of new sensation. "Nothing."

"Hmm. All right, then, we'll move on. Does the vibrator have batteries?"

I test it out, and find that it purrs nicely in my hand. "It does," I say, and immediately cringe. I sound far too eager, and I know from Damien's chuckle that he both heard and understood.

"And the mask," he says. "Go ahead and put that on."

"All right." I slip it over my eyes, and the world goes dark. "Okay, I—holy fuck." The oil that I thought did nothing is now doing considerably more than nothing. "That oil, it's . . . well, it's very wow."

"Tell me."

"It's like mint, I guess. Like if you sucked on one of those really strong mints and then went down on me. Oh, wow. It feels amazing, sensitive—oh, god, Damien, please."

"Please, what?"

"Everything. Anything." I squirm, wanting simply to relieve this growing pressure, this demanding sensation. "Please, sir, can I touch myself?"

"Oh, yeah. We're going to use the vibrator. Your fingers. I'm going to tell you how to touch yourself, baby. And you're going to let me hear you come."

I am awash with gratitude. I've been holding the phone, but now I put it on speaker and set it beside me, peeking out from under the blindfold just long enough to make sure I push the right buttons.

"Slide your hand up your thigh," he says, "then gently stroke your clit. Are you doing it?"

"Yes." I can barely speak.

"Can you turn on the vibrator?"

"I—I think so."

"Fuck yourself with it, baby. I want it inside you. I want you imagining it's me. Holding you, fucking you, burying myself deep in you."

Oh my god. I fumble, turned on, frantic, weak with longing. I switch to my right hand, and stroke my clit with my left. The oil is amazing, and . . . "I'm close," I say. "God, Damien, I'm so close."

"I know, baby. Come the rest of the way for me. Let me hear it."

"I—" But I can't talk anymore. I've done as he asked with the vibrator, and it fills me, the dual sensation of the vibration and my finger stroking my clit coupled with my fantasy of Damien, and his voice on the phone telling me to "Come for me, baby, come for me," is too overwhelming. I let my head fall back, and grind my hips, lost to everything now but the need for release that is close, so close, so very close, and then—

I explode, and as I do, I cry out Damien's name.

"That's it, baby," he says. "That's it. Keep touching yourself. Don't stop. Don't stop, baby, you can come again."

I've turned off the vibrator and tossed it onto the seat, but I do as he says and stroke myself. I'm so desperately wet. Wet and wide open and wishing that Damien were right here.

I still have the mask on, but I can hear the mechanical sound of the privacy screen starting to descend.

What the fuck?

"Damien!"

"I hear it, too. It's just the privacy screen. Don't stop. Don't put your legs together. Stay like that, baby. Open and wide."

"Are you crazy? *Edward.*"

"I believe we agreed that you needed to be punished."

"*No.*" I pull my legs tight together and rip off the mask even as I slide sideways, out of the line of sight of the driver.

And when I do, I realize that it isn't Edward behind the wheel, it's Damien.

He turns to glance, and I take deep, gasping breaths as I try to reconcile fear and relief and anger.

"Bastard," I finally say, though that hardly covers it.

"Slide back to the middle."

"And if I don't?"

"Suit yourself." He starts to raise the privacy screen.

"Fine." I'm pissed, but I'm not stupid. And, yeah, I'm still turned on.

As he drops the screen, I slide back to center.

"Spread your legs," he says, and as I do, he adjusts his mirror. "Now, that really is a beautiful view." There is awe in his voice, and it makes me feel beautiful. Despite being exposed, despite the scars on my thighs. Damien makes me feel like the most beautiful woman in the world, and that is just one of the things that makes me love him.

"Wider," he says. I comply, and I hear Damien's sharp intake of breath. He may be playing with me, but there's no denying that he's turned on, too.

"Are you excited, Ms. Fairchild?"

"Yes," I admit. "Except for that one moment of terror, yes."

"You should know me better. And you should listen better."

"Listen?" And then it hits me. "The bag. How would you know about the goodie bag if you weren't in the car?"

"Exactly. I gave you that clue. It's not my fault if you were too distracted to pay attention."

I manage a smirk. "Actually, I think it was your fault."

He chuckles again. "Maybe so."

I start to bring my legs together.

"Oh, no, Ms. Fairchild. That's how you sit for the rest of

the ride. It's your punishment—and my reward," he adds, tapping the rearview mirror.

"In that case," I say, and strip off my sweater, shirt, and bra.

"Jesus, Nikki," Damien says, as I sit naked on the backseat, feeling suddenly very smug.

"I thought you needed to be well rewarded. After all, you earned it. I mean, you've been sitting in an empty limo all afternoon while I was inside drinking and watching hot guys."

"Best not to remind me of your infractions," he warns. "And the truth is, I wasn't just sitting in the limo."

"Oh?" I lick the tip of my finger and slowly circle my nipple. I'm pretty sure I hear a low growl come from the driver's seat. "What were you doing?"

"You were with the girls," he says, his voice unnaturally tight. "I was with the guys."

"Were you?" I let my finger trace down, down, down. Slowly, I stroke my sex, thrusting my finger deep inside, then withdrawing it to tease my clit.

I started this little show to torment Damien, but I'm also tormenting myself. "So, um, who were you with?" Honestly, it's getting hard to think.

"Alaine, Charles, Preston. Jesus, Nikki, do you have any idea how hard I am?"

I allow myself the pleasure of a satisfied smile. "Anyone else?"

"Ryan, Evan, Blaine. A few others."

"Mmm." I force myself not to drift, not to let myself come. I want him hard and hot. I want to turn the punishment around on him.

I want to keep control.

"So, um, tell me about Evan. Jamie was certainly checking him out."

"Tell her to stay away," Damien says sharply, and my hand pauses.

"Why?"

"Actually, I take it back. Don't tell her anything. Knowing Jamie, telling her to stay away would just make her more determined."

"All right," I agree. "But why? What's wrong with him?"

"Not a damn thing. I like him, a lot. But he has an edge."

"An edge? What kind of edge?"

"The dangerous kind."

"Oh." I want to ask more; however, I know better than to try to get information out of Damien that he doesn't want to give. "To be honest, I think Jamie's appreciation is more aesthetic than active. I'm pretty sure she's got her eye on another guy."

"Who?" Damien asks.

I shrug. I don't answer, but I'm thinking of Ryan.

For a moment I think Damien will press the point, but all he says is, "We're here."

I glance out the window and see that we've entered a drive-in movie lot. I laugh out loud. "Where are we?" I ask, tugging my skirt and shirt back on. I don't bother with the bra or underwear. At the moment, they seem superfluous.

"The Vineland Drive-In. City of Industry."

"Don't you have to pay?"

"I called ahead and made arrangements."

"You planned this all along," I say, which is pretty much stating the obvious. "Why?"

He opens his door, gets out, then joins me in the back.

"Why?" I repeat.

"So we could make out in a car at the drive-in," he says simply.

I laugh, because as corny as it sounds, the idea is also exciting. "Interesting. I think I'd like that."

"Would you?" He reaches over and begins to unbutton the

shirt that I just put back on. I lean toward the console so that I can raise the privacy screen.

"No," he says as he peels the shirt off.

"Damien!"

His fingers unbutton my skirt, then tug down the zipper. "Do you really think that someone is going to lean on the hood, press their face to the glass, and peer all the way back here?"

"They might," I say, though I agree it's doubtful.

"They won't. But doesn't the possibility make you wet?" He slides his hand up my skirt. "Yeah," he says. "I think it does."

I lick my lips, refusing to admit the excitement that's building inside me. "I was already wet," I say.

"Mmm-hmm."

I feel my cheeks heat. "I thought you didn't do public sex."

"I don't. And I'm not going to. We're in a limo. No one's looking in. But I like the fantasy," he admits. He leans forward and kisses me, even as he slides two fingers deep inside me. "And so do you."

"I do," I admit, both because it's true and because I don't want to have secrets from Damien. "You are my fantasy, Damien. You know that, right?"

"And you are mine," he says, after kissing me softly. "We're lucky, you and I. There were so many places where our lives made wrong turns. And yet all those turns, all those horrors, all those days that we want to forget—they all add up to this moment. To you in my arms." He strokes my hair, his expression tender. "I have no regrets for the past, Nikki. And when I'm with you, the only thing I can see is the future."

"Damien," I say, the word soft like a prayer.

"Yes?"

"Kiss me."

"Whatever you want, sweetheart," he says before his mouth closes over mine and I slide down into the bliss of his arms.

Chapter 7

I sit in the silence of the Malibu house, sipping a sparkling water as I work at a small desk in the library. The library is my favorite room in this house, and it's not really a room at all. Instead, it's a level—a mezzanine—broken into a variety of sections. The comfy chairs and coffee tables are by the wall of windows overlooking the ocean. The bookshelves line the area that is visible from the massive staircase leading up from the entrance hall. The work areas are farther back, hidden from view, and it is in one of those quiet corners that I now sit.

It is late—barely three in the morning—and Damien is asleep in our bed.

I couldn't sleep, and though I stayed in bed for hours, warm in Damien's arms as I drifted in and out of a hazy dream state, I never managed to fall into slumber. I'm not sure if it was nerves or too much bourbon or the persistent thoughts of my mother, but in the end I gave up and came down here. Now I am sitting in the light of my laptop monitor putting the finishing touches on the gift I intend to give Damien on our wedding day—a scrapbook of our time together.

I've been working on it for months, even before we were engaged, and have managed to gather and edit photos ranging all the way from our very first meeting at a Dallas pageant to the present. I had originally intended it to be entirely electronic, but once he proposed and I realized that this was the perfect wedding-night gift for the man who owns everything, I decided that it needed to be tangible. I bought a leather-bound scrapbook with thick, archival paper, and have been carefully pasting in the images and writing captions and notes to him with my very best effort at penmanship.

Right now I am searching the computer for a picture of the Vineland Drive-In, because that is a memory I want him to keep, though I don't think either one of us had any idea what movie was playing. Instead, we made out like teenagers in the backseat, kissing and exploring, touching and groping. And when Damien finally thrust hard inside me—when I came in sudden release and exultation—I am certain that my cry was at least as loud as the movie soundtrack.

The hairs on the back of my neck prickle, and I know without turning around that Damien is here. His walk, his scent, his presence—I don't know what it is, but there is something in him that calls so profoundly to me that I am never unaware of him. If he is in the same room, my body knows—and wants.

I gently close the scrapbook, then tuck it into a drawer before turning to him.

"I don't like waking up without you," he says.

I smile. "Now you know how I feel." Usually it is me who wakes up to find the other side of the bed cold and empty.

"What are you doing?"

"Just working on something." I lift a shoulder. "I couldn't sleep."

"Oh, really?" He lifts a brow and eyes the desk.

"Don't even think about it, mister. You'll see it on Saturday."

"Saturday," he murmurs, the hint of a smile playing around his mouth. "Seems like there's something I'm supposed to be doing on Saturday."

I laugh, and fly out of the chair to smack him playfully on the chest. He pulls me into his arms and kisses me, gently at first and then with increasing fervency. "I reached for you," he says. "You weren't there."

The words are matter-of-fact, but to me they seem thick with meaning. I lean back so that I can see his face more clearly. "What's wrong?"

"I could ask you the same thing," he says, deflecting my words but not my worry. There is something on Damien's mind. He tucks my hair behind my ear. "Tell me what's keeping you awake."

"Bourbon," I say. "Bridal jitters."

"Not your mother?"

"That, too," I admit.

"Whatever you want to do, you know that I support it. All I ask is that you remember this is your wedding, and it's the only wedding you're going to have." He strokes my cheek, the touch melting me as much as the words. "Consider that when you decide how to handle your mother."

I nod. "You're right." I take his hand. "And you? Is it wedding jitters that are bothering you? Is something going on at work?"

He turns, looking out toward the rows of polished bookshelves now standing like sentries in the dark. He doesn't answer right away, and I'm starting to suspect he isn't going to answer me at all. Then he says, "It's Sofia."

I try not to react, but I have no control over the quickening pace of my heart, and I'm certain that my eyes have gone unnaturally wide. "What about her?" I ask carefully. Sofia is so far off my list of favorite people, it isn't even funny. Still, she was important to Damien when he was growing up, and despite a lot of recent shit, I know that she's still important to him.

"I got an email from her. I saw it right after we got home. She wants to come to the wedding. She thinks that it could be arranged."

The words hang in the air, like one of those cartoon anvils that is defying the laws of gravity and simply hovering, waiting for the moment when it will drop and crush the hapless coyote.

I open my mouth, close it, then try again. "Oh," is all I can manage.

"That pretty much sums it up," he says. He's wearing pajama bottoms tied loosely around his waist, and he slides one hand into a pocket. With the other, he massages his forehead with his thumb and finger.

"Do you want her to come?" I finally ask.

He lifts his head, looking at me as if I've gone insane. "No."

A moment passes, and then he lets out a soft curse. "No," he repeats, "and the not wanting makes me sad." He meets my eyes. "But I meant what I said in the limo, about our choices and the people in our lives leading us to this point. To each other." He steps closer to me. "It saddens me—hell, it angers me—but I have no regrets."

"I don't, either," I say, thinking of my mother. Of who she is, what she's done, and what I want. It's all a turmoil inside me. A storm. I know what I should do, what I want to do. But I'm not certain it's what I can do.

And though he hides it better than I do, I know that a similar storm is raging within Damien. How can it not be? He thrives on control. It is his lifeblood, his sustenance, and yet just the mention of Sofia's name conjures the specter of everything that spun out of control, cutting a path of destruction through his life as effectively as a spinning propeller breaking loose from its axle.

"Damien," I say, and I hear both longing and helplessness in my voice.

I see the heat flare in his eyes as he moves even closer to me. I take an automatic step backward, but am foiled by the desk. I stop, breathing hard, as he cages me in. I am wearing the button-down shirt that he abandoned on the floor when we went to bed. The tail hits me mid-thigh, and he uses his finger to trace the line of the hem, slowly easing it up, higher and higher.

My pulse quickens, and I feel the effects of his touch shimmering through me, hot and electric and alive.

Without thinking, I shift my stance, widening my legs. I want his hands upon me. I want his cock inside me. I want everything he has to give, and I want him to take everything he wants.

His hand slides between my legs and cups my sex, finding me desperately wet. "Tell me you want me," he says, sliding his fingers inside me. I almost melt with pleasure.

"Always," I say truthfully, and I know with absolute certainty that there will not ever be a time when I don't respond to Damien's presence. To his proximity, his heat. When I won't open like a flower to him. When my body won't crave his touch.

He thrusts another finger inside me and I grind down, shamelessly wanting more. But he denies me, and I hear myself whimper as he pulls his hand away. And then my whimper changes to a gasp when he grabs either side of the shirt and tugs it open, baring my breasts and sending buttons flying.

"Beautiful," he murmurs, and I close my eyes in expectation of his mouth on my nipple. But the touch doesn't come. Instead, he turns me around, then pulls the shirt the rest of the way off so that I am naked in front of him. I am facing the desk, my ass pressed against his erection, now hard steel beneath the thin pajama bottoms.

"I wanted you in the limo," he says. "But I need you now. Do you understand what I'm saying?"

"You know I do." I turn to look at him as I speak, but he shakes his head.

"Eyes forward. Bend over. Hold on to the far side of the desk."

I do as he says. I feel vulnerable. I feel *him*.

"I don't think we ever took care of that little issue of punishment," he says.

I lick my lips, my body already tight with anticipation and my sex clenching with desire.

"Is that what you want, Nikki? Shall I spank your ass? Shall

I punish you with the sting of my palm, turning your ass pink and sweet, making you hot?"

"I'm already hot," I say honestly. "And yes. Please, yes." We both want this. Hell, we both need it. He needs to take back some of that control, and I so desperately need to give it to him. Because I need the storm to settle inside me as much as he needs my submission.

I do not turn around, but I can hear the soft rustle of material as he slips off the pajama bottoms. He steps closer, and the tip of his cock rubs along the crack of my ass. "Maybe I should just take you, fast and without warning."

"Yes." There is no hiding the need in my voice, and Damien chuckles.

"Soon," he says, and then lands his palm sharply against my rear.

I cry out, more from surprise than pain, and then brace for the second blow. It comes fast, and then Damien's palm is caressing the point of impact, smoothing out those brilliant red sparks, making them flow inside me, shifting from pain to a vibrant pleasure that pulses through me.

"More?" But he doesn't wait for an answer, just spanks me again, and again. Eight more times, until my rear is red hot and sensitive and my cunt is so wet that I can feel my desire coating the inside of my thighs.

I am bent over the desk, my breasts rubbing against the wood with every impact, and now my nipples are as tight and hard and sensitive as my clit. I'm awash in sensation, my entire body sparking like a live wire, and with the right touch, I know that I will shatter.

I expect another smack, but this time his hands grab my hips instead. With his knee, he roughly shoves my legs apart. One hand comes down on my back, holding me in place over the desk. The other strokes my sex, opening me, readying me, though that is hardly necessary—as I am so ready for him to be inside me, I can hardly stand it.

"Damien, please," I beg. "I need you in so many ways, but right now, I just need you to take me."

He does, thank god. Gently at first, just the tip of his cock sliding into me as my muscles clench greedily around him. He withdraws, and I moan, immediately regretting the loss of him. Then, without warning, he slams into me, our bodies coming together brutally, violently, and I can feel his body tightening as his climax draws close. "Come with me, baby," he says, his hand snaking around to stroke my clit.

It is that touch in combination with the sensation of being filled by Damien that sends me spiraling off the cliff, then grabbing on to the edge of the desk as Damien thrusts into me, faster and faster until he explodes as well, then collapses onto the carpet, clutching me around the waist and pulling me down with him.

I land on top of him, and he grins. "Again, Ms. Fairchild?"

"I could be convinced," I say, though I am still breathless.

He lifts himself just high enough to kiss me. "Marry me," he says, then grins.

"Yeah," I say happily. "I think I will."

"All I am saying is that there is a reason that tradition exists," my mother says as we enter Phillipe Favreau's Rodeo Drive boutique.

I am regretting not only having her come along today, but also that I answered her questions about my flower choices for the wedding. She has been harping on it ever since I explained that the cupcake tower would be decorated with wildflowers because that was the overall floral theme.

Wildflowers, in the world of Elizabeth Fairchild, are an epic fail where weddings are concerned.

"Orchids, lilies, gardenias. Darling, those are all lovely and elegant and classic."

"I like what I've picked out, Mother." I glance around the studio. There are only three gowns on mannequins and one very thin woman working behind a tall glass table that doubles as a desk. "Now, would you drop it?" I glance at the woman. "I'm Nikki Fairchild. I have an appointment with Alyssa for an alteration on a gown that arrived this morning."

"Nikki Fairchild?" she repeats, looking a bit more flummoxed than is usual for store clerks on Rodeo Drive. "The Damien Stark gown?"

I frown. "Um, well, I'm going to be the one wearing it, but Damien ordered it, yes. Why? Is there a problem?"

She smiles an overly perky smile, and little knots of dread form in my stomach. "I'll just get Alyssa. One moment."

"Even magnolias," Mother says.

"Would you stop it?" I am practically snarling, and Mother's eyes go wide.

"Nichole! You need to learn to control yourself."

I suck in both a breath and my temper, and refrain from telling her that she needs to learn to shut up. "I'm a little nervous," I say. "I think there may be something wrong with the dress."

"Nonsense. I'm sure it's lovely. Do you have a picture?"

I glance sideways at her, thrown off kilter by the fact that she's actually being soothing. "Um, sure." I pull out my phone and call up the photographs we'd taken in Paris, both of Phillipe's sketch and of the basted-together version that I wore for the initial fitting. Just seeing it makes me smile. It has a fitted bodice with a low neckline that reveals a hint of cleavage. The sleeves are slim and hug my arms. The skirt is not a traditional princess style, but is instead sleek in the front and over my hips, showing off my curves. The back has a modified bustle that supports a train.

The neckline and the hem and the lower line of the bodice are embroidered with tiny flowers accented with pearls, giving the pure white dress a touch of the whimsical. I think it's an exceptional dress, and I cannot wait for Damien to see me in it.

I glance over at my mother, expecting to see approval in her eyes. I should have known better.

"Well," she says with a sniff, "I suppose this is to be expected, considering your choice of flowers and cake."

"I—" I snap my mouth shut. I have no idea what to say. No idea what insult to hurl that will cut her as deeply as she is cutting me, each word like a new wound.

All I want is one tiny crumb from my mother. Approval, compassion, respect. But there is nothing there, and there never has been.

And yet I have been foolish enough to let that flame of hope keep burning. God, I'm an idiot.

I turn away so as to not let her see that my eyes are bright with tears.

"A longer train," she says. "And a fuller skirt. This is one of the few times you can completely hide those hips, Nichole. You should take advantage of it."

I cringe, wanting to scream at her that just because I'm no longer a size four does not mean that I have to start wearing caftans. I'm young, I'm healthy, I'm pretty, and if she's too goddamn stupid to see that—

My wild thoughts are interrupted by the door to the back room bursting open and a tall red-haired woman hurrying in.

"Nikki," she says, holding out her hand. "I'm Alyssa."

I start to hold my hand out as well, only to discover that I've clenched it so tight that I've left indentations from my nails in my palms. I flex it, then extend it to her. "Is there a problem?"

"I'm afraid so," she says. "This is terribly embarrassing, but your dress is missing."

"Missing," I repeat stupidly.

"We hope it's just a clerical error in customs, and we're doing everything we can." I halfway tune her out, still stuck on that one word: *missing*. My dress is missing.

". . . have been other shops with items missing . . ."

What the hell am I going to do? This is my dress. My *wedding* dress. I mean, I can't just run to Target.

". . . customs or the shipper, but we're looking into it, and . . ."

And it's not even just a wedding dress. It's the dress I bought during my trip to Europe with Damien. It's the dress we bought during our days and nights in Paris. The dress made by the designer who assured Damien that he would go faint with awe when he saw me in the gown. This is not a dress I can lose, nor is it a dress I can replace, and I can feel the panic, the anger, the futility rising inside me.

One goddamn thing after another, and I can't even lash out. Because it's not this poor girl's fault—hell, she's mortified, too. But everything is just piling on: the photographer and the music and the flowers. Those goddamn flowers that my mother has been talking about for the last hour.

"Ms. Fairchild?" Alyssa says, her voice ripe with concern. Her fingers brush over my arm, and I use the touch as an anchor to draw me out of my thoughts and back to reality. "Ms. Fairchild, are you okay?"

"She's fine," my mother says firmly. "This can only be considered a good thing. It gives her a chance to find a dress that might actually flatter her figure."

Alyssa's eyes are wide, and she's staring at my mother like she's never met such a creature before. Hell, she probably hasn't.

"Come on, Nichole. This is Beverly Hills. I'm sure we can find you a gown."

"Get the hell out of here." I did not plan the words, but I

know the moment that they are out that I mean them with all my heart.

"Excuse me?"

"Texas," I say. "Go back to Texas, Mother. Go now."

"Texas! But, Nichole, how—"

"It's *Nikki,*" I snap. "How many times do I have to tell you? You don't listen."

Beside us, I see Alyssa lick her lips and then fade into the background. At the glass desk, the thin girl seems overly interested in the single piece of paper on the surface.

I really don't give a shit. Right then, decorum is the last thing on my mind.

"I can't possibly go to Texas now. I'd miss the wedding."

"That's the idea," I say. "I'll have Grayson fly you. You'll need to leave today so that he can be back in plenty of time. He is invited," I add, my voice syrupy sweet.

"Darling, I'm your mother. You can't ask me not to be at your wedding."

I hesitate for just a moment, just long enough to hear Damien's voice in my head talking about choices and paths and where they lead. And this choice leads to my wedding day. To a day of celebration. Or to a day with my mother harping in my ear. The woman who has, in so many ways, gone out of her way to steal the joy out of so many moments in my life.

"Nichole, don't do this. I need—" She cuts herself off, her lips clamping tightly shut.

I take a deep breath, suddenly realizing that I've been more of an idiot than I thought. My mother didn't come here because my impending wedding spurred her to repair our relationship. And she didn't come because she wanted to apologize for the horrible things she said to Damien.

She came because she spent every dime our family had a long time ago, and she sees a new cash cow in me. I don't know what it is she needs—a new house, a new car, investment capital. I don't know, and I don't care. She's not getting a dime of my money, and she's sure as hell not getting Damien's.

"Goodbye, Mother."

"Nichole, no. You can't do this."

"You know what, Mother? I can." I head for the door, my heart feeling lighter and my step springier. I glance back at her and smile. "And for that matter, why don't you go ahead and find your own way home?"

Chapter 8

"You're amazing," Damien says that night when I tell him what I did. "You once told me that you didn't have the balls to stand up to your mother." We're in the swimming-pool-size bathtub, facing each other, our legs touching.

"I still don't have balls," I say with a laugh.

"Sure you do." He reaches for my hand and tugs me toward him, then very deliberately cups my hand over his package. "These are all yours."

"Damn straight," I say, then capture his mouth in a kiss.

His arms go around me and he pulls me close, until I have no choice but to straddle him if I want to sit in any sort of comfortable position.

Not that straddling Damien is a hardship, especially when his erection is rubbing against my folds in a way that is very effectively taking my mind off the day's drama.

"I'm proud of you," he says, trapping me in the circle of his arms.

"I'm proud of me, too," I say. "I took control of the situation. I decided what I wanted for this wedding, and I did what had to be done." I kiss him. "I think I'm going to make a habit of going after the things I want."

"Haven't you always?"

I press a finger over his lips. "That's not the point."

"What is?" he asks.

"This," I say, reaching between us to cup my hand around his erection. Slowly, I stroke the length of him. "Taking control can be very rewarding," I say.

"Oh, yes." His voice sounds raw.

"Something wrong, Mr. Stark?" I ask innocently. "You seem distracted."

"On the contrary," he says. "I'm very focused. Very aware."

"Are you?" I increase the pressure on his cock, then tease the tip with my thumb.

He sucks in air, and I see the shudder cut through him and the heat in his eyes.

He looks at me, and I smile, slow and easy and with all sorts of promise.

"Kiss me," he says. "Ride me."

Now it's my turn to shudder in anticipation. I rise up, capturing his mouth in a kiss that is hot and deep and demanding. His tongue wars with mine, thrusting and teasing. I lower myself onto his cock and ride him, lifting myself up and down in a frantic rhythm that sends water sloshing around the tub.

Over and over, deeper and deeper, until I have no choice but to break the kiss, because I have to arch back simply from the weight of the pleasure that is shooting through me.

When I do, his mouth closes over my breast, and his teeth nip at me, the pain sending hot wires of pleasure down through my body to my cunt, to that deep place inside me that he's touching, thrusting against with every stroke, building a delicious pressure that grows and grows until finally we explode together, sending water flying out of the tub and me collapsing back against Damien's chest in utter satisfaction and release.

We stay that way until we fear that we will shrivel in the tub, then Damien lifts me out, dries me off, and carries me to the bed, tucking me gently under the cool sheets.

"You haven't told me what you're doing about your dress," Damien says moments later as we twine together in the bed, half drifting off to sleep.

"I went back inside after Mother left," I tell him. "It's not perfect, but they had a dress that was my size in the back."

"Do you like it?"

I shrug. The truth is that it's a lovely dress that any bride would be thrilled with. But it's not *my* dress, and what girl is happy with sloppy seconds?

"I'm sorry, baby," he says, kissing my bare shoulder.

"It's okay, really. I promise you'll think I'm stunning."

"I always do."

I smile, and I'm still smiling as I start to drift off. I'm just about to slide into the sweet oblivion of sleep when I remember one other thing. "You still awake? I have a brilliant idea."

"I'm always awake for brilliance," he says.

"I got the idea from those tweets of us from Raven."

"Us?"

"Us girls," I clarify.

"Uh-huh. If this is about inviting the Raven men to the wedding, I'm going to exercise my veto power."

"Very funny. No, I was thinking about our photographer problem. I know I told you I wanted to make sure we had wedding portraits, but we can sit for a portrait anytime. Besides, I want to remember the day, not a pose. And I was thinking that we could do the same thing all those folks did in tweets."

"Which is?"

"Candid shots. We give each guest a camera as a wedding

souvenir. And then we have them drop the memory cards in a bowl before they leave. We'll get a ton of fabulous pictures of our friends, us, dancing, eating. They won't be professional, but they'll be fun. And they'll be *us*. And not the kind of tacky pictures that the paparazzi will snap from the beach. What do you think?"

"I think you're brilliant," he says. "Brilliant and beautiful. And I cannot wait to be your husband."

I smile in contentment and love. "Me, either," I say, and then, finally, I close my eyes, snuggle closer to Damien, and let sleep tug me under.

Damien is already gone when I wake up on Friday. He's left word with Grayson that he has some business to attend to before we leave on our honeymoon and that he will either be at the office or looking at various properties with Mr. Black.

I put a waffle in the toaster—which pretty much sums up my culinary skills—and eat it without syrup on the patio while I make some morning phone calls. The first one is to Sylvia, and I explain my plan about the cameras. She thinks it's brilliant, and swears that she has plenty of time to handle it.

"I'll make sure they're delivered by morning. Seriously, Nikki, don't worry about it. Rest a little today. You deserve it. And you'll need it for your honeymoon."

I roll my eyes, but since she's right, I don't argue. Instead, I actually do the delegation thing and email her the names of three bands I auditioned, liked, but rejected. It's not a perfect solution, but it is a low-stress one. She promises to call them, see who's still available, and to pick the best one.

I thank her and sign off, then try to decide on the appropriate form of pre-wedding relaxation. I actually managed to finish Damien's scrapbook last night, so that's out. And while my own work has been stacking up, somehow the idea of getting on to the computer and programming just doesn't appeal.

About the only thing that does, actually, is a walk along the beach. And since I don't want to go alone, I head downstairs to the first-floor guest suite, knock, and then head into Jamie's darkened room.

Normally, I'd let her sleep. But since this is my last day as a single best friend, I figure an exception is in order. I pull the covers back and give her a little shake.

"Mmm, Ryan . . ."

I lift my brows, because that's a very interesting development, but Jamie doesn't indulge me by talking in her sleep again. Instead, she bolts upright, springing awake.

"Holy fuck, Nikki," she screeches. "What the hell are you doing?"

I shrug. "Wanna take a walk on the beach?"

Fortunately, Jamie is easygoing. She shoots me a couple of dirty looks for good measure, throws in a curse, but gets dressed. We're down at the beach within fifteen minutes.

"So, do you have anything to tell me?" I ask.

She stares at me like I'm a loon. "The moon isn't made of green cheese. Masturbation doesn't make you go blind. Jethro Tull is a band, not a guy. How do those work for you?"

"Not bad," I say. "I was thinking more along the lines of Ryan."

She slows her step. "What about him?"

"Ever since Damien had him take you home that time, you've had this thing."

I expect her to deny it. Instead, she shrugs. "So?"

"So there really is a thing?"

"Not as far as he's concerned," she says, her tone frustrated. "As far as I can tell, I'm invisible to him."

I hook my arm through hers. "I can't imagine you being invisible to anyone."

"I know, right? I mean, what's up with that?"

I laugh. "So what are you going to do?"

"About Ryan?"

"About you."

She slows her pace. "I don't know. I didn't get that commercial that Caleb is directing, but it felt nice doing the audition thing again. But I don't want to get back on the same hamster wheel, you know? And I'm—" She glances at me, then clams up.

"What?"

"Nothing."

"James . . ."

"Fine. Whatever. It's just that everything changes with you getting married."

"I'm still your best friend." I stop walking, and tug her to a stop, too.

"Well, duh," she says, in a way that sends a shock of relief running through me. "I just mean that I don't think I'd do that great living by myself. In case you hadn't noticed, I have a tendency to run a little wild. And you're off the roommate market. I thought about living with Ollie, but that might be weird."

"Ya think?"

She waves a hand. "Nah, that's over," she says, referring to their romps between the sheets. "But it still might be weird. Where is he, anyway? He's coming to the wedding, right?"

"He's supposed to be at the dinner tonight." Since we're not doing a big wedding, we're not having an official rehearsal dinner. But we are getting a whole slew of our friends together. "He's been in New York. Depositions, I think he said."

"And Damien's cool with him coming tonight?"

"Like you said, it might be weird, but on the whole it's okay. They aren't ever going to call each other up to go have a beer at the corner pub, but I think we can manage the occasional dinner and social event."

"Good." She crosses her arms over her chest. "Change sucks."

I think about the changes in my life since Damien entered it, and the ones that are coming. A wedding. Hopefully a family. I smile, then start walking again, tugging Jamie along beside me. "No," I say firmly. "You'll see. Change doesn't have to suck at all."

Le Caquelon in Santa Monica is closed tonight for our private party. Alaine, Damien's childhood friend and best man, owns the fondue-style restaurant, and has graciously offered it for this evening's party.

I love the place, with its funky decor and wild colors. The last time I was here, Damien and I shared a very private booth. Tonight, everyone is gathered in the main restaurant. We are laughing, talking, and toasting. And, of course, indulging in the various fondue pots that Alaine has scattered throughout.

He has turned off the restaurant's normal New Age music in favor of piping Rat Pack tunes from the speakers. Apparently he is aware that Damien and I share a love of Sinatra, Dean Martin, and the rest.

I smile at Damien, who is talking to Ollie and Evan across the room. He leaves them, then strides to me and pulls me close, easing me around the makeshift dance floor before dipping me, much to the amusement of the other guests. "I am a genius," he says.

"So I've been told."

"I also own a stereo," he adds.

"This is also a fact that I'm aware of. I assume there's some sort of connection coming."

He points to the speakers. "We don't need a band tomorrow. We just need a DJ."

I gape at him. "You are a genius. Except I already told Sylvia to hire a band."

"She didn't have the heart to tell you, but they've all been booked." He leans closer, nips my earlobe, then whispers, "I think you may be exhibiting signs of stress. My assistant was trying to protect you. I can't say I blame her."

I laugh and push him away, then immediately pull him back into my arms. "You're in a good mood."

"Of course I am. Haven't you heard? I'm getting married tomorrow."

"Lucky man," I say.

"Very," he replies, and the intensity of his gaze acts like an underscore to the word.

"I have something for you," I say, tugging him to the far side of the restaurant where all the women have piled our purses. I had brought a huge tote, and now I pull out the present wrapped in silver paper.

He takes it, his expression so much like a boy on Christmas morning that I laugh with delight. "Go ahead," I urge.

He peels off the paper, studies the book, then slowly opens it. I know the first image he sees—a snapshot of the two of us in Texas six years ago. It was an offhand shot by a local news reporter and it never even made the paper. I lucked into it after a call to the paper's morgue. "Nikki," he says, and there is awe in his voice. He flips through the pages, and the love I see in his eyes makes my knees go weak.

I watch as he examines every page, every memory. When he is finished, he closes the book with reverence, sets it gently on the table, and then pulls me close. "Thank you," he says, those two words holding a lifetime of emotion.

He kisses me gently, then leads me back to the crowd. "I have a gift for you, as well," he says, then looks at his watch. "I need about fifteen more minutes."

My brow furrows as I wonder what he could be up to, but I nod. "That gives me plenty of time to make the circuit and eat more chocolate. Come with?"

"Of course," he says, then follows me to the chocolate fondue station. Alaine is there, and we chat for a while. Then Alaine and Damien go off to talk with Blaine and Evelyn. Since I have something to ask Evelyn, I almost follow them, but Ollie approaches, and I pause to give him a hug.

"Hey, deposition guy. How goes the wild and woolly world of civil litigation?"

"Wild and woolly," he replies with a grin. "And over. At least for a few weeks." He waves to Charles Maynard, his boss, then leads me into a corner. "Charles asked if I wanted a transfer back to New York."

"Really? Why?"

"Courtney, I think. I asked for the transfer to LA originally to be closer to her. Now that we're not a couple . . ." He trails off.

"Are you going to take him up on the offer?" Ollie and I haven't been as close lately, but I know that I will miss him if he moves.

"Thinking about it. But I'm on the fence. I love Manhattan, but LA has its perks, too." He looks at me as if there is something else he wants to say.

"What?"

He hesitates, then barrels forward. "Do you think there's any chance of repairing the damage with Courtney?"

I feel my shoulders sag. "You fucked up, Ollie. Big time. We all love you. Hell, she loves you. But I don't know if that's enough."

"No," he says. "I don't, either."

I squeeze his hand. "I'm here if you need me."

"I know," he says, then hugs me. "I'm glad."

I return the hug tightly, thinking that this is another nice thing about weddings—it lets you clear out the last of the ghosts lingering in your past.

I make the circuit, chatting with Ryan and Edward, with Steve and Anderson. Charles and Blaine come up and I try to get some sense of where Charles stands on Ollie's move, but he's saying nothing.

Sylvia and Ms. Peters and others on Damien's staff are here as well. And, of course, there's Evelyn.

"I've been trying to corner you all night," I say to her.

"Funny, I was just thinking that you were the popular one." She steps back and examines me in that sentimental way folks have of looking at brides before the wedding. "You're good for him, Texas. Hell, you're good for each other."

"Yes, we are," I say. "Did Damien tell you about my mother?"

"I heard some of it from him," she admits. "I think I heard the rest from Jamie."

I grin. That doesn't really surprise me.

"I sent her packing," I say. "And I never asked her to walk me down the aisle, even though she's the only parent I've got."

"Parent?" she repeats. "You know better than that, Texas. Family's what you make of it, and that woman may have given birth to you, but she's not your family, not really."

I look around this room filled with friends and have to nod. "I know," I say. "But you're family, and I love you." I take a deep breath. "Would you walk me down the aisle?"

I think I see tears in her eyes, but I don't say anything. I just give her a moment to gather herself, even while I'm holding close to my heart the knowledge that my request moved her. "Hell yes, Texas," she finally says. "You better believe I will."

Moments later, Damien calls me over to where he stands chatting with Evan. He pulls a flat silver box out of his pocket and hands it to me.

"I can open it?"

"Of course."

I rip the paper off. I lift the top off to reveal a beautiful necklace with a silver chain and sunshine-yellow gemstones.

"Damien, it's lovely." I glance down at the emerald ankle brace-let I always wear, feeling spoiled.

"I remembered the flowers on your wedding gown. I thought this would match them."

My heart twists at his thoughtfulness. "But that was the first dress," I explain.

"I know," he says, as Evan reaches over and grabs a large box off the floor. He sets it on the table, and I look between the two men with curiosity. "Go ahead," Damien urges. "Open it. I think you'll find the necklace appropriate, after all."

Wary, I pull off the lid, and find myself gazing down at my beautiful, missing wedding dress.

"How—?"

"I have a few friends who have a unique ability to track down internationally shipped items that have gone missing," Evan says.

"Oh." I glance at Damien, wondering if that means what I think it does. But his face reveals nothing. To be honest, I really don't care how or where he found my dress. I'm just glad it's arrived.

"Alyssa's coming to the house in the morning. She'll take care of any alterations on-site," Damien adds, and I lean over and kiss him impulsively, this man who takes such exception-ally good care of me.

"Thank you," I say to Damien, then turn to include Evan. "Thank you both. You saved me."

A sense of relief sweeps over me, and for the first time since I started this wedding planning thing, I feel truly stress-free. It feels nice.

I reach out and hold tight to Damien's hand. *This*, I think, *is the only thing that's important.*

The party continues until well into the night, and it's al-most two by the time we get home. I'm about to strip and fall into bed when I realize that I've missed a call. I put the phone on speaker and listen as the message plays.

"Hi, Nikki, this is Lauren with the flowers for tomorrow. I just wanted to let you know that we're all set. It was last minute, but we were happy to make the change."

I frown and glance at Damien, who looks as confused as I feel.

"So we'll be there in the morning to set up, this time with the lilies and gardenias. And we're sending a selection over to Sally, too, for the cake. Thanks again, and we can't wait to see you tomorrow. Congratulations again to you and Damien."

The call ends, and I stare at the phone like it is a serpent.

What the fuck?

What the bloody fuck?

"She switched them," I say. "My mother actually fucked with my wedding." I meet Damien's gaze. I know mine is angry. His is murderous. Not because of the flowers—I sincerely doubt he cares about sunflowers versus gardenias—but because of what that woman has done to me over and over and over.

"It's like she's reaching out from Texas and twisting the knife. Like there is no pleasure in her life unless she's screwing with me."

I stalk around the bedroom, trying to get my head together. I feel cold and angry and out of control. Whatever pleasure I'd felt when Damien and Evan presented me with my wedding dress has been swept away. It's as if this wedding will never truly be my own. And now I either have to endure a wedding with my mother's stamp upon it, or I have to spend my wedding day sorting out this mess.

"Dammit," I howl.

"It will be okay," Damien says, pulling me into his arms.

"I know it'll be okay. It's not like we're talking about curing cancer. But that's not the point. She just went and turned the whole thing around on me."

"And at the end of the day, we'll still be married," he says reasonably.

I am in too bitchy a mood to listen to reason, but it's still there. Inescapable and true and hanging in the air between us.

I stalk around the room a bit more, while Damien eyes me with trepidation, as if I'm a bomb about to go off.

Smart man.

Finally, the bubbling anger cools, leaving calm calculation.

I feel the prickle of an idea, and slowly it grows. After a few more laps around the room, I stop in front of Damien.

"I can fix this," I say.

"What do you mean?"

"I can howl and complain that she fucked up my wedding. Or I can turn it around on its ear, flip my mother the bird, and say that she didn't fuck up my wedding, she did me a favor."

"Did she?"

My smile is slow. "Yes. And I'll tell you why." I grab the collar of Damien's shirt, pull him toward me, once again feeling light and free. I kiss him hard. "I can tell you," I repeat, and then flash a smile full of wicked intentions, "but you're going to have to make me."

Chapter 9

I stand on the third-floor balcony looking out at the calm Pacific. It is a beautiful evening, perfect for an outdoor wedding.

It is almost sunset. Just about time for the ceremony to begin.

Damien is beside me, his arm around my waist. The expanse of his property, lush green fading to pale sand, spreads out before us.

Usually, the beach is empty this time of day. Right now, however, it is dotted with white tents and glowing lanterns. Guests mingle, indistinguishable from this distance, and I hear the soft strains of Frank Sinatra drifting up to us. Beyond the line of tents, the paparazzi are camped out, ready to pounce.

I can't help but smile at the thought that we're pulling something over on those vultures.

Beyond them, the Pacific glows a warm purple tinged with orange from the swiftly setting sun.

Soon, I think. *Soon I will be Mrs. Damien Stark.*

"You're sure this is what you want?" Damien asks as the air fills with the thrum of his helicopter. It swoops down in front of us to settle gently on the helipad.

I take one more look at the panorama spread out before me. "I'm sure," I say, raising my voice to be heard over the rotors.

Below us, Gregory and Tony are loading suitcases into the bird.

I rise up on my toes and kiss Damien, hard and fast and deep. I pull away, breathless, and smile at the irony—it took a shove from my mother to drive home something I should have realized all along.

I press my palm to Damien's chest, wanting to feel the beat of his heart beneath my hand. "It's not the walk down the aisle that matters—it's the man waiting for me when I get there. You said it yourself, it's the only wedding I'll ever have, and this is the way I want it." No stress, no drama, no paparazzi. No polite chitchat, no worries about music or food or flowers or unexpected relatives showing up out of the blue. Just Damien and those two little words—*I do.*

"And all the work you've put into the reception?" he asks, even though we talked about this last night—about how I'd been working so hard for perfection that I lost sight of what Damien already knew—that so long as we end up as man and wife, "perfect" is a given.

Still, I indulge him by answering again. I understand he needs to be certain that I am sure I want to do this.

"The party's important, too," I say. "And they'll have a great one." I nod toward the beach. "Trust me. Jamie has it under control. If anyone knows how to make sure a crowd has a good time at a party, it's my best friend." I smile more broadly. "I asked Ryan to help her. They'll party through the night, and anyone who has a mind to can watch us get married in the morning. And Evelyn promised to spin the crap out of it for the press."

Damien's smile is as wide as my own. "I love you, Ms. Fairchild," he says.

"You won't be able to say that much longer. Soon it'll be Mrs. Stark."

He takes my hand and tugs me toward the stairs. "Then let's go," he says. "The sooner, the better."

We hurry hand in hand down the stairs, then sprint for the helicopter, heads down, laughing. Damien helps me aboard, and once we're strapped in, he signals the pilot and the bird takes off.

So, with the guests waving goodbye from the beach and the paparazzi snapping wildly, we elope into the sunset, leaving our wedding guests to eat our food, drink our champagne, and dance into the night.

Damien and I stand on a beach beside a foaming sea that is shifting away from the gray of night into a cacophony of colors with the rising sun. That was something else I'd realized: I couldn't get married at sunset. I had to have a sunrise wedding.

I am wearing my wedding dress and the necklace that Damien gave me, and when I saw the look in Damien's eyes as

I walked the short distance down the aisle to him, I knew that whatever trouble it took to rescue the dress was worth it. I feel like a princess. Hell, I feel like a bride. And in Damien's eyes, I feel beautiful.

I am not wearing shoes, and I curl my toes into the sand, feeling wild and decadent and free. There is no stress, there are no worries. There is simply this wedding and the man beside me, and that is all that I need.

In front of us, a Mexican official is performing the ceremony in broken, heavily accented English. I am pretty sure I have never heard anything more beautiful.

"Do you take this man?" he asks, and I say the words that have been in my heart from the moment I first met Damien. "I do."

"I do," says Damien in turn. He is facing me as he speaks, and I can see the depth of emotion in his dual-colored eyes. *Mine,* he mouths, and I nod. It is true. I am his, and always will be.

And Damien Stark is mine.

A few feet away, a small boy who has been paid some pesos is holding Damien's phone, streaming video of our wedding back to Malibu, where Jamie is projecting the ceremony onto one of the tent walls, just in case any of the guests are still sober and awake after a long night of partying.

Here on our beach, the official pronounces us man and wife. The words crash over me, heavy with meaning, filling my soul. "That day," I whisper, my heart full to bursting. "That day when you asked me to pose for you—I never expected it to end like this."

"But it hasn't ended, Mrs. Stark. This is just the beginning." His voice sounds full to bursting, and his words are absolutely perfect.

I nod, because he is right, and because I am so overwhelmed by the moment I can manage nothing else.

"I'm going to kiss you now," he says, then captures my mouth with his. The kiss is long and deep, and all around us the locals clap and cheer.

I cling to Damien, never wanting to let go, as the sun continues to rise around us, casting us in the glow of morning.

Perfect, I think. *Because the sun will never set between Damien and me. Not today, not ever.*

have me

Chapter 1

Mrs. Damien Stark.

Those three simple words fill my thoughts as they have all morning, ever since I spoke the magic words that transformed me from Nikki Louise Fairchild, a single woman, to Nikki Fairchild Stark, a wife.

I feel the tug of muscles as my mouth curves up into a grin, followed by the tightening of Damien's hand around mine. "You're smiling," he says.

"I can't seem to stop," I admit. We have been walking side by side along a Mexican beach, the cool water of the Pacific rising up to froth around our ankles, then rushing back out again in a rhythm as old as time.

Now I turn to face him, and my breath catches in my throat even as my pulse picks up tempo. I have looked at him so many times, and yet every glimpse is like the first. He is power and perfection, love and honor. He is the culmination of my dreams, the embodiment of my fantasies.

He is the future, I think.

Most of all, he is mine.

He is standing with his back to the ocean, the blue sky spread wide behind him as the waves churn around his feet. He wears swim trunks low on his hips and an open short-sleeved button-down. It catches the breeze, the white material emphasizing his athletic build and the sleek, tanned chest that my fingers itch to stroke.

Even dressed so casually, Damien looks like a mythical god rising from the sea, a being so powerful that even the elements cower at his command. And in a moment of giddy certainty I know that this man would have been as successful on a battlefield as he is in a boardroom.

Not for the first time, I think about the fragility of circumstance. What if we had been born a hundred years apart, or even twenty, or ten? What if he hadn't judged that beauty pageant so many years ago? What if I had caved to my mother and become a model instead of pursuing my dreams? And what if I'd slapped his face instead of accepting his offer of one million dollars in exchange for a nude portrait of me?

I would have survived, yes, but surviving isn't the same as living, and with Damien, I am vibrantly, brilliantly, happily alive.

I tell him my thoughts, wishing I had the words to truly describe the way my heart swells with both relief and gratitude when I think about how even the tiniest snip of the threads in the tapestry of time could have sent our lives spiraling down different paths.

"You're a miracle," I conclude, hoping that he understands despite the inadequacy of my words.

"No," he counters. "*We're* the miracle." His words make me shiver, because Damien Stark gets me in a way no one else ever has, or ever will. And that, I think, is the real miracle.

I watch as he glances at his wrist, then grimaces in wry

amusement when he doesn't find a watch there. I laugh. "Out of your element, Mr. Stark?"

"Happily roughing it," he counters, then turns toward the horizon. "What time do you think it is?" he asks. "Almost eleven?"

The sun looks down upon us from above, and I tilt my head back, shielding my eyes with my hand as I gaze at its white-hot heat. This is the time of day when the sand glitters and light sparkles off the ocean's froth like liquid fire. Appropriate, I think. Because right now, I want nothing more than to burn in Damien's arms.

"That's probably about right," I say. "Why? Do you have some pressing engagement?"

He grins in response to the amusement in my voice. "As a matter of fact, yes."

I raise my brows in legitimate surprise. "Oh, really?" I'm certain he hasn't planned a lunch. After all, we had a romantic breakfast on the beach right after our wedding ceremony, and that was only a few hours ago. We'd indulged in everything from delicate crepes to plump berries to coffee with thick, heavy cream. No way is he hungry again already.

"All right," I say. "Out with it. What's up?"

He says nothing, but merely hooks his arm through mine. "We should be getting back."

I narrow my eyes, but fail at my effort to look stern. Because, of course, I know what he has planned. Or at least I know the gist of it. This is our wedding day, after all. And there are certain traditional ways of passing the time immediately after tying the knot. Frankly, I'm all for that plan. What I don't know are the specifics of what Damien has in mind.

I examine his face, noting in particular the determined gleam in his eyes. "You're not going to tell me, are you?"

His mouth twitches as he fights a smile. "Not even if you beg." He leans toward me, then brushes his lips over mine.

"And I do like it when you beg," he adds, his voice full of wicked promises.

The kiss is soft and teasing, but my reaction is anything but gentle, and I have to fight the urge to press myself hard against him as a familiar heat pools between my thighs. "Damien," I say, and I hear something close to desperation in my voice. Passion is never far beneath the surface with the two of us, and just that simple kiss has sent fire rippling through and over me.

I reach out and grab his shirtfront, then use it as a lever to pull him closer even as I move toward him. The air between us is charged, and I feel the surge of electricity rush through me as I press against his bare chest, now slick from the heat and humidity.

Beneath the thin material of my bikini top, my nipples tighten, and I make a small sound of longing. I changed out of my wedding dress before breakfast, and now I am wearing only this small top, tiny bikini bottoms, and a sheer pink sarong wrapped around my hips and knotted at the side. But even such minimal attire is too much. I want nothing but skin on skin, and I ease my hips forward, desperate to feel him against me.

He is hard, his erection straining against his baggy trunks. I shift my hold on him, cupping my hands on his ass and pulling him tighter, closer. He groans, the sound so full of desperate need that my entire body quivers, and I think that I might come simply from the force of his desire.

But no—I want more. I want to pull him down with me into the sand. This man who is my husband.

I want his hands upon me, his cock inside me. I want his lips, his touch. I want his heat.

I want everything he can give and more.

Best of all, I know that he wants it, too.

"Damien," I whisper, then release him as I fumble at the knot on my hip. The sarong is thin and gauzy, but it will suffice as a makeshift blanket.

His hand closes over mine, and I tremble with anticipation. I draw my hand away, then close my eyes, more than willing to let him undress me.

Except he doesn't.

I stand for a moment, confused and disoriented, then open my eyes to find him looking at me. I see the desire on his face, as vibrant and wild as my own need. And yet he makes no move to touch me again. On the contrary, he takes a single step back, his eyes never leaving mine.

He is denying us both, and that simple fact both pisses me off and turns me on.

I gather self-control around me like a cloak, then lift an eyebrow. "Playing games, Mr. Stark?"

"Absolutely," he says with a wicked grin. "And just in case you've forgotten, I don't play if I can't win."

"Really?" I say, enjoying myself. "And what's the prize?"

He steps closer, still not touching me, but so close that I can hear my own heartbeat echoing against the hard breadth of his chest. "You are."

My heart flutters in my chest. Even now—even married—he makes me feel as deliciously alive as I did the first time he touched me. "In that case," I whisper, the words thick with the weight of truth, "you've already won."

He reaches out and strokes my cheek so gently I'm not sure that I can truly distinguish his touch from the breeze. "Yes," he says. "I have."

He twines his fingers with mine, then starts to lead me across the sandy beach toward a boardwalk.

"At least tell me where we're going."

"Back," he says.

I start to say that I had already figured that much out. We are on a secluded beach, in a remote part of Mexico that I can't pronounce and couldn't ever find again. After deciding to skip the wedding drama and elope, we'd left LA in one of Damien's private jets. We'd left it at a fair-sized airport with Damien's regular pilot, Grayson, who I presume has taken it back to the States. Damien and I had been chauffeured across the airport in a Jeep, then boarded a small, single-engine prop plane with only two seats and a tiny cargo area. Damien himself had taken us the rest of the way.

Damien explained the switch in aircraft by telling me that the runway where we were going couldn't accommodate a jet. As it turns out, "runway" was a bit of an exaggeration. The landing strip was little more than a length of packed dirt. I'd been terrified that I would die before we arrived and could take our vows. Damien had been exhilarated.

And while I might have preferred a plane with more than one engine and some asphalt to land on, I wouldn't have traded the look on Damien's face for anything. Not the joy I saw as he maneuvered the craft, nor the pride and expectation when we deplaned, climbed into a waiting Jeep, and drove the short distance to the remote—and utterly spectacular—resort.

The property is small, with fewer than ten guests at any time. It caters exclusively to couples looking for a romantic retreat, and from what I've seen so far, the owners know their business well. For although our personal concierge told me that the resort is fully booked, neither Damien nor I have seen any sign of the other four couples. Instead, it is as if we are alone on this remote stretch of beach—or as alone as one can be with a staff who caters to your every whim.

I'd seen a map of the property upon arrival last night, and the overall area of the resort resembles a hand. It is set on a remote section of beachfront with five peninsulas that protrude like fingers. Each bungalow occupies its own peninsula, giving it both privacy and a stunning ocean view from three sides.

Though we'd arrived after dark, I'd been impressed from the first moment I saw the resort. But when I stepped into our bungalow and saw the three-sided ocean view revealed by walls and walls of glass, my breath caught in my throat. It was like standing on the deck of a boat with miles of pitch-black ocean stretching toward forever, broken only by the moonlight dancing on the curl of the waves.

Our bungalow is the farthest from the main building, which houses the staff offices, a spa, and a restaurant that rarely has patrons but does a huge business in room service. Even without the breathtaking view, the bungalow is stunning. It features a luxurious bedroom dominated by a huge bed covered in bright pillows of pink and turquoise. A remote control operates a set of blackout blinds that drop the room into complete darkness. Since I see no reason to block the view at night or during the day, I don't expect that Damien or I will make much use of that technology.

As for the rest of the place, there is a fully stocked, state-of-the-art kitchen, a living room that features an indoor-outdoor fireplace, and a covered patio with a huge two-person lounge chair from which to enjoy both the view and the ocean breeze.

"Do you own this?" I'd asked Damien after we'd arrived and I'd had time to catch my breath. He'd smiled, but then surprised me by shaking his head.

"I almost bought it years ago when it was stumbling," he said. "I ended up giving the owners a loan to help them get past a hump, do some upgrades, and rebrand the place as an exclusive—and very upscale—getaway destination."

"They succeeded in spades," I said.

"Yes, they did," he said. I heard the note of pride in his voice and looked at him curiously. "This property has been in the same family for over three generations. There's a history here, not to mention the kind of work ethic that would have found a way to make the property viable. I just pushed the process along. I didn't want to alter what the family had built, but I did want to make sure that what they'd established would continue to flourish."

I nodded, remembering what he'd once told me about a small gourmet wine and cheese company. He'd loved the product and had wanted to help the company, so much so that he had partnered with them, letting them run autonomously, but with the full weight and resources of Stark International behind them. It had been a mistake. Suddenly, the small local company that had been praised in the press was vilified, with critics claiming it was actually big business pretending to be small and family-owned. Damien had pulled his resources and sold Stark International's share back to the owners, but the damage was done, and it had taken many years for that company to recover.

Now, as we approach our bungalow, Damien draws me close. "There was another reason, too," he says.

I frown, trying to follow his train of thought. "For not buying the resort, you mean?"

He nods. "I wanted a place to come when I needed to be completely alone. No work. No obligations. A respite."

"Like now," I tease.

"Like now."

I pause on the path, then hook my arms around his neck and rise up onto my tiptoes. "In case it escaped your attention, you're not alone."

"But I am," he says.

I open my mouth to say something light in response, but then stop. I can see by his face that he is serious.

"A man is never more himself than when he is alone," Damien says, in answer to my unspoken question. "That is when the mask comes off. Shut the door, and the persona drops away. Alone, you reveal your soul. You and I know that better than most people."

I nod, but say nothing.

He brushes his lips over mine in a kiss so soft it makes me want to cry from the sweetness of it. "You, Nikki, are the only person I can be with and still be alone. You see me—the core of me. And not only do you see me, but you love me."

"Yes," I say, and only when I taste my tears do I realize that I am crying, after all. Throughout my entire life I have played a part. Social Nikki. Beauty Queen Nikki. Dutiful Daughter Nikki. But with Damien, I am only Nikki.

"I am alone with you," he says. "And at the same time, neither of us will ever be alone again."

I blink away the tears. "It's perfect," I say. "You could have searched forever and still not found a better place for us. It—it fills me up." The words are inadequate, but when he squeezes my hand and says, "I know," I think that perhaps he understands.

When we arrive at the bungalow, my thoughts are still on Damien's words and this place. I meant what I said about the location being perfect. Ever since his murder trial, things have been just a little crazy. And he's right, this is a well-deserved respite for both of us. Time to be alone together. A chance to stop the movement of the earth for just a little bit. I grin at the thought.

"What's that for?" he asks, brushing the corner of my mouth with his fingertip.

I lift a shoulder casually as he opens the bungalow door for me. "I was just thinking about how easily you control the universe. Stopping the earth's rotation is no mean feat."

He chuckles. "Is that what I do?"

"Mmm-hmm." I take his hands and pull him inside. "But right now, I don't want the earth to stop. Just the opposite. Make the earth move for me, Damien," I say, pressing my body against his. I draw in a deep, self-satisfied breath as he shifts against me, his erection hard against my abdomen. "I want you to make me fall apart," I whisper. "Please, Damien. I want you to make me scream."

"As you wish," he says, in the kind of low voice that makes

me tingle in anticipation. "After all, Mrs. Stark, this is your wedding day."

Chapter 2

As it turns out, I don't scream. Instead, I squeal as he scoops me up and holds me tight against his chest, my arms hooked equally tight around his neck. I laugh and kick as he carries me toward the bedroom.

"I'm not going to make you scream, Mrs. Stark," he whispers with mischief in his voice. "I'm going to make you beg."

"Because you like it when I beg." My voice is breathy as I repeat what he said to me on the beach.

His mouth curves into a grin, but he doesn't answer in words. Instead, I see the truth in his eyes. *Oh yes,* I think. *This is going to be fun.*

I expect him to deposit me on the bed, and I'm prepared to cling to his shirt and pull him down on top of me if he even thinks about stepping away, even if only to undress. Instead, he surprises me, moving through the bedroom to a sliding wooden door. He shifts his grip on me just long enough to open it, revealing the most spectacular bathroom I've ever seen.

I'd seen enough of it last night to know that it is amazing, but it had been dark when we arrived, and I'd been more interested in the man I was eloping with than in architecture and plumbing, no matter how incredible.

This morning, I'd had no occasion to come through these doors. Damien had roused me before sunrise and handed me over to two local women who had hurried me into the living area, which had been converted into a makeshift dressing room. They'd washed my hair in a portable beauty shop–style chair, then did my makeup in the smaller, but still luxurious, bathroom off the kitchen.

I was primped and polished, then decked out in my wedding dress and hustled to the beach for a sunrise ceremony so quickly and efficiently that my memory of this morning before the vows began is a blur.

Then, as now, I'd wanted only Damien.

Now, however, my desire for the man is both underscored and enhanced by the scene in front of me. "Damien." The word comes out as an awed whisper. The room is romantic. Magical.

As perfect as the man himself.

I tilt my head up to find him smiling down at me, and in that moment my heart is so full that I have to cling to him more tightly for fear that it will burst.

This is like no room I've ever seen before, and I am a bit in awe. Last night, in the dark, I hadn't really thought about the floor, and if I had I would have assumed it was solid. Instead, it is slate leading up to a rectangular wading pool that fills most of the bathroom, but extends beneath a sliding glass wall to dominate the back patio as well. Beyond its infinity-style end is the ocean, and from the perspective of someone standing inside the house, the rocky shore that slopes down from the bungalow is completely invisible.

In some ways, this space reminds me of Damien's house in Malibu. *Our* house, I think, mentally correcting myself. It's similar in appointment and elegance, and yet it's different, too. Exotic. It is the perfect place for a honeymoon, and I whisper as much to Damien even as I continue to gaze around in delighted awe.

A small stone bridge stretches across the pool to the giant, modern tub that sits in the middle like an island.

But it is not these architectural enhancements that have stolen my breath and teased my heart. Instead, it is what Damien has made of the room. Because it is awash in rose petals. They cover the floor and they peek out from the bubbles that fill the tub. Incredibly, they also float on the water of the infinity pool. Beside the tub, a tripod champagne bucket rises from the water. A bamboo tray rests across the tub. On it sit two champagne flutes.

The tub has no shower, but I can see that there is one outside. Right now, the room is open, with the glass wall pushed aside so that the breeze flutters in, cooling my heated skin.

Unlike the room, which is more stone flooring than pool, the patio is mostly pool with only a few stone islands. One supports a chaise lounge that is little more than an outdoor bed, and which has, for that reason, drawn my attention. The other stone island is near a freestanding wooden wall from which a showerhead protrudes, as well as some hooks on which hang loofahs, bottles of shampoo, and other spa-style bath items.

Because the patio is completely open, there is no privacy here other than that offered by the stretch of empty beach and the wide open sea. It is wild. It is free. It is civilization stripped bare, and everything about this room—from its appearance to its rose-petal scent to its promise of decadent pleasures—has captured me utterly.

As Damien said, we are completely alone, and the knowledge that he can take me here with the ocean breeze kissing my skin and the wide open sky witnessing our pleasure makes me so weak with longing that I am even more grateful that Damien is holding me, as I doubt I could stand otherwise.

He crosses the stone bridge, then puts me down gently near the edge. I start to move, but he shakes his head, then slowly reaches behind me to untie the two knots that hold my bikini top in place. It falls into the water, and though I raise a brow in surprise, Damien simply continues.

His fingers skim lightly over my breast, making me draw in air, then shiver as his caress continues down my side and over my waist, making my skin prickle with need and anticipation.

He unties the sarong and lets it fall, as well. It floats on the surface of the water, and I watch as it flows outside, the sunlight catching it and making the fibers sparkle.

"The rest," Damien says, and I lick my lips as I comply, easing the bottoms down over my hips to pool around my ankles. I step out of the tangled fabric, then stand naked in front of my husband.

He smiles, soft and easy and full of promise, then pulls me to him. With practiced ease, he lifts me up and then gently places me into the tub. The temperature is perfect, and I sigh in ecstasy, letting the slightly oiled water sluice over my skin. I scoot back to lean against the smooth side of the tub and make room for Damien to join me.

Except, of course, he doesn't.

"Damien," I protest.

"Hush. Let me take care of you." He takes the champagne and opens it, very deliberately letting the cork fly out of the room, and sending foaming bubbles splashing down upon me.

I laugh. "Isn't that the uncouth way to open champagne?"

"Perhaps," he says. "But it's much more fun." He fills the two flutes, then hands one to me before picking up the second. His eyes skim over me, but the humor I'd seen only moments before is gone, replaced by something both soft and deep.

"Damien?"

His eyes meet mine, then, and I see the heat—and the love. He raises a glass in a toast. "You are my heart," he says, his gaze never leaving mine. "You are my blood. You are the air that I breathe and the strength inside me. You are not just my wife, Nikki, you are my soul. You are my world. You are my life."

I draw a shaky breath, nodding foolishly as if that will keep the tears at bay. "And you are mine," I say, then extend my flute to clink with his. "I love you," I add, wishing that I had his eloquence, but knowing that he understands what is in my heart even if I can't quite find the words.

"I know," he says as he moves to kiss the top of my head.

"Will you join me now?" I ask. I want his touch. I want him wrapped around me, lost with me in this warm and wet embrace.

Instead of answering, he sets down his champagne flute and picks up a glass container and pours some scented oil onto his hands. Then he moves behind me as I make a low noise of protest. But not as adamantly as I could have—while I do want him in the tub with me, I certainly can't deny the appeal of being bathed by Damien.

"Lean back," he says. "Close your eyes."

I comply, then sigh in utter delight as he gently rubs my shoulders. His fingers are strong and hot, and I lose myself in the pleasure of his touch and the rich scent of vanilla. He is tending me, seducing me, and right then I am more than willing to be seduced.

"Are you familiar with how honeymoons got started?" he asks, lifting my arm out of the tub and focusing on my hand.

I shake my head, too aroused by both the gentle pressure he is now exerting along each finger and by the not-so-gentle direction of my thoughts to form words.

"Years ago—back in tribal times—a man would take the woman he claimed for his wife to a secluded spot, where he would very thoroughly seduce her."

As he speaks, he draws his oil-slick hands up my arms, then eases them down over my collarbone until his palms cup my breasts. I draw in a stuttering breath as my nipples tighten, wanting more.

Thankfully, Damien doesn't disappoint. He moves his hands in small circular motions so that his palms brush lightly over my erect nipples, sending sparks of pleasure shooting through me. I shimmy a bit in the tub, trying to quell the need that started out as a soft hum between my legs but is now a throbbing demand.

"She probably wanted to run," Damien says, and I can't help the small sound of demur. Certainly *I* have no desire to run.

My eyes are closed, but I can still hear the chuckle in Damien's voice as he continues. "But he wants her, and in his determination, he keeps her for a month. One full cycle of the moon."

"Honeymoon," I murmur.

"It's a long time to be a captive," he says. "Most likely she wanted to hate him." He slides one slick hand from my breast down into the water. He continues south, teasing my abdomen until his fingers brush the line of trimmed hair at my pubic bone. "But he was determined to ensure that she would stay. And so he set out to satisfy her."

His hand slips between my thighs to stroke me lightly. "She was probably scared," he comments as I gasp, arching up toward his touch as the first electrical sensations of an orgasm dance through me in a glorious hint of more pleasure to come. "But he did his best to soothe her."

"Yes," I say, feeling deliciously soothed. My head is tilted back, my eyes still closed. My breathing is shallow now, my body primed.

The pad of Damien's finger traces small circles on my sex, teasing my clit in a way that makes me whimper, but which doesn't bring the satisfaction I now crave.

Frustrated, I shift my hips, seeking gratification as I silently beg for more. I am wild with need, shameless with desire.

"All of his focus was on erasing her fears. On making her warm and weak and wanting."

I want. Oh, dear god, I want.

He eases a finger inside me, and I release a moan of both demand and pleasure as I arch up, then fall back into the tub. Water sloshes over the sides, undoubtedly soaking Damien, but I don't care. All I want is this moment. All I want is for him to take me there.

"His every thought was on her," he says, thrusting another finger inside me even as his thumb teases my clit in the most subtle of motions. "His only goal was this woman."

"Yes," I whisper. I slide one hand down between my legs and press my palm over his hand, silently urging him to go deeper. Harder.

He does, thrusting those two fingers roughly inside me as the tip of another finger dances along my perineum. I gasp, writhing with pleasure, my body poised to explode. I'm close, so very close, and I slide my hand up to grasp my own nipple, tugging hard in an attempt to force myself over the edge even as Damien teases and torments me.

But this is Damien's show, and as he uses his free hand to cup my breast and still my fingers, I open my eyes to see my own wildness reflected back at me in Damien's expression.

"Please," I say, but he simply shakes his head, his mouth curving into the kind of arrogant smile that I know only too well. The kind of smile that promises abundant pleasure and unimaginable delights—but all on Damien's terms. And Damien is a man who knows how to prolong a seduction.

"He would take her to the edge," Damien says slowly. "Making her crave him. Making her want him. Pushing her to the very height of sensual pleasure, promising her the explosion. Taking her so far that she would surrender to him, give herself over to the promise of pure pleasure in the arms of this man."

"Yes," I say. "Oh, yes."

He withdraws his fingers from my sex, and my muscles tighten in protest, my body wanting to draw him back in. He cups his hand there, the pressure making it hard for a cogent thought to form in my head.

"And only when he is sure does he claim her fully, take her completely." He draws his hand away, and I have to bite my lip to stifle a moan of protest.

He reaches into the tub and scoops me up, one arm beneath my knees, the other around my back. I hook my arms around his neck and snuggle against him, wanting to be as close to this man as humanly possible.

"He plies her with softness and seduction," Damien says, and I murmur a protest against his throat. "What?" he asks.

I tilt my head back and look at him through heavy lids. "I'm not complaining," I say, "but I'm not so sure that men in history saw it entirely your way."

His lips twitch. "No?"

"I think they just took what they wanted, and the woman be damned." I lift an eyebrow, teasing, and he dips his head to kiss my forehead.

"Perhaps," he says. "Or perhaps I'm not finished telling you my story. It's one thing for him to make her crave him. It's another thing entirely for him to finally claim her. For her to truly understand that she is his."

"Oh," I say, as a sensual tremor cuts through me.

"The height of pleasure," he says slowly, the words so heavy with meaning they make me weak. And, yes, they make me wetter. "The precipice of passion. He would take her there, again and again, until she was desperate with longing, all resistance lost, all hesitation erased. She would know only him. Want only him. And she would beg for the relief and explosion that only he could bring her."

We're on the patio now, and he carries me to the shower, then puts me down. He turns on the tap, and pleasantly warm water begins to fall from the rain-style showerhead. I tilt my head up, enjoying the way it washes over me, then look down to watch as the last remnants of the bubbles that clung to me from the tub are washed away down the drain.

Beside me, Damien is still in his swim trunks and open white shirt. He's soaked, and the thin material now clings to him in the kind of magazine-cover-model way that makes me want to simply stare at him and bask in the knowledge that he is mine.

"Here," he says, turning me to face the wooden wall from which the showerhead protrudes. He takes my wrist and raises my arm above my head. It is only then that I notice that the hook that I saw holding shampoo is actually a slipknot. He takes the bottle of shampoo out, then slips the rough rope around my wrist before pulling it tight, effectively trapping me in place.

"Damien," I say, and I can hear both trepidation and excitement in my voice.

He hears it, too, and I see the hint of a smile as he takes my other hand and repeats the process so that I am standing there naked and bound, facing the freestanding wooden wall.

He steps back, watching me from just to my left, far enough back so that I have to turn my head to see him.

"He claims her," he says slowly. "Claims her and possesses her. Takes her and commands her. Teases and taunts until she understands that he is her life now, just as she is his."

I swallow, hearing both reality and history in his words. "And if she already knows it?"

Our eyes lock and the air between us seems to shimmer. I can feel it touching me, the tickle of electric fingers dancing over my body. I am alive with this man. My husband.

I am alive, and I am his.

And we both already know it.

For a moment, I think that he will say something else. His eyes narrow in what I can only assume is amusement. Then—without saying another word—he turns and walks away from me, carefully stepping on the stone path that leads the way across the infinity pool.

I watch him go, determined not to call after him. I don't know what game he is playing, but I am certain that there *is* a game. I'm also certain that while Damien might deny me simply for the pleasure of making me beg, he won't deny me for long. Not today. Not when he wants me just as badly as I want him.

Still, just in case, I give a firm tug to my bonds, managing only to tighten the slipknots. Well, damn.

And then, as if to prove my hypothesis, Damien returns. He's changed clothes, and now he's wearing khaki shorts and nothing else. He seems to glow in the sunlight, and I think to myself that he is sun kissed. At the moment, all that thought does is make me jealous of the sun.

He crosses purposefully to me, and even on this beachfront patio and dressed so casually, there is no question but that he is a man to be obeyed. More than that, I know that I will willingly do so.

He's carrying one of the champagne flutes, and now he comes to stand just to the side of the wooden wall so that I can look at him more easily.

"You're beautiful," he says, with such reverence in his voice that it makes me go weak.

"Is this how you like me?" I ask, lifting my chin. "Naked and bound and wet for you?"

One eyebrow arches slightly as he takes a step toward me. "Are you?"

Yes, yes, oh, dear god, yes. I don't say that, though. Instead I just smile. "Come and find out."

"Tempting," he says, moving even closer, and with each step my anticipation rises and my body fires just a little bit more.

"Please," I say, when he is close enough to touch me, but maddeningly doesn't do so.

"Please what?"

"Touch me," I say. "Fuck me."

"Feeling desperate, Mrs. Stark? Dear god, I like the sound of that."

"Desperate?" I quip.

"Mrs. Stark," he says firmly, and takes a sip of the champagne. "I'm not sure there are any two words in the world that give me greater pleasure." He lifts the glass to me. "A sip for the bride?"

I nod and ease forward. He puts the glass to my lips and tilts it for me to drink. I swallow some, but most of it dribbles down my chin and onto my breasts.

I shiver slightly from the unexpected splash of cool liquid, then shiver even more when Damien moves closer, pressing one hand to my lower back to hold me in place as he licks the champagne from my cleavage.

I do not recognize the sound I make. It is wild. Feral. It is a demand, a plea, and if I were not bound to this wall I would fall to my knees and beg him to take me hard, to take me fast.

With his free hand, he cups my breast as his tongue laves my areola before his mouth closes over my nipple. He suckles me, sending electricity shooting down to my clit, making my already throbbing sex go almost painful with need.

I struggle to move my hands because I want to touch him. To stroke his back and bury my fingers in his hair, but I am bound, and I can only feel and want and need.

Damien.

I don't realize that I've said his name aloud until he looks up at me, his lips still pressed against my breast, his face full of wide-open desire.

"Pleasure," he says, then bites down on my nipple. "And pain."

I cry out as his teeth dig into my sensitive flesh, but at the same time, my breast tingles with arousal, and my body hums as if every erogenous zone is interconnected. A web of sensuality crisscrossing my body, from my clit to my breasts, to my mouth, to my fingers. Over and through me as pleasure and pain combine to bring me closer and closer to something that has the power to both destroy me and make me whole.

"Tell me what you want." He straightens, his body pressed hard against mine so that I can feel his erection through his shorts. "Tell me what you need."

"You," I say. "Hard. Please."

Our eyes meet, and he cups his hand behind my neck then tugs me forward into a kiss so violent that our teeth clash and I swear I taste blood.

"You are my wife, Nikki. My heart, my life."

"Say it again," I beg.

"Wife," he says, understanding perfectly what I need to hear. He moves behind me, his palms stroking my shoulders, my back, my ass. "Mine," he adds as he presses against me from behind and slides his hand around to stroke my sex. I am drenched, desperately turned on, and a wild tremor shakes my body.

We're one, he and I. And right now I need him inside me, as if in proof of that simple truism. "Please, Damien. I need you."

"Not yet," he says, and I hear the rustle of cloth as he takes off his shorts. He moves back in front of me now, and as he goes to unbind one of my hands, I take the opportunity to drink in the perfection that is Damien Stark. He's impressive dressed; naked and erect, he's perfection. And I am selfishly, greedily, gloriously happy that he is mine.

"You're smiling," he says.

"I have reason to."

"We both do."

One of my hands is still bound, but he turns me so that my back is to the wall. He kisses me gently, his tongue exploring my mouth even as his hands graze my body, as if he is just discovering me for the first time.

With my free hand, I clutch the back of his head, keeping him close to me, not wanting this kiss to end, but also not wanting it sweet. I want it hard. I want to be fucked.

I want to be claimed like a bride of the honeymoons of old.

"Claim me," I say. "Please, Damien, take me now. I need you to. I need to surrender."

It is as if my words are an invocation; he deepens the kiss, taking as much as I can give, demanding everything I have.

Roughly, he presses me back so that I am against the wall, then takes my leg and lifts it so that my thigh rests on his hip and I am open to him. He fingers me, and I arch back from the glorious sensation of being explored. "I love how wet you are," he murmurs, and before I can respond, he closes his hands around my waist and lifts me up and thrusts his cock deep inside me. I cry out, taking all of him and wanting more.

He slams us backward, pressing me hard against the wall as he pounds deeper and deeper into me. I clutch his shoulders and cling tight, my body open to him, my need for him just as savage as his for me.

This isn't about romance and wine and roses and moonlight. This is wild. This is primitive.

This is wonderful.

He is claiming me. Marking me.

He is giving me what I need—*everything* I need—and I willingly surrender to both him and to the waves of pleasure that rise up, higher and higher as we continue to move together, the storm building inside both of us.

"Say it," I demand as my body reaches the crest. "Oh, god, please, I need to hear you say it."

Our bodies slam together again in one final, brilliant thrust even as the word I crave crashes over me, pushing me over the precipice and sending me hurtling toward the stars in an explosion of light and color.

"Wife," he cries even as his own release takes him. "You are my wife, my life, my love."

And Damien . . . Damien is my husband.

Chapter 3

The sea is calm and I am floating, my head tilted back and my eyes open to the sky. Clouds move lazily above me, drifting upon the air as I drift upon the sea. I cannot see Damien, but I can feel him, and I know that he is near and that I am not alone.

It is him as much as the water that buoys me, and I breathe deep, then close my eyes, warm and safe and alive.

I do not know how long I drift, I only know that when I open my eyes, it is dark and the stars wink down at me, not soft and gentle, but with a devious malice, as if they hold a secret that I am not allowed to share.

I tremble, suddenly aware that I can no longer see or feel him, and a bubble of panic rises in me. I tense, my breathing becomes shallow. I struggle to stay afloat, but it is no use. As if the water has claws, it pulls me under, and I start to sink, coughing and sputtering as my head dips below the surface and I struggle to rise.

I am wild with panic, flailing and fighting, and it is only when my bare feet touch sand that I realize that the water is shallow. Relief washes over me like the tide; I am not drowning. I am only floundering, and once I find Damien, I know that I will be steady again.

I regain my balance and press my palms to the ocean's surface, feeling it pulse beneath my skin with the motion of the waves and the pull of the tide. A current tugs at my ankles, silently urging me to let go. To melt into the water and submit to the power of the ocean.

Damien, *I think, certain that I have found him.* He is the ocean. *He is power and motion and grace and beauty, and the reason I cannot find him is because he is already there. Surrounding me, stroking me, urging me to come to him.*

I relax and give in to his sensual lure, letting the water tug me down, down, down, until my entire body is below the crystalline surface. I open my eyes and realize that I can see all the way to eternity. The world here beneath the waves is vibrant and alive, an explosion of colors despite the darkness of night above. I watch in awe as an orange and red coral reef rises above me. Fish dart to and fro, as if late for important engagements.

I have forgotten to breathe, and I panic, then realize that breath is not required at all. This is where I belong. Here, in the nether land. Here, where Damien surrounds me.

Except . . .

Except it is not Damien I feel around me. Not his comfort, nor his warmth. On the contrary, I feel cold. Lost.

Most of all, I feel afraid.

A little frantic, I search the ocean. I want to cry out, but the water presses against me, and I cannot. My heart pounds a fearful rhythm in my chest, and the vibrations radiate out, causing the sea to churn.

I reach to steady myself, but there is nothing to hold. I grapple, searching for purchase and finding none. I try to cry out, to beg for Damien to hold me, but no sound comes out.

And then I see him, and my heart twists.

He is standing near me, his torso rising above the water while his feet are planted in the sand. I watch from my odd perspective beneath the water as the waves buffet him. He reaches out a hand. At first I think it is to steady himself, and then I realize that he is reaching for me. I slog forward, my own hand extended. I can almost touch him. Just a little bit closer . . .

My fingers brush his, and I almost weep with relief—and then he is pulled away, the current taking him, and I cry out in horror as I try to swim toward him, only to find the way blocked. The reef, the wildlife, the tide. Everything in this new universe is conspiring to keep us apart, and when they finally move away and my vision clears, he is gone. There is nothing but ocean as far as the eye can see.

No! No, I can't have lost him!

I open my mouth to scream, then choke as the ocean moves in to drown me. I struggle, rising, and suck in air, my ribs aching from the pounding strain of my lungs. I am still coughing out water when I see him floating facedown in front of me.

I do not hear the scream that is ripped from my throat, but I know that I am slogging through the water, trying desperately to reach his side. I do not know how, but my arms end up around him, and then we are on the beach and I am over him, my mouth on his as I give him air—sweet, sweet air—and beg him to please, please, please come back to me.

But he doesn't. He just lays there, cold and wet, staring up at me with eyes that should twinkle like the stars but now are as flat as stone.

"No!" The word is ripped out of me, and I pounce on him again, unwilling to give up. Not able to even conceive that he could be gone.

I press my lips against his again, determined to give him life. To give him mine, if it comes to that. To do anything and everything to bring him back to me, because there is no way—no way in hell—that I can go on without him.

But there is nothing.

Despite my fighting, my pleading, my crying—there is simply nothing.

But I do not stop. I press on. I push. I plead. I threaten. And, goddammit, I will *him to come back, and I do not stop. I cannot stop, because if I stop, then there is nothing left of the world, and I will float off into space, a shell of myself. Lost. And truly and completely alone.*

"Don't you dare," I say, the words ripped from my throat as I thrust the heels of my hands down over his heart. "Don't you dare leave me."

A tear trickles down my nose, but I do not stop to wipe it away. It falls, landing on Damien's lips. I blink, and another tear follows the first.

His lashes flutter. Color returns to his cheeks.

And then his lips move in a word so broken and soft that I almost do not recognize it—"Nikki."

He is alive. He is back.

He is mine.

Chapter 4

I sit bolt upright, my skin covered in a thin sheen of sweat, my breath coming hard and fast. We are on the oversized patio chaise lounge, and Damien's arm is around me. He pulls me back down to him, his voice so soft and gentle that I understand only the sentiment and not the words. *It's okay. I'm here. You're safe.*

I close my eyes, letting his strength fill me. And when I have taken all I need, I turn to him. "I'm okay now," I say. "You can let go."

He brushes my lips with a kiss. "Never."

I burrow closer, then smile against his shoulder. That one simple word is as comforting as a down blanket in winter, and I am content, the rough edges of the dream finally smoothed away by this man who loves me.

"Do you want to tell me about it?"

"No," I say, then find the words coming anyway. How he was pulled away from me. How everything in the sea seemed to conspire to keep us apart. How I found him dead in water that had been comforting only moments before, but then turned suddenly menacing.

"I couldn't bring you back," I say, feeling the tears well again.

"But you did," he says. He pulls me close and captures my mouth with his. The kiss starts out sweet, then turns hot and hard, demanding and possessive. "You *did*," he repeats once he has released me. "And you will never have cause to bring me back again, because I will never leave you. I was foolish enough to do that before, and it just about killed us both."

I nod, then take another deep breath, steadying myself. Because I know the truth in what he is saying. Damien wouldn't leave me any more than I would leave him. And yet fear still clutches me, its sharp talons digging in and taking hold.

Now that I have shaken off sleep, I think I understand the nature of my fears. Despite being married—despite being taken, claimed, *possessed* by this man that I love so dearly—I am desperately, horribly afraid of losing him, no matter how determined we are to stay together.

I finger my wedding ring. I thought that I would have no fears once he slipped it on my finger. But even matrimony cannot erase reality, and I know that there are still things out there. Things like Damien's murder trial. Yes, the case was dismissed. But what if it hadn't been? He would have been ripped from me, forced to spend his life behind bars. And there is neither a vow nor a ring that can protect us from that.

The trial, thank god, is in the past. But there are still horrors lurking in the world. Things that could tear him from me. Things that could crash into our lives, trying to force us apart. His father, for one, who surely isn't done trying to get a piece of Damien. Or Sofia. I can't blame her, his childhood friend, for loving Damien, but I can damn well blame her for trying to rip us apart. She's locked away now, her past and the world having taken their own toll, and while Damien receives regular reports from the doctors that say she is improving, I don't think she will ever be well enough to hold tight to sanity in a world where Damien and I are together.

And yet at the same time, I know that Damien still loves her like a sister, even though what she did came close to destroying both of us. He declined her request to come to our wedding, and although he had sounded casual when he told me, I know that the necessity of keeping her away hurt him. I can only imagine how much it had angered her, and I stifle a shiver, more glad than I like to admit that she is far away, bound to her treatment by court order.

As if that weren't enough, there is also my mother, the paparazzi, ex-bosses, ex-lovers, the press, competitors, and god only knows who else. It's a big world, and when you cast as long a shadow as Damien, you make a lot of enemies. And Damien's enemies are mine now, too.

I was wrong in the dream, I realize. The ocean wasn't Damien. The ocean was the world. And the world is brutal.

When Damien's hand closes over mine, I realize that I have been unconsciously stroking one of the long scars on my thigh. I wince, both embarrassed and disturbed. I do not cut anymore— with Damien, I don't need to. Not even when my thoughts turn dark and fear seeps into me.

Yet here I am, groping for that pain, barely even conscious of the need to find my center, and that simple fact scares me. Because I do not understand the insecurity that has led me to touch that most horrible of souvenirs.

I wait for Damien to comment on it, but he doesn't. Instead, he gently traces my wedding ring. After a moment, he says only, "I was wrong back in Malibu."

I frown. "What are you talking about?"

"I told you we didn't need the ceremony. That it was just a formality because you and I were already one. I was wrong."

I cock my head. "We're not one?"

He chuckles. "About that, I was right on the money. But I was wrong about not needing the ceremony."

"You were? How?"

"How many times have we faced the world together and survived?" he asks, and I know right now that he understands my fears. "How many times has that world tried to tear us apart? Your mother, Sofia, the past?"

I don't answer, but it doesn't matter; he is not expecting me to.

"Our wedding is our bond. Our promise and our proof. It's a symbol to the world around us that we'll fight and that we'll win. Most of all, that we are one."

He spreads his fingers, his eyes locked on his own ring. "A simple silver band," he says. "But it's made of titanium, and that's about as strong as it gets." He meets my eyes, and I am awed by the ferocity reflected back at me. "There's nothing to be afraid of, sweetheart. Not anymore."

I look down at my own ring, a platinum band accompanying a stunning diamond solitaire. "Maybe I should trade this in for titanium."

"Not necessary," he says, as he takes my hand, holding it so that our two rings touch. "I will always give you the strength you need."

"I know." I wish there was a way to fill the sound of my voice with everything that is inside me. I clutch tight to his hand and pull him toward me as I stretch out on the chaise. "I want you now," I say. "I want to feel my husband inside me."

His grin is slightly wicked and slightly amused. "Convenient," he says. "Because at the moment I'm overcome by the urge to ravish my wife."

I manage a fake yawn and pat my hand over my mouth. "*So* unoriginal. After all, you did that just a few hours ago."

"And you have a better idea?"

"As a matter of fact, yes." I shift on the chaise so that I am straddling him. "I was thinking that I should ravish my husband."

"Were you?" He is on his back, and I am sitting just above his pubic bone. I feel his cock twitch, teasing my ass. I rise up, then scoot backward just a bit. He is fully erect now, and I hold his cock with one hand while I wiggle my hips to position myself. I keep my eyes on Damien as I do and watch the storm building. He knows what I'm up to—how could he not?—but that doesn't stop his groan of surprise and pleasure when I quickly lower my body, impaling myself on his steel-hard cock.

"Yes," I say in answer to his question. "I was."

My voice is breathy, and I rock a bit as I speak, using my knees to rise up and down. I ride him hard and fast, my back arched, my breath coming in ragged bursts. I do not close my eyes, and in unspoken agreement, neither does he.

Damien Stark is as necessary to me as my blood. He is what makes me whole, what makes me alive. And as I move on him—as I feel him hard inside me, so vibrant and vital—I watch the passion burn like fire in his eyes and know with unerring certainty that it is the same for him.

"Now." Without warning, he grasps me by the hips. I cry out as both pain and pleasure rock through me when he slams me harder against him, thrusting his cock even deeper so that I feel the shock of him through every cell, filling me until I'm right on the precipice.

"Come with me now," he says, and the passion and need in his voice push me that rest of the way over. My sex clenches tight around him, and I cry out from the force of the explosion that rips through my body even as Damien's hips thrust up and he empties himself into me.

I fall forward, my heart pounding and my body trembling as the final shocks of both my own orgasm and his rumble through me. "Damien," I murmur.

"I know," he replies.

Later, we spoon together, drifting in that place that is neither sleep nor wakefulness. He is behind me, his body tucked against mine, making me feel safe and warm. So much so that I make a soft noise of protest when he pushes himself up on an elbow.

He chuckles in response to my protest, and I am about to voice my objections even more loudly when he begins to trail his finger lightly over my side, along the curve of my waist and hip. I sigh and snuggle backward, ensuring maximum contact. Right then, I feel so light, warm, and sated, so satisfied I think I could simply melt into the mattress. "Please tell me that I never have to move again."

"I could tell you that." I hear the hint of a tease in his voice. "I could probably even make it happen, though it would be an expensive proposition. Another couple has rented this bungalow, and I believe they're scheduled to arrive in just under five hours."

I roll over in his arms. "Another—"

"And if you never move again we'd undoubtedly miss our plane. Not to mention the honeymoon I've planned."

I sit up, enjoying the way the cool air caresses my heated skin.

"Well," Damien says. "I do like this view." He traces his finger lightly over my breast, and my already erect nipple becomes even tighter.

"Honeymoon?" I repeat. "I thought this—" But I cut myself off. Of course this isn't our actual honeymoon destination. While I had been planning our wedding, Damien had been planning the honeymoon. But our decision to elope had been last-minute, and Damien had taken care of that, too. Only now do I realize that I had been assuming the two destinations were one and the same. Clearly, that assumption sat somewhere to the left of reality.

"Okay," I say after making all the necessary mental readjustments. "Where are we going?"

"Where? Were you not listening earlier? Honeymoon tradition. Remote location. Intense seduction." He draws a lazy pattern on my bare breasts, leaving a trail of heat and renewed desire.

"I'm all for intense seduction," I admit. "But if you're expecting to get me out of bed, you're going at it all wrong."

"You may have a point." There's laughter in his voice, and he's sporting a smug grin as he eases off the chaise lounge. "I can't tell you, but maybe a hint."

I watch as he moves back inside, then returns moments later with a small jewelry box. He hands it to me, and I open it slowly, wanting to savor the surprise. Inside is a delicate bracelet with a single silver charm.

The Eiffel Tower.

I gasp, then throw my arms around Damien's neck. "We're really going to Paris?"

"We really are," he says.

I laugh, delighted. *"Merci,"* I say, drawing on my rusty high school French. And though he knows it already, I add, *"Je t'aime. Beaucoup."*

"I love you, too," he says. "So very much."

Chapter 5

The buttery leather of the Bombardier's passenger seat envelops me, and I breathe deep, frustrated by how antsy I am despite feeling at home in Damien's private jet. Correction, *one* of Damien's private jets. As best I can tell, he has a fleet of them.

Correction again—*our* private jet, as Damien keeps reminding me. I never aspired to own a jet—and I have a sneaking suspicion that Damien's accountants and lawyers and other Big Important Advisor Types would say that I still don't—but I can't deny the coolness factor. After all, not so long ago I was driving a battered Honda with an equally battered transmission. I think a private jet definitely constitutes a step up in the world.

Damien had flown us out of the resort in the prop plane, and we'd met up with Grayson, who was now in the cockpit, along with Damien and the co-pilot. Damien has co-piloted the jet before, but that is not on the agenda today. Instead, he's only gone up front to attend to something, and I am anxious for him to return.

I press my hand onto the leather of the seat beside me and am comforted by its warmth. With Damien beside me, I was fine. But now the dream has moved back in, small wisps of fear that Damien's simple presence had battled back, but which can run free and wreak havoc when he is away from me. Intellectually, I know that he is only discussing the flight plan with Grayson and generally making sure that all of our travel arrangements are in place and confirmed. But even knowing that, I can't help but think that my dream was a portent, and that no matter how desperately we might want our honeymoon to be a romantic bubble, the world is going to put up a fight.

I grimace and tighten my grip on the stack of magazines in my lap. *Yeah? Well, bring it on. Because together, Damien and I can face anything.*

"Is there anything you need, Mrs. Stark?"

I jump, startled, and look up to find Katie, the fleet's senior flight attendant, smiling at me. I glance down at my hands, and see that my knuckles are white against the dark cover of this month's *Wired* magazine. I try to relax. "I'm fine. Just tired."

"Of course," she says, and though her face remains perfectly polite, I can't help but think I hear a hint of amusement in her voice, and my cheeks heat in response. I'm a newlywed, after all. "The stateroom is made up for you now."

"Oh," I say stupidly. I've flown on this jet a number of times now, so I'm perfectly familiar with the stateroom, and often spend the trip back there once we've reached altitude. What I'm wondering is why I'm going there without Damien.

My question must be all over my face, because now Katie does smile. "Mr. Stark said that he'd join you there momentarily."

"Right," I say, feeling a little foolish. I tuck my stack of magazines under my arm, then ease out of the plush seat and head toward the back of the plane. I think of Katie's promise that Damien will be coming soon, and my body warms with pleasant anticipation. The flight to Paris will take approximately ten hours. Considering how hard and fast we've been going since we left Los Angeles, I know that we should get some sleep if we don't want to pass out from jet lag and exhaustion right there on the rue de Rivoli. But even if we crash for a full eight hours, that still leaves two delicious hours all to ourselves.

I hurry the rest of the way, but when I open the door I see that once again, Damien Stark is ahead of the curve. The room glows with candlelight, an unexpected reality that makes me laugh out loud. Who but Damien would think of candlelight on an airplane?

Of course, these are faux candles, but the illumination is just as romantic, and the flickering light from dozens of scattered candles gleams off the room's polished wood and casts dancing shadows that under other circumstances could seem menacing, but tonight are both inviting and comforting.

The narrow bed is still made, the pristine white duvet covered with rose petals. I smile, thinking of the tub back in our Mexican bungalow. Our honeymoon, it seems, has a theme.

There is no champagne, but the small bedside table is

topped by a bottle of eighteen-year-old Macallan next to two crystal highball glasses, and I grin. Before meeting Damien, my drink of choice was bourbon. More recently, though, I've discovered the pleasures of single malt Scotch.

All in all, the room is a delight, and I can't help but think that we will likely be getting less than our full eight hours, after all. Not a problem; I'm more than willing to sacrifice sleep for Damien.

I pour myself a shot of Scotch, neat, then sit on the edge of the bed and sip it, savoring the slow burn and the way I can feel the heat spreading through me. I toss back the rest, then close my eyes and let the slow buzz tingle through me. We didn't eat dinner, and the Scotch is strong. Not as strong as my thoughts of Damien, though, and between my buzz and my desire I am beginning to squirm a bit in frustration.

My nipples tighten, rubbing almost painfully against the fitted bodice of my sundress. I reach up, cupping my breasts, imagining that it is Damien's hands upon me. Damien, who knows my desires as well as I know them. Maybe even better.

I think of the way he took me in the shower. Of the tub filled with scented water and rose petals. This cabin filled with candlelight.

He did that for me. To please and seduce me.

I smile to myself with just a hint of mischief. *Now*, I think, *it's my turn.*

I stand just long enough to unzip the sundress and slide the spaghetti straps off my shoulders. I wriggle it off my hips and then toss it across the room so that I am standing naked in front of the bed. I'm not wearing underwear—a nod to the game that Damien and I used to play—but he hasn't yet discovered that little secret. That's okay, though. There's plenty of time for discovery once we get to Paris.

Right now, I have a different kind of surprise in mind, and since I don't know how much longer Damien will be in the cockpit, I know that I have to hurry. I turn and assess the bed, trying to think. I have something in mind, and after a few seconds of mental gymnastics, I think I've figured out how to pull it off.

By the time I hear the light tap at the door, I am ready.

"Who is it?" I call, just in case it is Katie.

"It's me," he says, and because I am already so desperate for him, the simple sound of his voice makes my body tremble and my sex clench with need.

"Come in," I say, but it doesn't matter. He has already turned the knob and the door is pushing inward.

"Sorry about that," he says, still in the hallway. "There was some mix-up with the flight plan, and—"

He breaks off, sucks in air, and shuts the door fast behind him. Then he stands frozen, his eyes taking in every inch of me, the examination so slow and methodical that I almost believe that his gaze is a physical touch.

I am naked and mostly spread-eagled on the bed. The thing about jets is that seat belts are required, and though Damien and I routinely sit in the more traditional main cabin during takeoff and landing, even the stateroom's bed has belts that can be used in the case of turbulence.

Or in the case of seduction.

It had only taken a few moments to use the straps and buckles on the far end of the bed to secure my ankles. Much trickier had been the task of securing my left hand above me. But I'd managed it. Now that arm is extended and bound, leaving me more or less immobile. Only my right hand is free, and I can tell simply from the rhythm of Damien's breathing that he is well aware of the way the fingers of my free hand are stroking my very wet, very sensitive sex.

"Christ, Nikki."

I just grin, feeling both desirable and very, very smug. I know damn well what he is looking at, and the surge of feminine power at having both surprised and silenced Damien Stark makes me more than a little giddy.

"Hi," I say, my voice low and sultry. "I poured you a drink. Why don't you get it and come over here?"

"I don't know," he says. "I'm having a fine time just standing here and watching."

"Really?" I keep my voice light, but soft. And as I speak, my fingers never leave my sex. "I'm having a nice time, too."

"So I see."

"Mmm." I slide a finger deep inside myself, lifting my hips and releasing a low, desperate moan as I do. My plan may have been to get Damien worked up, but it's working equally well on me, and I'm so damned aroused right now that it is all I can do not to take myself all the way, then watch Damien's face as I shatter in front of him.

But no. This isn't a solo act. I want his hands, his mouth. I want to feel him on top of me. I want his cock inside me.

I want the wildness, the release. I want to see Damien Stark's famous control shatter, and I want to know that I am the one who did that to him.

Wife, I think.

Damn right.

I keep my eyes on his face, then withdraw my hand. Slowly, I trail my finger up my belly, then over my cleavage. When I trace a circle around my nipple, I see a muscle tighten in his cheek. But when I bring my hand to my mouth and draw my finger in between my lips, his composure breaks and he actually growls even as he crosses to me in one long stride.

I laugh, delighted, then slowly slide my finger out from between my lips. I smile up at him, my eyes wide and innocent. "Feeling a bit desperate, Mr. Stark?"

"With you, always."

I sigh with satisfaction. I feel exactly the same way.

He is standing even with my shoulder, his hip brushing the

side of the bed. Now he reaches out to trace his fingers up my bare arm until he reaches the strap that binds my wrist in place. "Interesting," he murmurs, then steps backward, letting his fingers trail behind him as he moves, so that he is lightly stroking my ribs, my waist, my hip.

After a moment, though, he steps away from the bed, leaving me bereft when his fingertips leave my skin. I suck in air, only then realizing that I'd forgotten to breathe. He goes to the table, picks up his glass of Scotch, then takes a sip. Throughout it all, his eyes never leave me.

I lay there—I can do nothing else—and as I do, my skin begins to tingle. There is never a time when I am not aware of Damien. When I can't conjure the sensation of his fingers on my skin or his lips upon my cheek. I have only to think of him, and I can feel him.

But this is different. This is anticipation mixed with need. This is heat. This is the knowledge that I have offered myself for him to do with me what he will—and I do not know how far he will go with that. I only know that wherever he takes me, I will go willingly.

"I wonder," he says, and then says no more.

I try not to respond, but the word comes despite my efforts. "What?"

His smile is slow and wide and just a little devious. His dual-colored eyes crinkle a little, adding a bit more devilish flair. "I wonder what you would do if I just stood here for the rest of the flight and enjoyed the view."

I'm not worried. He's wearing loose-fitting shorts, but they don't hide his erection. My husband wants me as much as I want him. "We've barely gotten underway," I say. "Ten hours is a long time to stand. And there's no other seat in this room."

He glances around as if to verify my observation. Then he moves back another step so that he is leaning against the door. "I'm sure I can make do. I'm capable of putting up with all types of self-denial. At least so long as the prize at the end is worth it."

"Oh." I shift a bit uncertainly on the bed. I know damn well he speaks the truth. I know even better that I am the prize—his wife, hot and wild and a little bit crazed with desire, all the more so because she has been teased and tempted, and yet denied.

I drag my teeth over my lower lip as I watch him. He's not smiling, and yet there is no denying the spark of amusement lighting his face. "You wouldn't," I say, projecting a note of certainty in my voice that I don't actually feel.

"Wouldn't I?" He takes a sip of Scotch, studying me. "Funny, I thought you knew me better than that."

"Dammit, Damien," I say, not certain if I'm pissed or amused. The only thing I am certain of is the feel of my body. The way my skin seems to fit just a little too tight and my breasts are a bit too heavy. My nipples are so damn sensitive that even the faint movement from my heartbeat makes them tingle in a silent demand for more. And my sex—oh, Christ, I'm so damn wet, so swollen, so painfully, desperately, needfully turned on, that even the lightest brush of my fingertips sends shock waves through me and makes my cunt throb in demand. I want him inside me—no, I *need* him inside me. But if he's going to torment me . . .

"No," he says, as I boldly stroke myself, imagining that my touch is Damien's, and then arching up as a series of sparks like tiny fireflies begin to dance inside me, a precursor to the lightning storm that is coming.

He crosses to the bed and takes my hand, his thumb brushing lightly over my sex in the process, like some form of casual torment. "No," he says again as he lifts my hand above my head, then uses the same seat-belt strap that I'd used for the left one to bind this hand as well.

I am completely immobile now. My hands are strapped

above my head, bound together at my wrists. My legs are bound on either side of the bed, leaving me wide open and ready. I am naked and helpless and entirely at Damien's mercy.

I am wild with anticipation, and so aroused that the tightness in my nipples is almost painful, and my sex is so primed for his touch that I fear I will come from nothing more than the weight of his eyes upon me.

"Well," he says, as if to himself. "What does a man do when faced with unlimited possibilities?"

I don't answer. I'm too entranced by the expression on his face, like a man who has just opened an incredible gift. It is a look—among so many others—that I have come to know well. It's a look that says he loves me. More than that, it's a look that says he desires me.

He pours himself another shot of Scotch, and then takes a sip, as if pondering this knotty dilemma. I continue to watch him, my breathing shallow, my anticipation building. After a moment, he steps beside me again, his glass raised. I expect him to take a sip, but instead he very slowly tilts the glass above me, allowing a thin stream of liquid to fall. It splashes on my breasts, then trickles down my belly, some pooling in my navel, and some easing over my waist to dampen the sheet beneath me.

It is not cold, but I still gasp from the shock of contact, my eyes going to Damien's. I see heat and purpose, and I watch, mesmerized, as he sets the glass aside, and then slowly removes his shirt, his shorts, his briefs.

I have little enough time to enjoy the view, though, as he tells me to shut my eyes. I consider protesting, but since I know it will only earn me a blindfold, it hardly seems worth it.

And then there is his touch.

The stroke of his hands lightly over my skin, running along my sides as if to steady me. His fingertip strokes a pattern on my stomach, circles and swirls drawn with the Scotch, cooling my heated skin as the liquid caresses me.

He is touching neither my breasts nor my sex, and yet the sensation is so wildly sensual that he might as well be. I feel his touch throughout my body. Heating the flesh between my inner thighs. Making my nipples so painfully tight.

I writhe against my bonds, wanting more. Wanting everything. Wanting Damien.

And yet I can find no relief from the growing pressure of desire. This building firestorm inside me that he is so slowly and so deliberately stoking. I can only ride this wave, losing myself to the painfully sweet torment of his touch.

"Damien, please," I murmur, but he only brushes his lips across mine.

"Frustrated, Mrs. Stark?"

"You know I am."

He says nothing, but I swear I can hear his smile. This is what he wants, to take me to the edge, to keep me hovering there, and then—when he finally sends me spinning into the abyss—to be there to catch me as I tumble back to earth.

He lifts his hand from my body, and I whimper a bit.

"I could stand here all night, simply looking at you." His voice is as soft as the caress he has withdrawn, and it sends shivers over me. "Seeing the way the color changes on your skin when you are aroused. The way your nipples peak and the way your stomach muscles tighten in anticipation of my touch. Every inch of you is ripe with need for me."

"Yes," I whisper.

Slowly he traces his fingertip from the indention at the base of my throat all the way down to my navel. I arch up, his touch sending shock waves through me, and when he stops—so close to where I crave both his touch and the explosion I know it will bring—I moan in frustration.

"I control an empire," he says, "and I will not deny the thrill of holding that kind of power. But it is nothing compared to the way I feel when you respond to me. When my words make you smile, when my touch makes you wet. And when you are like this, bound and open, so full of trust and desire, giving yourself so completely to me—god, Nikki," he says, his voice quivering just slightly. "I swear it's you who has the power, because only you can break me."

I open my mouth to speak, but there are no words. And when his mouth closes over mine, I fall hungrily into the kiss, then moan in protest when he withdraws to kiss his way down my body, his mouth following the trail of the Scotch.

The sensation is as delicious as the man, and I writhe against his touch, wanting more, so much more. And Damien, thank god, delivers.

With agonizing slowness, he kisses his way down my leg, paying particular attention to the soft skin behind my knee. My muscles are tight, straining for him, and yet I can do nothing but withstand the storm of his touches.

When he reaches my ankle and undoes the bond, I have to bite back a protest. I want the freedom to move, yes, but there is no denying the pleasure of being at Damien's mercy.

I hear his soft laugh and realize that he knows exactly what I'm thinking. "Don't worry, sweetheart. I'm not even close to done with you."

He releases my other ankle, then eases onto the bed so that he is between my legs. I am spread wide open for him, and though he is my husband—though he has seen me this intimately countless times—I cannot help the heat of a blush that spreads over me.

"Beautiful," Damien murmurs as he lifts my legs to his shoulders. He tries to tug me closer, but I am immobile thanks to the bonds on my arms, and so he leans in, driving me crazy when he gently blows on my clit, making me gasp and squirm and then cry out as his mouth closes over my sex and his tongue sets my senses on fire.

I arch up, because it is too much, but he refuses to relent. He sucks and laves, his expert tongue teasing and tasting, pushing me higher and higher until I am so close that I can almost taste the sweetness of the coming explosion, and I long for it, pushing toward it, wanting and craving it.

And then he stops—and that swirling disk of pleasure that has been hurtling toward me fizzles, dissolving in front of me in the dark abyss of lost pleasure.

"Damien." His name is a curse, a protest, but my words neither wound nor move him.

"Soon," he says calmly. "Anticipation, remember?"

"Bastard," I tease, but the word catches in my throat as he starts to lower me so that my rear is on his thighs and his fingertip skims lightly over my sex.

"I haven't fucked you like this," he says. "You on your back, legs up, helpless. Me on my knees, holding you close, slamming deep inside you. Tell me, sweetheart, would you like that?"

I say nothing—his finger is wreaking too much havoc with my senses to let me lasso the power of speech—but my answer is in my body, and Damien well knows it. With a small chuckle, he leans sideways and opens one of the small drawers that line the cabin-side of the bed.

He reaches in and pulls out a familiar bag. It takes me a second to recognize the gift that my best friend, Jamie, and my other girlfriends presented me at my bachelorette party.

"Damien! Oh my god."

"A goodie bag of sex toys seemed like something we should take on our honeymoon."

We've not had the chance to play with the contents, and now he peers inside and pulls out a bullet-style vibrator and some lube. Considering how wet I am, the lube is hardly necessary. Unless . . .

"Damien . . ."

"Shhh. You're mine, remember. To have. To fuck. To do with what I will. Isn't that why you greeted me the way you did, laid out and bound for my enjoyment?"

I lick my lips. The man does have a point.

He is kneeling on the bed, and my legs are spread open on either side of him. Now he turns on the bullet and it softly vibrates in his hand. He palms it, then slides it slowly along my inner thighs. The sensation is incredible, all the more so when he brings it to my sex, teasing near but not actually stroking my clit.

Pleasure swirls around me, lifting me higher and higher as Damien teases me with the bullet until, yes, I'm literally begging to be fucked.

"Every way," he says. "All the way."

I nod. "Yes. Oh, god, yes."

"Legs up," he says, then lifts my hips and guides himself inside me. I've not been in this position with him, and as he thrusts into me, his eyes looking into mine, I have to admit I like it. I am on my back, my ass rubbing his thighs, the contact on my clit as he enters taking me higher and higher with each powerful thrust.

"Do you want more?" Damien's voice is low and sensual and rolls over me like a touch.

"I want everything."

I hear the buzz of the vibrator, then feel the cool gel on his fingertips as he readies my ass. I bite my lower lip in anticipation, forcing myself to relax as he inserts the bullet. I sigh with pleasure from the sensation of being completely filled by both Damien and this toy, and also from the exquisite tingle of the vibrations dancing inside me, growing stronger with each of Damien's thrusts inside me.

"Dear god," he says, and the deep groan that lights his voice lets me know that he can feel it, too.

The sensation builds, growing so wild and burning so hot that I am not entirely sure if it is pleasure or pain. All I know is that it lifts me. That it takes me. And that it is not just this jet that is making me soar. It is the man inside me.

Harder and harder he thrusts, and I meet each motion, drawing him in, deeper and deeper. I want to get lost in him. Already I do not know where I end and he begins. All I know is pleasure. All I know is Damien.

Damien, who sets the world spinning wild around me.

Damien, who commands the earth, the stars, the universe, and me.

Damien, who has brought me to the brink.

"Damien," I cry as everything that I am shifts and tilts and bursts in a wild cacophony of light and sensation that wash over me with such violence and joy it is a wonder that I can survive.

And yet I do, and it is Damien who pulls me back. Whose soft touch strokes me. Whose gentle kisses bring me down. Who holds me close and keeps me safe. "Damien," I murmur, as the softness pulls me under and I succumb to the warm, languid pull of exhaustion. *I am his,* I think. *I am loved.*

Chapter 6

When I come back to myself, Damien cleans me up and frees my arms, and I stretch, reveling in the sensation of once again having the use of all my limbs. The bed is small, but I like it. I curl up behind him, my face snuggled up against his shoulder and my legs twined with his. I am floating somewhere in that state between waking and dreams, and idly wondering if it is really necessary to ever move again. At the moment, I think I could stay like this forever, drifting through the sky with the man I love.

"Thank you," I whisper.

"For what?" His voice is soft, too, and I think that if I close my eyes and let go, I will find him right next to me in that dream world.

"For loving me."

He is silent for a moment, then rolls over so that we are facing each other. Gently, he brushes a stray lock of hair away from my eyes. "I've seen what's in your heart," he says. "How could I help but love you?"

I let his words glide over me, as warm and soothing as a blanket. "You're very good at that, you know."

"At what?"

"At making me feel as special with your words as you do with your body."

"How many times have I told you, Nikki? I will always give you what you need."

I ease forward and press a soft kiss to the tip of his nose. "Thank you for this honeymoon," I say. I'm not sure what answer I expect. A smile, perhaps. Or a tease. Even some romantic words.

Instead, I see a shadow in his eyes.

"Damien?"

He shakes his head. "Sorry. I was just thinking about our hotel in Paris."

"Problem?"

"I certainly hope not."

I frown. I'm still confused, but tell myself that there must have been some sort of snafu that was troubling him. But even that seems odd, because Damien is the kind of guy who simply tells someone to fix something, then forgets about it, knowing damn well that his staff will make it happen. Then again, this is our honeymoon. So perhaps he's taking more of an interest in the details. I snuggle closer, the thought pleasing me.

"Don't go to sleep just yet," he says, though his voice sounds as lazy as I feel.

"I'm not sure I have a choice in the matter. You've thoroughly relaxed me."

"I know the feeling, and while I do want you well rested for when we land, the fact is that Katie will be here soon with our dinner. And before she comes, I have a present for you."

"Really?" Despite the fact that I'm already feeling deliciously spoiled, I'm as delighted as a child at the idea of a gift. I sit up. "What?"

He chuckles, obviously amused at my eagerness. He sits up as well, then trails his fingers casually over my bare thigh before standing and moving to the door. There is a leather folio on the ground. It wasn't there before, so he must have entered with it, and I was too lost in a sensual haze to notice.

I make a small noise of satisfaction as he bends over, naked, to pick up the folio. "If my present is this view, I like it already," I say.

"Minx," he counters, making me laugh.

He returns to sit by me, then places the notebook in my hands. It is leather bound and zips around the edges. On the cover, embossed in the leather, are the words, *To Nikki. Because you are my world, I give you the world.*

My heart seems to skip a beat, and I look up at him, my eyes wide so as to prevent the tears that I know are inevitable.

He brushes a soft kiss over my lips. "Open it."

I unzip the case and open it, revealing the map of Europe he gave me the day he asked me to marry him. On that day, there were stickers only on Munich and London. Now the map is splattered with stickers, as if a wash of confetti has fallen atop it.

I tilt my head to look at him, pleased but not entirely sure I'm seeing the bigger picture.

From the twinkle in Damien's eye, I think he understands my confusion. He reaches over and turns the page, revealing a map of North and Central America. South America is on the next page, then Asia, then Africa, then Australia.

"I only gave you Europe, when I'd wanted to give you the world."

"You gave me that a long time ago," I say, feeling sappy and romantic and warm and loved. I flip back to the page with Central America and put my finger on the dot covering Mexico. "It was a beautiful wedding," I say. "And an exceptional wedding night."

His arm goes around my shoulders and I lean against him. "Are there more stickers?"

"In the back," he says, and I flip to the end and find a little pocket with a sheet of colorful dots. I peel one off, then find the page for Europe again. The continent is as colorful as a rainbow, and the only real gap is directly over Paris, the one major destination we didn't spend any time in during our Grand Tour. I'd expected we would—after all, Damien had taken me there to meet the man who designed my wedding dress—but we'd gone straight from the airport to Favreau's studio, then spent a night in a nearby hotel before I returned to the studio the next day to try on the basted-together dress that Favreau had worked on through the night. Once both Favreau and I were satisfied, Damien had whisked me back to the jet.

When I'd asked why we were rushing off to Italy, Damien had been surprisingly vague. I had considered telling him that I wanted to stay—that I wanted to see the sights and soak in the atmosphere of that famous, vibrant city. But I had seen something in Damien's eyes, and so I had remained silent, confident that wherever Damien took me, simply being with him would be enough.

Now I carefully put the dot over Paris.

I tilt my head so that I am looking at him again and grin. "I can't wait," I confess. "I've always wanted to explore Paris."

His smile seems hesitant, and for just the flicker of an instant, I think I see shadows in his eyes again. I take his hand. "If you'd rather go someplace else, that's okay. We didn't do Japan, and you sounded pretty keen on that."

His brow furrows in what I recognize as genuine confusion.

"I just mean—it's our honeymoon. I want us to go somewhere that we both like. . . ." I trail off, now as confused as Damien looks.

His expression fades quickly enough, though, and he laughs out loud, all trace of the earlier shadows erased. "Sweetheart, I love Paris."

"Oh."

"I would say I'm sorry that we didn't spend time there on our last trip, but I'm not," he adds, making me even more confused. He knows it, too. And he's enjoying himself, the bastard.

I narrow my eyes and cross my arms over my chest, trying to look stern but probably not managing too well. "You love it? Then why on earth didn't we sightsee or go to restaurants or take a stroll along the Seine when we were there? I mean, we traipsed all over Europe. We couldn't squeeze in an extra day or two after my dress fitting?"

"One, I don't traipse," he says, making me laugh out loud. "And two, I wanted to save it."

"For what?"

"For you."

I am truly baffled now. Smiling, Damien lifts my hand and kisses each of my fingertips. "Paris is light and love and romance," he whispers. "And so are you. I knew from the first time I touched you that I would explore Paris with you. But only as my wife."

His words squeeze tight around me, constricting my chest

with the force of our shared emotion. I open my mouth to say his name, but my throat is too thick, and even that one simple word cannot escape.

Slowly, a tear trickles down my cheek. I think of everything that fills his world, from high-level, high-stress business deals to the employees who rely on him for their livelihood, and yet there is never a time when he doesn't put me first. When he doesn't make me feel treasured and special.

He gently brushes the tears from my face. "That's not the reaction I was hoping for," he says, his smile as soft as his voice.

"You fill my heart, Damien." The words come in a whisper, but on their heels a laugh bubbles out of me. "Don't mind the tears," I say. "I'm just overflowing."

He takes me in his arms and I hug him tight, my face pressed against his chest, the steady rhythm of his heart like a coded message, promising me that nothing can ever, ever come between us.

I'm not sure how long we stay like that—possibly a few minutes, possibly an eternity—but we move only in response to a sharp knock at the door and Katie's crisp voice saying from the hall, "I'm so sorry to interrupt, but there's a satellite call from Ms. Brooks," she says, referring to Damien's assistant, Sylvia.

Damien sighs as he stands and runs his hands through his hair. "I thought I was clear, Katie. Unless there's an emergency, I'm not to be disturbed."

"I know, Mr. Stark. But the call isn't for you. It's for Nikki—I mean, for Mrs. Stark. And Ms. Brooks is convinced that it's urgent."

Chapter 7

"A lawsuit," I say numbly for what has to be the billionth time. I turn to Damien, not certain if I'm angry or scared or just plain gobsmacked. "How the hell can this be happening?"

"We'll get to the bottom of it," he says, and his voice is so precise that I know he is even angrier than I am. "It's either a mistake, or someone is fucking with you."

We're back in the main cabin where I had gone to take the satellite call, and now I shift even more on the leather love seat so that I am facing him directly. "Fucking with me?" I manage a mirthless laugh. "I'd say that sums it up nicely."

When Sylvia had first told me that a company named WiseApps Development was threatening litigation, my mind couldn't process it. I spend months and months developing all my smart phone apps, and the idea that I had blatantly stolen the coding for my most popular app was not only absurd but insulting.

It had to be a joke. My best friend, Jamie, being a goof. Or Ollie stretching his lawyer wings to give me grief on my honeymoon.

Except that is bullshit because neither of my friends would pull such a mean joke. This is real. And it's serious. And the thought of getting embroiled in litigation—of being accused of doing something so incredibly heinous—is more than I can process. I'm lost in the mist of unreality, and if it weren't for Damien's hand in mine, I fear I would never find my way back to reality.

"Nikki." His voice is gentle but firm. I take a deep breath, certain that my eyes are glassy, my skin pale. "It will be okay."

I want to believe him, but I can't wrap my head around it, and so I just stare at him, hating the attorney who has been calling Sylvia, terrified of the foundation of lies that must exist in order for WiseApps to have convinced an attorney to get involved.

"Nikki," Damien repeats, and this time his voice is sharp. He releases my left hand, then reaches across my body to take my right.

I glance down. I'm wearing nothing but a robe, and it has fallen open, leaving both of my thighs exposed along with the angry scars that mar them, souvenirs from another life, when it was pain and a blade that kept me centered.

Now, I'm surprised to see that I've been digging my nails into my thigh, so viciously that I've come close to drawing blood. I try to relax my hand so that Damien can pull it away, but I can't seem to manage it. I'm untethered, and I need the pain to anchor me.

"No," Damien says, and though I know that he is referring to the way I am hurting myself, I hear the word as if in contradiction to my thoughts. *No, I do not need the pain.* And he is right, I think. It's not the pain that is my anchor. Not anymore.

It's Damien.

I turn to him suddenly. Urgently. "Tell me it will be all right."

My hand is tight in his, and I see the flash of relief on his face. The recognition that I have returned to him from a dark and lonely place. "You've done nothing wrong," he says. "Of course it will be okay."

"It makes me feel dirty," I say. "And no matter what happens, if it gets out, that's what people will remember. That there was a scandal, and that I was involved."

"I know." I appreciate that he doesn't offer platitudes or tell me that it is ridiculous to feel that way. He gets it, in part because he has been there himself, but also because he understands me. How I think. How I feel.

I straighten my shoulders. The truth is, I've survived scandal before, and a pretty damn juicy scandal at that. I can weather this, too. With Damien beside me, I can survive anything.

I draw a calming breath. No matter how horrible this is, at least I am not alone.

"What do you mean that someone might be fucking with me?" I ask after I've drawn enough breaths to feel capable of carrying on a reasonably coherent conversation.

"Just that it's interesting timing, isn't it? You've just gotten married. You want to enjoy your honeymoon. And you have access to more than enough money to easily pay off a nuisance lawsuit."

"Access," I say with a mirthless laugh. "If by access you mean that I can cozy up to my mega-bazillionaire husband and ask him to pay the son of a bitch off, then yeah. I guess I have access."

Damien knows damn well that I have no intention of using his money to take care of my business. But that doesn't change the fact that his expression is entirely serious when he nods and says, "If you ask, you know I'll give you whatever you need. But I hope you don't ask."

I'm not surprised. Damien isn't any more inclined than I am to kowtow to blackmail.

I pinch the bridge of my nose as exhaustion starts to settle on me. The travel, the stress. It is all beginning to wear me down. "Maybe it's just a misunderstanding," I say.

"I sure as hell hope so. Because if it turns out that someone is fucking with you—" His voice is as sharp as a blade.

"Damien." My voice rises with warning. I know what he is capable of—the lengths he has gone to in the past to protect me from those who would hurt me. And while I don't give a rat's ass what happens to somebody who is trying to use my company and my reputation to scam a settlement from me, I don't want to see Damien thrust back into the mire.

I start to say that to him, but he shakes his head and tightens his grip on my hand. He meets my eyes. His are fierce. "I will slay your dragons, Nikki. I will keep you safe."

"I know," I say. What I don't add is that that is what scares me.

I raise our joined hands to my lips and press a soft kiss to his knuckles. I am thinking of my dream—of the world trying to pull Damien and me apart—and I shiver.

"What?"

But I only shake my head and conjure a wan smile. "Just the whole thing," I say. "I've never been sued. I don't much like it." True words, and yet not a true answer.

He doesn't comment on my obfuscation, and yet I think he knows. How could he not? This is the man who can see into my heart.

He watches me for a moment, then nods. I tuck my feet under me and rest my head on his shoulder, exhaustion suddenly overtaking me as the adrenaline rush fades. I know that I would be more comfortable in the stateroom, but my body is limp and heavy and I doubt I can move. Damien brushes his lips gently over my temple. "We still haven't had dinner."

"Feed me in France," I mumble, so tired I'm barely able to form words.

"It's a date." He tucks an arm around me and pulls me closer. "Sleep now," he says.

And I do.

Chapter 8

Skin against skin.

A brush. A stroke. The butterfly touch of lips against my ear.

And a voice, soft but firm.

"Nikki. Sweetheart, we're landing in less than an hour. Time to wake up."

"Mmm. Sleep," I protest.

"Food," he says, trailing his fingers lightly over my lips. "And clothes. Parisians are pretty open-minded, but I think registration at the hotel might go more smoothly if you're wearing more than a bathrobe."

His words seem to float over me. I know he's right, and yet I want to stay here in this soft place between sleep and dreams. There are heavy things out there—scary things—and right now I know only vaguely that they exist, and that for this brief time I have escaped them. I am safe here in sleep, with only Damien's voice to blanket me and the gentle caress of his fingers to soothe me.

"Five more minutes." My words are a soft mumble, and I shift a bit closer to him.

He says nothing, and once again the thrum of the jet's engines starts to draw me down into the sweetness of sleep, safe beside this man whom I love.

My descent is halted, however, by the soft stroke of his hand. His fingers ease down my neck in a gentle caress that makes me shiver. He tugs the shoulder of my robe down, exposing my skin. He kisses me there, gentle touches designed to sweetly tease me. Then he slides his hand down, moving slowly over my breast, making me gasp in delight and then sigh in regret when his hand continues on, having merely teased my nipple into tight, sweet arousal.

"Damien." I'm not sure if the word is a protest or an exultation. All I know is that he has loosened the tie of the robe and now spreads it open. "Damien," I say again, but this time the word is little more than breath, because his hand has slipped farther down and he is stroking me, playing me. I close my eyes and sigh as I let the power of my husband's touch send sparks scattering through my body.

I'm aware of every part of me, as if every cell is crying out for more contact, and in answer to my own desires I raise my hands to my breasts, teasing my nipples, then tugging harder as the pressure of Damien's touch increases, as the storm gathers, coming closer to releasing all of its fury inside me.

"Tell me you like this," he demands.

"Yes," I say as I raise my hips, urging him not to stop. To touch me harder, faster, deeper. To take and take until I am turned completely inside out. "God, yes."

"You're close, sweetheart," he says, and I make some sort of noise in response. "Close," he repeats, gently removing his hand and making me gasp at this sudden withdrawal of pleasure. "But not ready."

I moan in protest and frustration. "Clearly you're not familiar with the definition of ready."

"Then educate me," he says. "What are you ready for?"

"You."

His smile is wide and satisfied and wonderfully sexy. "I like that answer. Stand up."

I hesitate only a moment, because now I understand. "Yes, sir." I stand, then move to the middle of the cabin so that I am right in front of where he sits on the love seat, his back to the side of the plane and a row of windows open to the night. I hope we don't hit turbulence, but I am not overly worried. There are worse things than stumbling into Damien's arms.

"Take off the robe." He is wearing loose khaki shorts and an ancient Wimbledon T-shirt. His arms are spread out along the back of the couch, giving him a casual air. His legs are slightly spread, and I can see the tight muscles of his thighs. He's been working out more and his always exceptional body is even more toned.

But even though his posture is casual, his expression is anything but. He is watching me with something that can only be described as hunger. And I am all too happy to be devoured.

"The robe," he says, making me jump. I haven't yet complied. I've been too caught up with watching my husband. Now I hesitate for different reasons, my attention turning toward the front of the plane and the now-closed door to the galley. It's one thing to be naked under a robe that I can yank closed. It's another to be naked altogether.

"Is there a problem, Mrs. Stark? I believe I told you to ditch the robe."

I start to speak, but force the words back. I think about Katie. About the privacy of the stateroom. And about this wide-open cabin, separated from the crew's area by just one thin door.

But this is Damien. He'll push my boundaries—I know that. But he won't cross them.

I let the robe fall to the floor, my eyes never leaving his. "Yes, sir," I say, and see the heat of fire in his eyes, then feel it burn my skin as he slowly lifts his gaze from my feet to my head, examining every inch of me, and making me even wetter in the process.

"Good girl." His voice is rough, and I can hear the need. I glance down, and feel a wave of satisfaction upon seeing the unmistakable bulge of his erection straining against his shorts. "Now tell me what you want."

I almost sag with relief, because what I want is what I always want. Where Damien is concerned I am insatiable.

I want him inside me. I want it hard and wild and just a little bit crazy. I want there to be room for nothing inside me except Damien. Not my dream, not the lawsuit, not any of the realities of the world that have started to seep back into my mind now that wakefulness has caught me.

Damien, I think. *All I want is Damien.*

I start to say as much, but then stop myself. Because as much as I want him—and oh, dear god, do I want him—that isn't all I want.

No, I want him just as crazed as me. I want to make him desperate. I want to hear him beg. I know that he needs me—I stopped doubting that long ago—but I want to see that need in his eyes, and I want to see the satisfaction of his desires when he explodes inside me.

I take a step toward him.

"Tell me," he repeats. "Tell me what you want."

"I'd rather show you." I walk toward him as I talk, my eyes never leaving his. One step, then another. I see his expression shift, wariness edging toward pleasure.

And then, as I kneel in front of him, there is understanding. Mostly, there is desire.

He starts to speak, and though I don't know if he intends to protest, I don't wait to find out. I press my finger to his mouth and gently shake my head. "No. My turn. Not a word."

He nods, just a small movement of his head, but I revel in the power. I just might be the only person on the planet to whom Damien Stark will willingly submit.

I lean forward and with slow, deliberate motions, I unbutton the shorts and then lower his zipper. I slip my hand in and stroke his cock through his briefs. He is hard as steel, and when I let my eyes dart up to his face, I see that his jaw is tight and know that he is fighting for control.

I draw his cock out, steely hard and incredibly thick. Damien makes a low noise like a growl of need, and my stomach quivers in response. My entire body throbs with want of him, but not yet. Not until I taste him.

I lick the very tip of his cock, and am rewarded by the way he arches back and the way his fingers reach for me and twine tightly in my hair. Feminine power surges through me, and I look up to see muscles in his chest straining against the shirt. He looks like a man on the precipice, aroused and wild and ready. And I am the woman who took him there. Who will take him further.

I lick him, cupping his balls and following the vein that bulges in his cock up to the tip. He shudders under my touch, then gasps when I open my mouth and take him in, sucking and licking as I try to take all of him, wanting the sensation of making him go over like this, lost to my whim and the pleasure I am giving. I can't manage, though. He's too big and I am not at a good angle. More than that, I am driving myself crazy, because as much as I want to take him there, the truth is that I am craving the feel of him inside me. And the more I imagine the feel of him deep within me, the more I know that I have to have him. Dear god, I have to have him now.

"Straddle me."

The words are little more than a whisper, but they wash over me with the force of an answered prayer. I tilt my head back and find him looking at me with such intensity it seems to burn. "I need to be inside you," he says.

"I know," I say as I rise. "I need it, too."

I hold on to his shoulders and put my knees on the love seat on either side of him. With my eyes never leaving his, I position myself, teasing the tip of his cock and then—oh, dear god, yes—impaling myself on him. Deeper and deeper until I feel like I will lose him inside of me, and me inside of him.

"Christ, Nikki, you feel so good." His hands cup my breasts as I arch back and we rock together, slow and sensual moments that swirl pleasure around us, as heady as a cocktail.

"I can never get enough of you," he says. "I know you so intimately, and yet never stop discovering you."

I close my eyes, surrendering myself to the wonder of his touch and the power of his words.

"There is never a time when I don't see you and lose myself utterly to you. You're mystery, Nikki, and you're truth. Look at me," he says, and I hear the change of tone in his voice.

I open my eyes and see the intensity on his face.

"We're together now." His voice is firm and thick with meaning. "Neither of us is alone. We're one. And whatever you have to face, I will face it with you. Whatever battles you have to fight, I will fight them with you. I will see us through this."

I swallow, thinking of how I wanted nothing more than to stay asleep, hiding from whatever new horror awaited me out in the world. Hiding from Damien, too, even as I felt protected in the shadow of his arms. I should have known better. I should have known he would see right through me—and that he wouldn't let me hide.

"Do you understand?" he asks.

"Yes."

"Does that bother you?"

I think about it, then shake my head. "No," I say truthfully. "It makes me feel safe. I have no more secrets from you." I'm not entirely sure that Damien can say the same thing. And, yes, there was a time when that would have bothered me, but no more. I will happily spend the rest of my life peeling back the layers of this man.

He watches my face for a moment, as if trying to convince himself that I am being forthright. Then he nods. "I'm going to have my attorneys deal with this bullshit."

"Damien—"

"No. It's your lawsuit, and I get that. But you don't have a litigator on retainer, and I have an entire team. I am not coddling you, but I am helping you." He cups my chin. "Okay?"

I glance down to where our bodies intersect, then look up at him with a cocked eyebrow. "You pick the strangest times to have these conversations."

"It's the mark of a good businessman." The corner of his mouth curves up. "Find your opponent's weakness and exploit it."

I roll my eyes.

"Okay?" he asks. And because I am not a fool, I nod.

The truth is, before, I simply wanted to hide. To make it all go away. But Damien has reminded me that I am not alone. More than that, he's reminded me that I'm stronger than I think.

Even better, I am stronger with him.

I want to say all that to him, but instead I simply say, "I love you."

He pulls me forward to catch me in a kiss, and I take the opportunity to shimmy a bit on his lap. "What was it you said about how we were going to be landing soon? Maybe I should stay like this for touchdown. Might be interesting."

"Maybe you should," he says, and for a moment, I think he means it.

Then he pinches my ass. "Then again, that probably violates some FAA regulation. Best not to tempt fate. Besides, I believe Katie's been keeping dinner warm for us."

Again, I'm reminded that she is just past that little door and could come in at any time.

Once again reading my mind, Damien glances up, silently reminding me of the privacy button. It has ensured that she didn't come in. But at the same time, my cheeks heat with the certainty that she knows exactly what is going on in here.

"We are newlyweds, after all," Damien says. "And to be honest, I don't think I'm quite finished working up an appetite."

"Oh, really?" I say, lifting myself a bit and then lowering, slowly at first and then gradually increasing speed. "And what is it you're hungry for, Mr. Stark?"

"Funny you should ask." He takes my hips and guides me, increasing the tempo and impaling himself deeper and harder inside me. "Right now, the only thing I'm interested in is you."

"Good." I put my hands on his shoulders, letting our rhythm build and our passion grow. Our eyes are locked, and neither of us looks away, both too entranced by the storm that we are building in each other.

"There," he says, as if he feels what I feel. As if he saw within me that electrical sensation spreading down my inner thighs, a precursor to the explosion.

But I see it inside him, too. More, I feel it in the way his cock hardens, in the quickened rhythms of his thrusts. My body responds in kind, tightening around him. Giving as much as I am taking and moving faster and faster in a sensual dance that breaks us both into a frenzied explosion of light and passion.

"Damien." His name is a cry, a prayer, and as I cling to him, my body shaking as the storm rips through me, I hear my name, too, as Damien's release fills me, and then there is silence as his mouth closes over mine and he kisses me feverishly until we both pull away, spent and gasping for air.

"Well," I say, after my body stops quivering. "I think I've got one hell of an appetite now."

"Funny," he says. "I'm still only hungry for you. But I suppose nutrition counts for something." He gently lifts me off him, then reaches for my robe to clean us both off. I raise my eyebrows and he chuckles. "You don't need to put it back on. I'll toss it in the laundry bin later. And I rather like the idea of watching you walk naked to the stateroom."

I release what I hope sounds like a snort of disapproval, but is really laughter. And just to show him up, I make my way to the back, adding a little more swish to my hips as I go.

I pause outside the stateroom and look back. He is watching me, his expression full of love and longing, passion and heat.

I breathe deeply, feeling calm and centered. Yes, there's a lawsuit, and yes, that sucks. But that's just a blip. A chapter in the book of my life. Hell, a footnote.

Damien is the whole story. And our life together is epic.

Chapter 9

As it turns out, we don't just take a limo to the hotel. We first take a helicopter from the airport to a helipad in the city center. I've done many things with Damien, but so far we've not commuted over Paris by helicopter. And, yeah, I'm a little giddy.

I lean toward the window, one hand on the glass, the other tight in Damien's hand, and watch as the pilot brings the bird down gently. After just a few more moments, the staff has unloaded our bags and is escorting us to a waiting limo. It's smooth and seamless and definitely one of the perks of traveling with Damien.

The limo's interior is completely frosty, but I barely notice it. I'm too busy gazing out the window at the city that is passing by us. The Arc de Triomphe, the stunning architecture, and even a glimpse of the Eiffel Tower. I feel like a little girl with her nose pressed to the window, not a woman who recently returned from a very similar trip.

All too soon, our drive ends. The limo pulls up in front of what looks like a private residence, but the uniforms on the two men standing by the door make it clear that this is a hotel.

The two livery-clad bellmen hurry forward to retrieve our bags, then whisk them away while Damien and I walk more slowly into the hotel. A distinguished man with a small mustache hurries to greet us. I learn that he is the manager of the Hôtel Margaritte, and that this exclusive hotel just off the rue du Faubourg Saint-Honoré has only twenty rooms and was once an eighteenth-century private residence.

Damien and I will be staying in the penthouse.

The manager escorts us there, taking us through the lobby, which is still furnished as it would have been centuries ago, with tapestry and gilt, crystal and elegance. I walk with my head in constant motion as I look this way and that, trying to take it all in.

But whatever awe I feel for the lobby fades when we reach the penthouse. It is, in a word, incredible. Taking up the entire top floor, it is luxury personified, with no detail overlooked in the beautiful furnishings, the antique mirrors, the modern kitchen well-concealed behind decorative, period-style doors.

The real showstopper, however, is the huge bay window that arches up into a skylight, giving the living room the illusion of being outdoors. And, as if to remind us that we are in Paris, we have a stunning view of the Eiffel Tower.

"This room was the conservatory at one time," the manager says. "Mademoiselle Margaritte, the hotel's namesake, kept it filled with flowers."

"It's lovely," I say, thoroughly delighted.

He finishes giving us the tour, then leaves us in privacy. Only then do I realize we never stopped at the front desk. That pedestrian form of checking in is apparently one of those pesky things that only those who don't have the means to own small countries have to put up with.

"Do you own this place?" I ask Damien when we are alone.

"I don't, no. Why? Do you think I should?" He pats his pockets. "Let me check my wallet. Maybe I have enough cash. . . ."

"Oh, sure," I say. "You can laugh. But I've seen you buy some pretty amazing things on the spur of the moment." When we were in Italy, he'd heard about an authentic Michelangelo that was going to be put up for auction. He'd contacted the seller, made the kind of deal that couldn't be refused, and then donated it to a Los Angeles museum on the condition that he could take it on loan for two months out of every year to tour his properties, kept under watchful guard in the lobbies of his offices all over the globe, and thus giving the general public a chance to come view a masterpiece.

"True," he concedes. "But I rarely buy real estate on impulse."

"There's always a first time," I say lightly. "But seriously, why aren't we staying at one of your hotels? You have one not far from here. Or at least Stark Properties, a wholly owned subsidiary of Stark International, does."

For a moment, he looks confused, then he grins. "You've been reading my corporate magazine."

"Maybe," I admit, because there were a few copies on the plane. "But it would still have been a good guess. Because, honestly, where *don't* you own property?"

"Greenland. At the moment, I'm completely without holdings in Greenland."

"Ha-ha." I turn to examine the suite some more, taking in the plush furniture, the wide-open spaces, even the grand piano that I have absolutely no idea how to play. "I'll admit this place is exceptional, but why not stay at one of your own?"

"Because this is our time," he says. "No one knows us personally. No one will knock on the door if there is a crisis. It's not possible to be entirely anonymous with you," he adds, taking my hand and tugging me toward him, "but I'd like to at least try to be invisible."

I lean back against him, then close my eyes as his hands

tighten around my waist. We stand like that for a moment, swaying slightly, the top of my head tucked under Damien's chin.

"Are you tired?" he asks.

"Mmm. That depends on why you're asking."

His low chuckle rumbles through me. "That's definitely one reason to stay awake. But I confess that I was thinking of something a bit more public."

I turn in his arms. "What about being invisible?"

"I'm sure we can blend," he says. "Maybe I'll even buy you a hat to go with your dress."

"*Un chapeau*," I correct, "and I'd like that." The dress I chose on the plane is a vintage style shirt-dress, with buttons running the entire length and a belted waist that creates a very full skirt. I'm feeling rather Audrey Hepburn, and a hat would be just the thing.

"You're the one who'll be recognized," I point out. "I've only become a celebrity by default." Damien, however, has been in the spotlight since he was a kid, and he played enough tennis and did enough commercials in Europe that I doubt I'm exaggerating the chances of him being noticed. Especially when you factor in how widespread the coverage of his recent trial was.

"I have a disguise." He grins as he says it, then crosses to the leather backpack that doubles as a briefcase when he travels.

I watch, amused, as he pulls out a white cap with a French flag imprinted on the front.

I laugh and shake my head. He's still Damien, no question about it, and I think he looks damn hot. But on the whole it's not a bad disguise. He rarely wears caps, and if he adds some sunglasses—and if we both carry daypacks—we'll look like any two tourists out exploring the city.

"So do I look like just an ordinary guy?"

"You'll never be ordinary," I say. "But close enough."

The hotel is located near dozens of high-end shops, but it's only just past eight in the morning, so nothing much is open yet. Damien promises me a day of shopping later, and I am fine with that. I may be hesitant to use my husband's money to fund my business, but I am not so proud as to turn down designer clothes.

Right now, though, we stay primarily on the side streets, enjoying the local ambiance. We are holding hands, and though I feel as though we are wandering aimlessly, Damien assures me that he knows where we are going.

"So what is on our agenda?" I ask. "It's Paris, after all. There are about a million things I want to do."

"What's on your list?" he asks, as an amazing yeasty scent draws us off the street toward a tiny café with charming outdoor seating.

I start to rattle off everything I can think of, from the Louvre to the catacombs to the Seine and the Eiffel Tower. "And Versailles," I add as we take a seat at one of the tables. "And Montmartre. And the Left Bank and the Metro and—oh, hell, I don't know. How does everything sound?"

His smile is indulgent. "Sounds reasonable to me."

When the waitress arrives he orders two *café crèmes* and two *pains au chocolat*. I'm impressed, but not surprised, when he orders in what I assume is perfect French. *Stark International*, I think, and grin. Why wouldn't he speak French?

"I'm not quite fluent," he admits as we sip our coffee and watch the people on the charming avenue. "But I can get by."

After we've finished our pastry and coffee, we meander down small streets and alleyways until we cross a wider, busier avenue, then follow a half-hidden path into a lovely garden.

"It's like an oasis," I say. I had grabbed my camera on the way out of the hotel, and now I make Damien stop as I take a few shots. It is as if we have wandered into a fairy tale, and I want to capture the magical aura on film.

"This is one of my favorite shortcuts," Damien says, as he leads me down a tree-lined path. "And for exactly that reason. It's an escape. A respite from the crowds and the noise."

"So where are we?"

"It's called the Jardin de la Nouvelle France. I think it was set up in anticipation of the 1900 World's Fair, but don't quote me on that. I come for the way it looks, not the history."

As interesting as the history might be, I have to agree, and as we follow the path—taking a few side trips just for the sake of adventure—I can't deny the joy I feel simply being in this cool, green space. I keep my camera out, delighting in the play of light and shadow, and taking so many pictures that I will undoubtedly have to buy new memory cards before this trip is over.

We wander farther in and find a lovely little bridge, not to mention an actual waterfall.

"Here," Damien says, taking my hand at one point when I'm certain that we've managed to get horribly turned around. "I'll show you my favorite place to sit." He leads me to a small pond shaded by a weeping beech. There is a small stone bench, and we sit for a moment, his arm around my waist and my head upon his shoulder.

"Thanks."

"For what?" he asks.

"You said you were giving me the world. Thank you for giving me these hidden treasures, too."

When we finally stand to continue on our way, I'm surprised to realize that it's after ten thirty.

"Slow and easy," Damien says when I comment on the time. "Just like a honeymoon should be."

I take his hand and squeeze. Because, really, I can't argue with that.

We emerge from the park onto the Cours la Reine, and follow that street for a while before crossing at the avenue Winston Churchill. That road goes to the Seine, and turns into the Pont Alexandre III.

"Are we crossing?"

Damien shakes his head. "We can take the stairs down and walk along the water for a while or stay on street level and check out some of the sights. We'll pass the Louvre in a few more blocks."

"Can we go in?"

"We can," he says, then kisses my forehead. "It's already on today's agenda. But there's someplace else I want to take you first. You still okay with walking? We can catch a cab."

"I'm great," I say, meaning it. There is nothing I enjoy more than walking in a new city, unless it's walking in a new city with Damien.

We stay on the street level until we've passed the Place de la Concorde and I've *ooh*ed and *aah*ed over the Obelisk and taken a dozen more pictures. Then we go down the stairs and walk along the Seine until we reach the Pont des Arts. We head back up the stairs, begin to cross the bridge, and then I stop, confused by the odd appearance of the bridge's railing.

"What's that—locks?" I've stepped to the side, and Damien is beside me, as I realize that the odd metallic jumble I'm looking at is in fact a collection of padlocks that are attached to the bridge railing like barnacles.

I tilt my head to look up at Damien. "What on earth?"

"This is the bridge for lovers," he says. "You've never heard of it?"

I shake my head even as I look farther down the bridge, not able to fathom just how many lovers have come here to pledge their devotion.

"They come. They write their names on a lock. They attach it to the bridge, and they throw the key into the Seine."

"For luck?" I ask, and he nods.

"Is that why you've brought me here?"

"It is," he says, and those two words warm my heart. "But I want to switch it up just a little."

I frown a bit, confused, but nod.

"Not too long ago, part of the bridge fell off—it collapsed under the weight of the locks."

My eyes widen. "Love is a heavy burden," I quip, then immediately frown. "Was anyone hurt?"

"No, but even so. I thought we could start our own tradition. Carry our own weight, you might say."

I cock my head, smiling as I wait for him to explain.

He draws a small box from his pocket, then opens it to reveal a silver charm in the shape of a lock. I pick it up, and see that it has our names engraved on it. "And it has a key, too," he says, lifting the velvet to reveal the tiny key. "It's for you, from me. And once I put it on your bracelet, I thought we could throw the key into the river."

My chest swells and my throat is thick with tears. I nod stupidly because I can't get the words out. It is romantic and sweet, and I lift my wrist for him, the little Eiffel Tower dangling there as he attaches the lock charm next to it.

"I love you," I say as he puts the key in my hand.

"And I love you." He cups his hand over mine. "On three?" he asks, and we start to swing our joined hands. Once. Twice. On the third time, we let go, and the tiny key goes flying.

"Forever," Damien says.

"Forever," I agree.

The rest of the afternoon feels just as soft, just as romantic.

We wander along the Seine, looking at the street vendors' wares, taking silly pictures of each other, and holding hands. Once or twice I see people looking at us—a few even snap pictures—but I tell myself that it is nothing. That if there are less than a dozen people who recognize us, then we are having a good day.

We spend two hours in the Louvre, and I gasp in awe at the

majesty of some of the paintings, and then gasp in surprise at how diminutive the *Mona Lisa* is, certainly not as big as I expected given the enormity of her reputation.

After, we buy cheese and wine and have an afternoon picnic in the Jardin des Tuileries, where we do nothing but laze about enjoying the weather, the surroundings, and each other.

As night approaches, Damien takes me back to the Seine and we take an evening cruise. We sip champagne and watch the lights of the city come on. And when the Eiffel Tower lights and sparkles on the hour, we toast to love and laughter and romance.

As we are heading back to the dock, Damien receives a text, and since he has ordered strict silence except in emergencies, he glances at the screen. I watch him, dividing my attention between my husband and the Parisian skyline.

The muscle in his cheek tightens, so I know it is not good news, and he taps out a reply quickly, his fingers practically attacking the screen. But when he turns back to me, the frustration is gone and he is simply Damien again, a man sharing champagne with his wife on their honeymoon.

"How do you do that?" I ask. "You must have a million things going on and a trillion fires to put out, and yet you can just shut it all down. Turn it all off." I wish that I could do the same. Because although I have reveled in every moment of this day, the truth is that the threat of that damn lawsuit has been lying under the surface, clinging to my enjoyment like tar.

"I don't know," he says, brushing my cheek. "I simply will it away. It isn't gone. Only shelved."

"I can't even manage that." I press against him, sighing as his arms go around me. He smells of fresh air and grass from the garden, and his body is hard and hot against mine. "Make it go away," I murmur as I feel the need rise within me. "For just a little while, make me forget everything but you."

I lean back just enough so that I can tilt my head up to look at him. His eyes are like molten steel, and I quiver simply from the thought of his touch.

"There's somewhere I want to take you." I hear the strain in his voice, as if he is fighting back the urge to touch me. The boat has reached the dock, and he leads me off, then pauses on the *quai* to study me. "I wasn't sure, but, Nikki—yes. Come on."

I'm not at all sure what he has in mind, but I go willingly. Eagerly, actually.

On the street level, we catch a taxi and Damien instructs the driver to take us to À la Lune in the Quartier Pigalle. I note the way the driver glances back, his expression almost a leer, and I raise my brows. Damien only shrugs. "Think red light district."

"Oh," I say, and then settle back in the upholstered seat. I have no idea what Damien has planned, but I'm completely confident I will enjoy it.

It's not a long drive, and soon we are in a neighborhood that reminds me a little bit of Bourbon Street and a little bit of Times Square. On one corner, I see a red door and a small neon sign for À la Lune. The driver lets us out without a word, but when Damien pays him, his eyes stay on our faces for just a bit longer than I'd like. I tell myself it's nothing. If he'd recognized us—if he cared—he'd have pulled out his phone and snapped a picture. As it is, he drives away.

Damien takes my hand and leads me toward the red door, but stops a few feet away on a section of the sidewalk submerged in shadows. "I meant what I said before, about Paris being a city of romance and wanting to share that with you on our honeymoon. But it also has a libertine side. A bit wild. A bit decadent."

"And that's a good thing?" I tease, easing up against him, so close I can feel his erection. He cups my ass and pulls me closer.

"It is," he says, with more seriousness than I anticipated.

"Do you remember what you said back in Malibu the other day? We were eating breakfast."

I grin, certain I finally see where this is going. "I said it felt very domestic. That I liked that." I ease closer, then grind my pelvis against his. "What's the matter? Already feeling shackled by matrimony?"

"Shackled wouldn't be a problem," he says, "though I'd prefer it was you and not me. And no. But I don't ever want us to become . . . settled." As he speaks, he steps back so that he can run his finger down my dress. He eases the skirt up, then growls low in his throat when he finds that I'm not wearing underwear.

"I don't want to be settled, either," I say huskily.

"Dear god, I love you." He tightens his hand around my waist and I arch back, letting him explore me, letting his touch excite me. I know that we are outside, but it is dark and this is Damien, and I don't care. I want this. I want him. And I want the passion to fire so hot between us that it burns away everything else.

"Inside." His voice is rough. "If I don't get you inside right now, I swear I'm going to fuck you right here against this wall."

I'm tempted to see if he means it, but I notice some people walking across the street. I don't think they've seen us, but no sense tempting fate. "All right," I say. "Let's see just how decadent Paris can be."

Chapter 10

As it turns out, it can be pretty damn decadent. The club caters to couples, who can either choose to share partners or not. We are definitely on the "or not" side of the equation, a fact that

Damien makes clear to the couple who enter the club at the same time we do.

The hostess greets us in French, then switches seamlessly to English. She explains that she will take us to the dressing rooms where we will put our clothes and belongings in lockers. She makes a particular point to stress that my camera must be locked away, and I am fine with that. I don't want to take pictures any more than I want someone taking pictures of me.

The club provides robes, sarongs, and towels. We can choose what to wear, or wear nothing at all. She continues to explain the rules, which are basically nonexistent. Anything goes. Anything, anywhere. Except for the hot tub, where actual intercourse isn't allowed, a statement that drives home that it is allowed anywhere else.

"Are there private rooms?" I ask.

"There are. But you do not have to be concerned about your privacy no matter what you do or where you do it." She flashes a bright smile, then nods to Damien. "Our members understand discretion." It is the first time that I realize she knows who we are. And that Damien has been here before.

I glance sideways at him, but he only shrugs. If I want answers, I'm going to have to wait, because we are already on the move and we are following our hostess to the dressing room, women on the left of the plush joint sitting area, men on the right.

She smiles, nods, then leaves.

"I was wondering how you found this place," I say. "But I guess a member would know where it is."

"Renewed member," he says, not at all perturbed by the green fire of jealousy that has crept into my voice. "It's been years since I've been here, but I called yesterday and reinstated my membership."

"Oh." I tell myself I'm not going to ask, but then I completely ignore my own sound advice. "Who did you come with?"

"Carmela," he says, referring to the bitch of an Italian supermodel he dated many years ago.

"Oh." I swallow. "And about that couples thing. Did you, um, share?"

"I did," he says. He takes two long steps to end up right in front of me. Gently, he cups my chin, then kisses me so sweetly it almost makes me cry. "Why wouldn't I? She wasn't mine."

His words soothe me more than I want to admit. "I don't like thinking that there were other women before me," I admit, though I know it is a foolish thought because Damien Stark is about the furthest thing from a monk on the planet.

"There weren't," he says. "There may have been women—they may have even shared my bed—but there was no one before you."

I nod, still feeling foolish, but also incredibly happy. I wipe a tear away with the edge of my thumb.

He tells me to go change—"not naked; I don't intend to share even the sight of you"—and to meet him back in this sitting room.

I do, returning in a sarong, and more than happy to find him with a towel wrapped around his waist, the bulge at his crotch making it more than evident that he is ready for whatever delights are on the agenda.

He leads me through a space with couches and chairs and people in various states of undress, all touching and stroking and teasing. I'm not sure what the etiquette is here, but I can't stop looking. Damien sees me, and pulls me back into an alcove, one of many in this room, and clearly set back for this very purpose. There is, in fact, a small curtain that can be pulled across the opening, turning it into a small but private space, almost like a little dressing room.

"Have you ever watched other people make love?" Damien asks.

I shake my head. "No. I mean, yes. Some porn, but that's different."

"It is," he says. He stands behind me, so that we are in the shadows and I am looking out over the room. Hands stroking. Lips meeting. I don't know why, but watching these strangers makes my own temperature rise.

"I don't want them," I say, as Damien cups my breasts through the thin material of the sarong. "I don't want anyone's touch but yours."

"But it turns you on," he whispers, and I nod.

"Why?" I ask.

"They're a mirror. You see passion on their faces and you want it. You see the burn of heat on their skin, and you want to feel it. You hear them cry out when they come, and you want to go there, too."

"Yes," I moan, as the truth of what he says washes over me. I've never thought I had any voyeuristic tendencies, but watching these people—their hands stroking slick skin, their mouths meeting—is like kindling to the fire already growing inside me. "God, yes."

I lean back against Damien, feeling the press of his erection against my rear. His fingers tighten on my nipples and I cry out, the cry shifting to a desperate moan as his other hand snakes down to my crotch. "Please," I say. "Touch me."

"Are you sure?" he asks, and I hear the hard edge of want in his voice.

I nod. I do not want to be the one being watched, but I so desperately want to feel. "The shadows," I say. "And the sarong is open at the side." No one will be able to see, I tell myself. But the truth is, I'm not sure I care anymore if they do.

The slit in the sarong is over my hip, but Damien turns it so that it is over my thigh, just barely covering my sex. He slips his hand under the material and strokes me. I bite down on my lower lip to keep from crying out. I am so hot, so sensitive, that I fear I will explode right there in his hand.

"Nikki, oh, god, baby." He uses the hand that was on my breast to pull my sarong up from the back.

I know I should protest—but I don't want to. I want the thrill. I want Damien. I want him to fuck me in this dark corner with this cornucopia of sex spread out in front of us. I want the wildness.

I want it all.

"Yes," I say, and lean forward so that I can hold on to the edge of the alcove. I yank the curtain partly closed—a nod to privacy—but I do not want to block our view.

I am still wearing the sarong, and Damien is behind me, so I know that we have some privacy, but when Damien grips my hips and thrusts himself inside me—when I cry out from the delicious intensity of taking him in and having him pound hard inside me—I know that anyone who looks toward us must know exactly what we are doing.

I don't care.

All I want is Damien.

All I want is to feel, and I reach around, taking his hand off my hip and easing it into the sarong, silently demanding that he stroke my clit even as he fucks me from behind.

"Don't close your eyes," Damien demands, and I don't. Instead I watch. Passion watching passion. Heat locked onto heat.

He teases my clit as his cock fills and strokes me. He is working me into a frenzy, and his touch combined with the surroundings pushes me over the edge so hard and so fast that I am certain that without Damien to hold me up, I will tumble and fall to my knees.

As the orgasm blasts through me, my body milks him, muscles clenching in a desperate need that takes him the rest of the way, and he explodes into me, his hands closing tight on my shoulders as he cries my name.

He closes the curtain then, and I turn in his arms, then melt into his touch, into his kisses.

"I love you," he says.

"I know," I say, then snuggle closer. I am content. And right at the moment, I'm not feeling domestic at all.

We stay a bit longer, enjoying the sauna and the hot tub. Making love slowly in a pirate-themed private room where I let Damien take me captive and then ravage me. It is late when we leave, and I am feeling well-used and wonderful.

"How did you know?" I ask as we exit onto the sidewalk. "How did you know I would like it?"

"How do you think?"

I stay silent; we both know the answer. Because Damien knows me as well as I know myself. And as far as I am concerned, that is a glorious feeling.

I take his hand and pull him to a stop, then lift myself up to kiss him, planning a soft buss, and then laughing as he captures me long and slow and deep.

A bright light flashes, turning the world inside out, and it takes me a second to realize that the light came from the flash of a camera. It is followed in quick succession by a lightning storm of flashes, and I stumble backward, realizing only after the fact that Damien has pushed me aside.

Damien is in the street, and his fist slams hard into the photographer's face even as I process the words that have been hanging over my head like a cartoon bubble since the first flash went off—"Fucking A. Stark pays for her, then he shares her."

The accent is heavily British, and when I see the multiple cameras around the guy's neck as he stumbles backward, his nose a bloody mess, I realize that he is a celebrity chaser from one of Britain's tabloids.

I don't even have time to feel sick before I see Damien lunge for the guy.

"Damien, no!" I shout, but my words come too late. Damien grabs the guy by the shirtfront and pulls him back. He seems to hesitate, and then instead of breaking the guy's face, he grabs one of the cameras and breaks that instead.

"Get the fuck out of here." His words are low and very, very dangerous, and it's obvious that the photographer knows that. He turns, then breaks into a run. I grab hold of Damien's shirt, afraid that he will run after him.

"It's over," I say, breathing hard and starting to shake. "Just stop. It's over."

But even as I say the words, I know that it is a long, long way from over.

Chapter 11

"I'm sorry," Damien says in the taxi on the way back to the Hôtel Margaritte.

"For not stopping? For breaking his camera?" I make a face. "It's okay, really. I don't give a fuck about him. I just don't want you to get in trouble."

"Not for that," Damien says. "For bringing you here."

It takes me a moment to understand what he's talking about. "You mean to Paris? To the club?" I tighten my grip on his hand. "Damien, that's ridiculous."

"Is it?" His words are tight. Clipped. "I almost canceled this entire trip after I saw your face in Mexico. How much you enjoyed the beach, the solitude."

I remember the shadows I had seen on his face when we had talked about leaving the resort, and everything falls into place.

"And then to bring you to a city crawling with press—to put you back in that spotlight," he continues. "And worse, to take you to that club. It was like opening a damn door for every lowlife asshole—"

"No." I press a finger over his lips. "I love Paris," I said. "And dear god, Damien, I loved going to À la Lune with you." I remember the way he'd touched me, the over-the-top eroticism of feeling Damien inside me while we watched those strangers and knowing that we were just as exposed. "And there was no way you could predict that some asshole with a camera—"

"Couldn't I? There's always some asshole with a camera, Nikki. It's part of the package. The cameras and all the shit in my past. It's all there, and I'm so goddamn sorry that it's part of your life now."

"Damien, it's okay," I say fiercely. "I don't want to be cloistered, and I don't need to be. You take me places—in the world, inside myself—and I don't want you to stop."

I see something that looks like hope on his face, but then it fades, replaced by both anger and regret. "At the very least I should be able to give you a respite on our honeymoon."

"No." My voice is hard. Firm. "Dammit, Damien, don't you get it? I don't want to escape your life. I love you. All of that shit, it's just part of the man you became."

"Fertilizer?"

I roll my eyes. "I'm serious. You're a whole package, Damien. And maybe I don't have warm and fuzzy feelings for the paparazzi, but I do love you. And that makes it easier to put up with them. You know that," I add, feeling just a little panicked, because he *does* know that. "I've told you that over and over. Don't you know I mean it?"

Damien, however, doesn't answer, and my throat is thick with tears as I look into his eyes. This is about more than the paparazzi, I realize. I may not like them, but I'm getting used to them, and Damien damn well knows it.

I frown at him. "What aren't you telling me?"

He is silent for a moment, and when he does speak, my chest is so tight that I am certain I have forgotten how to breathe.

"Sofia," he says. "She's the one behind the bullshit lawsuit."

"How the hell do you know that?"

"My lawyers managed to trace it back. That's what Sylvia texted to tell me earlier. I was going to tell you later. I didn't want to spoil Paris." He makes a rough sound in the back of his throat. "So much for that."

He runs his fingers through his hair. "At any rate, it's been shut down, and her attorney knows how he was duped. But she started it. She's behind it. Because she wanted to fuck with you."

I'm still trying to take it all in. "I—I don't understand."

"WiseApp? Try WiseAss." There's anger and hurt in his voice. "God*damn* her."

"She's messed up," I say, though the words are hard to choke out. I can't help but remember what she said to me—that Damien didn't love me, that I should give him up and turn to a blade to ease my pain.

I force myself to bite back the fury. It's useless now. Because she is sick, and all her antics are doing is hurting Damien now. Damien, and me.

I rest my hand on his leg. "It's not your fault."

"She should be in a facility that doesn't allow her access to the internet or telephones. She's got someone pulling strings for her. She's too damn smart; too damn manipulative."

"It was only a nuisance," I say, though it was a hell of a lot more than that. "You've put an end to that bullshit lawsuit before it could get really bad."

He turns to face me square on. "And how bad is too bad, Nikki? Everywhere we turn, my past is reaching out to hurt you." He twines his fingers in my hair, and I wince, remembering when I took the scissors and violently chopped it off. He slides his hand down to cup my thigh, and I force myself not to cry as I think of the scars—of the times when the paparazzi, the shit with Sofia, and all the other crap has brought me so close to cutting. I shiver, but I shake my head.

"But I haven't," I whisper. "I haven't because of you. You're my strength, Damien. You know that."

"And your dream?" he asks, and I have to force myself not to shudder with the memory of it.

Instead, I manage a shrug. "Everyone has nightmares. Not everyone is as lucky as I am to have a man like you to soothe them."

His hand closes around my upper arm, his eyes boring straight into mine with the kind of heated ferocity that makes me breathless. "There is no fire I wouldn't walk through for you, Nikki. But that doesn't mean I want you to burn, too."

"I already burn *for* you, Damien. Of course I'll burn *with* you, too."

For a moment, his grip tightens so much that I almost wince. Then he pulls me violently toward him, and his mouth is hard against mine. His palm is at the back of my head, his fingers twined tight in my hair. Our teeth clash, his tongue invades my mouth, and I want this—this heat, this wildness. I need him to know that I can take it. Him, this life, this place. All of it.

"Do you have any idea how much I love you?" he asks as the taxi pulls to a stop in front of the hotel.

"At least as much as I love you," I reply.

I start to edge toward the door, but Damien's hand stops me. I follow his glance through the window and see the gathering of paparazzi near the entrance, their cameras aimed at us.

Well, hell.

"Go," Damien says, with a firm smack of his palm to the glass divider between us and the driver.

To his credit, our driver continues on, leaving the vultures gaping. He takes us around back and delivers us to the service entrance. The decor is significantly less stunning as we walk through the kitchen and past the laundry, but at least it's a photography-free zone.

We head for the service elevator to take us up to the penthouse, and as we're waiting for it to arrive, Damien pulls out his phone and checks a text message. "Goddammit."

"What?" I ask, but he is too busy opening apps and checking something.

I edge closer to see, and come face-to-face with the image of Damien's hand on my breast, his other inside my skirt. And thank goodness for the shadows, because nothing beneath my skirt is visible. Not that anyone needs to see what we're doing; it's pretty obvious. My face is alight with passion, after all, and the very clear sign for À la Lune glows neon orange behind us. I recognize the image—it's from before we entered the club.

I don't recall making a noise, but I must have, because Damien looks up from his phone, his expression somehow both angry and sad, both cold determination and tender vulnerability.

"No," I say. "This isn't your fault."

"The hell it isn't."

"We're married," I say. "What the hell do we care if it's on Facebook?"

"It's everywhere," he says. "Sylvia says it's gone viral. They'll be dragging out the story about the painting soon, too," he says, referring to the way the press vilified me for accepting a million dollars in exchange for a nude portrait of myself.

My stomach twists, but I tell myself it will be okay. "All that picture shows is that I love you and I want you. That you turn me on desperately. All it will do is make every other woman in the world jealous that I'm the woman in your bed. I can live with that," I add with a sharp thrust of my chin.

"I don't like seeing you exposed," he says. "Especially when I'm the one who exposed you."

"I can deal with it," I say. I don't mention that *can* deal and *want to* deal are two entirely different things.

"Doesn't mean you want to," Damien says, effectively reading my mind as always.

We're in the elevator now, and it slides to a stop at our floor. I take Damien's hand and squeeze it lightly. "We'll be fine," I say. "We're together. How can we be anything else?"

His answering smile warms me. *Yes,* I think as the doors open inside our suite. *This will be okay.*

And then I see the room.

"Back in the elevator." Damien's voice is hard and dangerous, and he is in front of me in less than a second. I have barely registered the state of the room—all I know is that it is in shambles. Our luggage wide open, our clothes scattered everywhere. We hadn't taken the time to unpack. Apparently someone decided to do it for us.

"Damien—"

"In," he says, backing me in, then jamming his finger on the button to close the elevator door before pressing the button to ring security.

"I think they're gone," I say. "Whoever did that to our room, I think they're gone."

"I'm not taking chances with you. Come here. You're shaking."

I fall into his outstretched arms and burrow close as he wraps me tight against him.

When the elevator doors open on the ground floor, we are met by hotel security. A team has gone up in the main elevator already, we are told. We wait, and I can see from the tightness in his cheek and the stiffness of his body that waiting is not sitting well with Damien. He wants to be up there. He wants to know what is happening. He wants action. And the only reason that he is not already in full motion is because of me.

Static bursts from a walkie-talkie, followed by a string of French much too fast for me to catch even a single word. The guard responds, looks at Damien, then at me. "The perpetrator is no longer in your room," he says in clear but formal English. "We cannot at this time determine what is missing other than the . . . intimates."

"Intimates?" I repeat.

He clears his throat. "It appears that whoever broke into your suite took intimate apparel. Underwear, bras." His nose goes a bit pink and he makes a point not to look at me. "There may be more, of course, but . . ."

Damien stands beside me, rigid with fury. As for me, I don't know if I'm going to laugh or cry. I think the laughing will win, but I'm not sure if that's humor or hysterics.

No one speaks as we return to the room. When we arrive, we see that our things have been stacked neatly. The order doesn't lessen the feeling of having been violated.

"How did this happen?" Damien says, his words sharp and clipped. I know what he means, and it is clear that both the guard and the hotel manager who have joined us also understand the unspoken part of Damien's question—how the hell did someone get into our room in a hotel of this caliber with the kind of security that Damien demands when he travels.

"I assure you, Mr. Stark, we will be interviewing staff throughout the night, and will have answers for you by morning."

By morning, I am certain, our underwear will be all over eBay. I catch Damien's eye and see that his expression mirrors my own. *Fuck.*

"In the meantime, if there is anything that you require—"

"Privacy," Damien says, and the manager is astute enough to know that now is the time to stop with the platitudes and just get the hell out of there.

Damien's facade remains intact until the manager and his staff leave. The perfect embodiment of a wealthy man who is very put out. Only I see the volcano boiling beneath, and as soon as the elevator doors have closed behind them, Damien picks up a decorative metal bowl and hurls it across the room to shatter the huge mirror that hangs behind the dining table.

As it breaks apart, I release a breath I have been holding. I do not begrudge him his anger. On the contrary, I want to toss a bowl myself. Except I don't. Not really. What I want is to fall to the ground. What I want is to grasp one of those shards. What I imagine is the sting of glass against flesh—and *dammit,* I don't want to feel that or imagine that or be that girl. And yet there it is, laid cold and harsh all because the paparazzi are fucking with us and Sofia is a stone-cold bitch.

"*No.*"

Damien's voice seems to reach me through a tunnel. It starts far away and then it is right beside me. The voice and the man. I am standing still, a bit shell-shocked, and suddenly his hands are on my arms. He spins us around until my back is against the wall and his mouth is on mine.

One hand slides between my legs, cupping my sex through the material of my skirt. Not sensual, but hard. Demanding.

Wild.

And I am just as wild as Damien.

I yank my skirt up, and he never once breaks our kiss. As his fingers thrust deep inside me, his mouth bruises mine and his other hand closes tight on my breast. So tight that it is not just trails of pleasure that shoot from my breast all the way down to my clit, but pain, white-hot and familiar.

Damn me, I want more. I want it hard. I want to spin off

into an away place—and I want Damien as the tether to bring me back.

Damien, I know, needs that, too. He needs to dominate, to regain control.

And I need—god help me—I need the pain to get centered.

"Yes," I say, and that one word is like a trigger. I feel his muscles tense, his body tighten, both with need and with trepidation.

"Nikki." He backs off, the increased distance almost imperceptible, but to me it is a dangerous gulf.

I pull him back. "Yes," I repeat. "You need it. And so do I." I meet his eyes, knowing that he understands the depth of my craving. The extent of my need. Knowing also that I understand that he needs this just as much as I do. "You're the only one who can take me there."

"And the only way you will ever go there." His voice is harsh and firm, but he is right. I will never turn to the blade again. I don't need it. I have Damien.

I do not respond; I don't have to. Whatever fears he had about my need have been either soothed or overwhelmed by his own desire. By his need to lash out and grasp firm to the strands of our life that have been whipped into a frenzy, spinning wildly out of control.

I am those threads, and by claiming me, he can take back that control. And I—I can find the center that I crave, lost in the storm that is Damien.

My dress buttons up the front and I hadn't bothered to replace the belt when we'd dressed at the club. Without warning, Damien clutches the material and rips the dress open. I gasp as buttons fly, then suck in air as he turns me around, then pulls the garment free, tossing it negligently aside before turning me around again and thrusting two fingers roughly inside me.

I arch my back, my mouth open in a moan, and I grind down on his hand, wanting him to fill me.

He withdraws, pinching my clit and sending shocks of pain colored as pleasure racing through me.

I gasp, overwhelmed by this new sensation, then cry out in surprise when he lifts me up and carries me to the sofa, bending me over the back. I start to put my arms down to balance, but he is having none of that. "Behind your back," he says, and I use my right hand to clasp the wrist of my left. It is uncomfortable; I feel unbalanced. But I know that is how he wants me to feel. Unbalanced, shaky, off-center. Because if I am not, how can he make me whole again? He stands behind me, and I hear the metallic glide of his zipper as he strips, then feel the warm press of his hand on my ass, stroking, exploring, teasing. He slides it down slowly, sensually, then finds my core, so wet and ready for him.

"Is this what you want?" he whispers. "Do you want my fingers inside you? Stretching you, playing with you? Do you want me to fuck you, Nikki? Do you want me to take us both over the edge?"

I do—but that is not all that I want, and Damien knows it. I say nothing.

"Tell me," he says, bending over me so that I feel the warmth of his skin over my rear and over my arms as his weight presses them down into my back. I could stay like that forever, warm and enveloped within him. But he asks the question again, his lips now brushing my ear so that his voice makes me shiver. "Tell me, Nikki. Tell me what you need."

"You know," I say, because I do not want to put it into words. I do not want to crave what I do—to need the pain to drive me back to center. But he already knows, because he understands me as well as he understands himself. "Please."

"You are mine." The words are a whisper, so soft I can barely hear them and yet those three words crash through me, full of love and hope and longing. "Mine," he repeats, louder this time as he stands up, breaking that contact between us and leaving me longing for the warmth of his touch again. "Mine," he says as his hand comes down sharply against my ass, sending hundreds of fiery pinpricks through me to gather between my thighs.

"Mine," he repeats, as his palm strokes my ass, soothing before rising again to spank me over and over, the sting building inside, the fire of contact shooting out like lightning, making me cry out even as I focus on it, grabbing hold and pulling it back in, taking it over so that it is not the pain that controls me, but me that controls the pain.

"Mine," he repeats as my body lights up with sensation and desire. He moves closer, his cock pressing against my rear as he spreads my legs and strokes my core, the touch sending shock waves rippling across my skin. "I take care of what's mine," he says, the words spilling over me as he thrusts hard and fast inside me.

I cry out as my body welcomes him, tightening around him to draw him deeper. But this isn't slow and easy. This is hard and fast, and he pulls out, then slams into me again, our bodies coming together in a violent impact that sends me spiraling up out of myself.

He holds my hips tight with one hand, the other reaching around to stroke my clit as he pounds relentlessly into me. He is using me, and I am using him, and together we are leading each other through this horrific forest that has grown up around us.

I can feel everything inside me—everything inside him—and it builds and builds until the explosion is inevitable, and I know that if we were to explode like this without each other, we would be lost.

But Damien and I are each other's bread crumbs, and we will always lead each other back.

After, he pulls me gently to the ground. I lay on my back and look up at him as he strokes my face and then gently, so gently, enters me again. He is no longer controlling me, but controlling himself, and I submit willingly, letting him go where he needs, and letting him take me with him.

I close my eyes, lost in the sweetness as he moves in soft and subtle motions, letting my pleasure build slowly and gently until it breaks over both of us, not an explosion this time, but a gentle rainfall that washes all the harshness away.

With a sigh, I curl up beside him on the floor, my body pressed against his. "How is it that you can make my world so right even when everything is going wrong?"

"Because you love me," he says. "And I love you. That is our talisman, our charm. We may still break a little, you and I. But so long as we are together, neither of us will shatter."

I close my eyes and breathe deeply, because he is right. With Damien, I will always be made whole.

We lay there in silence until I cannot stand it any longer. "What are you going to do?" I finally ask.

"The news will have leaked," he says. "Even if no bra or panty shows up on eBay, already the tabloids have heard. We'll be the story of the moment, for however long the moment lasts."

"Add in the picture of us outside the club and you taking a swing at that photographer . . ." I trail off. I don't really need to go on.

"Do you want to stay?"

"Yes," I blurt, then immediately say, "No." I grimace. "I want Paris," I admit. "And I meant what I said before—the scrutiny and the photographers all come with the package. I'm your wife, Damien, and I will handle whatever I have to handle because I will never give you up. But—"

"I know," he says. "And the truth is, if my money can't buy us an escape, then what the hell is it good for?"

I prop myself up on an elbow to squint at him, wondering where he is going with this.

"I can't make the social media blasts go away," he says. "And I can't shoo away the photographers. I can't even promise it will be better the next time we come. But what I can do is make it better now."

His words are like a soothing balm, swathing me with hope.

"Will you trust me to make it right?" he asks, his eyes fixed on mine. He says nothing else, and I know that this man who single-handedly rules an empire is leaving this to me.

"You're my breath," I say, telling him what he already knows. "You're the beat of my heart. You are the essence of me. And I will always trust you."

Chapter 12

I push my windswept hair out of my eyes and take the captain's hand. He is a huge man, his coffee-colored skin slick with sweat. His smile flashes a hint of gold as he helps me from the boat to the unstable, floating dock that shifts beneath me as I step onto the weathered wood.

Damien follows, then pauses long enough to pay the man and thank him for bringing us over.

"I be bringing your staff, too, you just say the word, mon."

"No staff," Damien says. "Not this trip. But I'll radio when we need you to come back for us." He splays his hand against my back, and I can almost feel his thoughts in the pressure of his fingers. *Alone. Together. Paradise.*

I turn my head to smile at him. That sounds like heaven to me.

The captain returns to his little boat as Damien and I step from the dock to the white sand. I am wearing shorts and a tank top. My feet are bare. The captain unloaded our luggage onto the dock, but we leave it there for the time being, too intent on exploring this wide-open, nearly wild island in the Bahamas.

The sand is warm beneath my feet, and Damien and I walk across it to the water's edge. There are barely any waves; instead, the turquoise water sits as still as a painting, wide-open and vibrant and never-ending, this fabulous tableau broken only by the silhouette of similar small islands in the distance.

Behind us, the sand rises toward a line of vegetation, and I see a rustic path cut through the brush. I follow it with my eyes and can just make out a small stone house.

"That's the only structure," Damien says. "It needs a bit of fixing up, but it's perfectly livable. The cay is seven acres of undeveloped wilderness and pristine beaches. And there's not a soul here other than us."

"You really bought it?" I'm still in awe.

"I really did."

I wade out until the warm water hits me just below the knees, then look back at him with a grin. "I thought you didn't impulse-buy real estate."

"I don't. But you have a way of shifting my priorities and undermining my equilibrium."

"Oh, do I?" I reach down and scoop some water with my hand, flinging it toward him. "Should I apologize?"

"Hell, no," he says, then splashes me right back before taking my hand and tugging me toward him. I laugh and stumble into his arms, then hold on to him as we both tumble to the sand.

Damien is on top of me, and our lighthearted playfulness changes to heated longing as easily as flipping a light switch. Suddenly I am breathing hard, my skin tingling, and my body aware of every point of contact. My blood pounds, and the island noises—the birds, the surf—are muffled by the overwhelming beat of my own heart.

"I bought it for you," he says, his voice rough. "But I was selfish, too."

"How so?"

He is straddling me, and his hips move now, almost imperceptibly, but enough to send sparks through me. "I want to make love to my wife on the beach. I want to walk naked in the surf. I want the freedom to take you anytime, anyplace and know that there are no cameras, no paparazzi. No one watching us. No one paying any attention to us at all."

I nod, too overwhelmed to speak. He did this for me. He bought a freaking island for me. I'm having a hard time wrapping my head around the magnitude of that, and all I can say is what's in my heart. "I love you."

His smile is radiant.

"But how?" I ask. "I mean, how did you find it? It was only last night that we found the room ransacked, and only this morning that we flew to Nassau. Do you keep a list of Really Expensive Places I Might Decide to Buy?"

"Something like that," he says, his lips twitching as his fingers smooth my hair. "I looked at it about six months ago as a potential resort site. I didn't think it worked for that, but I had Sylvia call the agent last night to see if it was still available. It was—and now it's ours."

"It's so much." I can't even imagine how much an entire island must have cost him.

"I promise we can afford it. And what's the point of working hard to build a fortune if you don't enjoy the money once you have it?"

Since I can't argue with that, I don't. Instead, I lean up long enough to hook my arms around his neck and pull him even closer to me. I meet his eyes, so full of heat and power they rival the sun that beats down on us. "Make love to me, Damien," I whisper, and feel the immediate tightening in his body and the concomitant awakening of my own.

"With pleasure," he says, flashing a sexy Damien Stark smile. Then he claims me with a kiss so bold and hot and deep that it clears my mind completely, erasing everything but this moment and this man and those three simple words that I cling to with such desire and wonder—*Mrs. Damien Stark*.

Now, on this island, with only the sun and the sky to witness our passion, I lose myself in the pleasure of this man that I married. And, yes, I am content.

play my game

Chapter 1

Sunlight pours into the kitchen from the east-facing windows, and through the open glass doors on the west side of the house, I can hear the rhythmic pounding of the Pacific as it batters the Malibu shore. It is just past seven on a Sunday morning in February, and though I had awakened with both a smile and a plan, the smile is fading and my plan is floundering. I fear that it is time to face the terrible, horrible, inescapable truth—I can't cook my way out of a paper bag. And my plan to treat my husband to breakfast in bed is crashing and burning.

Or maybe just burning, I amend, as I realize that my waffles are doing just that.

I use the built-in handle to flip the waffle iron over, then open the top with the tines of a fork. The thing inside doesn't resemble any food product I've ever seen. It's black and bumpy and looks vaguely like the underside of a hiking shoe.

"Well, shit," I say, then add on an even more colorful string of curses when I realize that the eggs are burning and that smoke from the bacon is going to set off the fire alarms any second now.

I lunge sideways toward the stove and hit the button for the vent, then narrow my eyes toward the ceiling, daring the alarm to start screeching. Because even if breakfast consists of black coffee and dry toast, I *am* going to manage it. And nothing—not a smoke alarm, not the scent of burning batter, not even my muttered cursing—is going to roust my husband of almost three weeks out of bed before I am ready to surprise him.

A heartbeat later, I know just how wrong I am.

I have not yet turned around, but I don't have to. I know that he is awake, and I know that he is standing behind me. I didn't hear him approach. I didn't catch his scent. There is nothing tangible to announce his presence to me. But that doesn't matter.

I simply know.

Maybe it's a shift in the density of the air.

Maybe it's the way that the heat from his body makes the molecules around him spin faster.

Maybe it is the simple fact that he is Damien Stark, my husband, my love, and I could no more be unaware of his presence than I am of my own body.

For a moment, I simply stand there, my back still to him. I had wanted to surprise him, and so I will admit to a small tingle of disappointment. But that is quickly conquered by the desire to see him. To savor him. To let the image of him that fills my mind now fill my reality.

I turn slowly to find him leaning against the wall that separates the third floor kitchen from the open area. He is wearing a pair of thin gray sweatpants tied loosely at his hips and absolutely nothing else. His athlete's body glows with a lingering tan, courtesy of the island that was the last stop of our honeymoon, and the light on his burnished skin highlights the sculpted planes of his chest and abdomen.

Damien's prowess in business came after his fame as a professional tennis player, and looking at him, it is easy to see how he excelled at both. He is power and strength and beauty combined, and I stand like an idiot, absorbing the sight of him, then sigh with the same kind of full, sensual pleasure brought on by a sunset or a symphony or the stars filling a country sky. Damien Stark is a feast for the eyes, a concerto for the senses. And though I know him intimately—though he is mine, and I am his—I still go weak at the sight of him.

"This is an exceptionally nice scene to wake up to." His eyes skim over my inappropriate cooking attire. Bare feet, one of his dress shirts, and a white apron with a rather unoriginal *Kiss the Cook* logo.

"Funny. I was just thinking the same thing." That's an exaggeration, because the truth is that I'm having a hard time thinking at all. Or, rather, my thoughts are all primal in nature. *Need. Want. Take.*

He closes the distance between us in three long strides, then slides his arms around my waist. His grin warms me like sunshine, but when he pulls me to him and closes his mouth over mine, I am warmed by a much more dangerous kind of heat. "Good morning, wife."

My lips tingle from the intensity of his greeting, but I respond in kind, loving the way these words sound. "Good morning, husband."

He trails his fingertip along my jawline. "You have batter on your face," he says, before slipping his finger in his mouth. "Tasty."

I roll my eyes as he leans in to kiss my ear.

"And flour in your hair."

"I would have managed eventually," I say. "You're the one who got out of bed and spoiled my surprise."

He glances behind me at the brick of a waffle. "Believe me, I'm surprised."

"Careful, mister," I say, but I'm laughing. We both know that my cooking skills are nonexistent.

"It's the thought that counts," Damien says. "And I like this thought very, very much."

He pulls me in for another long, slow kiss. The kind that makes me think that getting up early on a Sunday morning was really not one of my more stellar ideas.

"I know how to fix this," Damien says.

"Does it involve getting naked and going back to bed, and you assuring me that you didn't marry me for my culinary skills?"

"Actually, no, though I think that should definitely be added to the day's activities."

"Oh, really?" I lean closer, relishing the way his arms tighten around me, pulling me against him so that I can feel him hot and hard and close. "And what else is on the agenda?"

He slides one hand down over my shirt until he finds my bare thigh, then slowly trails his fingers up, under the light cotton. "It's our last day before we go back to the real world." His voice is as soft as his caress, and I moan softly as his hand moves between my thighs and his fingers stroke and tease me. "I want to spend it making love to my wife. Touching her. Caressing her. Burying myself deep inside her."

My knees are weak, and it's a good thing that Damien is holding me up. "I approve of your plan for the day. I approve so much, in fact, that I think we should get started on that right now."

The tip of his tongue traces the curve of my ear, sending shivers racing through me. "But first, we're going to go get breakfast."

It takes a moment for my fuzzy brain to register his words. "Go?"

"I told you. I can fix this." He kisses me lightly, then releases me. I sigh in disappointment at the loss of contact even as Damien nods at the rather unappetizing mess I've made in the kitchen. "Pastries and coffee and fresh-squeezed orange juice. After all, we'll need energy to survive the rest of the day I have planned."

"I like the sound of that," I admit. We've been back home from our honeymoon for a few days, but neither one of us has gone back to work officially yet. I've done some coding at home, but not much. Just minor tweaking of a few of my smartphone apps. And Damien, of course, has fielded dozens of phone calls and read god-only-knows how many emails. But considering all he usually handles in the course of running the universe, his work activities over the last several weeks have been nonexistent by comparison.

He takes my hand to lead me out of the kitchen and toward the bedroom, then pauses in front of the stack of cat food that I've moved from the pantry to the counter.

"Please tell me that's not your secret ingredient."

I know he expects me to laugh, but I just can't manage it. Instead I lift a shoulder. "I'm going to box it up to take to Jamie."

Damien presses a soft kiss to the top of my head, obviously understanding my mood. "I know, baby. I miss the fluff ball, too."

Technically, Lady Meow-Meow belongs to both Jamie and me. More technically, she belongs to Jamie, who was the one who actually rescued her from the shelter when she was a one-month-old ball of white fur. I'd taken temporary custody when Jamie rented out her condo and set off for Texas to get her shit together.

That didn't work out as planned, though. Texas turned out to be more of a pit stop than a relocation, and not long after she'd moved in with her parents, she was back in LA. She'd come for my wedding. She'd stayed because of Ryan Hunter, Damien's security chief, who as far as I can tell is head over heels for her. And the feeling, thank goodness, is mutual.

Now, it's the two of them and the cat living in the tiny Venice Beach house that Ryan has rented for years. According to Jamie, it's a temporary arrangement until her tenant moves out in a few months. Then she'll move back to the condo.

She hasn't said as much, but I expect that Ryan will go with her. We had drinks with them the day after we got back to California; I've seen the way he looks at her. More important, I've heard the way she talks about him. And I couldn't be happier for both of them.

But that doesn't mean I'm not sad about losing the cat.

I tilt my head back and smile up at Damien. "I'm fine. It's all fine. I just saw all the food in the pantry and it made me sad. Besides, it gives me an excuse to have lunch with Jamie," I add with a devious lilt in my voice. "I haven't seen her alone since we got back, and I have to fill her in on just how spectacular our honeymoon was."

Damien laughs. "Two best friends discussing a honeymoon. Why do I feel like I'm facing a performance review?"

My grin is pure wickedness. "Don't worry, Mr. Stark. As always, you scored a perfect ten."

He kisses me again, long and lingering, then pulls me close. I sigh happily and lean against him, trying as always to absorb the fact that this is my life now. *He* is my life now.

"I love you," I say softly, then feel the tightening of his arms around me in response to my words.

"You're my everything, Nikki. And I love you desperately." He takes my hand and leads me back to our bedroom. He tugs the apron over my head, then slowly unbuttons the shirt I am wearing. He eases it off my shoulders, and it falls gently to the floor behind us. I'm naked beneath it, and the material caresses my back as it falls, making me shiver from both the sensuality of the moment and the anticipation of Damien's touch.

He doesn't disappoint. He tilts his head down as if to kiss me, but then only brushes his lips across mine in the lightest of touches. I want to protest, but the words die in my throat as he moves to trail kisses down my body. The curve of my neck. The sensitive skin along my collarbone.

He pauses at my breast long enough to tease my nipple with his tongue. It is as if he has opened a conduit, and threads of electricity go racing through me, making my nipples tighten with need and my clit throb with demand. I close my eyes and part my lips, concentrating on breathing. On not losing all control and begging him to just take me right there.

But then his kisses move lower, and his tongue dances down my abdomen, then over my pubic bone, and then—oh, dear god—his tongue flicks over my clit, and I have to reach back and grab the iron footboard of our bed in order to remain upright.

I spread my legs, wanting and expecting more, but he pulls away, letting his fingers trail sensually up my body as he stands. I am gasping. Hot and needy. But when I reach out and brush my fingers over the erection that is straining against those goddamn sexy sweatpants, Damien just takes a step back and shakes his head. "Later," he says, making the word sound like both torture and a promise.

"Christ, Damien. How am I supposed to do anything today other than want you?"

"Sweetheart, there's nothing else today that you need to be doing."

I take a moment to gather myself while he heads into the bathroom. I find him in the closet, where he hands me a pair of capris and my favorite light sweater.

"I should grab a shower," I protest as I watch Damien slide into a pair of jeans and a threadbare Wimbledon T-shirt.

"Casual Sunday morning," he says. "And you look amazing as always. Besides," he adds with a wicked gleam in his eye, "if you want a shower later, I'll be happy to help you out. Make sure you get very thoroughly clean."

"I bet you would." And though I'm laughing, I already know that's an offer I absolutely will not refuse.

We're both hungry, and so we drive to the Upper Crust, a charming local bakery about a mile up the beach. It's one of my favorite places in Malibu, and while Damien orders, I find a table on the wooden deck with a wide-open view of the ocean.

Damien's house—*our* house—has an equally stunning view, but is set much farther back from the beach. One thing that I love about the bakery is that it is built practically on top of the dunes, so that all you have to do is descend the stairs at the back of the deck to be on the sand.

I mention that to Damien when he returns with big mugs of coffee and two flaky chocolate croissants.

"Then we'll build a bungalow right at the edge of the property. I'll talk to Nathan about drawing up plans," he adds, referring to Nathan Dean, the architect who designed the main house.

I gape at him. "I was just making conversation."

He looks almost confused. "So you wouldn't like that? I would." He reaches out to wipe a stray bit of chocolate from the corner of my mouth, then licks his fingertip. "I can't tell you how many times I've wanted to strip you naked on that beach, and yet I had to wait until we were all the way up the hill. But if there was a conveniently located bungalow . . ."

I shake my head in mock exasperation. "Clearly I'm going to have to watch what I say around you, Mr. Stark. I mean, what if I'd said that I wanted a pied-à-terre on the moon?"

"I'm certain that can be arranged." He twines his fingers with mine, then kisses my knuckles. "I think this is my favorite part of being married."

"Croissants?"

"Spoiling my wife."

I only smile. As ridiculous as Damien building a bungalow because of an offhand comment might be, I can't deny that it makes me feel all warm and gooey inside. Then again, simply being with the man makes me feel that way.

"Do you want another?" I ask, nodding at his chocolate-stained plate.

"Offering to wait on me?"

"Anything you want," I say. "Anything you need."

He squeezes my hand. "I have everything I need."

My smile is so wide that it almost hurts. Around us, I see other customers watching us and grinning, too, as if our passion is infectious. I recognize a few as neighbors, who undoubtedly know that we are newlyweds. Then again, considering how much the tabloids and social media report on our every move, I imagine that the whole world knows we're newlyweds.

I swipe my finger through the chocolate that is left on Damien's plate, then lift it to his lips. His brows rise ever so slightly, and then he draws my finger in, lightly sucking and sending such sparks of ecstasy through me that it's a wonder I don't moan with pleasure.

When I pull my finger gently away, I can't help my smile of victory. I'm quite certain that at least someone on this deck has a smartphone and a Twitter account, and that picture will be all over social media within the hour. Normally, that would bother me.

Right now, I not only don't care, I want it.

I want the world to see us in love. To see the way we look at each other. The way we complete each other.

I'm happier than I've ever been, and if I can't shout it from the rooftops, then I'll just let the world shout it for me on social media.

"You're smiling," Damien says.

"Why wouldn't I be?"

"Good point." He stands. "Ready?"

I nod, then start to head for the door into the bakery. He tugs me to a stop and nods to the stairs. "I'll come back for the car when I go for a run later. Right now, let's walk home."

I love Southern California. Although it is technically winter, the temperature is already in the mid-sixties, with the forecast predicting highs in the seventies. I take off my shoes, and Damien does the same, and we walk in the surf, where the water is frigid no matter what the season.

We hold hands and talk about everything and nothing as we walk home. "Hard to believe we're already into the second week of February," I say, thinking that we've just come back from our honeymoon and now it's almost Valentine's Day. I feel a bit like a kid whose birthday is the week before Christmas. "I wasn't even thinking about the timing when we picked our wedding day."

"You mean the weather? It's usually a bit colder this time of year, but it's always comfortable."

I glance sideways at him, wondering if he's really that clueless. His expression, however, is entirely unreadable.

"I just meant—" I cut myself off, frustrated.

His brow furrows. "What?"

Communication, I think. *Marriage is all about communication.*

"I was just thinking that our first Valentine's Day is almost here."

"Not even close," he says.

"Um, less than a week. That's right around the corner."

I don't realize that he's stopped until I've gone a few more steps. I turn back. Damien actually looks a little worried, and I confess I'm surprised. This will be our first Valentine's Day together, and knowing Damien and romance, I'd anticipated him doing it up big. I tell myself it's stupid to get my feelings hurt, especially since there's a week to go, and Damien could pull off amazing with only five minutes' notice.

Still, I can't help feeling disappointed. Which is completely and totally unfair, but there you go.

I draw in a breath and plaster on one of my best pageant smiles. "Actually, you're right," I say. "As far as you and I are concerned, a week is practically a lifetime."

"Nikki. Come here." His voice is low and apologetic, and I keep my face bland because now I am certain that he forgot. He just . . . forgot.

People forget things, though, right? Even newlyweds.

Even Damien Stark.

I move into his arms, in part because he asked me to, but also because I want to be close enough to him that if I tilt my head down he won't see the stupid, foolish, idiotic tears that are starting to well in my eyes.

He slides his hands over my arms, moving them until I'm cupping his ass—along with the small, square box tucked into his back pocket.

"Take it out." His voice is firm, but I think I hear a faint hint of amusement.

I blink, then do as he asks. It's a small, white cardboard box, the kind that department stores use to package jewelry. Confused, I look up at Damien, and I no longer wonder if he's amused. It's very clear that he is.

"Open it."

I'm starting to feel very foolish, but I do as he asks and gently tug off the lid to reveal a necklace on which hangs a tiny glass bottle. Inside the bottle is a rolled up piece of paper.

I look up at Damien, confused. "It's lovely."

"Take out the scroll."

"Really?" I don't wait for his reply, but use my fingernails to pull out the tiny cork. The paper is harder to get out, but Damien fishes a little army knife out of his front pocket, then passes the tiny pair of tweezers to me. I realize as he does that he'd brought the knife in anticipation of this moment.

Even with the tweezers, it takes some skill to fish out the paper. I finally manage, though, and I unscroll it, then squint at the tiny writing.

> *For my wife for Valentine's Day,*
> *A proposition, if I may—*
> *Three clues for you,*
> *You know what to do—*
> *And if you want your present to claim,*
> *You're going to have to play my game.*
> *Now here's the clue that I speak of:*
> *Tell me, darling Nikki, what is sweeter than Love?*

"Damien." My voice is soft, muted by the happy, astounded tears that have clogged my throat.

"I can't claim to be a poet," Damien says, though I think the poem is charming, and all the more wonderful because Damien wrote it.

He hooks his finger under my chin and tilts my head up so that there is no way I can hide my tear-filled eyes. "Three clues. Six days. I think you'll make it."

My heart has swollen so much it seems to fill my chest, cutting off my ability to breathe. "You didn't forget."

The softness I see in his eyes just about slays me. "Oh, baby. I could sooner forget my own name than our first Valentine's Day."

"I love you." The words seem thin compared to the emotion that pours through me.

"And I you. But, Nikki," he adds, and now his voice takes on a harder edge, belied only by the slight twitch at the corner of his mouth. "You doubted me. I think that deserves a punishment."

I cock my head, wary, then squeal when he smacks my bottom. I laugh and take off toward the house at a run.

But not too fast. After all, I'm hoping that Damien will catch me.

Chapter 2

Since Damien is in exceptional shape—and since I'm not exactly trying hard to get away—he catches me easily enough. He tugs me to a stop, then scoops me into his arms. I kick and squirm a little just for form, but there's no denying that I am a very willing captive.

I keep my arms hooked around his neck as he carries me up the path and then surprises me by veering off onto the newly constructed tennis court.

There is a plush lounge chair on the sidelines, which I have recently realized he put there so that I would have a place to sit and watch him practice. That's not all it's good for, though, especially as it is as wide as a twin bed and at least as comfortable.

"Damien," I protest as he pulls my sweater over my head. "It's broad daylight." I don't add that there is still a chill in the air. The temperature may be in the sixties, but right at this moment my skin is so heated that I could be naked in Antarctica and not even notice.

"So it is." He doesn't even slow down, however. Instead he reaches for the button on my pants. He unfastens it, then eases the zipper down. He tugs the capris down over my hips, then moves lower until he reaches my feet, still bare from our walk on the beach.

He brushes a finger over the arch of my foot, making me

squirm. Then he pulls the pants fully off, leaving me in only a bra and my very tiny panties.

Damien's eyes skim over me, the heat in his gaze affecting me as potently as if his hands were skimming over me. I feel my body go soft and wet, and when his focus turns to my crotch, I moan softly in anticipation of his touch.

Slowly, he peels me out of my underthings until I am naked on the lounge chair and burning under Damien's gaze.

"Beautiful," he murmurs, and I feel the warm current of a blush as it creeps up my skin.

Slowly, he traces his fingers over my body. Up my shin, over my thigh, then along the soft skin of my inner thigh. He moves with casual ease over the scars that once embarrassed me, but that I rarely think about now with Damien. And then his hands are traveling up, over my belly, up my rib cage. He slows at my breasts, using the tip of his finger to stroke and tease before lightly pinching my nipple and sending a shock of pleasure through me that is so sweetly profound it makes me arch up, but whether that is because the sensation is too intense to endure or because I am trying to make it last even longer, I do not know.

"Stand up," he finally says. "I want to see you."

I do, standing naked on the court at the foot of the chaise, my body soft and ready. My breasts are tight, my nipples like pinpoints of need. And my clit is so sensitive that even the slight breeze is driving me a little mad. I am wet—so wet—and my sex throbs with demand, my arousal growing with each beat of my heart.

"This isn't fair," I say, though I'm not entirely sure how I have managed to form words. "I'm naked, and you're not."

"I'd hate for you to think I'm inequitable, Mrs. Stark."

I watch, mesmerized, as he eases out of his clothes. He is exceptional when he is fully clothed. Naked and erect, he is like a god, wild and virile and powerful.

He lies on the chaise, then crooks a finger to call me. I don't hesitate, and I ease over him, my knees on either side of his hips so that his erection strokes me, making me tremble. Making me even more wet.

Since I am pretty much certain that I will die if I don't have him inside me right this instant, I take his cock in my hand—intending to stroke and position him against my sex—but I am foiled by the shake of his head and the crisp way that he says a single word. "No."

"I—what?"

He makes a spinning motion. "Turn around and come here. I want to taste you."

I hesitate, not sure why I feel suddenly awkward. It's not like Damien's never gone down on me. As far as I'm concerned, his tongue is magical.

But to straddle his mouth, and backward . . .

The thought is both arousing and a bit disconcerting.

"Nikki." He says my name in the kind of voice that brooks no argument, and I comply, both because he has ordered me to, and because I want it, this new intimacy. With Damien, there is nowhere he can take me that I won't go, and so help me I want to go everywhere with him.

His hands cup my rear, and I understand the benefit of this position the moment his tongue strokes me, soft and teasing. Because although Damien is holding me, I have more control. I can shift and move, and make the pleasure build fast or slow.

More than that, I can see him. His long, muscular thighs. That gorgeous chest with just the slightest hint of hair. Those rock-hard abs that my fingers know so well.

And the beautiful cock, so hard now that I think it must be painful. And what kind of a wife would I be if I didn't give my husband just a little relief?

Feeling both aroused and mischievous, I lean forward at the waist, which has the added benefit of moving my hips slightly even as Damien's tongue thrusts inside me. I swallow a moan as my body tightens around him. *Christ, yes, I want his cock*. If not inside me, then in my mouth. I want to feel him get harder. I want to taste his arousal. I want to make Damien feel as wild and crazed as he is making me feel.

And so slowly, I lick the crown, then smile in satisfaction as he grows even harder. As he groans against my cunt before teasing me more, his tongue working magic on my clit.

I take him in, almost coming merely from the taste of him, all heat and male, arousal and spice.

Above us, the sun shines down. I feel the warmth on my back, and the knowledge that we are outside, so deliciously intimate, makes me even more aroused. A tremor runs through my body, and I know that I am close. That the storm is building and soon Damien will take me over the edge, and I so desperately want him to go with me. I use my tongue, laving and stroking, and I feel him getting harder, tighter. Closer.

Then it's right there—so close, I'm so goddamn close—

And then his touch is gone, and I'm left stranded on that precipice, aroused and ready with no one to take me over.

Damien has managed to extricate himself from beneath me, and now he is stretched out beside me. And though he looks just as aroused as I feel, there is no denying the amusement that flickers in his eyes.

"What the hell?" I demand and earn a laugh from my husband.

"I'm pretty sure I told you this was a punishment. For doubting me, remember?"

I open my mouth, fully prepared to call him a nasty name, but then he tells me to bend over his knee.

I stay quiet. And then, because I'm feeling bold, I say huskily, "You do realize that's not a punishment at all."

"I know," he says, and the dark promise in his tone makes me shiver.

He moves to sit at the foot of the chaise, and I eagerly bend across his lap, already more aroused than I was just moments before. It's not about the anticipation of pain, though there is no denying that I will always want the pain. But I do not need it nearly as often as I used to. Now I want it only from Damien's hand.

But this is not about battling my demons. This is about letting go. About surrendering to Damien. About letting him take me and fill me.

And, yes, it's about pleasure. About passion.

And as Damien and I know better than most, pleasure and pain have the same core. And I willingly surrender to both of them.

The first spank makes me gasp, the sting spreading out, and then calming down as Damien rubs the curve of my rear, softening the sting. He smacks me again, just a little harder, and I feel my sex clench with longing. He slides his hand between my legs to stroke me, and I know that he is aware of how aroused he is making me. Of how much I want this—and how much I will want him after, once my ass is red and he has had his fill.

Again and again. Five more spanks and I am on fire, from the sting of flesh against flesh, but also from the erotic need to be fucked, to be taken.

"Damien." I only whisper his name, but it is enough, and he helps me up, then settles me on his lap, my knees on either side of him so that I am straddling him as he sits on the end of the lounger, his hands at my back keeping me steady.

"I want to watch it build in your eyes," he says. "I want to see the moment when we float away."

"Yes." I rise up on my knees, then lower myself onto him, slowly at first and then faster and faster until that precipice looms in front of me again, and I can see the explosion building in his eyes, my own passion reflected right back at me.

"Now," he demands when we are both at the edge. "Now, Nikki, dammit, come with me."

I arch back, a slave to his demands, and burst into a billion pieces even as he explodes inside me. He holds me tight, keeping me from getting lost in the ether and providing a tether to bring me back to myself.

I collapse against him, breathing hard, relishing the comfort of his arms, strong and safe, closing around me.

"Damien." That's all I can say, but it is enough.

"Yes," he says, his voice so tender it brings tears to my eyes. "I know."

Later, he carries me up to the house, because I am not at all convinced that I will ever have the power to walk on my own again.

I manage to stand for a shower, then dry off and settle back on the bed, naked, as Damien stays in the bathroom to shave.

I drift off, sated, only to be roused by his voice wafting over me. "Now, that is a very lovely view."

I stretch and roll over, opening my eyes to find him naked in the doorway—and once again fully erect.

With a laugh, I prop myself up on an elbow. "You, Mr. Stark, are insatiable."

"You make me insatiable," he counters, coming to sit beside me on the bed. "I could spend the entire day here with you. Maybe the week, the month, the year."

"I like it. Though we'd have to figure out how to eat."

"Oh, I intend to eat my fill," he says, nipping his way down my belly.

I squirm, delighted by his touch, and then I tense. I cock my head as something pokes at my memory. Something about eating . . . about sweetness . . .

About love.

I twine my fingers in his hair. "Wait—"

He lifts his head, one brow cocked.

I glance at the clock, see that it's still early enough, and grin at my husband. "Sorry, sweetheart, I'm cutting you off."

"Oh?" His expression is vaguely amused. "And why is that?"

"I've nailed the first clue." My tone is smug. I am certain that I'm right.

"Really?" He eases his way up my body until I am trapped beneath him. "Tell me."

I shake my head. "Nope."

He kisses my neck. "Please?"

"Not a chance, buddy. At least not until you buy me a meal."

"A meal?"

"Lunch," I confirm. "In Beverly Hills. And after my meal," I add with a wide, smug grin, "I want my dessert."

We end up having a late lunch at one of the outdoor tables at 208 Rodeo, and we split an order of sweet potato fries and a burger while we do the people-watching thing, scoping out both tourists and locals as they stroll along Rodeo Drive or wander up the stairs to Via Rodeo. Not surprisingly, there's a significant amount of reciprocal watching, and I catch sight of more than a few people taking surreptitious snaps of us with their phones. A few even stand boldly across the street and aim powerful zoom lenses in our direction, clicking furiously as they rattle off shot after shot.

Again, I don't care.

It's a gorgeous day. I'm with my husband on a Valentine's Day scavenger hunt. And I'm still basking in the glow of some outstanding morning sex.

Seriously, life is good.

A perky waitress who looks like she's ready to star in her own sitcom bounces to our table. "Can I get you some dessert?"

I meet Damien's eyes. "Thanks," I say. "But we've already got a plan for that."

We settle the check, and then stroll the two short blocks to Love Bites, the exceptional bakery owned by Sally Love. She's been featured on every food program known to man and has graced the pages of wedding and food magazines. She's known Damien for years, and I adored her—and her cakes—from the moment I met her. And after just one bite of her dark chocolate and Kahlua cupcake, I knew that no one else could cater our wedding.

I'm convinced that *what is sweeter than Love* leads like an arrow to Sally Love and Love Bites. Valentine's Day and love go together—and love leads to weddings. So how could the bakery that catered our wedding not be where the clue leads?

But though I might be certain, Damien, damn the man, has steadfastly refused to either confirm or deny.

Soon enough, though, I'll know if I'm right.

I'd called Sally just seconds after my *aha* moment, and though the bakery is technically closed on Sundays, she said that she was on-site getting ready for a luncheon she's catering tomorrow and invited me to stop by.

"Look at you two," she says the moment she tugs open the glass doors to her sugar-scented shop. "The very picture of marital bliss."

I simply grin and return her enthusiastic hug.

"Now, what's this all about?"

"Apparently my wife has a craving for your cupcakes."

"Does she?" Sally says, her brows rising. "I'm flattered, but what brought this on?"

I look between the two of them, suddenly unsure of myself. "Um, it's just that nothing is sweeter than love, right? So that must mean your cupcakes."

She points a finger at me. "Now, there's an excellent slogan for an ad campaign. Mind if I borrow it?"

I glance toward Damien. "You'll have to ask him."

"It's all yours," he says.

"Easiest deal I've made all day," she says with a wide grin. "But seriously, what do you need from me, Nikki?"

I hand her the tiny piece of paper and watch as she squints at the words. When she looks up at me, I see both interest and confusion on her face. "This is from where?"

"From him," I say, pointing toward Damien.

"Oh, really?" There is laughter in her voice, as if the very thought of Damien Stark writing silly poetry and organizing a scavenger hunt is beyond the realm of possibility. She looks so perplexed, in fact, that I'm about to tell her that I must have made a mistake.

That's when I see the tiniest smile touch her mouth.

"Oh, you are *so* playing me," I accuse. "Both of you."

She holds her hands up in mock surrender. "Sweetie, I swear I have nothing in the store you'd want tonight. But if you'd like to special-order something for delivery to your office tomorrow . . . well, I'm sure I can come up with a treat that will intrigue you."

I keep my own expression businesslike, but inside I'm jumping with glee. I *knew* I'd figured out the clue. I'd just done it faster than she or Damien had expected. "That sounds great. I always need a sugar boost by the afternoon. Why don't I let it be chef's choice?" I add, smiling innocently.

She holds my gaze, then nods. "I think that'll work out just fine."

Damien and I spend a few more minutes chatting with her, and when we leave, I have a chocolate cupcake in hand—one that she said was leftover from the catering job she was preparing in the back.

"It's delicious," I say to Damien, who has taken my wrist and is starting to lift the confection to his mouth for a bite. "And it's all mine." I tug my arm very firmly out of his grasp.

"Oh, really?" The humor is plain in his voice. "And why is that?"

"We both know I got it right. You're just keeping your mouth shut to torment me."

"Tormenting you is one of my favorite activities, Mrs. Stark."

"I know that very well, Mr. Stark," I retort, keeping my voice and my expression prim despite the heat that his sultry tone has sent coursing through me. "But this time it's my turn to torment you. No sharing unless you play nice." As if to illustrate my point, I take another bite of the cupcake.

With a laugh, he tugs me close. "You can withhold chocolate," he says, dipping me. "Just don't withhold anything else."

And then—as the well-heeled Rodeo Drive crowd looks on and applauds—my husband licks the chocolate from the corner of my mouth before kissing me long and deep and very thoroughly.

Chapter 3

Despite having weeks of work stacked up on my desk and an email inbox that is full to overflowing, I am having a terrible time concentrating at my desk on Monday. I manage to spend the morning getting some work done, then eat lunch at my desk as I plow through emails. But by mid-afternoon, I've lost my focus. Instead of computers, I'm thinking about cupcakes. Not to mention the present that I have planned for Damien—and yet haven't had nearly enough time to work on.

The problem with buying presents for a man like Damien Stark is that if he doesn't already own something, then it's probably not something he'd want anyway. I considered naming a star for him, or stealing him away for a romantic weekend, or even donating in both our names to one of his favorite charities.

But while I have no problem with any of those ideas in theory, none are intimate or original enough for our very first Valentine's Day.

No, I'm going with handmade—more or less—and personal.

Unfortunately, the "handmade" part has been giving me some trouble, and I've realized that I'm going to have to break down and ask for help.

Since that is at least some distraction from wondering about Damien's present to me, I pick up the phone and call Sylvia, Damien's personal assistant.

"Nikki! Hey, welcome back. He's spending all day on nineteen with Preston," she says, referring to the head of acquisitions for Stark Applied Technology. "But if you hold on, I'll call down and let him know you're on the line."

"No, that's okay," I say. "I called to talk to you." Sylvia was one of the first people to learn that not only was I the model for the life-size nude portrait that hangs in the Malibu house, but that Damien paid me a cool million dollars as a fee. When she told me that Damien had gotten off cheap, I knew she and I would get along fine.

And after she attended my bachelorette party at Raven—a local male strip club—any lingering wife-of-the-boss awkwardness was soundly swept away. Once you've shared the experience of having a half-naked cowboy's package gyrating in your face, it's hard not to be friends.

"What's up?"

"You know the photographs that hang in the thirty-fifth floor reception area? The redwood and the bicycle and all the others?"

"Of course."

"Damien told me they were done by a local photographer. Out of Santa Monica, I think. Do you know his name?"

"Sure, but can I ask what's up?"

"Valentine's Day," I admit. "I've got this idea to do a photograph of me. Kind of artsy—I have a pose in mind. And then I'll adjust the color on Photoshop and add a caption. I know I've waited till the last minute, but I've set up the self-timer a dozen times, and I just can't get the composition right without me being behind the lens."

"He'll love it," Sylvia says. "Perfect for the man who just acquired the very last thing on earth that he wanted."

"What's that?" I ask, completely confused.

Sylvia laughs. "Duh. You."

"Oh." I feel a blush of pleasure rising up my neck because the truth is, I know that she's right.

"His name is Wyatt Reed, and I'm happy to give you his number. But I happen to know that he's out of town. He's on a shoot in Australia until March."

"Oh. Well, damn." I consider my options. "Do you know any other photographers? Someone in the PR department or—"

"I could do it."

"Really?"

"I don't take a lot of shots of people, but I've been into photography for years. Architecture, mostly. But if you show me what you're going for, I'm sure I can make it work."

"That would be amazing," I say. And not only because she would be solving my problem. How cool that she is into photography, too.

"Listen, I've got a call coming in. Shoot me an email and let me know when you want to do this thing, okay?"

I agree and end the call just as Mrs. Crane—the receptionist for my shared office suite—buzzes me. "Ms. Archer is here."

"Really?" I'm not expecting Jamie, but I can't deny that I'm glad to see her. I'd called her last night to schedule lunch and gossip for later in the week, and then, of course, I'd given her the quick-and-dirty rundown on Damien's scavenger hunt, the first clue, and my frustration.

"So?" Jamie asks as she bursts into my tiny office. She looks around—as if shocked that the decor hasn't changed in the few weeks since she's been by—then flops down on the little sofa. "Has the cupcake come yet?"

I shake my head. "Why are you here?" Her condo is just a few miles away, but she's been staying in Venice Beach, and that's way the hell and gone from Sherman Oaks.

"One, I am loving this scavenger hunt thing—I'm totally stealing the idea."

"You can love it without driving to the Valley," I point out.

"Which brings me to reason number two. Audition," she says, then holds her hand up for a high five, which I happily supply.

"Seriously? What for?"

"Pilot for a new drama. I've actually got a really good shot according to Evelyn," she adds, referring to Evelyn Dodge, one of my absolute favorite people who is now also Jamie's agent. Jamie makes a face. "Of course with my luck that means I'll get the job, I'll kick serious ass, and the network won't pick the damn thing up."

"Sorry," I say. "This is a no-pessimism zone. Only positive thoughts once you walk through that door."

She rolls her eyes, then curls her feet under her, tilts her head back, and starts to chant.

"Jamie, what the hell?"

"I'm visualizing. Shut up for a second. I'm about to give my speech at the Golden Globes."

I snort back a laugh, but I'm saved from having to think of a snarky comeback by the sharp buzz of the intercom again. This time, Mrs. Crane announces a delivery for me, and Jamie and I both spring for the door.

"It's okay, Mrs. Crane," I say. "I've been expecting it."

I yank open the door, probably terrifying the skinny guy standing there in a delivery uniform. Once I have the package and have sent the guy on his way with a tip, Jamie and I take the box back to my desk. I sit in my chair and she perches on the wooden desktop beside me.

"Well?" she says. "Open it."

Since I'm not sure what I'm waiting for, I nod, then use a letter opener to slice through the tape that is holding the decorative pastry box closed. It's only slightly bigger than a cupcake, and when I open it, I'm surprised to see that it holds exactly that—a cupcake.

Specifically, a lovely cupcake with green fondant icing and the numeral "4" printed perfectly across the top in blue icing.

I glance at Jamie, who looks just as baffled as I feel.

"That can't be all of it." I reach for the cupcake. "There must be a message underneath."

But if there is more to the message, it's not on the box beneath the cupcake where I expect it. So when Jamie very reasonably suggests that the clue might be baked into the cupcake, I use my iPhone to snap a picture of the treat—just in case—and then I use the letter opener as a knife and carefully cut the cake in half. There's nothing hidden inside. No secret message baked in the cake.

But as soon as we've both picked up our halves to feast upon, I see the carefully printed website written on the bottom of the paper muffin cup.

"I *knew* it." I am feeling so smug and triumphant that I have to battle the urge to call Damien and gloat. I don't, though. I'm not home free just because I've found a website.

"Well?" Jamie sounds impatient.

"I'm on it." I pull my laptop closer to me, then type in the URL as she comes around my desk to look over my shoulder, then mutters, "Well, *fuck,*" when all that pops up is an input box for a username.

I echo her sentiments as I lean back in my chair, thinking. "This has to be it," I say. "Somehow, this leads to the next clue."

"I adore Damien," Jamie says, "but couldn't he have just taken you out for dinner and a movie like a normal guy?"

"I thought you loved the scavenger hunt idea."

"Well, sure. Until it got hard."

I laugh and shake my head. Not only is Damien a far cry from your average guy, but I'm so delighted by this game—which plays to both my romantic and geek sides—that if I weren't already full-up with love for my husband, I would fall even further.

"Four," I say, even as I type the numeral into the box. I glance at Jamie, hit *enter,* and cross my fingers.

A moment later, the screen changes, and I feel a little tug of glee:

Welcome, Nikki Stark
Please Enter Password

My glee fades when I realize there is yet another hurdle.

Once again, I meet Jamie's eyes, but she's already on it. She's snatched the box and is examining every last inch of it and the muffin cup. "Nothing," she says. "Do you think we ate it?"

I don't answer. I'm too busy typing a four into the box. I hold my breath, hit *enter,* then both laugh and curse when I hear Damien's voice saying, "Try again, sweetheart."

"Oh my god," Jamie says. "You *so* have to figure this out. Like right now."

I agree. I can picture Damien at work today, doing whatever

master-of-the-universe thing is on his agenda. But even while he's buying Argentina, he's secretly smirking about the fact that he has befuddled his wife.

The image only makes me more determined to figure this out. And fast.

"Paris?" Jamie suggests.

I try. Nothing.

I try "Stark," "Wife," and "Malibu."

And then, I realize.

"I know what it is," I say, then type in "Sunset," the safe word that I picked my first night with Damien. That's sort of like a key, after all.

I hold my breath—and then smile with satisfaction when the log-in screen disappears and text fills the screen.

> Congratulations, Nikki, you solved clue number two,
> Interpreted the hint just right.
> Now that you know what to do,
> I'll tell you that this clue,
> Is only available at night.
> Are you enjoying this game, please say that you do,
> And know that I'm exceptionally fond of you.

"Fond of you?" Jamie wiggles her eyebrows at me. "That's got to be the key. Because that man is so beyond 'fond' it isn't even funny."

I don't disagree, but neither have I got an inkling about where this clue leads. And a solid minute spent staring at the screen isn't helping any.

I'm about to close my laptop and offer to walk Jamie to Starbucks for a good-luck-at-the-audition latte, when my email pings.

"I bet he knows you got in," Jamie says, looking over my shoulder at the name of the sender: Damien J. Stark.

I realize it must be a new account, because Damien has never used his middle initial on his emails, and I assume it's one he set up for this game.

I open the email—and immediately go cold.

The subject line reads *Mine*.

And under that, filling the body of the email, is a grainy photograph of my husband with his mouth on Italian super-model Carmela D'Amato's breast. They are both naked, and the look of ecstasy on Carmela's face is one that I have seen and felt on my own.

I clap my hand over my mouth, certain I'm going to be sick.

"Hey," Jamie says. "*Hey*. He didn't send this. You know he didn't send this."

I nod, numb, as Jamie closes my laptop.

"She's that supermodel, right? The one Damien screwed around with back in the day?"

I nod. "I saw her again not too long ago."

"Really?" Surprise laces Jamie's voice. "Where?"

"Damien's hotel room in Munich."

"Wait. What?"

I shrug, going for nonchalant. In truth, just the memory makes me edgy. "We came back to the room and she was waiting there. All ready to get down and dirty with Damien again. Apparently, she was on a standby list when he traveled to Europe."

"Nikki . . ." Her voice trails off into sympathy.

"I know. I'm fine." And I am. I'm not even jealous. Not really. Except I am. I'm jealous of every woman who had time with Damien. Not because I think he still wants them, but because I covet those lost hours that could have been mine.

I mutter a curse and reach to open the laptop again, but Jamie stops me. "Dammit, Nikki, don't do this to yourself."

"I'm not." My voice is shaky, and I take a deep breath to

steel myself. "You're right—Damien didn't send this. I want to know who did."

"And looking at that fucking picture is going to tell you?"

I shake my head, then open the lid and maneuver my finger on the trackpad to click on the sender. "There," I say, when the full email address pops up. It's his name, all right. But it's not from Stark International or any of Damien's companies.

No, the domain that this email came from is WiseApps.

Jamie lets out a low whistle, and I nod my head in agreement. WiseApps Development is the name of a company that threatened me with litigation just a few weeks ago, effectively putting a nasty gray cloud over my honeymoon. As it turned out, the company—and the lawsuit—were bullshit. A stunt pulled by Damien's batshit crazy childhood friend, Sofia.

"I thought she lost internet privileges," Jamie says.

"I thought so, too." When I say "batshit crazy," I mean it in the literal sense. Sofia is currently locked away in an institution outside of London, and after the fiasco with the threatened lawsuit, the security around her was amped up and her privileges were knocked down. But Sofia is as brilliant as she is crazy, and if anyone could figure a way around an internet ban, she'd be the girl.

"This picture must be years old," Jamie says, as if to console me.

"I know. Don't worry, James. I can handle this."

"Damn straight you can, Nicholas. But you don't have to handle it alone. For that matter, you shouldn't. Someone is fucking with you. You need to tell Damien. Hell, you need to tell Ryan."

I tilt my head up to look at her. "Ryan?"

"He's Damien's top-dog security dude, right?"

I nod.

"I may not know Damien as well as you do—"

"I certainly hope not."

She snorts, but otherwise doesn't falter. "But I do know that Damien's not the kind of guy who would consent to that sort of picture. And I doubt that he would have been any different half a dozen years ago."

I nod. She makes an excellent point. "Someone hid a camera, and then bided their time for years. Sofia?"

"She's in London, right? And has been for a while? Look at the coffee table."

Needless to say, I hadn't noticed the furnishings on first glance. Now I see that she's right. A copy of the London-based *Financial Times* is on the table, along with a magazine called *London Today* that looks like an in-house hotel publication.

"Like I said," Jamie says, "you need to tell Damien. *Go.*"

I do, but not before giving her a hug and telling her to break a leg at her audition.

Then I'm out the door, shouting to Mrs. Crane that I won't be back until tomorrow.

As I race to my car, I think about the cupcake and the message that sent me to it: *what is sweeter than Love?*

I sigh. This isn't the day I expected, not by a long shot. But at least I'm heading toward Damien. And with him at my side, I know I can handle whatever is coming.

Chapter 4

I race downtown in Cooper, my still-new Mini Cooper, and ignore the parking garage in favor of the valet parking service in front of Stark Tower. I toss the valet my keys, then race inside.

Joe waves from his perch behind the information desk. "Good to see you, Mrs. Stark."

"Hi, Joe, sorry, Joe. In a hurry!" I jab my finger on the button, then rush up to the nineteenth floor and the reception area for Stark Applied Technology.

As soon as I walk off the elevator, I see Preston Rhodes step out of the closest conference room.

"Nikki," Preston says. "Good to see you. I was just telling Lisa we need to have you two over for drinks so we can hear all about Paris."

"We'd love that," I say. "But right now, I really need to talk to Damien. Do you mind if I borrow him for a few minutes?"

His mouth quirks with irony. "I'd like to borrow him myself."

I frown, confused. "I thought he was in meetings with you all day."

"That was the plan. Apparently something came up." He tilts his head back, as if looking to heaven. "He said he was going to the apartment. Something he had to take care of."

I feel an unpleasant twisting in my stomach, but tell myself I'm being foolish. Damien handles a dozen crises a day. There's no reason to think that my crisis has already exploded.

I use my card key to call Damien's private elevator to take me to the top floor, which is divided between Damien's penthouse office space and his downtown residence. As soon as the car arrives, I press the button to indicate my destination, ensuring that the elevator doors open onto the apartment side.

It whisks me upward, and I hold on to the rail for both balance and support. Because despite my stern admonition to remain calm, the higher we rise, the more my nerves are fluttering.

I hear voices the moment I step into the foyer. Damien's, clipped and curt. And another voice, softer but agitated. A woman, perhaps?

It's hard for me to tell, but I'm not wasting time playing guessing games. I pass the flower arrangement that never seems to wilt, then step into the living room.

I expect the familiar furniture. The vase with a crystal red rose. Damien's science and business magazines scattered across the coffee table. And, of course, I expect to see the man himself.

I do not expect to see Carmela D'Amato, and when I do it is immediately as if she is the only thing I *can* see.

Suddenly, I realize what I should have known all along— bitch from hell Carmela has teamed up with uber-bitch Sofia to screw with me and Damien.

Well, fuck *that*.

As I rush toward Carmela, I vaguely hear Damien calling my name, but it's like white noise behind the sound of blood rushing through my head. It's not until my hand has lashed out and slapped her soundly across the cheek that the world snaps back into focus and my legs go weak.

I'm falling to the ground, but I feel Damien's arms go around me. As always, he is there to catch me when I fall.

"Do you know what she's done?" I snarl. "What she's sent?"

He is behind me, so I cannot see his face. But Carmela is in front of me, and I see the way she looks at him, as if the world is suddenly caving in around her.

I'd braced for her to lash back at me. Instead, she looks soft and a little lost.

And when she drops to the couch and presses her face into her hands, I know that I have stepped into Neverland.

"Damien?"

I steady myself, then turn in his arms so that I can see him. *He* does not look soft. On the contrary, he is angry and tight. He is an explosion waiting to happen, and in that moment I know that the only reason he's managing to hold it together is because Carmela is in the room with us.

His fingers are tight around my upper arm, almost to the point of hurting. I don't object, though. I understand that this is his way of keeping me close. Of protecting me from whatever is happening—because whatever's going on is bigger than one emailed photograph sent to Damien Stark's new wife by his crazy childhood friend.

"Damien," I repeat. "What's happened?"

He doesn't answer. Instead, he lets go of my arm and then says very slowly and carefully, "Why did you come here?"

At the question, Carmela looks up at me. Her eyes are red, but the softness is fading, and as she awaits my answer, I can see her hard edges clicking back into place.

"I got an email," I say. I pull out my phone and hand it to him. As I was planning to do that all along, the email is already open on my screen. The note—*Mine*—and that horrible, sensual, brutally raw image.

"I opened the email thinking it was from you," I say.

"*Son of a bitch.*" He smacks his hand hard against the wall, and I'm grateful it's not the one holding my phone.

"You saw the domain name?" I ask. "When I saw Carmela, I thought she'd teamed up with Sofia." I no longer think that. Because it's very clear to me that Carmela isn't calling the shots here any more than I am.

"She didn't," Damien says. "And this email didn't come from Sofia."

"You're sure?" Since I know WiseApps was a domain that she set up, I thought my assumption was pretty damn reasonable.

"She doesn't own it anymore. Transferred it while we were on the island," he says, referring to the island getaway he took me to for the last leg of our honeymoon.

"Because of you."

"Because of me," he confirms, and I wonder how many lawyers he'd sent swooping down on her after the fiasco in Paris and my mini-meltdown at the thought of being sued.

"She could have transferred it to someone who's pulling this shit for her," I say.

"I don't disagree. But she's been in tight lockdown since we left Paris. I called to confirm. Just hung up before you got here, actually."

I nod, taking it all in. "And the reason you called to confirm that was because you got an email, too, didn't you?" I feel like my brain is mush, but I'm slowly catching up.

Carmela has been silent through our conversation, but now she passes me her phone. It's open to an email showing the same image, but her message is different. *$200,000 by 10 p.m. PST on Feb. 13 or it goes public at dawn on Valentine's Day. And all the others, too. Wiring instructions to follow.* Like my email, this was supposedly sent from Damien.

"I got the same email," Damien says. "It came from you. Nikki Fairchild Stark."

"Fuck," I say, then drag my fingers through my hair. "What does he mean by 'the others'?"

"More pictures, presumably," Damien says, and his tone is so calm and so even that I know he is very close to losing it.

"Our blackmailer did not send them." Carmela finally speaks, her accent almost musical despite the horrific circumstances. "But I imagine they are . . ."

"More graphic." My hand reaches for Damien's. "Yeah. I get that." I glance between the two of them. "So what now?"

"Now, I go." Carmela eyes Damien. "You will let me know what you decide?"

"I will."

With a nod, Carmela moves to a table by the window and picks up her purse, then swings it over her shoulder as if she's here in the apartment for nothing more than an afternoon coffee. "Nikki, would you mind walking me down?"

Beside me, I feel Damien tense, but he makes no objection.

I hesitate, then step away from Damien and toward Carmela, a woman I'd never thought I would have an ounce of sympathy for.

Damien's fingers linger on mine as I leave, and before the elevator doors close, I look back and meet his eyes. I see the storm brewing, and I almost tell Carmela that I cannot leave him. Not now.

But then he nods, and the doors shut, and I clutch hard to the handrail as the elevator starts its descent.

For a moment, neither of us speaks. Then she turns to me. "We did not know. That there were cameras, I mean. Even then—even when he was with me—he never would have done that if he had known he was being filmed."

"I know." What I don't know is why she is being so conciliatory. I draw a breath. "What did you mean? When you said Damien would let you know what he decides? Don't you have a say?"

"I leave it to Damien to decide what to do. Whether to pay or whether to let the pictures be released."

I simply stare at her. "And you're okay with that? With just letting him choose what happens to a pretty goddamn intimate photograph of you?"

"I cannot lie," she says, her voice as hard as stone. "I was upset when I got the email. I do not like being used. And I would happily strangle the fucker who has put us in this position. But, yes, I will let Damien decide."

"Why?"

She lifts one shoulder in an elegant shrug. "I am not ashamed of my encounters with Damien. We were both single. And we both look quite nice, yes? Under different circumstances, that image could practically be an art print."

Her words are matter-of-fact, but I hear the hard edge of reason and anger underpinning them.

The elevator arrives at the lobby. Before the door opens, though, I press the stop button, then use my card key to deactivate the alarm before it can start to squall. It's a handy trick I learned from Damien, who has stopped this elevator on several occasions when we just couldn't wait to get up to the apartment.

When Carmela realizes that we're staying in this plush box until our conversation is over, she exhales loudly, then continues. "The truth is that I've posed nude before. And while you don't seem the type who would know it, there's a sex tape of me that has made the rounds. A bastard of a manager I screwed back in the day." She waves a hand as if wafting away smoke. "These photos are tame by comparison."

"You didn't seem to think so when I arrived."

Her smile is thin. "Just because they are tame does not mean that I'm not angry."

I nod. That much, I understand. "And Damien?"

"He has always been careful. Private. But why ask me? You know Damien Stark better than I do."

I tilt my head, surprised that she would admit as much.

She sighs. "Look, I know that I was a bitch in Munich. What can I say? I like him. And I very much liked to fuck him."

My hand tightens around the rail. "If this is supposed to be a friendly conversation—"

"My point is that things have changed. He's married now. I don't screw around with married men." She shoots me a wry smile. "And we both know Damien wouldn't be interested anyway. Not now. Not since he's with you."

I nod. And while I'm not sure that I've gone from completely detesting her to genuinely liking her, I will at least grudgingly concede that she's not a total bitch.

"The thing is," she continues, "despite his penchant for privacy, under other circumstances, Damien might say fuck it and let the picture out. Why not? He looks damn hot. And it's no secret that he used to screw around. More important, we both know that Damien's not the kind of man who bends over and takes it in the ass when someone threatens him."

"No. He's not. So what's changed?"

She looks at me as if I'm an idiot. "You, of course. These pictures get out, and you'll be drawn through the muck, too. And he's so damned in love with you that the thought of that just about kills him."

My heart squeezes with her words, because they're true, and I know it well. What surprises me is that Carmela sees it, too.

"Don't look so shocked," she says, as if reading my mind. "You have cast a spell over him, and the whole world knows it."

Since I'm not sure what to say to that, I just smile and flip the switch on the elevator, allowing the door to open.

She pauses on the threshold. "You know, under different circumstances, you and I might have been friends."

And although I never would have believed it before, in that moment, I think she might be right.

It's an interesting detente, and I'm amused when her parting gesture is an air kiss.

Then I place my card key against the pad and let the elevator whisk me away, knowing full well the storm that awaits me upstairs.

Chapter 5

Damien is there the moment the elevator doors open, and before I even have time to draw a breath, he has taken my hand and pulled me out. I gasp, only to cry out again a moment later when he slams me against the foyer wall, stretching my arms above my head as his mouth finds mine and his body presses hard against me.

"Christ," he says, when he breaks the kiss. "Oh, Christ,

Nikki." His hands are all over me—cupping my breasts, following the line of my waist, sliding hard between my legs so that I grind down against him and moan with arousal and a wildly desperate need.

"Yes," I say, though he has asked me no question. The word is an invitation. An admission. An acknowledgment. I want his touch—I want everything. And I need it, dear lord, how I need it right now.

Most important, I know that he needs it, too. He needs to take me. To claim me.

He needs to bury himself deep inside me and know that no matter how fucked up the outside world becomes, this passion between us will never fade. That I will always be there for him, whenever and however he wants.

"Yes," I say again, even as he undresses me, not bothering with buttons or zippers but yanking me out of my skirt and ripping my blouse open so that only seconds pass before I feel his mouth close over my breast.

He is wild and hot and though I know the source of this—though I know that this intense need stems directly from all the shit that has been piled upon us—I cannot deny that I love the way he is making me feel.

"Tell me," he says, breathing hard as he cups my face. "Are you okay?"

I nod, because I understand the foundation of his question. This is not only about Damien regaining control, it is about him giving me what I need—wild, hard, fast sex. Intense. Hot.

Pleasure and pain—but right now, it is not the pain that I need.

"I'm fine," I say. "I swear I'm fine." An odd laugh bubbles out of me. "I didn't even think of it," I realize. "I never thought of a blade, never imagined its weight in my hand or the sensation of metal slicing through flesh. Damien," I murmur, and my heart is beating fast as the full realization of what I am saying washes over me. "I didn't think of it at all. All I thought of was you. All I wanted was to get to you."

It is a big thing, and Damien knows it. Before, I've fought the urge to cut, using him as a weapon. This time, I didn't even crave the blade, only the man.

I crave him still, and when he looks at me with heat and wonder in his eyes, I pull him close and beg him to please, please fuck me. "I need you," I say. "Only you. And I know that you need me." I brush my lips over his ears. "Anything you want, Damien. Anything you need."

I see the heat in his eyes, but I am unprepared when he lashes out, slams his hand so hard against the wall behind me that it shakes. "God*dammit*." He backs away from me, as if horrified that he brought violence so close to me, and then kicks over the coffee table, sending all the magazines tumbling.

"Damien!" I go to him and catch his wrists. "Damien, talk to me."

He pulls me hard against him, then presses my head to his chest, his fingers twined in my hair. I can hear the beat of his heart, fast and steady, and I want to kiss him all over. Kiss him and make it better, even though this is something even the most fervent of kisses won't fix.

"All I want to do is keep you safe from them," he finally says. "These goddamn vultures—and yet they're everywhere. They've followed us from day one. Before we were even married. On our honeymoon. Now this."

"These pictures aren't about me," I say.

"The hell they're not."

I swallow, because I fear that he is right. Didn't Carmela even hint at that very thing?

"All I want is to fucking protect you."

His words reverberate through me, and I pull my head back so that I can see his face. "You do. Christ, Damien, how can you not know that you do? I'm safe with you. I'm whole with you."

He stares down at me, his dual-colored eyes so wild that I fear the storm will consume us both.

Then something seems to shatter in him and he kisses me hard before pulling me close. "You're my blood and my breath, Nikki. You're my life. I will always fight for you. I will always come to you. And I will happily destroy anyone who tries to hurt you."

"Do you think I don't know that?"

"I need you." His voice is raw, and I can feel the heat rolling off him. "Christ, Nikki, I need you now."

"Yes." It's all I say. It's enough.

He takes me to the window and puts my hands on the glass. "Close your eyes," he says, as he starts to ease kisses down my spine.

I shiver as sparks of electricity ricochet through me, priming me for his touch and leaving my body begging for more.

"Do you feel it?" he asks. "The cool glass against your hot skin, your nipples tight and needy. There's a whole world out there, and you are naked before it."

"Yes," I murmur. He's taken me in front of a window before, and he knows that I like it. I hadn't expected to, but there is something so wildly freeing about the world falling away even as passion takes you higher.

His kisses have reached the base of my spine and now he uses his hands to silently urge my legs apart. He strokes me, teasing my clit with a single fingertip but not slipping inside me despite the way I wiggle my hips, my soft moans of longing coming even without conscious thought.

"Turn around," he demands, and when I do, he lifts me up so that my thighs are resting on his hips. He holds me steady by cupping my ass, and I arch back as he thrusts into me, the back of my head brushing the glass wall as I do.

I clutch his shoulders, my fingernails digging into him as he thrusts again, the movement pushing my back against the window so that I am pinned there between him and the glass. Unlike a bed, there is no give, and I feel the power of each of his thrusts, so deep and hard that it seems as if he will split me in two, and oh, god, how I want that.

I close my eyes and give myself over to the pleasure of his touch, of his power. I want him to take me, to have me. Maybe the world outside is going crazy, but in here, I am his.

I am always his.

And between us, the world is exactly as we want it.

Tension fills his body, then bursts out of him as a powerful orgasm rocks him. I hold on, letting his release roll through me, relishing the way he looks and feels when he loses control, all barriers down, all control surrendered to me, to this moment.

"I love you," I cry as my own release takes me, and I cling to him until the waves of passion slow and I can breathe normally again.

"I know," he whispers, his lips brushing my ear. "We love each other."

Gently, he cleans me up, then we curl up together on the couch, a blanket draped over us as we look out over the city in the distance.

"You know that there's nothing I wouldn't sacrifice to keep you safe," he says. "Nothing I wouldn't do to make you happy."

"I know," I say. "But don't do it, Damien. Don't pay. The thought of you paying extortion money makes me ill, especially if you think you're doing it for me."

"I've done it before."

I shake my head. I know he's thinking of Eric Padgett, the man who'd claimed that Damien was involved in his sister's death. "That was a settlement," I say. "And I may not be a god of all things business like you, but even I know that businesses and people pay money to settle for a whole lot of reasons, and that doesn't make it extortion. It just means that they made a business decision and their reason won out."

He looks at me, as if trying to read something in my expression. "I have a reason to pay to keep those pictures out of the press," he finally says.

"No, you don't." I cup his face. "Do you think I don't understand what it would cost you to pay? To give in to this bullshit?" I hold his gaze hard, because I do understand, and I want to make sure he realizes that.

"For better or for worse, Damien, remember? Those wonderful wedding vows. And honestly," I quip, "how bad could it be? Half the women in America are already jealous of me. Once they see that picture of you, the other half will be, too."

He is quiet for a long time, and when he speaks, his voice is both soft and urgent. "Are you sure?"

"I wouldn't say it if I wasn't." And I *am* sure. I can survive those pictures being out there, and so can Damien. But if he gives in to whoever is yanking our chain, he will not only be sacrificing his own principles on my account, but he will start to slide down a horrible, slippery slope. "I'm certain," I repeat, just to make sure he understands.

His eyes never leave my face. I hold his gaze, understanding that he is trying to see if my words match my truth.

Finally, he nods. Just once. And then he bends over and kisses me lightly. "You're amazing. You know that, right?"

"Of course," I say airily. "But feel free to tell me as often as you want. And honestly, I'm pretty fond of you, too," I add, reciting back the words from the clue that had come with the cupcake.

It's when I say them out loud that something shifts in my mind.

Fond of you.

Fond you.

Fondue.

I toss the blanket off us and start to stand up. Damien takes my hand. "Where are you going?"

"We," I correct. "Where are *we* going?"

"Oh?"

"I think we should have an early dinner," I tell him. "At Le Caquelon."

Chapter 6

Damien is deliberately closemouthed, but as we take the elevator up to Le Caquelon, the Santa Monica–based fondue restaurant, I know that I'm right, just as I'd been right about the cupcakes. I'd had to wait for the proper moment, but I'd been right.

Hopefully the proper moment for Le Caquelon isn't tomorrow night.

Still, even if it is, we'll have had a lovely dinner tonight, not to mention visiting another stop on our own personal memory lane.

That's what Damien is doing, of course. Each clue leads to something or someplace that has meaning for us. The bakery where we got our wedding cake. This restaurant, where he took me after Blaine finished painting the portrait of me that hangs on the third floor and where we had our pre-wedding party.

I wonder what the next clue will be, and as I think back over the richness of our time together, I can't help but acknowledge that there is a wealth of possibilities.

"Smiling, Mrs. Stark?"

"I like your game," I admit.

He doesn't have time to answer before the elevator doors open, but I see his smile of pleasure as he takes my arm and leads me to the stunning aquarium that serves as a maître d' station.

The hostess, Monica, beams at us, her multicolored hair complementing the wild colors that fill this space. "Mr. and Mrs. Stark, it's so wonderful to see you again. I have your booth ready, so if you'll just follow me."

"Our booth?" It occurs to me that Damien assumed I would make it this far tonight and has planned ahead. He, however, says nothing.

The booth that Monica leads us to is, in fact, *our* booth. It's the very one that Damien brought me to the night that Blaine finished my portrait. And I happen to know that it is very well soundproofed.

These private dining areas are set up like tiny rooms. Each is a booth, with walls at the diners' backs and a door at one end of the table and a window overlooking the ocean at the other. Access is controlled by a red light/green light system, and when the red light is engaged, privacy is ensured.

The area is not entirely a booth, though. If you slide all the way through, there is a small space between the table and the window that is sufficient for standing. I look at it now, remembering the way it felt to be pressed up against that glass with Damien's hands upon me.

I shiver slightly, and when Damien's hand presses lightly against the small of my back, I am certain that he knows exactly what I am thinking.

I tilt my head up to look at him. "Even if I'm wrong and there's no clue here, it's worth it just to be back."

His smile is soft with silent agreement, but I can't tell from his expression if this really is the right answer to the clue, and I resign myself to taking it in stride and simply going with the flow of the game. If this is where the next clue is hidden, sooner or later that will be obvious.

And if it's not?

Well, I'll just have to keep trying.

I slide into the booth, and Damien settles beside me. Monica tells us that the owner, Damien's childhood friend Alaine Beauchene, isn't on the premises tonight, but that he has taken the liberty of ordering for us, if that's okay.

It is, of course, and when our waiter returns with the wine Alaine selected, I take a sip and sigh with pleasure.

The tabletop is also a cook surface, and soon enough it is topped with a pretty copper fondue bowl filled with melted cheese, the delicious scent of which fills the room and makes me realize just how hungry I am.

Damien spears a cube of bread and dips it in the cheese, then blows on it before feeding it to me.

I am at his side, our legs touching, because I do not think that it is possible for me to be so close to Damien and not touch him. I shift a bit though, so that I am facing him more directly, and we touch and talk and eat, with Damien feeding both himself and me.

As we finish the cheese and move on to cubes of steak and pork in a fragrant port sauce, he tells me about the progress on Stark Plaza, a Century City office and retail complex that Stark Real Estate Development is working on. I fill him in on my progress with several apps I have in development, and with the details about a tech conference I'm hoping to attend in the summer.

The talk of trips reminds him that he may need to travel to New York soon to meet with the new production manager at one of his subsidiaries, and he promises that if I take the time to go with him, he'll take me to at least one Broadway play.

I let him know in no uncertain terms that I will travel anywhere with him, play or no, and then give him the general rundown on my to-do list, most of which can be done on the road
with a laptop.

It's comfortable. It's normal.

Hell, it's even married—and I love this cozy familiarity and
affection.

But none of it is bringing me any closer to figuring out what
the next clue is, though I am absolutely certain that it is hidden
here somewhere. All I have to do is figure out where.

My frustration has spiked by the time the waiter clears the
table of the main course, and I decide that it's time to get more
aggressive in my search. I slide down and look under the table,
then hear Damien's amused, "Now, that has all sorts of interesting possibilities."

"I'm checking for a hidden package," I confess as I scan the
area for envelopes taped to the bottom of the table.

"I'm not saying a word," Damien says, and as I ease back
out from under the table, I see the way his mouth twitches with
amusement.

I roll my eyes, realizing my unintended double entendre,
then cup my hand over his crotch. "Well, *this* package isn't hidden at all," I say, and am rewarded by the sensation of his cock
hardening beneath the press of my hand.

My body warms with familiar longing, and when I see the
corresponding heat in Damien's eyes, I think that perhaps this
booth should be put to better use than eating and chatting. I'm
about to follow up on that thought and switch the booth's light
from green to red, when there is a tap at the door and it slides
open.

"Can I offer you dessert?" Monica asks.

I look at Damien. Right then, he's the only dessert I want.
"No, thanks," I say, even as Damien says, "Yes, definitely."

I narrow my eyes, then look between him and Monica, realizing as I do that Monica is not our server. For that matter, she's not a server at all.

"Yes," I amend. "I think I'd enjoy dessert."

"I'm so happy to hear it."

She hands us each a dessert menu, then slips away. I open mine, unsurprised to see that the usual text has been replaced with a single piece of parchment on which the third clue is set out in fancy script:

> *Paul Simon, Beyoncé, the Beatles, too.*
> *They'd all see it when looking at you.*
> *Fire and ice, brilliance and flame,*
> *I'll dress you up to solve the game.*

I read it twice, then shift in my seat to gape at him. "Are you kidding me?"

His expression is entirely too innocent. "Problem?"

I wave the menu. "I don't have a clue what this means."

"Well, that's a shame." He takes a sip of his wine. "I was looking forward to you finding your present."

I scowl, but study the words again. Singers, but what did they have in common? And it says they would see it. But see what?

I have no idea, and so I move on. Fire and ice. Brilliance. Flame.

All of that seems very familiar, and I'm regretting my choice to have wine with dinner, because apparently I need a clear head to figure this out.

I'll dress you up.

What do you do when you dress up? Fancy clothes, fancy shoes. I close my eyes and imagine I'm in our monstrosity of a dressing room. Makeup. Hair.

Jewelry.

I smile because now, the singers make sense, too. Paul Simon's "Diamonds on the Soles of Her Shoes." Beyoncé and "Single Ladies (Put a Ring on It)." And, of course, "Lucy in the Sky with Diamonds," courtesy of the Beatles.

Ha! Nailed it.

I turn to him, certain that victory is written all over my face.

"Yes?"

I hold out my hand. "I need your car keys and your phone."

At that, he looks baffled, but he complies.

"What about the clue?" he asks.

"Oh, I solved that." I'm certain of it. But I'm not willing to tell Damien just yet. Because I'm enjoying this game too much. So much, in fact, that it's inspired a little Valentine's Day game of my own.

I scroll through his contacts until I find Edward. I could have used my own phone, but I'm going for dramatic flair here.

"Mr. Stark," Edward says, answering on the first ring.

"It's Nikki," I correct. "But it's Mr. Stark who needs you. He's at Le Caquelon, and needs a ride home as soon as you can get here."

"Of course, Mrs. Stark. I'm on my way."

I thank him, then hang up and give Damien back his phone.

"I need a ride home?"

"You do." I dangle his keys. "I'll meet you there."

His eyes narrow. "What exactly do you think you've figured out?"

"The clue," I say. I'm absolutely positive that whatever my present is, it's in our closet in one of the velvet-lined drawers that Damien had custom made for all the jewelry he buys me. Specifically, the drawer on the top left where I keep the diamond jewelry.

"And we're going home separately because . . . ?"

But at that, I only smile, then kiss him lightly even as I slide my hand down between his legs, stroking his now-stiff cock. "I'll see you at home, Mr. Stark."

And then I'm gone, leaving behind one very baffled husband.

Chapter 7

We drove into town in the Jeep Grand Cherokee, and though it is the easiest car for me to drive, I wish we'd brought the Bugatti. Right now, I want speed, because I'm racing to get home before Edward gets on the road with Damien.

I'd called Edward again as I waited for the valet to bring the Jeep around, and he promised to text me the moment that Damien is in the limo. He doesn't know what I have planned, of course, but I think it amuses him to be in on my conspiracy, whatever it may be.

When I reach the house, I don't bother parking in the garage. Instead, I leave the Jeep in the circular drive and use the key code to enter the house. Though we have a butler/valet/ all-around general house guy, Gregory does not live on the property. On the contrary, Damien has rented an apartment for him nearby, and is building a small bungalow on the eastern portion of the property that will become Gregory's home.

All of which is fine with me. I like Gregory. But I like being alone with Damien a whole lot more.

I take the stairs two at a time, then race into our closet, which is really more of a dressing room. For that matter, it's really more of an apartment, considering the entire space is bigger than the efficiency I lived in for one semester during college.

The jewelry drawers are against the back wall, and a single code unlocks all of them. I punch it in, then pull out the black velvet–lined drawer that holds the various bits of diamond jewelry that Damien has given me. Right now, that means it has a pair of earrings and a stunning necklace that he bought for me when we attended a charity function.

Sometimes, the emerald and diamond ankle bracelet he gave me even before we were officially together is in this drawer, but usually it is exactly where it is now—on my leg, a permanent reminder that I am his.

At first glance, everything appears as it should. Then I realize that there is an additional piece of black velvet in the drawer. I run my finger over it and feel the bumps of something hidden beneath.

I grin, because I know damn well that I have found the prize.

I peel the velvet back to reveal a strand of pearls and a pair of silver nipple rings, connected by a serpentine chain. My body flushes with desire and memory. He'd given me the pearls in Germany and put them to deliciously erotic use. As for the nipple rings, he'd introduced me to those in the condo I used to share with Jamie, and I'd been astounded by how much my body responded to the intense sensation of not only the constant pressure on my erect nipples, but also to the demanding tug when Damien pulled on the chain.

Just remembering makes me wet, and I drag my teeth over my lower lip, thinking that both of these things fit in perfectly with my plans for the night. And, more, thinking that I want Damien now—like right this very instant—and I am grateful when my phone buzzes with Edward's text letting me know that they are on their way.

Thank god.

The last thing in the drawer is an envelope that was underneath the jewelry. I take it out and open it to find an airline itinerary. Not a ticket, as that's not necessary for a man who owns his own fleet of aircraft. But according to this, we're leaving for Nassau tomorrow evening, then taking a puddle jumper to an island resort called *Serafina Spa Retreat*. We're staying there three nights, then returning home on Valentine's Day.

I sigh with pleasure. Damien took me to an island for part of our honeymoon, and while it was heavenly, the location was remote—just the two of us in a small cabin on an otherwise uninhabited island. Perfect for a honeymoon, and perfect for escaping the world.

But I can't deny that a spa sounds absolutely delicious, as does three nights on an island with Damien.

Right now, though, I have something else delicious in mind.

I want to change, and so I do that quickly, ultimately wrapping myself in my favorite white, fluffy robe. Then I move into the bedroom and put my phone on the mattress beside me. I put it on speaker, and dial Damien's number.

He answers on the first ring.

"Where are you?"

"At home. In bed."

"Are you?" I hear the tinge of interest in his voice.

"But I'm imagining I'm with you," I say. "Tell me, Mr. Stark, is the privacy screen up?"

There is a pause before he answers, and when he does, the heat in his voice is unmistakable. "It is now."

"Close your eyes," I tell him. I close mine as well, remembering the first time that I was alone in his limo with Damien's voice stroking me, caressing me, getting me off. "Can you imagine me there? Sitting beside you? My hand on your thigh?"

He says nothing, and I take that as acquiescence—a sign that he is willing to surrender to my game.

"I'm sliding it up," I say. "Moving slowly over your slacks. Closing my fingers over your cock. Tell me something, Mr. Stark." My voice is breathy, and it is all that I can do not to slip my hand down between my legs. "Are you hard?"

"Very."

"I know. I can feel it. Can you feel me? I'm stroking you. Making you even harder until you're begging me to tug down your zipper and slip my hand inside. Do it," I whisper.

"Jesus, Nikki."

I allow myself a satisfied smile but otherwise don't pause in my seduction. "I'm unfastening your belt and unbuttoning your pants. I lower the zipper so carefully and slide my hand in to free your cock. Do that, Damien. Do that and imagine it's me."

He doesn't answer, but I can hear him breathing.

"You're hard and soft, like velvet on steel, and I'm gliding my hand over you, teasing you, bringing you so close that you want to explode. But not yet," I say. "I want to taste you."

"Holy Christ." His voice is raw, and I'm squirming on the bed, worked up not only by my words and the power they are having on him, but by what I'm wearing under this robe.

"Can you feel my tongue on you? Licking your balls, then tasting every bit of you as I lick you just like candy? I suck your crown, then draw you in, so deep, and you taste so amazing and I can't get enough, and you're getting harder and harder and—"

"Not just yet." His voice is tight, and I am certain that he is fighting not to come. "You want this? You want to take me there?"

"Yes," I whisper.

"Then you're going there with me. Tell me what you're wearing."

I hesitate, because this wasn't the game I had planned, but I cannot deny that it has its own appeal.

"Tell me," he repeats.

"A robe," I say. "The thick white one."

"Take it off."

"Will you watch while I do?"

"You know I will."

"It's off," I say, as soon as I have dropped it off the side of the bed.

"Are you naked?"

I lick my lips. "No."

"What are you wearing?"

"Funny you should ask," I say. "I found the most interesting things in my jewelry drawer."

"Did you?"

"So right now, I'm wearing a pearl choker and nipple rings."

"Are you? I'm looking forward to seeing that. And nothing else?"

I know that he expects the answer to be yes, but instead I say, "Well . . ."

"Oh?" I hear the interest in his voice. "Tell me."

"Well, it's just that I thought I should accessorize. After all, if I'm wearing the pearl necklace, then surely I should wear the matching panties."

I trace my hand down to the thong that he once gave me, a delicious little piece of lingerie with a string of pearls in the most interesting of locations.

"Oh, baby," he says, and I can't help the bubble of laughter that bursts free.

"Make me squirm," I say, "and you'll make me come."

"Slide your hand down," he orders, "but touch nothing but the pearls."

I do, moaning a little because the sensation is exquisite, all the more so because the pearls are slick with my own arousal.

"Very nice," he says. "But, baby, as much as I'm enjoying this game, I think it's time for us to give it up."

"Oh." The disappointment practically floods my voice, and I hear his low chuckle of understanding.

"I'm on the property," he says.

"Oh!" I may have been enjoying the game, but I cannot deny that I'm ready to have the man and not the fantasy.

"I want you on the bed." The command is clear in his voice, and I melt just a little bit more. "Legs open. Arms at your sides. And your eyes closed."

I comply, though it is hard to stay still when I hear the security system beeping, signaling that he has opened the door.

I've tucked the folded itinerary under the band of my thong, but I'm otherwise exactly how he wanted me to be. I hear his footsteps and force myself not to open my eyes and watch him approaching me. And when his weight shifts the mattress, I bite my lower lip and breathe deep as he trails kisses up my leg, finally taking the itinerary in his teeth before straddling me and dropping it on my chest.

"You've been a very naughty girl," he says, then lowers himself to kiss me, long and hard. "I like it."

I laugh, then open my eyes as I hook my arms around his neck and pull myself up for another kiss before taking the itinerary and setting it aside. "I like my present. A spa getaway with my husband. It's perfect."

"You're perfect," he says. "And right now, I'm not interested in spas or islands or getaways." He starts to kiss his way down my body. "Can you guess what I am interested in?"

I press my fingertip against the corner of my mouth. "Hmm. Let me think."

I lift my head long enough to meet his eyes. "I love you."

"I know you do," he says. "And that knowledge is what fuels my days and lights my nights. Now put your head back, baby, and close your eyes. I want to make you fly."

He is as good as his word, and as his fingers and mouth set my body on fire, I stretch my arms out and close my fists around the bedclothes in defense against the pleasure that is rising like a storm inside me.

Down and down he moves until his tongue is stroking the string of pearls that makes up the thong of these exceptionally intriguing panties. And though he is not touching me directly, the pearls are moving intimately over me, making me even more desperate for him than I already was.

"Dammit, Damien, now," I beg, but I tormented him in the limo, and he is not going easy on me now. This is torture by seduction, and it is glorious.

From the floor where it has fallen, my phone chirps, the distinctive cricket sound that I assigned to Jamie's texts. "Ignore it," I say, then make a mental note to strangle my best friend after she repeats the text three more times.

I'm about to tell Damien to go ahead and toss my phone out the window when his phone rings. Another distinctive tone, this one assigned to the Stark International security department.

"Shit," he says, but since I happen to know that the number is for emergency purposes only, I know that Damien will answer. As he reaches for his phone, I decide to grab mine and see what Jamie says.

All her text reads is *9-1-1*.

I frown, and turn to look at Damien, who now wears an expression that could bring down a small nation.

"What's happened?" I ask as soon as he ends the call.

"Get dressed," he says, pulling his clothes back on.

"Tell me," I demand as he tugs me toward the closet.

"Jamie and Ryan got an extortion email, too. Another two hundred grand or else the sender releases a sex tape."

"Of her and Ryan?"

"Of her and Douglas," Damien corrects, referring to the rather sleazy next-door neighbor that Jamie banged on more than one occasion.

"Oh, shit," I say, as I pull on a knit skirt and a T-shirt.

"Yeah," Damien says as we head toward the stairs. "I think that about sums it up."

Chapter 8

We start out heading toward Venice Beach, assuming that both Ryan and Jamie are at his house. But a text from Jamie soon has us changing course. Ryan, apparently, has taken off for Studio City. And according to my best friend, he's gone with the intent of beating the crap out of Douglas.

Fortunately, we're not yet to Santa Monica, so we abandon PCH once we reach the Getty Villa and Highway 27, and careen through the hills toward the 101 Freeway.

We arrive right before Jamie, who is squealing to a stop in front of our old building. She's in the Ferrari that Damien and I gave her as a going-away present, and I know damn well that she pushed that machine to the limit to get here that fast. I know, because we did the same thing.

"Ryan's here," Damien says, nodding toward a Mercedes parked at an odd angle across the street.

"He's gonna kill him." Jamie is hurrying toward us. Her eyes are red and her makeup blotchy. "I've never seen him so mad."

"He has reason to be," Damien says darkly. "Come on."

The building entrance is enclosed now, thanks to Damien's contribution to building security, but Jamie has the key code. She taps it in, and we three hurry inside, then up the stairs to Douglas's condo, right next door to the one Jamie and I used to share.

Damien tries the knob, then pounds on the door when he finds it locked. "Dammit, Ryan. Open up."

Jamie joins him in pounding. "Hunter! Open the door!"

For a moment, we hear nothing. Then the door opens, and I see Ryan, looking completely wrecked.

Immediately, Jamie launches herself at him. He catches her, then holds her close as she sobs against him.

Ryan meets Damien's eyes, and I can almost hear the question that is passing between them—*Did you do something I'm going to have to clean up?*

And, yes, Damien would clean it up—of that much I'm certain. If Ryan Hunter beat the shit out of Douglas the Sex Tape Prick, Damien would do everything in his power to see that Ryan not only got off easy, but that the women of this city threw him a fucking parade.

For a moment, Ryan doesn't move. Then he just shakes his head before stepping aside, silently letting us pass.

Inside, Douglas is on the sofa clutching his stomach, his face so drained of blood it is almost translucent. "Fucker kicked the shit out of me."

"And you deserved it," Damien says.

"I didn't do it," Douglas says. "Kung fu boy there says I threatened to sell a tape of me and Jamie to TMZ or some such shit, but it ain't true, man."

"Bullshit," Jamie says. She looks stronger now, and although she's still holding tight to Ryan's hand, she's standing on her own, and her face is on fire with anger. "You made that thing without telling me. You really think I'm going to believe your bullshit now?"

"Hey, it's true. I don't know how anyone got their hands on that file. Musta hacked my computer or something, because it wasn't me. I mean, shit, my whole life's about getting pussy. How much do you think I'm gonna get if word gets out I'm taping chicks without their knowledge?"

"How much pussy are you going to get in jail, you sick perv?" Jamie retorts.

"Jesus, fuck. Shit." He drags his hands through his hair, making it stand on end. "This isn't on me. Christ, I swear."

In an instant, Ryan is across the room. He has Douglas by the collar and hauls him to his feet. Douglas looks so terrified that I'm surprised he hasn't pissed himself.

For a moment, no one in the room breathes. Then Ryan

tosses him back down. "You're not even worth it," he says, then turns away. He walks toward the door, taking Jamie's hand as he does, and wordlessly leaves.

I start to follow, but then stop when I see Damien lagging behind. He meets the other man's eyes and says, very slowly and very calmly, "I'm going to find out who threatened to leak that tape, and if it comes back to you, that kick in the gut will seem like a gentle kiss good night compared to the hell I will put you through. Do we understand each other?"

If I'd thought that Douglas was pale before, I'd been seriously wrong. I watch now as every last bit of blood fades from his face. He starts to nod, but Damien has already turned away; he's made his point.

Once we are on the sidewalk with Ryan and Jamie, Damien puts his arm around Jamie's shoulders, then meets Ryan's eyes. "I'll pay."

"Damien, no!" Jamie's protest is fast and sounds sincere, but Damien barely even acknowledges that she's spoken. Instead, he's looking straight at me. I swallow, grateful that he jumped to protect Jamie, but at the same time hating the fact that he is breaking from his usual pattern. Because Damien Stark is not a man who gives in to this kind of bullshit. Or, at least, he wasn't before I entered his life.

"There's no point in risking that tape getting out. I said I'll pay." He shifts his attention to Ryan. "That's final."

Ryan nods.

"But—" Jamie's protest dies as Damien turns back to me.

"We're leaving."

I give Jamie a quick hug, and hear her whisper, "Don't let him do it," but Damien tugs me away before I can respond. He opens the car door for me without saying a word, then gets in on his side. Immediately, the car is full of the power of his rage, and when he grips the steering wheel, I see that his knuckles are white.

I open my mouth to say something, then close it again. I understand why he is angry—hell, I'm angry, too. More than that, I understand his need to lash out. To push through. To figure out a way to get on top of this and say "fuck you" to the world.

So I am not surprised when he tears away from the curb with all the speed of a rocket.

Instead of turning toward the 101, he follows Laurel Canyon up into the foothills, then turns on Mulholland Drive. That doesn't surprise me either, and I simply hold on tight as he maneuvers the curves and straightaways before finally jerking the steering wheel and skidding to a halt in a turnout.

I'm breathing hard—I trust Damien, but this road is brutal. No guardrails, sharp curves, and the city spread out like a net below us.

Slowly, I reach for him and am relieved when his fingers close tight around mine. I want to speak, to soothe. But the truth is I don't know what to say.

Finally, I say the only thing that I am certain must be said. I tell him what Jamie said to me. "You don't have to pay. I don't want you to pay. And Jamie doesn't want you to pay, either."

His eyes are flat when he looks at me. "I'm paying." There is a beat—just one moment of silence—and then he gently tugs his hand free. He opens the door and gets out of the car, then moves to stand near the drop-off and look out over the city. The headlights are still on, and the light is hitting his back, illuminating him like an angel and casting his shadow down upon the world.

My chest tightens, and I wish that I had a magic potion that could make this entire mess go away. Because the truth is that both options suck. Damien isn't the kind of man who willingly pays blackmail. And though it is true that Jamie will survive if that tape goes public, that is not the kind of thing that she should have to be strong for.

I realize that I have been sitting stiffly, my fingers clenched into my thighs so that the pressure from my nails digs into the skin just below the hem of my skirt. *Shit.*

I sigh. There is no magic potion. There is just me and Damien and our friends and the world. And right now, the world has infringed too much.

I force myself to relax, to loosen my fingers and shut away the pain. I tell myself I don't need it now—not really. I may be a cutter, but it has been a long time since I have cut. I have Damien now to anchor me. Even more, I have found strength inside myself.

I will survive this. And so will Damien. And so will Jamie.

Telling myself that, I open my door and move to stand beside him, though this time I do not touch. This time I will wait for Damien, because I know that he will take what he needs from me, just as he lets me take what I need from him.

A moment passes, and then another. Finally, he speaks. "I will pay," he repeats, as if he is responding to a question I just posed. He has been facing straight ahead. Now he turns to look at me, and what I see in his face is no longer flat, but fierce. "You say that you're strong enough to handle seeing that shit with me and Carmela, and I believe you. But this . . . no."

"I can handle whatever comes." My voice is soft, but strong. "With you beside me, you know I can. And so will Jamie. She made her choices, and she knows they were bad ones. She gets it. And she understands what it will cost you to pay extortion money. And, Damien, it's not even your choice. The file was sent to Jamie, not you. Not me."

He manages a twisted smile. "You and I both know who they expected to pay."

Since I can't argue the point, I don't. "Even so, it's not your decision."

"I'm making it my decision."

"Dammit, Damien—"

"*No*. She made bad choices? She damn sure did. But she's turned it around. She doesn't deserve this. And I won't have her tossed out there to the wolves any more than I will have you hurting for your friends. Not when I can fix it."

"It's blackmail."

"It is, yes." He takes my hands and pulls me close. "Dammit, Nikki. Do you think I didn't see?" He brushes my cheek, and I shiver from his touch. "You were fine when it was just about us—you can stand it because you're strong, and because you've stood it before. But where Jamie is concerned—when you are shouldering pain for a friend—baby, do you think I don't know how it wrecks you? Don't you know by now how clearly I see you?"

I nod, my eyes flooded with tears, because I do know how well he sees me. Just like I know that Damien will do whatever it takes to protect me and mine, no matter how much a sacrifice that protection is.

But this isn't a sacrifice I want him to make. "It does wreck me," I admit. "But I will get through it. So long as I have you to anchor me, you know I will. But what I can't survive is knowing that you did something like this for me, when doing it will chip away at the core of the man I love."

He doesn't answer me. But I see the anguish on his face.

"I love you," I whisper, but I barely get the words out before his mouth finds mine. The kiss is brutal, wild, and claiming. And I know that I was right—Damien will always take what he needs from me, and he knows that it is already his.

"Nikki." My name is a moan, and I cannot respond. Not when he has claimed my mouth again, his tongue warring with mine, teasing and tasting, so deep and wild and hot that I can feel the power of this kiss reverberate through me, exciting every part of me so that I feel as though I will die if I don't feel his hands upon me.

"Yes," I say. "Oh, god, yes."

He pushes me back roughly so that my legs are against the hood of the car. His fingers tangle in my hair, his palm cupping the back of my head as he bruises my mouth with wild kisses.

This is passion, but it is also punishment and domination. Because I had a moment when I needed the pain and I didn't go to him. Because someone out in the world is fucking with us, and he can't find them or make them stop, and swimming in someone else's stream is not something Damien handles well.

I understand all that, and I want to give him what he needs. But right now, this isn't about control or anger or frustration. It's about heat and need. It's about touch and demand.

It's about the absolute certainty that I will not survive one minute longer if Damien doesn't take me right now, and I really don't care that we're on the side of the road with the sky open above us.

"Please," I beg.

And Damien, who will always be there for me, does not disappoint.

He turns me around, pressing me down against the hood of the car. I spread my legs and lift myself on my toes. My skirt is up around my waist, the pearl thong absolutely soaked.

He rips it off, and I hear pearls scattering across the turnout. I don't even care. Right then, I'm lost in the feel of his fingers stroking my sex. I'm wet, and his hand slides over me, then thrusts inside. I moan with pleasure, but it's not enough. I want all of him, and tell him so. Begging. Demanding.

I'm rewarded by the sound of his zipper and then—thank god—by the hard press of the crown of his penis against my slit.

He enters me. Just a little at first, and I bite down on my lower lip, wanting more. Wanting all of him. And yet he is going so painfully, teasingly slow.

It's driving me crazy. Which, of course, he knows.

Then, without warning, he thrusts hard, sliding deep inside

me. I cry out, my voice filling the night air. As I do, I arch up, and in that moment, Damien leans over me, his motion driving him even deeper into me. I try to thrust my hips back, wanting everything he has to give. He is filling me completely, and I cannot help but wonder how I survive even a second when I am not so intimately connected to Damien.

Except I am; I always am. Even when I am not touching him, I am connected to him.

The thought makes me soar, and as he cups my breasts in his palms—as he bites lightly on my neck and pounds hard into me—I shatter into a billion pieces, then cry out in passion and relief and exultation as Damien explodes inside me.

And the last coherent thought that I have is that no matter what, Damien and I give each other what we need, and we always will.

Chapter 9

"You're sure that you aren't going to get in trouble?" I ask Sylvia. "And there's no chance he'll walk in and see what we're up to?"

We're in the living room of the Tower apartment, and Sylvia is parked behind the tripod on which I've mounted the Leica that Damien gave me.

"I told you, he's in meetings all morning."

That much I know. Those meetings—including some video conferences that started before dawn—are the reason that we stayed in the apartment last night. "What if he forgot something?"

"It's my job to make sure he didn't," she says. "And I promise, he's booked solid. He's doing nothing but meetings until the chopper gets here. But if you're that worried, shut up and let me take the picture. Then I can get out of here and you can be sure we're safe."

"Sorry," I say, genuinely contrite. "I just want it to be a surprise. And I really do appreciate you helping out."

"I'm glad to. The picture taking and the rest of it, too."

We've arranged that Syl will take several shots of me, which I'll download to my laptop from the memory disk while I'm on the plane to the resort. It's not a working trip, but I think it's a safe bet that Damien will have at least one or two business things to take care of. And when he does, I'll do a bit of work, too.

My plan is to manipulate the photo to the way I want it, add a caption, and then email the whole thing back to Sylvia. For her part, she's promised to have it printed, framed, wrapped, and delivered to the Malibu house. When we get back on Valentine's Day, it'll be right there for Damien to open.

Just thinking about it makes me grin. There's something about having to jump through all these hoops that makes the gift feel even more special. Hopefully Damien will enjoy the photo as much as I'm enjoying creating it.

Right now, though, I need to get on that whole "creating it" thing.

"Okay," I say. "Let's do it."

She nods and adjusts the focus. We've already checked the lights and filters, because I'm trying to minimize reflections and glare. The image I want is me in front of the window, the city spread out behind me. I'm wearing my most form-fitting dress, and one hand is flat against the glass as I stand at an angle so as to accentuate all my curves.

If the picture turns out like it is in my mind, it will be stunning. Unfortunately, things don't always work out that way.

I stay still as Sylvia clicks and adjusts, then has me move to various similar poses so that I will have others to choose from if I hate the original idea.

About the time that I think my arm is going to fall off from being extended so long, she calls it a wrap.

"Well?" I ask, and her answering grin is all I need to know.

"You're going to have a hell of a time choosing the best one," she says. "And Damien is going to love it."

I think about what she says as I pack a small suitcase. I hope she's right. Considering the game that Damien put together for me, I feel a little bit like a slacker. Then again, there's no reason I can't step up to the plate next year. Or even for his birthday. After all, surely I could come up with some sort of personalized iPhone app.

The possibility amuses me, and I'm so lost in thinking about apps for lovers and scavenger hunts that I don't hear Damien come in. I am sitting on the bed, my laptop bag beside me and my suitcase propped up in front of me like a desk, and I'm busily scribbling notes when he knocks lightly on the doorframe.

I look up, confused for a second, then leap off the bed and rush into his arms. He kisses me with equal enthusiasm, then nods at the notebook that has fallen to the floor. "What did I interrupt?"

"I'll tell you when I work out the details. Right now, I'll just say that you have inspired another app." I grin mischievously. "I'm certain it will be a best seller."

He looks at me, amused. "How could it not, with you designing it? Are you ready?"

I am, and we gather our things, then take the elevator to the roof. The helicopter takes us to the airport where the now familiar jet waits for us, along with Grayson, the pilot, and Katie, the Stark fleet's senior flight attendant.

We get settled in, and Katie brings us both champagne before she returns to the crew area and leaves us alone.

"I didn't have the chance to thank you yesterday," I say after we're airborne. "First, you distracted me—"

"I believe you started the distracting, Mrs. Stark."

"Maybe." I am unrepentant. "But after that we were distracted by less enjoyable things. At any rate, a spa getaway sounds like the perfect Valentine's Day present."

"I'm very glad you think so."

I lean over to kiss him. "So tell me about the Serafina Spa."

"Remember when I told you that I'd been looking at islands to acquire in the Bahamas with the goal of opening a resort?"

"Sure. Did you decide to just buy this one?"

He laughs. "No. It's an excellent resort with a fine reputation, but it caters to everyone. We're staying in the private section, which has its own spa, bungalows, and the like. But the main areas are available to anyone. Singles, spring breakers, couples, families."

"Sounds to me like my husband is trying to sneak in some business during our romantic getaway," I tease.

He chuckles. "I assure you that wasn't part of the plan. I've done enough research on Serafina already to know that not only is there plenty of room for a competitive couples-only resort to move in and still have both resorts flourish, but that Serafina is an exceptional spa and resort. And until I've built a Stark couples' resort in the area, Serafina is the one resort to which I will take my wife."

"Very nice save, Mr. Stark."

He shoots me a stern look, but it's clear that he's amused.

"You gave yourself away, though."

He frowns. "What do you mean?"

"You said it *wasn't* part of the plan. Does that mean business is part of the plan now?"

"You, Mrs. Stark, are too smart for your own good."

I smirk.

"Something unexpected came up. Would you mind? Just one short meeting if I can arrange it?"

I take his hand and squeeze. "Are you kidding? Of course I don't mind." I don't tell him that I pretty much expected it. "What came up?"

"I'll show you." He turns on his iPad and pulls up an image of a skyscraper. "The Winn Building in New York," he says, then taps the screen and pulls up another image, this one of a lovely building still partially under construction. "The Amsterdam Art and Science Museum."

"They're amazing."

"They are," he says. "The architect is Jackson Steele." Another tap and I see a still photo from what looks to be a television interview outside at a construction site.

I have to admit the man is exceptional. It's hard to tell from the grainy image, but I'm guessing that he's in his thirties. He stands straight, looking as if he owns the world, with a strong jawline and wind-tossed hair that appears to be as thick and dark as Damien's. But it's his eyes that are the most striking—a vivid blue that seems to burst off the screen, even despite the very poor quality of the image.

"I've had my eye on him for a while," Damien says, "specifically for the Bahamas resort."

"Really?"

"I think he'll jump at the opportunity." He passes me the iPad, and I scroll through the images. "He's done a number of projects, but nothing like I'm envisioning. An entire island redesigned. A blank slate. I think it will intrigue him."

"No kidding." I mean it, too. Steele's buildings are spectacular, but Damien's right. What he's describing is unlike anything that Damien has included in Steele's portfolio. "So you invited him to Serafina?"

Damien shakes his head. "Aiden called this morning," he says, referring to Aiden Ward, the vice president of Stark Real

Estate Development. "Turns out Steele is vacationing on Serafina this week. I'm hoping to steal an hour or so of his time." He squeezes my hand. "Unfortunately, that means I'll be taking time away from you, too."

"Are you under the impression that I resent your work?"

His smile is slow and wide. "No." He kisses me, then puts his arm around my shoulders and pulls me close. "No, I have never been under that impression."

I bump his shoulder lightly. "Of course, you will have to make it up to me."

He trails his finger up my thigh, sending little shocks of awareness through me. "Trust me, sweetheart. I fully intend to do just that."

A private jet makes traveling much more comfortable, but even my husband cannot change the speed at which the earth rotates and jets fly. Which means that even though we flew from Los Angeles to the Bahamas in fabulous comfort, it is so late by the time we get to Nassau and then to Serafina that we barely even look at our bungalow before we peel off our clothes and fall into the soft warm bed that dominates the master suite.

Morning, however, is a completely different story. I am awakened by the sun streaming in through the open windows. The ocean is just steps away, and even though I know that this is a resort, with the exception of Damien's voice filtering in from the next room, I can hear nothing that even hints at other people on this island.

Nothing except Jamie's voice, that is.

Jamie?

I frown and pull on one of the robes that hangs on a hook by my side of the bed, then head out of the bedroom to figure out why my best friend is inside my romantic getaway bungalow.

I realize soon enough that she's not, of course. Just her voice over a speaker and her face on Damien's computer screen.

I stand in the doorway, out of view of both of them, and listen as my best friend tells my husband that he's being an idiot.

"You can't pay, Damien. You never do that shit."

"I have my reasons, Jamie."

"What, you mean Nikki? No way does she want you to pay."

"Nikki is part of it, yes. But so are you. Have you considered that I don't want to see that footage of you spread all over the internet?"

I can see her face and the screen, and for a moment she looks touched. But the expression fades quickly. "I can deal," she says. "Seriously, you think I want that on me, knowing that you're caving—*why* you're caving? Trust me, I can handle it. I mean, dealing with shit like this is practically my hobby."

"My mind's made up."

"You're an idiot, Damien. I'm allowed to say that now because Nikki's like my sister, so that makes you like my brother."

"Fine. As your brother, I'm allowed to hang up on you. And that's what I'm doing now, Jamie."

She starts to protest, but he closes the screen. He sits for a moment, and though he doesn't turn in my direction, he reaches back and holds out his hand to me.

I walk to him and twine my fingers with his. "She's right, you know," I say quietly. "You pay to keep the tape from being released, and it's never going to end."

"It will end when I find whoever's behind this," he says darkly. "And I promise it won't end well. In the meantime, I will take care of the people I love." He turns to look at me. "Tell me you understand."

"I understand," I say. "But that doesn't mean I like it. And I hate that it hurts you."

He stands, then kisses me. "In that case, you know how I

feel. Let's leave it aside for now. I want to enjoy this time with my wife. Deal?"

"Deal."

Despite the fact that staying in our own private bungalow on our own private beach sounds deliciously romantic, we both want to explore. After all, Damien and I did the private island thing recently. Now we want to check out the spa, the bar, possibly even the tennis court.

"This section of the island is limited to couples and spa guests," Damien says as we walk down a path that runs along the beach. "It has its own shops, bars, sporting activities. There's a reef not far offshore. We can go snorkeling later if you'd like."

"That sounds fun," I say. "So long as snorkeling doesn't trump spa'ing."

"Never," he promises.

"And that's why I love you," I trill.

We spend the rest of the walk making a list of the things we want to do for the rest of the day, and I've just added *long bubble bath in the Jacuzzi tub* when we arrive at the restaurant.

It's buffet style, and as the hostess leads us to our table, I think of one thing we didn't factor into our plans. "By the way, when are you meeting the architect?"

"Not sure. I left a message for him this morning, but he hasn't called back."

"Probably out snorkeling," I quip. "Or maybe he's just having a late breakfast," I amend, then nod across the room toward the omelet station where a dark-haired man waits in line. "That's him, isn't it? That's Jackson Steele?"

His back is to me, but the commanding presence I'd seen in the photograph is more apparent in real life. It's a presence I'm intimately familiar with, as Damien has the same air about him.

"That's him," Damien confirms. "Come on."

He's still in line as we approach, and Damien steps in next to him. "Jackson Steele," he says, extending his hand. "I'm Damien Stark."

Steele looks Damien up and down, then his eyes cut to me before returning to Damien. For a moment, I think he's going to ignore Damien's offered hand, but then he reaches out and the two men shake. "I know who you are, Stark. I got your message this morning."

"I was hoping to find some time to talk to you today or tomorrow," Damien says, and though I can tell that he can't quite figure this guy out, I'm certain that no one else observing the conversation would be able to tell that he is currently reassessing his approach. "I've been a fan of your work for a very long time and I'd like to discuss working with you on a project that I think you'll find intriguing."

"I'm flattered. But the truth is I'm not taking meetings this week. I'm on vacation."

"Understood," Damien says as the restaurant hostess steps up to him.

"I'm sorry to interrupt," she says, "but there's a call for you at the front desk."

Damien frowns, but excuses himself, saying that he'll be right back.

I decide to take up the slack. "I hope you consider the project. We're both very impressed by your work and think you would be an excellent fit."

"I appreciate that," he says. "But I'm not sure that Stark International is the place for me. I'm sure you realize that your husband casts a very long shadow."

"Oh." I'm trying to decide how to reply to that when Damien returns, apologizing for the interruption.

"I won't bother you on vacation," he says to Steele, sliding back into the conversation. "But why don't I give you a call at your office when I get back to the States?"

"I'm sure that's not necessary," Steele says, and though I can't put my finger on the reason, I feel as though there is something off about the way he says it.

Steele glances toward the line, which has barely moved. "Since we're all here, why don't you just go ahead and tell me now."

As I sigh with relief, hoping that Steele is reconsidering what he'd said to me only moments ago, Damien describes his plan to locate and acquire an entire island that can be developed as a high-end couples' retreat. "You have a strong vision, Mr. Steele. I'd like to have you join the project at the ground floor. Your finger in every aspect of the project, including the selection of the island. I think it's an exciting venture, and would add something unique to your portfolio."

"It would," Steele says. "But I'm going to have to decline."

"Are you?" Damien says. "May I ask why?"

"I have my reasons," he says glancing quickly at me before focusing entirely on Damien. And though they both appear relaxed and at ease, there's tension in the air.

"A number of reasons, actually," Steele continues. "But as I told your wife just moments ago, you cast a very long shadow, Mr. Stark. And I don't want myself or my work to get caught underneath it."

I expect Damien to argue, so I'm surprised when he nods slowly in acquiescence. "I'm disappointed, but I can respect your reason. If you ever change your mind, the door is open."

"I don't foresee that happening," Steele says. "But I've learned to never say never."

He nods to Damien, then to me. And then he abandons the omelet line just as he reaches the cook.

Damien watches him go, and I watch Damien.

"Interesting," he says. "Did he say anything else to you?" I shake my head, and he continues, frowning. "I'm usually so certain about people, but I can't quite get a read on him."

"What do you mean?"

"I'm not sure. But I don't think there's a middle ground with Jackson Steele. If I had the chance to get to know him better, I'd either like him or hate him. No ambivalence. No casual association."

"You'd like him," I say firmly.

He tilts his head to look at me. "And why do you say that?"

"Because he intrigues you."

He chuckles. "Maybe he does. Why do you think that is?"

"Because, Mr. Stark, of all the people in the world, Jackson Steele is one of the few who have ever managed to look you in the eye and say no."

Chapter 10

Damien pampers me thoroughly on our last full day on the island.

We sleep late, then start with breakfast in bed, catered by the extremely efficient room service staff. After that, we move to the spa and a couples' massage in a cabana by the beach.

Damien disappears while I have a facial and pedicure, but when he returns he leads me to a small sailboat moored at the end of a whitewashed wooden pier. I look around and see no one but us.

He laughs. "Have a little faith. I promise you, I can handle a sailboat."

"So many hidden talents, Mr. Stark," I tease as I reach for his hand and let him help me onto the boat.

I know nothing about sailing, but it's soon clear enough that Damien does. He gets us untied from the dock and maneuvers us away from the island with the same kind of confidence and ease with which he does everything else.

"There's Steele," I say, pointing to the shore. I look at the sky. "Sun's straight overhead. No shadows right now."

Damien laughs, but after a moment, his expression turns thoughtful.

"Damien?"

He cocks his head and flashes a wry smile. "No shadows," he says, repeating my words. "Steele doesn't know the half of it."

He sounds so distracted that I'm getting a bit concerned. "What are you talking about?"

"Steele doesn't want to be in my shadow—doesn't want to ride on my coattails."

"Right." I'm still not following him.

"Whoever our blackmailer is wants exactly that. He wants to hide. Wants to stay in the dark, hidden in the shadows, secure in the belief that he knows me so well." Damien meets my eyes. "So damn certain that now that I'm married, I won't want a spotlight shining on my wife or her friends. And that I'll pay to keep all sorts of shit in the shadows."

"Are you saying you won't?" My words are tentative; I'm afraid to hope.

"No," Damien says. "I won't. I can't." I see the worry fill his eyes. "Once I do, it won't ever stop. Baby, tell me you understand."

I'm in his arms immediately. "I've been telling you that. So has Jamie. No matter what hits the tabloids, we'll survive."

He pulls me close and hugs me tight before easing back and then pressing a soft kiss to my forehead. "I'm still going to try to keep it from getting out."

"How?"

His smile is tight. "I'm going to play a hunch. And then I'm going to negotiate."

"You mean you're going to threaten."

"Sweetheart," he says. "You know me so well."

He pulls out his phone.

"What's the hunch?" I ask before he can dial.

"I'm willing to believe that Douglas isn't the brains behind this—that man couldn't find his dick without a woman or a map—but his claim that releasing the tape will destroy him is bullshit. That tape gets out, and suddenly he's the guy who screwed Nikki Stark's best friend. That's worth something to a worm like him."

"You think someone approached him?"

"I do," Damien says.

"Who?"

He shakes his head. "I have a few ideas, but no confirmation."

I swallow, and though I say nothing, my fear is that Damien thinks his father—a man who has about a million recent reasons to hold a grudge—is behind this.

"Will Douglas tell you who it is?" I ask.

"To be honest, I believe Douglas when he says he doesn't know."

"So someone approached him anonymously?"

"That's my guess. Which means that at the very least, Douglas has a way to get a message back to them." He pulls out his phone. "And I'm going to insist that he deliver mine. That he tell his handler that if Valentine's Day passes with no photos released to the media, then I will ignore this lapse in judgment on their part. But if a single photo turns up where it doesn't belong, I will not stop until I've made the life of every person involved a complete living hell.

"And then," he adds, with the scary kind of smile that makes me remember why he does so damn well in the shark-infested waters of corporate America, "I'll invite law enforcement to the party, just to add a little spice to the mix."

After Damien puts the fear of god into Douglas, he suggests that we put it away and enjoy the rest of our last day. After all, tomorrow is Valentine's Day, and we'll know soon enough if it worked.

"I think that's a wonderful idea, Mr. Stark. What do you have in mind?"

"Actually," he says. "I thought I'd teach you a bit about sailing."

As it turns out, I'm a hopeless student. I'm much more interested in watching Damien move, all masculine and athletic grace. His second item on the agenda, snorkeling, is much more my speed, and I follow him into the warm water as soon as the boat is anchored. The reef is teeming with color and life, and I watch all of it, mesmerized, and then delighted when Damien points out both a manta ray and a sea turtle.

Back on the boat, I sit on the deck, a towel wrapped around me as the sun sinks toward the horizon.

Damien is expertly maneuvering us back to the island, and I feel completely at peace out here on the wide, blue sea. Despite the dicey start to the morning, everything is calm now. We've both pushed it aside, I think. Hopefully, there will be no pictures released tomorrow, but if there are, we'll deal. If there's one thing I'm certain of, Damien and I can handle pretty much anything so long as we are together.

I'm surprised when he maneuvers the boat past the rental dock from where we'd departed. Instead, he follows the shore, and then brings the boat in to the small dock that extends from our private beach.

"Door-to-door service?"

"Only the best for you," he answers.

It's only once I'm off the boat and back at the bungalow that I see how seriously he means those words. The small pool in the bungalow courtyard is filled with floating candles, turning it into a magical fairyland. A bottle of wine is open beside a giant, round lounge chair designed for two. And beside the wine is a plate filled with cheeses and meats and covered with a clear glass lid to protect it from the elements.

Beside the pool, the hot tub bubbles, and I remember what I'd said about wanting to take a bath in the Jacuzzi tub. This, I think, is just as appealing.

"How did you do this?" I ask.

"I believe I've mentioned that I have a rather large bank account, which allows me to purchase a surprising variety of goods and services."

"Must be nice being you," I tease, then slide into his open arms.

"It's better now that I have you," he says, and I almost melt from the depth of emotion that fills his voice.

He tugs me to the lounge chair, and then slowly undresses me before telling me to lay back and close my eyes.

I do, and my reward is Damien's touch.

I cannot count the different ways that he has touched me since we have been together, but his touch tonight is deceptive, its simplicity hiding a power to drive me over the edge.

All he uses is a finger.

Slowly, he traces his forefinger over my leg, drawing soft patterns. Teasing me behind my knee. Stroking gently up my inner thigh, but not quite high enough. And though I moan a bit and squirm in silent demand, he does not stroke my sex.

Instead, his finger trails only in that soft area between thigh and genitals, but that is enough to send tremors running through me, shifting the rest of my body into a state of hyper-awareness so that innocent touches are suddenly anything but. Even his finger slowly circling my belly button makes my sex clench with longing.

Featherlight touches continue upward, caressing every inch

of me and paying extra attention to my breasts until my nipples are so hard and tight that I have to bite my lower lip so as to not beg him to close his mouth over me and suck my breast until I come.

Finally, that wonderful, damnable finger traces my lower lip, then teases its way inside my mouth. "Suck," he demands, that one word holding a world of erotic possibilities.

I do, drawing him in, and feeling the shock of sensation travel through me like an electric current that runs from my mouth to my cunt. There is no part of me now that isn't open to him. Desperate for him.

"Please," I whisper, and then tremble with need as he stretches out beside me so that his body is pressed against mine and all those erogenous zones that he has created sparkle and fire in anticipation.

"Tell me what you want."

"You know," I say. "I want to feel you inside me. Please, oh please, Damien."

"Anything you want, sweetheart," he says, slowly rolling onto his back and urging me on top of him. "Anything you need."

What I need is him. He has ministered to my body for what feels like an eternity and every cell in my skin is humming with desire.

And yet in all that time he has neither penetrated me nor touched my clit. I feel swollen with need, so ready to be filled by my husband that I fear I will go crazy if I don't have him right this very second.

I move to straddle him even as he moves onto his back. His cock rubs against me, teasing my rear, and I bite my lower lip, wanting everything. Wanting Damien.

Slowly, I rise up on my knees and then lower myself onto him. I gasp as he fills me, then cry out as his hips pivot up even as his hands on my hips push me down so that he fills me hard and fast and completely.

"Kiss me," he demands, and I lean forward, our bodies moving together as my mouth closes over his and my breasts brush against his chest, teasing my already sensitive nipples.

His hand slides between our bodies, and now his fingers do touch me, stroke me. He teases my clit as my body tightens around him, the muscles of my sex clenching to draw him in, hotter and deeper, and I can feel the tension building inside both of us until I can't stand it anymore, and I pull myself back up, then arch back so that I'm facing the sky as the force of my orgasm rocks through me and I grind against him, my muscles tightening around his cock and bringing Damien the rest of the way with me so that he calls out my name and I close my eyes as it echoes through the night.

When my body stops spasming, I fall down upon him again, then sigh as his fingers stroke my hair.

"It's midnight," he whispers, and I lift my head to meet his eyes. "Happy Valentine's Day, Mrs. Stark."

Chapter 11

Damien wakes me before dawn, though that is not an easy feat. It's his fault that I got so little sleep, and I feel no guilt about sliding down the bed even as I pull the covers higher.

I know we are on a schedule. But I also know that the plane won't take off without Damien. What's the benefit of being an ultra-rich lord of the universe who owns a fleet of planes if you can't adjust departure times in order to let your wife grab a few extra minutes of sleep?

I want to explain that, but all I manage is a murmured, "Fifteen minutes. Sleepy."

I hear the soft pad of his footsteps as he moves away from

the bed, and I slide back into sleep, secure in the belief that I've succeeded in begging more time.

Soon enough, I realize I'm wrong. He's back, and he's gently tugging the covers down. I peel open my eyes, and this time I pay more attention to my surroundings. My husband is already dressed in jeans and a crisp button-down. Behind him, I see his running shorts and a T-shirt on the floor near a half-packed suitcase. I put the clues together easily enough—despite not actually going to sleep until almost three in the morning, Damien is not only awake, but has both gone for a run and started packing our things.

Clearly the man is superhuman, but since I am a mere mortal, I still feel no guilt about closing my eyes again and trying to claim another minute.

He, however, is having none of it. He pulls the covers down, then scoops me into his arms. I protest for form, but it's warm and comfortable in his embrace, and so I simply snuggle closer. All too soon, though, he sets me on my feet, and then helps me into a robe. "Trust me," he says, then kisses me softly before leading me outside to our private beach.

"Damien." His name is little more than a breath. "It's wonderful."

I'm looking at a table draped with white linen, atop which sits a number of covered trays and a very large pot that I assume is filled with coffee. Tiki-style torches have been placed at each of the four corners of the mat upon which the table sits, providing a relatively sand-free surface. The sun has barely started to peek above the horizon, and the torches cast a golden glow over the tableau, making it seem all the more magical.

"Happy Valentine's Day," Damien says. "Since we're spending most of the day traveling, I thought we should start off with something special."

I smile up at him, feeling sappy and loved. "Every moment with you is special, Damien. Don't you know that?"

He doesn't say anything, but the tenderness I see on his face answers for him.

I take his hand and let him lead me to the table. And as we enjoy a breakfast of eggs and coffee and flaky croissants, we watch the sun rise on our first Valentine's Day together.

Because of our early departure and the time difference, we arrive home not long after noon. Damien has been checking social media since the sun rose in California, and so far he has seen no evidence that the photos or tape have been leaked.

We are cautiously optimistic.

Unlike the plane ride to the Bahamas, during which I'd managed to sneak in some work on my Valentine's Day present to Damien, I had no secret project on the return trip. So I spent the flight reading, napping, and trying to do a little bit of coding.

"Try" is the operative word, though, because Katie kept the mimosas flowing, and since it's Valentine's Day, I didn't hesitate to take them as fast as she wanted to bring them.

Which meant that the napping part of the plane ride soon overtook all other activities. And now, as we walk through the doors of the Malibu house, I am very well rested.

Damien takes my hand as we head up to the third floor, and as soon as we are high enough on the stairs to see the room, I gasp.

The entire space is filled with flowers. Not only that, but our bed—the lovely iron bed that was a prop for the portrait of me and that now lives in our bedroom—is back in this open area where Damien and I spent so many delicious hours together.

I turn to him, my smile so wide it hurts. "How did you do this?"

"Gregory. Sylvia. I have my ways."

"It's a wonderful Valentine's Day surprise."

His mention of Sylvia makes me wonder if with this minor redecoration she still did what I asked and left the package for Damien on the bed. From here, I don't see it, and I wonder if she put his present on the dresser in the bedroom.

But as we get closer, I see that the box is there, so flat and white that it blends in with the bedclothes, the only splash of color being a thin red ribbon.

Damien sees it, too, and glances at me curiously. He moves to the bed and lifts the package, then checks the tag. I know what it says, of course. Sylvia may have arranged to have the present wrapped, but I'd written the tag.

For my husband. For my love.

"Looks like I wasn't the only one who had the help of Valentine's Day elves."

I shrug innocently.

"Can I open it?"

"Of course."

He sits on the edge of the bed, and I climb on beside him. To be honest, I'm curious myself to see how it turned out. I'd managed to sneak time on the flight to Nassau to go over all the images that Sylvia took for me. I'd found my favorite, manipulated it in Photoshop to heighten the contrast so that my silhouette is even darker against the backdrop of the city, and to clean up the lingering glare from the glass.

Finally, I'd added text, a caption in lovely script on the left-hand side of the space so that it balanced my image on the right:

Anything you want. Anything you need.

I'd emailed the file to Sylvia with specific directions as to how to print it and frame it.

Now I can only hope that the end product is as lovely in real life as it is in my head.

Damien slowly unties the bow and sets the ribbon on the bed. Then he removes the wrapping paper to reveal the box. By now, I'm as anxious as if I were opening one of my own presents on Christmas morning, and I am biting my lower lip hard by the time he opens the box to reveal the framed photograph inside.

"Nikki." He manages to fill my name with awe. "My god, Nikki, it's stunning."

"You like it?"

He's been staring at it, but now he takes it out of the box, then turns to me, and I can see in his eyes that he likes it very much indeed. "It couldn't be more perfect."

"You're a hard man to shop for, Mr. Stark," I say. "I wanted to get you something special. Something us."

He cups my cheek with his palm and kisses me softly. "You did. It's beautiful. It's you."

He pulls me close and holds me tight. I hug him back, warmed by the fact that my single photograph—so small compared to a scavenger hunt and a spa retreat—has affected him so much.

"Thank you for my presents, too," I say. "If I haven't already said, I loved the treasure hunt, not to mention the retreat time with my husband."

"As did I," he said. "But that was more like an appetizer than the main course."

I lean back and frown at him, not understanding what he is saying.

"How could I give you your Valentine's Day present before Valentine's Day?"

"But—" I close my mouth as I regroup. "Um, okay. So . . ."

He chuckles. "The third floor pantry," Damien says. "Gregory assures me he put it in the pantry right before we arrived."

The pantry?

Damien's expression is both amused and smug. "Go on," he says, and since I need no more encouragement, I bolt toward the kitchen, desperately curious as to what he could possibly have gotten me. A personal chef, maybe?

I tug open the door, and then clap my hand over my mouth to stifle a scream of delight.

There, curled up and purring on a cushion inside a wicker basket is the tiniest, orangest, most adorable kitten I have ever seen.

"Damien," I whisper as the kitten opens its eyes, yawns, and stumbles out of the basket toward me. "Oh my god, Damien."

I glance back at him, and as I do, I notice the pile of cat food that I need to return to Jamie. Damien knew how much I missed having a cat around, and he got me a kitten.

I am overwhelmed. I'm in awe.

I'm in love.

"She doesn't have a name yet," Damien says, moving behind me and putting his hand on my shoulder. I scoop the kitten up, and am delighted when she immediately starts purring in my arms.

"She does," I say, snuggling close to my husband. "Her name is Sunshine."

We take Sunshine to the bed and the three of us pile on. I lean against Damien and laugh as we watch the kitten go through all her kitten-y antics. Attacking fingers and toes. Pouncing on imaginary prey. And generally being a bundle of cuteness until she wears herself out, turns in three circles, then settles down in the middle of the bed to purr herself to sleep.

"She's wonderful," I whisper as Damien leads me to the balcony. "She's perfect."

He stands behind me, his arms around my waist as I lean back against him. "She is," he says, but what I hear is *We are.*

I breathe deeply, relishing the feel of him. It is a soft moment, nice and gentle, but it doesn't stay that way for long. Soon Damien's hands slide beneath my shirt, and I draw in a breath as my skin tightens with longing and my heartbeat quickens.

He moves slowly, letting the anticipation grow, until his palms cover my breasts and he is stroking my nipples with his thumbs. The motion is almost casual, but my reaction is not. On the contrary, a wild heat is growing inside me, and if the press of his erection against my back is any indication, it is growing in Damien as well.

I murmur his name, and am rewarded by his soft "Shhh. Just relax." Easier said than done, but I close my eyes and let the sensation of Damien's expert touch take over, taking me all the way to the edge until, finally, he pushes me over and I explode in his arms as the sun sets on our first Valentine's Day.

I'm curled up in bed, wearing nothing but Damien's Wimbledon T-shirt, one leg tossed negligently across his thigh as I lick a chocolate ice cream–covered spoon.

Beside me, Damien has his laptop open and is scouring the internet as the kitten attacks our toes with military-like determination. "Still nothing," Damien says, squirming a bit under Sunshine's assault.

"Then it worked. You didn't pay, and they didn't release the photos or the tape."

"Looks that way," Damien says, though he doesn't look as happy about it as I feel.

"You still want to know who's behind it."

"Very much," he says.

"You'll find them. Ryan's on it, right?"

"He is. And eventually we'll find them."

"Damn right, you will," I say. "So worry about it tomorrow. I don't want those stupid threats touching any more of our day than they already have."

"Touché, Mrs. Stark." He sets the laptop aside, and grabs the red ribbon. He holds on to one end and tosses the ribbon toward the cat, who is immediately fascinated. She stares at the wiggling end of the ribbon, her eyes wide and her orange fur spiked out in attack mode. Damien and I both hold our breaths, swallowing laughter as her little butt wiggles, her tail spiky. Finally—after much observation—she pounces, attacking the end of the ribbon with all the panache of a jaguar going after its prey.

I laugh, delighted, and she abandons the ribbon just long enough to flop onto her back and wiggle.

Damien reaches down and scratches her belly and is rewarded by the kitten grabbing hold and gnawing his hand. He grins at me, and my heart melts a little.

"I could have sworn you told me you didn't want us to turn domestic," I tease.

"Is that what this is?" he asks, taking the ribbon and wiggling it again. "Domesticity?"

I offer him a spoonful of ice cream. "Yeah. I think it is."

He licks the spoon, then takes my finger and dips it into the ice cream. Then he offers my finger to the kitten, who runs her rough little tongue over it, making me laugh again. "In that case," Damien says, "I've changed my mind. I like domesticity very much."

"I like it, too," I say, snuggling closer. "And I love you."

He brushes a soft kiss across my lips and we lay together as the kitten climbs over us to find a spot on the pillow. And as the little ball of fluff settles in and starts to purr, I sigh with satisfaction.

This is us.

This is our life.

And it is exceptional.

seduce me

Chapter 1

I scowl at my calendar for today and wonder how I am possibly going to be able to cram everything into one workday. I have three meetings, half a dozen phone calls to return, a lunch appointment, and plans to meet my best friend, Jamie, for drinks at seven. And somewhere in there I have to schedule time to actually get work done.

Frankly, I'm not sure if it's possible without the aid of time travel devices or, at the very least, a part-time assistant.

I'm tapping the end of my pencil against the overfull sheet—because despite owning my own web- and mobile-app development company, I print my schedule every morning—when Damien approaches.

I know that he is there even though he has yet to say a word. Perhaps I heard his bare feet on the wooden floor. Perhaps the air shifted as he passed. Or perhaps he is simply Damien Stark, and I could no more fail to notice his presence than I could miss a tidal wave.

But more likely, I think it is because he has so thoroughly claimed me that there is never a moment when I am not blissfully and totally aware of him.

I am in the library on the mezzanine of the exceptional Malibu house that was still under construction when I first started dating Damien. Now it is our home, and every space within these walls is precious to me. I'm at the desk near the section where Damien has shelved his sci-fi/fantasy collection, tattered paperbacks tucked in alongside pristine, signed first editions. A few feet away, in one of the comfy leather chairs, the newest addition to our household is curled up into a tiny ball of orange fluff.

This is Damien's favorite place to work, and that's part of why I come here almost every morning—I like to feel close to him.

Right now, I feel very close indeed.

"You're amazing, you know." I speak without turning around, then smile when I hear his soft chuckle behind me.

"Because I can sneak up on you?" This time I do hear his footsteps as he moves even closer.

"I knew you were there. By definition, that isn't sneaking. Or, at least, it's not successful sneaking."

"You make a good point, Mrs. Stark." His hands press gently on my shoulders, and I close my eyes, just soaking up the feel of him. It's more potent than coffee, and if I could bottle this sensation, I'd be richer than my husband.

I haven't yet turned to look at him, but I don't need to. I long ago memorized every delicious inch of him. His lush, raven-black hair, so familiar to my fingers. His perfectly sculpted face, softened by the slightest shadow of beard stubble. His lean, well-muscled athlete's body that looks equally exceptional in jeans or a tux. And, of course, his dual-colored eyes that can look right to my core and see all my secrets.

It is not yet seven on a Friday morning and though I'm still in my typical morning uniform of a T-shirt and baggy shorts, I know that he is already dressed. I inhale, confirming that assumption. I smell the soap from his shower. The hint of musk from the cologne I bought him in Paris on our honeymoon, just a few months ago.

"So tell me, why am I amazing?"

"To properly answer that, I'd need PowerPoint, a projector, and at least two days." I tilt my head back so that I can grin at him, and my heart skitters when I see his face, even more perfect than the picture I keep tucked away in my mind. "But in this particular instance, I was referring to your time management skills." Damien accomplishes more in a day than most people do in a year. Frankly, I think it's highly likely that superpowers are involved.

"Busy day?"

"By human standards. For you, it's probably a cakewalk. But I'm going to have to do some juggling."

I stand as I push the chair away from the desk, then turn and lean back so that I'm half-sitting on it, my rear pressed against the edge. Damien's attention is entirely on my face, and there is such a look of hunger in his eyes that I have to smile. "Careful, or you'll be late for work."

"I find that's one of the perks of running my own company. There's no one to slap my hand when I break the rules."

I hear the thread of playfulness in his voice and match it. "Do you break the rules often, Mr. Stark?"

He lifts his hand, then brushes my hair away from my neck, so that his fingertips stroke my tender skin, tracing down along my collarbone. "As often as possible," he says.

I try very hard to continue breathing normally as his fingers drift lower, over the swell of my breast to linger on my nipple, now pebble-hard beneath the threadbare cotton of my favorite University of Texas T-shirt. He flicks it lightly, causing me to gasp. Causing a hell of a lot more than that, actually, as every nerve ending in my body suddenly seems to be connected to my breast by some sensual network that his touch has illuminated.

I say nothing, biting my lower lip against the instinct to cry out his name in demand and longing. He meets my eyes, his crinkling at the corners as his mouth curves up into a grin. He understands perfectly what I am not saying—what he is doing to me. He holds my gaze, his clever fingers traveling lower and lower until he slides his hand between my legs, cupping me intimately and making me moan. "What do you say?" he murmurs. "Want to break some rules with me?"

"Desperately," I admit.

He makes a low noise of approval, then eases closer, taking his hand away so that I can feel the length of his erection hard between my legs. He pulls me fully upright, his hands now cupping my rear as he grinds against me, a slow sensual movement like a sexy dance in a dimly lit nightclub.

I tilt my head back and he bends to press a kiss to the corner of my mouth, that simple contact as wildly erotic as the deepest kiss, the hardest fuck. And though the brush of his lips against my skin is feather soft, I feel the hard, demanding weight of it between my legs, and I press my hips tighter against his in silent, desperate demand.

He brushes his lips over my cheek to my ear, the sensation sending shivers of pleasure through me.

"I appreciate the sentiment, Mrs. Stark," he whispers. "But we'll have to wait to be naughty."

It takes a moment for my sex-fogged mind to process his words, and when I do, I turn my head to look at him, and see both heat and laughter on his face. I pull back, narrowing my eyes. "Will we?"

"The helicopter will be here soon. I have a meeting in San Diego at eight."

"You, Damien Stark, are a very cruel man."

"I can be." He steps back, fully breaking the contact between us and leaving me feeling soft and needy and very, very turned on. "But isn't it nice to know that your schedule is more flexible than you thought?"

I cock my head. "You're not off the hook, mister. There will be blowback."

"I look forward to your most creative punishment. Tonight, perhaps?" he says, and the eagerness in his voice makes me laugh out loud.

I'm about to tell him that he has no idea how creative I can be when my cellphone chirps in time with his. It's the automatic signal that is sent when someone uses a code to operate the gated entry to the property. Damien pulls his phone out of his pocket and glances at the screen. "Jamie."

"Really?" Jamie Archer is my best friend, and I have no problem with her popping by unexpectedly. I'm just not sure why she would, particularly this early. After all, she lives in Studio City, which is almost an hour away. More in morning rush hour, which in Los Angeles lasts from dawn until about lunch. Texting is more Jamie's speed, and so by the time she lets herself in the front door and is calling my name, my imagination has run wild with all sorts of horrible scenarios.

"What's wrong?" I call.

"Nothing. I've got news."

I glance at Damien, relieved. "Then meet me in the kitchen. I'll be right there."

The house actually has two kitchens, but I have never used the one on the first floor, which is huge and tricked out with so many amazing gadgets it would make Gordon Ramsay proud, not to mention easily serve up an intimate dinner party for two or three hundred.

I much prefer the normal-sized kitchen on the third floor. It was designed to be a space for caterers, as it is connected to the open area intended for entertaining. But it has become the kitchen that Damien and I use regularly.

From the mezzanine, I take the stairs that lead to an alcove near the kitchen. Damien and I arrive in the breakfast nook right as Jamie is helping herself to a cup of coffee.

"Okay," she says, "this is seriously awesome."

"The coffee?" I ask, and my best friend rolls her eyes.

"Gloria Myers. Do you remember me mentioning her?"

I scour my memory, but nothing comes to mind.

"She's the head of programming for the network affiliate in Dallas that offered me a job. You guys were on your honeymoon."

"Right," I say. "I remember." Jamie and I are both from Dallas. I came to LA to reinvent myself. She came to take the acting world by storm. It hadn't worked out quite the way she planned, however, and at one point Jamie had seriously considered returning to Texas to work as an on-air reporter while she got her shit together. She'd ended up staying, though, not in small part because her new boyfriend, Ryan Hunter, is doing a damn fine job of keeping her grounded.

"What about her?" Damien prompts.

"Gloria wants me to cover a tech convention in Vegas." Jamie bounces a little. "Just a couple of interviews, really. But it's a good break and a foot in the door. I told them months ago I wanted to be their West Coast correspondent, and I guess now they're taking me seriously."

"That's fabulous." I hurry over and give her a hug. "I'm so proud of you."

"It rocks, yeah. But the best part is that it's only a few hours of work tomorrow morning. If we go soon, we'll have two nights and almost two full days."

"We?" I repeat.

Damien is much quicker on the uptake. "So you came to whisk my wife away to Vegas? I don't know, Jamie. Sounds like a bad precedent to me." He is speaking in his corporate board-room voice, but I can hear the tease underneath.

"On the contrary," I say, "I think it's an excellent plan." I smile sweetly. "We can consider it your punishment."

"Oh, please," Jamie says. "Punishment? What? You two haven't heard of sexting?" She bats her eyes innocently. "That's what I intend to do with Ryan. It'll make the return home all the more delicious."

Damien puts on a mock scowl. "Is that why our corporate text rates are so high lately?" Not only is Ryan Jamie's boyfriend, he's also the chief of security for Stark International.

Jamie waves his words away. "Well?" she demands of me. "Are we on? If we leave now we'll hit Vegas early afternoon and have plenty of time to play. You should check out the convention, Nik. Mostly gamer related, but still right up your alley. And it's at the Starfire Resort and Casino," she adds with a meaningful look at Damien. The Starfire is a Stark International hotel. "Which means I figure you and I can snag one hell of a nice upgrade. So what do you say?" she asks me. "You can clear your schedule, right?"

I glance at Damien with a very smug grin. "Yeah," I tell Jamie. "As it turns out, I absolutely can."

Chapter 2

Despite Jamie's desire to hit the road immediately, it took us a few hours to actually get under way. For one thing, I had to shower and get dressed, which I did once I'd thoroughly kissed my husband goodbye and watched the helicopter whisk him off toward San Diego.

After that, I had to pack, which didn't take too much time

since we're staying only two nights. But the calls I had to make to reschedule an entire Friday's worth of appointments were another matter altogether. And while I sat at a shaded table by the pool with my phone and my laptop, trying to juggle my schedule with the schedule of everyone else involved, Jamie stripped down to bra and panties, then splayed out on a chaise lounge to work on her tan.

Honestly, it just didn't seem fair.

It was lunchtime when I finally got everything squared away, and we were able to pile into the limo. Damien had insisted that Edward drive us, and since the ride from Los Angeles to Vegas is infinitely more interesting in the back of a limo with alcohol, we hadn't been hard to convince.

Right as we got under way, we had Edward pull into Upper Crust, a charming local bakery and sandwich shop, where Jamie and I bought paninis for ourselves and Edward, then she and I settled in the back with our sandwiches, chips, and the well-stocked Stark International limo bar.

All of which goes a long way to explaining why, when we roll into Las Vegas at just shy of six in the evening, Jamie and I are just a teensy bit drunk. Not to mention very easily amused.

Which is why I burst into giggles when Jamie pulls out her phone, stares at the screen, and very plaintively asks me why there isn't even a smidgeon of sex in her inbox.

"Knowing you," I retort, "I find that very hard to believe."

"Okay, that's fair. If I scroll back I'm sure I can find some truly stellar sexts. But Ryan promised he'd send me something to keep him on my mind, and so far *pffft*. Nothing."

She flops back in the seat and pouts—or at least pretends to. I'm feeling a bit pouty myself, because I was certain that once Jamie planted the sexting seed in Damien's head he would jump all over that but my inbox is likewise sexless. Of course, sexting is like sloppy seconds compared to Damien's truly incredible phone sex skills. But that's not something I want to experience with Jamie in the limo with me. We're close. But we're not that close.

Truthfully, I'm not surprised that Damien hasn't checked in. His schedule was jam-packed today, what with zipping all over the West Coast. And right about now, I know he has a meeting with his assistant Sylvia. They have a conference call with a friend of Damien's at the Pentagon about buying Santa Cortez, a military-owned island off the California coast.

Most likely he's on that call right now, immersed in details and negotiations. It's really not the time for me to be bothering him.

Of course, I do anyway.

Just arrived in Sin City. Feeling deliciously sinful. Who knows where that will lead . . .

I hesitate only a second and then press send.
A moment later, my phone buzzes with a reply.

I'm intrigued. Take pictures.

I text back: *???*
I don't have to wait too long for his explanation.

If you're naughty without me, I want to know exactly what I'll be punishing you for later.

Oh.

I think of some of the very delicious ways that Damien might punish me and decide that a few selfies during this week-end jaunt will be well worth the trouble.

And no underwear. When I think of you, I want to think of you bare.

I lick my lips, my mouth suddenly dry. My soon-to-be-abandoned panties, however, are damp. I tap out a quick, *Yes, sir. Whatever you say, sir.*

Good girl. Meeting starting. Soon, Mrs. Stark. Until then, imagine me, touching you.

I smile, then tap my final reply: *I always do.*

When I look up, Jamie has her chin propped on her palm and is watching me.

"What?" I demand.

She just shakes her head. "You guys are so good together."

"Aren't you and Ryan?"

A wide grin lights her face. I'm girl-next-door pretty, with my blond hair and curves, but Jamie is movie star gorgeous. And when she smiles, it's a wonder that Hollywood producers don't drop from the skies and sign her to projects.

The smile she flashes now with Ryan on her mind is one of the most radiant I've ever seen. "Yeah," she says. "We are. Isn't that just the coolest thing?"

Considering Jamie's crappy track record with men, I have to agree that it is. And I am truly, genuinely happy for both of them.

"This is where we really got together," Jamie says, nodding out the window at the Starfire Resort and Casino, which we are approaching. "I mean, we fooled around in Malibu after your wedding, but it wasn't until Vegas that things really heated up." Her grin is wide and a little sappy. "So I really, really love this hotel."

"I'm very glad to hear it."

Although the Starfire is a Stark International property, I've only been a couple of times, and then on very short stays. The fact is, Damien owns so many properties in so many places that

I could visit one every day for the rest of my life and still probably not hit all of them.

It's a little daunting when I think about it. Which is why I usually don't think about it.

Edward turns off the Strip and into the drive, which circles a magnificent fountain that shoots jets of colored water into the sky to the delight of a crowd of people gathered around its edge.

We roll to a stop under the portico, and it's clear that although this limo has no identifying marks, the staff knows who we are. I'm treated like a queen, Jamie like a princess, and we are whisked through the lobby and down one of the long, tiled hallways to a set of elevators that access the penthouse suites.

Jamie and I are chatting as we walk, debating whether we want to go out for dinner or just have drinks in the bar and then go back up for room service. I pause, reaching out for Jamie's elbow.

"Did you see—?"

"What?"

But I shake my head, feeling silly. "Nothing. Just thought I saw someone I knew."

"Who?"

I shrug. "Probably no one." I hook my arm through Jamie's. "I say we go with shopping, then drinks, then grab some sushi." I point to a placard advertising a new Japanese restaurant that has just opened inside the hotel. "After that we can either crash in the room with a pay-per-view movie or go try our luck at the tables."

"Or we could find a club and go dancing?"

"You have to work tomorrow."

She makes a face. "True. Maybe tomorrow night."

I nod, though I'm secretly planning to veto that come tomorrow. I love to dance. But I love it most when I'm dancing with Damien.

We're in the owner's suite on the thirty-fifth floor, and the first thing we see when the bellman opens the double doors is the amazing view down the Strip through the wall of floor to ceiling windows. It's early March, so the sun has already set, and the lights of the city beyond the glass fill the room.

There is a huge kitchen, four bathrooms complete with Jacuzzi and steam shower, a living room, a media room, an exercise room, and two master bedrooms, each with their own private entrance.

The entire suite is more than twice the size of Jamie's condo, and despite having experienced the power of Damien's money many times over now, I have to admit I'm at least as wowed as my best friend.

I tip the bellman, who tells us to pick up the phone if we need anything at all, and when I turn back, I find Jamie in the middle of the huge living room, her arms out wide as she turns in a slow circle. She comes to a stop, meets my eyes, and then grins. "Can I just say how fucking awesome it is to have a best friend who's married to a bazillionaire?"

I match her grin with one of my own. "Funny, I was just about to say how awesome it is to actually be married to one."

Chapter 3

The bar closest to our bank of elevators is called Rain and has a water theme, including walls that feature streams of water running down them in what appears to be a permanent loop.

Jamie and I sit at the bar, which is made of a hollowed out

slab of marble filled with water and covered with glass. Goldfish swim in the water, back and forth in this makeshift river. It's whimsical and fun, though I have to wonder what the fish think about the whole thing.

"They love it," Jamie says. "I mean, they're goldfish. Usually the most they can aspire to is a bowl in some kid's bedroom. This is the big time for them."

I laugh and have to concede that she has a point. And then we both raise our glasses and toast the fish.

We've been down here for an hour, chatting and drinking and trying to firm up our plans for tomorrow.

"So shopping is definitely on?" Jamie asks. "I'm in the mood to do serious damage to my credit card. And you get some sort of discount here, right?"

"Only in the hotel stores. We go out into the mall, and you're on your own."

"Fair enough." She sips her martini. "After lunch, then? I have the first interview at ten and the next at eleven. And after that, I'm done."

"Are you ready?"

"Absolutely." She'd read over her prep material a little bit in the limo and then again before we came down here. "And I'll get up about six to give it another go-over. Don't worry. This isn't my first time playing a reporter."

"I just want you to rock it," I say. "This might lead to a full-time job, right?"

"Maybe. Gloria kind of hinted around. But I'm not going to get my hopes up. I'm just going to take my check for this gig and run. Straight to Michael Kors," she adds with a laugh.

I roll my eyes.

"You should come down with me tomorrow. Watch the interview. Or at the very least, scope out the trade show. It's mostly about games geared toward smartphone users."

"I'm tempted," I admit. "But I've pretty much decided that my goal for the weekend is to be as unproductive as humanly possible. So while you're slaving away, I'm going to be drinking mimosas by the pool."

"You bitch."

"And completely proud of it."

Jamie grins, then slides her hand into her purse. She stops mid-motion, then catches my eye, her expression sheepish.

I know exactly what she was doing—she was going to check her phone to see if she'd missed a call or text or email from Ryan.

I know, because I've done the same thing a half dozen times since we arrived at the hotel. And there hasn't been a single word from Damien.

"We're pathetic," I say. "Two fabulous, smart women out on our own, and we can't even go an hour without checking for a message from our significant others. Seriously, how girly and needy are we?"

"I'm not being girly and needy," she says firmly. "I just keep expecting him to ask me what I'm wearing under my clothes."

I raise a brow as I take another sip of my drink. "And what are you wearing?"

Her grin is slow and devious. "I'll never tell."

I laugh and we clink glasses. But I remain silent on my own relative state of undress. And, yes, I do feel naughty.

Which reminds me . . .

I reach into my purse and pull out my phone. "Not girly and needy," I tell Jamie, who is giving me The Look. "We need a selfie."

"Oh! Totally! With the drinks," she adds, which is easy for her to say. I end up leaning way back, holding the drink in my left hand and the camera in my right. Honestly, it would be easier to ask the bartender to take it, but Damien told me he wanted selfies, and for this particular game, I'm all about following the rules.

"Did you get us?" Jamie asks as I open up my photos.

"Hang on." It's a reasonable question. Photography is my hobby, but that doesn't translate to selfies. I tend to shift at the last second and mess them up completely. "Oh, check it out. This one's not too bad."

I pass her my phone, now open to the image of us, smiling and holding our glasses. Instead of shifting to the side, though, I apparently lifted my arm, because we don't fill the frame the way I had planned. Instead, we're in the bottom third, and the crowded tables in this popular bar are in the background. I figure that's even better, since it gives a sense of location.

"Nikki!" Jamie's voice is a low, startled whisper. "Did you look at this?"

"At what?"

"The picture. What's behind us."

"I—no." I frown. "What are you talking about?"

She slides the phone back to me. "Look."

I do—and then I turn toward her and grin.

"Don't turn around!" she says, as if I were planning to.

Of course, now that she has said that, the urge is powerful. Because now I know who's behind us. Now I know why neither of us have received any sexts.

Now I know that this weekend is going to be more interesting than I anticipated.

"I have to look," I admit.

"Yeah, me, too."

We both shift on our stools. And there, just sitting and talking as if they haven't got a care in the world, are Ryan and Damien.

They look up at the same time, and Damien's eyes meet mine. At first, his expression is flat. Corporate. Then his mouth curves up and his eyes darken, and I can see such promise of heat and pleasure that my stomach turns to butterflies and my mouth goes dry.

I expect him to say something. I expect him to come over.

I expect him to do anything but what he does next, which is turn his eyes away and continue talking to Ryan, as if I wasn't sitting right there at all.

I smile, suddenly understanding.

And this, I think, is going to be so much better than sexting.

Beside me, Jamie still isn't with the program. "Should we go sit with them?"

"No," I say with a grin. "That's not the game."

"The—*oh*."

Just as realization dawns, the bartender sets fresh drinks in front of us. "From the gentlemen," he says with a jerk of his chin, and we both turn to raise our glasses in a silent gesture of thanks. Damien, however, is the only one at the table.

I give him a little nod, then turn my back to him, hiding my grin.

Beside me, Jamie is about to lean toward me, presumably to ask where Ryan is. But that's when I see Ryan approaching her. He takes a seat on the open stool beside her, and I casually reach for my drink, then take a sip as I eavesdrop on my best friend.

"Haven't I seen you on television?" he says.

Jamie turns to him, her body language suggesting she gets this question all the time and is bored with it. "It's possible."

"I'm Ryan."

"I'm not the kind of girl who picks up strange men in hotel bars."

"No? I'm not a strange man."

"Too bad." Jamie's voice holds as much heat as a small nuclear reactor. "I like strange."

She slides off the stool. "You'll have to excuse me," she says politely. "I need to go to the ladies' room." She glances at me, her expression playful. "I'll be right back."

She walks away, and Ryan is left sitting alone at the bar.

"She's very particular about the men she dates," I say. "And she'll only fall for a truly spectacular guy."

Humor flashes in his eyes. "I'll keep that in mind." He inclines his head, then leaves. I take another sip of my drink and plan to tell Jamie that we really need to move on to food. Too many drinks and too little solid food is starting to mess with my head.

As I'm thinking about my increasing state of inebriation, someone moves up behind me. I know without turning that it is Damien, and when he asks, "Is this seat taken?" his low, familiar voice sends shivers through me.

"I suppose it is now," I say as he sits.

I turn to find him looking at me, his dark eyes burning with so much desire that it whips in fiery swirls all through me. I raise my glass, then take a sip. Frankly, I need it to cool down.

"I was hoping that drink would buy me an introduction."

I extend my hand. "Nikki Fairchild."

He takes it, and despite every way that he has touched me, this simple brush of palm against palm sends shock waves skittering all through me. "It's a pleasure, Ms. Fairchild."

I pull my hand away, feeling strangely unsettled. I want to play this game. And that means keeping my cool.

"Why did you want to buy an introduction?"

"I was hoping you'd have dinner with me."

"Were you?" I run my finger along the rim of my glass, my eyes never leaving his. "Why?"

He doesn't hesitate. "Because I was hoping you'd spend a few hours after dinner with me."

He reaches for the toothpick in my drink, then lifts it to his mouth, casually biting off the olive.

He has, I think, an absolutely perfect mouth.

"Ms. Fairchild?"

"I'm sorry," I say. "You have me at a disadvantage. Mr. . . . ?"

"Stark," he says. "Damien Stark." I like the way he says his name. He says it as though it belongs to me.

I put on one of my plastic smiles, the kind I practiced in my pageant days. "I've heard of you, Mr. Stark."

"Should I be flattered?"

"Tennis player. Entrepreneur. Womanizer?" I say the last as a question.

The corner of his mouth twitches. "Apparently I have quite the reputation."

He's put the toothpick on a napkin on the bar. Now I pick it up and brush it lightly over my lower lip, gratified when I see his gaze dip to my mouth. "Are you denying it?" I ask.

"Not at all. I've fucked a lot of women in my life, Ms. Fairchild."

"Oh." I lick my lips. "And do you want to fuck me, too?"

"Desperately. That, and so much more."

It takes a superhuman amount of effort, but I manage not to squirm. I am, however, hopelessly wet. And I'm quite sure that Damien knows it.

I draw a breath, gather myself, and look deep into those dual-colored eyes. "I'm not interested in being one of many, Mr. Stark."

"And any man who thought of you that way would be a fool. I'm not a fool, Ms. Fairchild." He takes my hand and presses light kisses against it, and it is as if coils of pleasure shoot straight from my fingertips all the way to my clit.

I can't help it, I actually moan. And when I do, I see victory dance in his eyes.

Bastard.

"About dinner," he says, trailing a fingertip lazily over my palm and driving me just a tiny bit crazy. "You still haven't answered."

I tug my hand away, then mourn the loss of contact.

"Sorry," I say. "I have plans with my friend."

His eyes narrow. "I don't believe you do." He nods, indicating something over my shoulder.

I turn, then see Jamie walking away from the bar with Ryan's arm around her waist. I stifle a laugh. Even when we're playing at seduction, Jamie is quick to jump into a man's bed. But what the hell. With Ryan at least, it's as safe as it gets.

I, however, am enjoying the chase too much to give in.

I reach into my purse and put a fifty dollar bill on the bar before sliding off my stool. "I barely know you, Mr. Stark, and it's been a long day. Thank you for the drink, but I think I'll just order room service."

I see genuine surprise on Damien's face, and as I turn to walk away, I don't even bother to hide my grin.

Yes, I think, this is going to be fun.

Chapter 4

I don't hurry to the elevator. Instead, I stroll past the hotel's stores, taking in the jewelry, the dresses, the designer handbags. I never turn around, but once or twice I see the reflection of Damien walking behind me, and I add a little swing to my step. I don't know what he has planned, but I do know it will be interesting.

When I finally reach the elevator bank, I turn into the elegantly appointed alcove, swipe my room key over the panel to call the elevator for the top floors, and then step on as soon as the car arrives. I press the button for my floor, then move back, waiting for the inevitable rise.

The doors are just about to close when Damien appears. He thrusts his arm through the gap to stop the doors, and then slides his whole body inside the car with me.

A car that suddenly seems much smaller than it is.

"Ms. Fairchild," he says, stepping toward me so that I am forced to either move backward into the corner or give up my personal space.

Damien's wife wouldn't move.

Nikki Fairchild—who is still being seduced—does.

His smile is slow, and suggests that he knows exactly what I'm thinking. He leans toward me, then reaches out to press his palm against the polished metal paneling just over my shoulder. "I'm not sure you understand the kind of man I am," he says. "I don't like hearing no."

I lift a brow. "In that case, I hope you're the kind of man who can handle disappointment. Because I'm not a woman who says yes easily." The elevator slides to a stop on the thirty-fifth floor, and I ease past him.

"I do love a challenge," he says as I step from the car and into the hallway.

I turn back, looking at him before the doors close and block the view. He looks magnificent in a tailored gray suit and an ice-blue tie. He looks like a man in control. A man who takes what he wants. And seeing him like that makes me feel a burst of feminine power that fuels both my desire for the man—and for this game.

"I'm glad," I say as the doors start to close. "Because you definitely have your work cut out for you."

I'm not certain, but I think I see him smile before the doors block my view.

In the suite, I head first to Jamie's room, but she has tied a red ribbon on the doorknob, and I have to laugh—it's our old symbol for Man in the Room. And while I'm a little jealous that Jamie has her boyfriend in her bed tonight, I'm not jealous enough to call Damien and end this.

I'm too curious to see how it plays out.

Since I'm alone, I decide to watch a movie in bed instead of in the living room, and I'm scrolling through a selection of truly uninteresting choices when my phone rings.

I glance at it, but it's not a number I recognize, and I'm really not in the mood to chat with a telemarketer.

I let it go to voicemail.

A moment later, a text flashes on my screen from that same number:

Answer your phone—D

I lick my lips and snuggle back against the pillows. Well, okay, then.

I wait. And then I wait a little longer.

And then—just when I've decided that he's intentionally tormenting me—my phone rings again.

"Mr. Stark," I say. "How did you get this number?"

"I have a knack for getting the things I want, Ms. Fairchild." The words are simple, but they are spoken in such a low, sensual tone that their effect on me is anything but. Quite the contrary, actually, and I close my eyes and just let the pleasure of his voice curl through me.

"Do you?" I ask, then lick my lips. "What is it you want?"

"I think we already covered that, Ms. Fairchild. What was it you said I wanted?"

I lick my lips, surprised that I find myself a little bit shy. This is Damien, after all.

Not now, though. Not tonight.

Right. I draw in a breath. "You said you want to fuck me."

"Very good. What else?"

"And so much more," I say dutifully.

His low chuckle rumbles through me. "Someone was paying attention."

"It was a very intriguing conversation," I admit. "So what is the so much more?"

"Where to begin? I want to touch you," he says. "Run my fingers over every inch of you, and then do the same with my tongue. I want to suck on your nipples until they're almost too sensitive to be touched, and then I want to do the same to your clit while I hold you fast in place. You'll want to squirm, to move, but you'll be trapped, a slave to every manner of pleasure that I can imagine, and all of it aimed at my ultimate goal of making you come."

I bite back a moan as I squirm on the bed, every inch of my skin on fire from his words.

He pauses, and the silence brings a sense of loss as potent as if he had taken his hand from my body. I don't admit that, though. Right now, I'm not ready to admit anything. Instead, I feign nonchalance. "Oh," I say, "is that all?"

He bursts out laughing. "Oh, no, Ms. Fairchild. I'm not buying it at all."

"Buying what?"

But all he says is "Mmm."

I shift on the bed, wanting his voice again. Just wanting more. "Mr. Stark?"

"I'm here. What are you wearing?"

"The same thing I was in the bar. A skirt. A blouse."

"Are you wearing a bra?"

"Yes."

"Underwear?"

I lick my lips. "No."

"No? How very naughty of you, Ms. Fairchild."

"Maybe I like to be naughty."

He makes a rough sound in the back of his throat. "Do you? I'll have to keep that in mind."

I hold the phone tighter, wondering just what that will entail.

"How naughty would you like to be tonight?" he asks.

"I don't know."

"There are rules," he says, reminding me of our first night when he sent me home in a limo with a cellphone. "And the first one is that you don't lie to me. Do you understand?"

I hesitate just a beat. "Yes," I say. And then because I do know some of the rules of this game, I add, "Yes, sir."

I can almost hear the smile of approval in his next words. "Now, answer the question. How naughty do you want to be tonight?"

"Very," I say. And then, because I'm feeling bold, "I want to get you hard."

"Baby, I'm already there. Put the phone on speaker and set it beside you. I want you to have both your hands free. Have you done it?"

"Yes," I say, glancing to where I've placed the phone just below the pillow.

"Now unbutton your shirt, just let it lay open on your skin. Are you doing it?"

"Yes."

"Good girl. Now I want you to stroke your exposed skin. Slowly, up and down, from your waist to your breasts. Gently," he clarifies. "Just let your nails trail over your skin."

The sensation is incredible, and I close my eyes and enjoy this sweet caress.

"How does it feel?"

"Amazing," I say. "Like it should tickle, but it doesn't. Like I'm coming alive."

"Tell me where you feel it." His voice is husky, raw with need.

"Everywhere."

"Are your nipples hard? Straining against your bra?"

"Yes."

"Is your cunt wet? Are you throbbing, wanting to be touched? To be fucked?"

I don't answer. I can only manage a whimper.

"Tell me, baby."

"Yes. God, yes."

"Pull the cups down on your bra. I want your nipples free. Then tease them with your fingernails, too. Just the same, very lightly."

I do, and I feel the pathways of pleasure opening up all through me.

"Now harder. Pinch yourself. Imagine it's my mouth on your breast. My tongue teasing you. My teeth scraping, biting."

It is all I can do not to cry out from the pleasure.

"You like that." It's a statement, not a question, but I still admit what he already knows.

"Very much."

"Suck on your finger. Harder, baby. Use your tongue. Imagine it's my cock. Christ, baby, I'm so hard."

I groan, but I don't stop sucking, and I can feel the pull all the way through me, all the way to where my muscles clench in demand, needing to be filled, to be fucked.

I imagine Damien touching me, stroking me. I imagine him filling me, and when his voice comes on the line again, a tremor of pleasure cuts through me, a tiny hint of the explosion to come.

"Draw your finger over your nipple next," he says. "Get it wet. Are you doing it?"

"Yes." The sensation is intense. Every inch of me is an erogenous zone, but my nipples are so sensitive I think I would come if Damien closed his mouth over my breast and sucked.

"Good girl. Now tilt your head down and blow lightly across your breast."

I hesitate, but then comply. And *ohmygod*.

I arch up, the unexpected sensation wreaking havoc with my already heightened senses, setting my body on fire, making me gasp with longing and need.

"I think the lady liked that," he says, when I stop saying, "Oh fuck, oh wow."

"Yes," I agree. "The lady liked that a lot."

"I want to see you," he says. "I want to see how wet you are. How flushed your skin is."

"Do you want to come to my room?"

He is quiet for just a little too long. Then he says, "So much I can't even tell you. But not tonight. Tonight, I want you to do something for me."

"What?"

"Stand up," he says, and since that's easy enough, I comply. "Now take your skirt off."

I reach behind me and find the zipper. I pull it down, then ease the skirt over my hips until it drops to the ground.

"Are you still wearing the shirt? Is it unbuttoned?"

"Yes."

"And your bra? It's still on with your breasts exposed?"

I nod. Then find my voice. "Yes, sir."

"Go to the window. Take the phone."

I do as he says, then stand there, half-naked, looking probably like some girl in a window in a red-light district. Only I'm thirty-five floors up and there's no one out there to see me.

"Send me a picture," he says, "just like that. Your breasts exposed. Your hand on your cunt."

I think I make a mewling sound.

"I want you in front of the window. I want to see the city spread out behind you."

"I—"

I close my mouth, unsure of what to say.

I want to do this, but at the same time I want to protest. I know it's a game, but at the same time . . .

"Come on, Ms. Fairchild." His voice, low and enticing, envelops me. "Don't you want to be naughty?"

Chapter 5

Do I? Do I want to be naughty?

I consider Damien's question, my body tightening with the thought of what he is asking me.

And the truth is that yeah, I do.

I love Damien, and I love being married to him. But this—this extra tinge of excitement—it fills me up and makes me float. It's shiny and new and tantalizing.

And while I would never go there without Damien, if he is holding my hand and keeping me safe, then well . . .

"Nikki?"

I close my eyes, smiling just a little. We are still playing the game; I know that. But this is the first time he has said my name, and I understand what that means. That he will always keep me safe. That he will never push me too far.

"Yes, Mr. Stark," I whisper. "I want to be naughty."

I stand as he told me, then use my free hand to hold the phone. I draw a breath, smile just a little, and snap the kind of naughty selfie that I never in a million years would have believed I had it in me to do.

I find it, then message it to Damien, being very, very careful to send it to the right recipient.

"Did you get it?" I ask, and then realize I'm holding my breath until I hear his, "Oh, holy Christ, yes."

My smile blooms. "I guess that means you like it."

"Fuck, yeah."

"Mr. Stark?"

"Yes, baby?"

I lick my lips, fighting shyness. "Are you looking at it now?"

"Oh, yes."

"Are you hard?"

I can almost hear his smile in the silence.

"What do you think?" he finally says.

"I think you are," I say, feeling emboldened. "Are you stroking yourself?" I press. "Are you pretending it's me? Are you getting off?"

"Christ, baby, you're damn sure tempting me. But no. I'm not coming until I'm deep inside you. And you don't touch yourself, either, until I tell you to. Are we clear?"

And just like that he has turned it back around. Taken what little power I'd grabbed and claimed it again with both hands.

Honestly, I can't say that I mind.

"Ms. Fairchild? Are we clear?"

"Yes." I have to force the word out past walls of arousal. "Yes, sir."

"Tell me you want to be fucked."

My cunt clenches in response to his words, and I make a low, needy sound.

"Please, Mr. Stark. I want to be fucked."

"Soon, baby. But tonight, I'm going to make you explode."

"Yes," I say, because right now that sounds pretty close to heaven. "Yes, please."

"Take the shirt off," he says. "And the bra. I want you naked."

I do as he says, and find myself standing naked in my bedroom, my body illuminated by the lights of the Las Vegas Strip, as I wait for my husband—my lover—to tell me what to do next.

"Tell me what you packed."

I bite my lip. "Packed?"

His low laugh rumbles through me. "I'm wondering what you tucked into your suitcase that we might find of use right now."

"Oh." I feel my cheeks heat and am slightly disconcerted. Which is ridiculous. Under the circumstances, the fact that I packed a vibrator is hardly going to rock Damien's universe.

"Tell me." And though his voice is demanding, I hear the undercurrent of amusement. "I like a woman who takes charge of her own pleasure," he adds, the words rescuing me from my slow slide into mortification.

"A vibrator," I mutter. "A bullet. It was a gift." I don't say that it was a bachelorette gift. He already knows that part very well. After all, we've played with this toy before.

"Interesting," he says. "Go get it. Then get on the bed."

I do, and I realize when I lie down that my heart is pounding so hard in anticipation that I can actually feel the bed pulse with each beat.

"Spread your legs, baby. I want you wide open. I'm right there with you, and I want to be able to kiss my way up your thighs. I want to be able to see how wet you are."

I close my eyes, imagining just that. His lips on my skin, his breath teasing my clit.

I shiver, and realize that I am very, very close.

"Turn on the vibrator now," he orders, and though I comply, I want to protest. Because as soon as he tells me to go anywhere near my clit with this vibrating bullet, I am going to come completely undone. And I'm not ready for that. I want this sensation to last.

But this is Damien's show, and so I say nothing.

And when he tells me to brush the vibrator lightly over my

nipple, I know that I should have trusted him to understand me. To know how to play me.

I do as he asks, and the feeling is incredible.

"Tell me," he says.

"I don't know how," I admit. "I—I've never done this. It's kind of amazing." My nipples are so damn sensitive that the sensation from the vibrator is sending shock waves through me, leaving my body trembling on the edge, but not going over. "It's like being suspended. Just waiting for the push."

"Do you want to go over?"

"Yes. No. I don't know."

He laughs. "Sounds like you want everything."

"Yes," I murmur as my body turns to molten lava. "Yes, please."

"Trail your fingers down, and tease your clit, baby. I want to hear you breathing. I want to feel you getting close. Tell me you're wet," he says when I gasp from that first stroke of my fingers over my slick flesh.

"I'm wet. I'm so very wet."

I let the vibrator fall, and it buzzes uselessly on the mattress beside me. I no longer care. Everything in my world is between my legs at this moment. My fingers. Damien's voice. And this wild, incredible rising passion that is threatening to consume me.

"That's me touching you, baby. My fingers stroking you, my breath teasing you. You taste so good. Can you feel my tongue sliding over you?"

I try to say yes, but the sound comes out garbled.

"Come on," he says. "I can hear your breath. I can hear your excitement. Tell me you want to come."

"I do," I say. "Oh, yes, please."

"Just a little more. Find that one spot, baby, and tease it. You're almost there."

It is intoxicating, this marriage of fantasy and reality, of being with the man who knows my body so well, while hearing the words of a new lover whispered in my ear. It's making me rise. Taking me higher. Leading me right to the edge.

And then, when Damien whispers, "Come for me now," I burst wide open and everything inside me spills out into the night until I am hollow and exhausted, ripped to shreds, and utterly and completely satisfied.

I float, just float for a while. And then, finally, I drift back down to earth.

"Oh, god, Damien," I say when I can find words again. Honestly, those are the only three words I can find.

"Good night, Ms. Fairchild." His voice is soft, and although that is all that he says, what I hear is, "I love you."

Chapter 6

Because spring has come early and it is unseasonably warm for March, I decide to spend the morning eating breakfast and reading the paper by the pool. I bypass the cabana that is reserved for the use of my suite—I'm not interested in being tucked away behind drapes—and pick one of the lounge chairs near the waterfall.

The area around the pool is beautifully landscaped with native plants and tropical flowers transplanted to make the area look lush. There are only a few of us out here this early, and I smile as I pass an elderly man in a golfing shirt reading a Harlan Coben novel and drinking a Bloody Mary.

I'm about to sit down when I see a flash of dark hair rounding the corner near one of the changing rooms. A woman. And though I do not recognize her, I am once again struck by the feeling of having seen someone familiar.

I consider getting up and following her, but I didn't see enough to be sure and, truly, if it's someone I know then I'll leave it to them to come say hi.

Once I'm settled, I peel off my T-shirt to reveal the bikini top I'd worn in the hope that the weather would feel just this nice.

I keep my skirt on, though. Not only is it not quite warm enough to strip all the way down to a bathing suit, but I don't do bikini bottoms in public. With Damien, I am no longer self-conscious about the scars that mar my hips and inner thighs. But that doesn't mean I want to invite the entire world to take a peek.

I pull today's *Los Angeles Times* out of my tote bag and set it on the table next to me. Then I wave my hand to signal a nearby waiter, who hurries over.

He looks to be a few years younger than me, and I guess that he's working his way through college. I order a bagel with cream cheese, coffee, and orange juice, then put my sunglasses on and tilt my head back, enjoying the feel of the still-rising sun against my skin.

I don't intend to doze, but I didn't get much sleep last night, and my eyelids are heavy, especially under the weight of the sun. I let myself drift, and suddenly it's not just the sun that is heating my skin. It's the memory of Damien's words in my ear last night.

For a brief moment, I regret not simply dining on the balcony that opens off my bedroom, because the temptation to slide my hands between my legs is very, very strong. I don't, however, want to give my nearby golfer a hard-on. Or, god forbid, a heart attack.

I hear the waiter's return and ask if he could bring me a glass of ice water.

"A little warm, Ms. Fairchild? From looking at you, I would have thought you were slightly chilled."

I open my eyes to find Damien smiling down at me. At my breasts, actually, and my rock hard nipples, very evident under my bikini top.

"You're staring."

"I'm enjoying the view." He takes a seat on the lounge chair beside me. "Thinking about last night?"

"Every delicious minute," I admit, and then swallow a smile of satisfaction when I see his eyes heat with my unexpected answer.

"And you?" I ask. "What are you doing this morning? Besides staring, I mean?"

"Staring, Ms. Fairchild?" His eyes flick up to my face, and then he draws his gaze down my body, moving so slowly and with such purpose that my skin tingles in the wake of his inspection, as if he is trailing a fingertip down the entire length of my body.

"Staring?" he repeats. "No, I'm studying. And planning."

"Planning?" I repeat. "Now I'm very intrigued. Do tell."

"Oh, just analyzing various strategies. How I'm going to touch you. What I'll do to take you to the absolute heights of exquisite pleasure. To get you close but not let you go over, so that you are reduced to whimpering in my arms and begging me for release." He looks at me blandly. "Things like that."

My mouth has gone dry, and all my blood has pooled between my thighs. But even so, I manage to latch onto one key point. "In your arms, Mr. Stark?"

"Noticed that, did you?"

"I'm a very good listener."

"I hoped that you would do me the honor of joining me for dinner."

I tilt my head, considering. Tonight is our last night. If I want to take this flirtation to the next level, it really is now or never. And, yeah, I want to see what he has planned.

"Are you going to behave?"

"That's highly doubtful."

I laugh, because that is absolutely the perfect answer. "In that case, Mr. Stark, I'd love to have dinner with you."

"How did it go?" I ask Jamie as we walk through the casino toward the hotel's main shopping area.

"I think it went great. Gloria said she'd call me about more interviews, so . . ."

She trails off and I pull her into a hug. "Jamie, that's awesome."

"Potentially awesome," she corrects, but she's grinning happily.

All around us, men and women are seated at blackjack and roulette tables or standing around the craps table. Dozens of them are playing slot machines, and the din is brutal. For that matter, so is the smoke that fills the air.

It's not even lunchtime, and yet this area is buzzing as if it were late at night. I suppose that's the idea of Vegas, but my idea of decadent runs in a more private direction, and I smile to myself as I look forward to dinner tonight with Damien and every wicked thing that will come after.

We walk a bit more before I pause and glance around. We've reached an intersection, and I'm trying to figure out which way to go. As far as I can tell, the basic design of pretty much any casino is to not provide an easy exit. That way, once someone is in, they have no choice but to stay and gamble.

"Starfire Promenade?" Jamie asks, pointing toward a sign that directs us to the left.

"That's it," I say. "Let's go."

We reach freedom in another five minutes, and emerge from the casino's relative dark to the well-lit sparkle of this high-end shopping promenade. It takes up three levels and every designer imaginable seems to have a storefront here, along with a variety of boutiques, restaurants, and even small galleries.

"What are you shopping for?" I ask.

She glances sideways at me. "You're not shopping?"

I think of my closet back home, which is about the size of my college apartment and completely stuffed with the clothes and jewelry that Damien is always buying me. Sometimes I think he won't be satisfied until I own at least one of everything.

"I might look for a present for Damien," I say. "Then again, in this weekend's reality, I don't have a Damien in my life."

"You're still playing?"

"Sure," I say. "It's fun. I take it you and Ryan aren't?"

Jamie lifts a shoulder. "Playing, sure. Pretending we picked each other up at a bar? Not anymore. Pretending other things . . ." Her voice trails off with a hint of a naughty lilt. "Well, a lady never kisses and tells. Or fucks and tells. Or blindfolds and tells. Or—"

"Jamie!" I slap my hands over my ears, laughing. "Stop. Please, stop."

She shrugs good-naturedly. "Hey, you asked."

I'm pretty sure I didn't, but I don't press the point.

"There," she says, pointing to a display of embroidered jeans in the window of one of the fancy boutiques on the other side of this wide walkway. "Let's check it out."

"Sure," I say and follow her. As we're about to go in, a dark-haired woman rushes past us as she hurries to catch up with friends. Seeing her reminds me, and I turn back to Jamie. "I had that feeling again," I say. "When I was by the pool this morning."

"What? Someone you know?"

"I have no idea, but yeah. It's a little disconcerting."

"It's probably nothing," Jamie says. "Or if you really are seeing someone familiar, they're probably just snapping pictures of you for Twitter. The price you pay for being married to a god of the universe."

I scowl, but have to concede she has a point. Since marrying Damien, I'm regularly all over social media.

"Listen, go on in," I say, pointing toward the store. "I want to look next door." The jewelry store window has a display of emerald and diamond jewelry, and I would love to find earrings to match the stunning anklet that Damien gave me when we first got together.

"I buy denim, you buy diamonds," she trills. "That pretty much sums up the differences in our lives these days."

I just laugh. "Oh, those aren't the only differences." I start to count on my fingers. "Beach house. Limo. Private jet. And don't forget the chocolate company in Switzerland."

"Well, now you're just being mean." She hip butts me. "Catch you in a few."

I grin, watching her go, then head into the store. It's larger than it looks from the outside and surprisingly crowded. A uniformed security guard stands at the door looking bored.

Glass shelving lines the walls full of pricey decorator items like handblown glass vases and porcelain statuary. The center of the space is made up of glass display cases arranged in a horseshoe, and the customers walk around the U-shape to scope out both the items on the shelves and those in the cabinets. Some are filled with brand-new pieces, others display estate jewelry. I find antique emerald and diamond drop earrings set in platinum and a matching bracelet that are almost exactly what I have in mind.

"They're stunning quality," the man behind the counter says. His nametag identifies him as Frederick Pyle.

"I'm looking for something to match this," I say, bending to remove my anklet. As I do, I see her again. My dark-haired shadow. And this time I am absolutely, one-hundred-percent sure that I know her. She has wavy hair that reaches her shoulders and a round face with prominent cheekbones. She's petite, and looks even smaller because she keeps herself hunched over, as if she is trying to hide from the world.

She's browsing the glass shelves, and I turn back to Mr. Pyle, both because he has brought out the pieces for me to look at, and also because I don't want to catch her eye while I'm still trying to remember her name.

Where do I know her from?

I try not to think too hard, because that is a surefire way to ensure that I don't remember. Instead, I put the anklet next to the bracelet. They are not a perfect match, but the settings complement each other beautifully. And, most important, I like them. "I'll take them," I say. And because I'm Mrs. Damien Stark and I never, ever do this, despite Damien telling me to buy whatever I want, whenever I want, I don't even ask the price. Instead, I just tell him to charge it to my room. Then I tell him my name, show him my ID, and fight not to smile when his already polite and deferential attitude ratchets up about a thousandfold.

"Of course, Mrs. Stark. Would you like to wait? Or shall I deliver the pieces to your suite after we've cleaned and packaged them?"

"I'd love to wear them," I admit. "How long?"

"Ten minutes. If you'd like to have a seat?" He points to a silk-upholstered divan at the back of the store. "Some wine?"

"I'll just browse," I say. "Thanks."

I stroll around the store, peeking into the glass cases, checking out all of the lovely, sparkly items. But my attention is only half there. Mostly I am racking my brain, trying to remember that woman's name. I'm trying very hard not to stare, too, which is good, as she keeps turning side to side, her eyes darting all over the place as if she is nervous.

Soon enough, I realize why.

She takes one of the handblown glass vases, and slides it surreptitiously into her purse.

Then she straightens her shoulders, browses the shelves for a few more minutes, and heads for the entrance. She's almost through, when the security guard steps in front of her.

"Excuse me, miss," he says. "I'm going to have to ask you to open your purse."

"Pardon?" Her voice rises, and even from across the store I can hear her panic. "Oh, golly," she adds, and in that moment, I know exactly who she is. Marcy Kendall from Dallas, Texas. One of the few girls in high school that Jamie and I genuinely liked. One of the few who was nice to me and didn't think I was stuck-up and bitchy just because I entered pageants. Somehow, she saw through all the bullshit and realized that my reserve wasn't bitchiness, and that the pageants were torture.

We'd never been close, but I'd liked her. And she'd been like a mirror on the world. A reminder that there were people who would see the real you, even when you tried to hide away.

I have no idea why Marcy Kendall is shoplifting a glass vase, but I'm determined to find out. First, though, I'm going to help her.

"Marcy!" I call, and then watch as she jumps almost a foot. She turns in my direction, and her eyes go wide.

"What—"

But I interrupt before she can say something stupid. "Where'd you put the glass vase? Did you give it to Mr. Pyle? Because I haven't paid for it yet."

For a second, her face is so awash in confusion that I am absolutely certain the guard is going to swoop down and arrest us both. But then it clears and the confusion shifts to such a profound gratitude that any doubts I may have had about helping her are firmly swept away.

"Oh," she says. "I thought you already had. I'm sorry." She laughs. "I told you that having mimosas at breakfast was a bad idea. I'm such a dope when I've been drinking." She smiles up at the guard, then pulls the vase out of her bag. "Sorry. Guess it looked like I was stealing it."

She starts to walk back toward me, and I think that all is well. But then the guard says, "Just one minute, miss," and he plucks the vase right out of her hand. He points to me. "And I'd like to speak to you, too, miss."

"Me? But I—"

I cut myself off. What the hell should I say?

Fortunately, Mr. Pyle chooses that moment to return. "Here you go, Mrs. Stark," and though I know he is using his outdoor voice so that he can share with the world—or at least these customers—that the fabulously rich Damien Stark's wife actually shopped in his store, right then all I can think is that his well-projected voice has reached the security guard. And that is a good thing.

The guard's mouth closes, and he hands the vase back to Marcy. "Sorry for the misunderstanding."

"Of course. My fault. Truly."

I look at Mr. Pyle. "Could you add that vase to my bill?" I smile sweetly. "She doesn't need it wrapped."

I take my package and hurry after Marcy, hoping that she won't run off in the time it takes me to get outside.

She hasn't.

I find her waiting for me on a bench across from the entrance to the store with Jamie's jeans.

She looks up as I approach, her smile tremulous. "Thanks," she says. "You really saved me."

I take a seat beside her. "What's going on, Marcy? Why were you stealing a vase?"

She lifts her chin. "Oh, I wasn't," she says, but I barely hear her words. She's done a decent job covering them, but in this lighting, I can see the bruises beneath her makeup. And now that I know what to look for, I see them not just on her cheek and neck, but also on her upper arm and wrist.

I keep my face impassive. I don't want her to know that I understand. Because I don't want her to bolt.

"I meant what I said about drinking in the morning," she is saying lightly. "I just grabbed it and walked out. Stupid. I would totally have paid."

I don't believe her, of course.

But I am determined to help her.

Chapter 7

I'm sitting with Marcy on a bench when Jamie bops out of the clothing store swinging a shopping bag.

She sees us, and her jaw drops open. "Marcy? Marcy Kendall?"

Marcy's smile is thin, but sincere. "Hey, Jamie. It's good to see you again."

Jamie looks between the two of us. "What's going on?"

"I bumped into Marcy in the jewelry store," I say. "She's my gremlin."

Marcy's brow furrows. "What?"

"I've seen you twice," I say. "Out of the corner of my eye. Yesterday in the lobby. This morning at the pool. It's been driving me crazy because I couldn't place you."

"Oh. And here I thought I was doing a good job just blending into the background."

I study her. Hunched over, hands clasped. Cuticles picked to ruins. Yeah, she looks like she wants to fade away.

I glance at Jamie, and I see the concern blooming on her face, too. I don't know if she's seen the poorly hidden bruises, but I imagine she has. Jamie's a makeup guru; that's the kind of thing she'd notice right away.

"So why are you in Vegas?" Jamie asks.

"Oh, I came with my boyfriend. Um, Jay. Jay Monroe. He's working one of the trade show booths."

"Is he a game designer?" I ask, and Marcy shakes her head.

"No. Just, you know, clerical, sales, that kind of thing. His boss brought him down, and I came along." She licks her lips. "He doesn't like when I stay at home. He gets jealous. That's another thing we're here for," she says brightly, though the sunshine in her tone isn't reflected in her eyes. "He wants us to get married. You know, a Vegas wedding. Maybe even one of those drive-through chapels."

Her smile, I think, is about the saddest thing I've ever seen.

"Where's home, Marcy?"

"Oh, Riverside, California, you know? But I miss Texas." Tears glint in her eyes. "I miss my mom a lot."

"Listen, we were going to grab some lunch. Want to come?"

"I'd love it," she says, and I can tell that the enthusiasm is genuine. "But I'm supposed to meet Jay for lunch. He only gets the one break today."

Jamie catches my eye, and I know she's thinking the same thing that I am—this girl would be *way* better off having lunch with us and blowing Jay off.

But right now, that's not something we can say to Marcy.

"What about dinner?" I suggest, though the thought of canceling on Damien makes me sad. Still, the thought of not helping Marcy makes me even sadder. And I would hate myself if I sent her back to her boyfriend without knowing exactly how she got those bruises—and how I can help this girl who was so nice to me in school.

"Oh," she says. "Um, that would be nice. But we're supposed to have dinner tonight after he finishes at seven."

"Maybe he could join us," I say. "It would be fun to meet your fiancé."

"Um. Sure. I guess."

I'm about to lock her into that plan, when I hear a man's voice bellowing, *"Marcy!"* down the promenade. The sound arrives first, but the man storms up immediately after. He's a big guy, solid muscle. The kind of man who looks good in his youth, then starts to fall apart. I predict jowls in just a few years.

"Jesus H. Christ, Marcy, what the fuck are you doing? I've only got forty-five minutes for lunch. What the hell part of 'at the beginning of the shopping area' didn't you understand?"

I glance down the promenade. We're only four storefronts from the beginning.

"I'm sorry, Jay. I'm really sorry."

I'm not sure how it's possible, but she seems even smaller.

"It's just that I bumped into friends from Texas."

"Hey," he says, barely looking at Jamie and me. He grabs her arm. "Let's go."

"We were hoping you could join us for dinner," I blurt. "You and Marcy with my husband and me."

He blinks at me. "We got plans."

"That's a shame. I just figured with you in tech sales we could maybe mix business with pleasure."

His eyes narrow. "You here for the trade show?"

"No, but my husband owns the hotel. He has a lot of business interests. And I do a lot of app work myself." I extend my hand, though I'm loath to touch him. "Nikki Stark," I say. "My husband is Damien Stark."

As I had hoped, the name works on Jay like a magic potion. He practically has dollar signs in his eyes.

"Oh, yeah. We'd love it, wouldn't we, Marce?"

"Sure," she says dutifully.

"That's great," I say. "Marcy's coming with me and Jamie to the spa at three, so we'll work out the time and place then."

Marcy's eyes go wide, and Jay doesn't look too happy. "Spa?"

"She mentioned you're working the trade show today," Jamie says. "We don't want her to be stuck all alone. It'll be fun. A girls' pampering session before y'all do the wedding thing. Congratulations, by the way."

"Thanks." He glances at Marcy. She smiles at him. Fortunately, she looks neither confused nor freaked out. "We should go to lunch," he says.

"Three o'clock," I say again. "At the reception counter for the spa. It's on the second floor, the other side of the atrium from the restaurant."

"Okay," Marcy says softly. She shifts her purse so that she is holding it against her chest. "I'll be there," she adds, and I understand what she hasn't said out loud—that she's coming because she feels like she owes me.

Which means that if I want to keep her listening to me after she arrives, I need to figure out pretty quickly what I want to say.

As soon as they've disappeared down the walkway, Jamie turns to me. "What the fuck?"

"She stole a vase," I say, then I tell her the whole sordid story. "You saw the bruises?"

Jamie frowns, her expression turning dark. "I saw. Guy's a prick." She drags her fingers through her hair. "I always really liked Marcy. What should we do?"

"Talk to her," I say. I draw a deep breath. "Talk, and hope she tells us the truth. Then maybe we can help her."

"You think she's actually going to show up at three?"

"I hope so," I say. "Because if not, we'll have to cancel our appointment to track her down. And I really want a massage and a manicure."

Despite the fact that I totally do want a manicure, I decide to ditch the mani-pedi experience in favor of Mission Marcy.

Jamie and I both want to get Marcy talking, and I just don't expect that to happen if we're in front of three strangers working on our hands and feet.

Instead, we opt for massages to loosen us up, and then plan to spend the next two hours in the relaxation room before moving on to the salon for pre-dinner blowouts and makeup.

"I've never had a massage before," Marcy admits after stage one of our spa adventure is complete. "That was really awesome. The thing with the rocks was kind of weird, though."

"I thought so the first time I had one, too," I admit.

Since Marcy was resorting to stealing vases, I figured spas weren't a common feature in her daily life and decided to splurge and get all of us ninety-minute Starfire signature massages, which incorporate hot stones. I think they're awesome—the stones heat up your back and make you that much looser—but being layered in rocks can be a rather odd experience.

Now we are all three wonderfully relaxed and kicked back in the steam room in the spa's women's changing room.

My plan is to steam for a while, then go relax with a glass of wine and some gossip. And more wine, if necessary.

"So how did you and Jay meet?" I ask.

"It was very sweet," she says, and for the first time she actually sounds as if she liked the guy once. "We met in a coffee bar and I'd lost my wallet. He bought me a latte, then helped me get home. Turned out my wallet was in my purse the whole time."

She lifts a shoulder. "That's why he thinks I'm so scattered all the time. First impressions." She rubs her hands over her face and then up, pushing her steam-slicked hair back. "Anyway, he did the full-court seduction press. Flowers. Sweet texts. Little presents. It was so nice. I felt really special. Like I was in a fairy tale."

"What changed?" I ask the question softly, and Marcy just keeps on talking. She doesn't even blink.

"I don't know. It was subtle. Slow. First he just wanted to

stay in and not go out with friends. And I thought that was because we were all cozy and new. And then he didn't want me to go out even if he was busy. He said my friends were catty and gossiped too much. But they don't, really. We just talk, you know, the way you do. And then he got mad when I burned a roast. And after that—"

She cuts herself off as if suddenly realizing what she is saying. What she is admitting to me.

"After that he started to hit you?" I ask. My voice is as gentle as if I were dealing with a scared puppy.

Marcy nods. "I—I'm getting really hot in here."

I hate losing the momentum of the conversation, but I also figure that's code for *I'm overwhelmed*.

So we step out of the steam into the cool area of the changing room, then wrap ourselves in the big fluffy spa robes and head into the relaxation area.

I get us each a glass of wine, both because I want one and because I know that after a massage and a steam, it will go straight to Marcy's head, thus inducing more talking.

We find a corner with three lounge chairs set up in a triangle with a table in the middle, and since the table is topped with a big bowl of fruit, it seems like the perfect place to relax. We lay back, sip our wine, and after a few moments I try coming at it from a different direction. "You wanted the vase so you could pawn it?"

"Yes." Marcy's voice is a squeak.

"So you could run?"

This time she only nods.

"Because he hits you."

And this time, she just looks at her hands.

"It's nothing to be ashamed of," Jamie says. "He's the asshole."

"I think he knows I want to leave. I think that's why he wants to get married."

"You should go to the police," Jamie says. "He can't hurt you like this and get away with it."

Marcy tenses up so immediately it looks painful. "No. He just gets mad. And I get better. And I'm not making excuses, really. But it's not like there's any proof. No doctors. I didn't tell anyone. Nothing."

"What about a counselor? You should talk to someone."

She shakes her head. "I should, I know. But I'm not ready."

I glance at Jamie, who nods almost imperceptibly.

"Do you still want to run?"

Marcy nods her head. "Yes. So much. I want to go home."

"Then run now. I'll give you some cash—no, don't argue. I want to," I say when she starts to protest. "And I can arrange a car to take you wherever you want to go. So tell me, Marcy, where do you want to go? Where would you be safe?"

"I want to go home," she says. "I want to go to Texas."

"Done." I smile at her.

"Just like that?"

"Just like that." I stand up. "But we shouldn't wait around. Let's get you out of here before he gets out of the trade show. Is there anything in your room you have to have?"

She shakes her head. "No. I've got my purse."

"Good. He'll see the stuff and figure you're in the hotel somewhere."

She blinks at me, her eyes wide and trusting. "This is really happening?"

"If you want it to."

"Yes." The relief in her voice cuts through me like a thousand sharp knives. "God, yes."

"Then let's go."

We dress quickly, and as we're walking out of the spa, I call down to the desk, then explain who I am and what I want. And, with typical Stark efficiency, everything is ready when we arrive at the main entrance—an SUV to take Marcy home with two drivers so that they can drive straight through to Dallas, and an envelope with two thousand dollars in cash.

Marcy stares at the SUV like it's Moses's burning bush. And as I look at her, I can't help but think of Damien. Our romance had been whirlwind, too. He had seduced me so thoroughly, sweeping me off my feet, showing me a whole new world. Just like Marcy's romance, it had been hypnotic and wonderful and like something out of a fairy tale.

But dear god, what different endings. Because now Marcy cowers when Jay is near, whereas I open like a flower for Damien.

He scares her, hurts her.

And as for me, there is nothing that I would not trust with Damien. My property, my soul, my heart. My life.

They are his, and I know that he will treat them well.

I reach over and give her a hug. "You're making the right decision. You deserve to be happy, not hurt."

Marcy's lips are pressed together tight, but she nods, and I'm certain she's fighting back tears.

"They'll really take me all the way home?"

"They really will," I say. "Here," I add, handing her my card. "Call me if you need anything. That's my cell on the back. And let us know when you're home."

"I will." She hugs me hard, then throws her arms around Jamie. "Thank you both," she says, her voice raw and breathless. "I'll text you when I get to Dallas."

"Do," I say. Then I give her one last hug and watch as she gets in the back of the SUV. I tip both the drivers ahead of time and tell them to drive straight through. They nod, then get in the car.

And as Jamie and I stand watching, Marcy disappears around the bend in the drive, past the fountain, and out into the Nevada afternoon.

Safe, finally. And that is a very good thing.

Chapter 8

I'm in an exceptional mood when Jamie and I return to the suite after seeing Marcy off in the SUV. Not that having a torrid weekend affair with my husband-lover isn't deliciously satisfying, but there's something about knowing that I really made a difference in Marcy's life that has me flying high.

I part ways with Jamie in the living room of our suite, and she goes off to her bedroom to take a nap. Frankly, I think she's sexting with Ryan, who took advantage of the fact that he was on site to schedule a meeting with the hotel's head of security.

I head into my room, and when I see the box on my bed, my mood goes from spectacular to fantabulous, especially when I open it and see the slinky, sexy dress and matching shoes that Damien has bought for me.

There's a note, too: *Looking forward to seeing you in (and out) of this dress - D*

I grin. I'm looking forward to that myself.

I spend the next hour getting ready. Since Mission Marcy took up my spa time, I have to do my own hair and makeup, but that's okay, and I finish with a good fifteen minutes to spare before I'm supposed to meet Damien in front of the restaurant.

I do a last-minute turn in front of the mirror, and have to admit that he picked out an excellent dress. It's sophisticated, yet comfortable. Sexy, but not slutty. And it's a wrap style, so there is a high slit over my right thigh, which adds an extra level of sultriness.

Then I'm out the door and hurrying to Periscope, a new seafood restaurant that has opened inside the hotel. It's located on the second floor of the hotel just over the reception area and across from the spa. What's intriguing, though, is that the ceiling in the reception area is three stories high. So Periscope is located along two sides of the perimeter, and has viewing screens that allow guests to see what is going on down below. Thus the name.

Damien and I are in a secluded booth right over the main entrance, so our view encompasses the entire lobby and even a bit of the casino. It's an interesting perspective, and makes you feel a little bit godlike, or at least like royalty. As if you are floating on a throne above the little people.

The booth is shaped like a C, and I am seated right next to Damien, my thigh brushing against his.

"I've been looking forward to this for a very long time, Ms. Fairchild," he says.

"Dinner?" I ask innocently.

"You, next to me. Me, touching you."

I lick my lips. "It seems to me that you've touched me plenty over the last few days."

"I've been looking forward to experiencing the reality, not the fantasy. Because as spectacular as the fantasy of you is, the reality is so much better."

I start to shift so that I can face him better, but he closes his hand over my thigh, holding me very firmly in place. "No," he says. "I like you right where you are."

"Do you? Why's that?"

He starts to answer, then stops when the waiter comes with our wine and appetizers. And all the while that Damien is using his right hand to lift the wine and taste it, his left is sliding very cleverly through the slit in my dress—and I am trying very hard to breathe normally. To not tremble in anticipation or longing. To not cry out with need.

But I want to do all those things. I have had the feel of his hands upon my skin so firmly burned in my imagination for the last two days that this new reality is shocking, and all I want to do is close my eyes and enjoy the sensation of his fingertips stroking my bare thigh.

"I think I like reality," I admit as soon as the waiter has gone away.

"Good," he says. "So do I."

As I watch, he dips his finger into the wine, then brushes his fingertip along my lower lip. I taste it, light and fruity, and though I haven't yet had even one sip, I already feel light-headed.

"Are you trying to get me drunk, Mr. Stark?"

"Of course."

I raise a brow. "So you can have your way with me?"

"Do you need to be drunk for that?"

"No," I whisper. "Anytime. Anywhere."

"I'm very glad you feel that way, Ms. Fairchild. Because I'm thinking here, and I'm thinking now."

"I—" I'm about to ask just what exactly he has in mind when his hand stroking lightly up my thigh makes his intent sweetly, perfectly clear.

"Damien."

"Hush. No one will know. No one can see."

He's right, of course. Our booth is secluded. But it's still decadent. Naughty.

And such a delicious turn-on.

"Close your eyes," he says.

I hesitate, but comply. I expect him to continue his fingers' inexorable trek up my thigh, but his hand has stopped just inches from the juncture of my thigh and pelvis. I swallow, hyperaware of the pressure of his fingertips against my skin. I'm wet, and I want to squirm. I want to silently urge him to move higher. To stop this tease.

But, of course, that is the whole point.

Damien will make me suffer—and that will make my ultimate satisfaction that much sweeter.

In the meantime, of course, I am silently cursing him.

"Open," he says, brushing something oily over my mouth. I part my lips, and he feeds me a piece of bread dipped in oil. Then a bit of shrimp cocktail. And then an olive from the antipasto plate. All delicious. All fire to my senses.

None are the touch I truly want.

"Damien."

That's all I say, but I sense the shift in him immediately. I have broken. I have begged.

And now I will get my reward.

That hand that has been so patiently waiting on my thigh, burning a hole in my skin, now slides up, leaving a trail of heat in its wake.

He hasn't touched me yet, but I tremble, the anticipation almost as powerful as the touch that I expect.

And when his fingers do slip over my bare skin, I hear his groan of surprise and satisfaction. "No underwear," he says. "Naughty girl."

"Is that what you like? Bad girls?"

"That depends how bad. Look at me," he says, and I open my eyes. The depth of passion I see in his eyes makes me gasp, as does the finger he slides inside me. My body contracts around him, wanting this. Wanting a hell of a lot more than this, but right now, in this restaurant, this is all I'm going to get. But when he slides another finger in, then teases my clit with his thumb, I have to bite my lower lip so that I don't cry out. And I have to clutch tight to the edge of the table so that I don't grind myself hard against his hand.

"That's it, baby. I want you to come."

I want to protest that we are in a restaurant, but right at the moment, I really don't care. I'm not caring about much, actually, except the way that he is making me feel. That, and trying to be at least a little bit modest. Not screaming would be good, but Christ, the way that the sensations are rising inside me, I'm really not sure that it's possible.

I look away, focusing on the lobby so as to maybe slow this down, maybe make it last, or perhaps get some control so I can keep myself from losing it completely.

And that's when I see her.

Marcy.

Jay is right beside her, and they are heading toward the main doors with their hand luggage.

Marcy looks utterly defeated.

And every ounce of blood and sensation fizzle from my body, leaving me cold and lost and frustrated in all the wrong ways.

"Nikki?"

There is concern in his voice, and I realize that I'm frowning.

"What's wrong?"

"I—" I swallow. I want so badly to say nothing. To pretend like everything is fine and slide back into the fantasy of this night with the Damien who has seduced me.

But I can't. Dammit, I know that I can't. And if I want to help Marcy, I need the man I married.

I reach beneath the table and take his hand, tugging it away from my core even as I slide sideways so that I can look at him directly. And as I do, I feel the warmth of his wedding ring against my palm. And in that moment, I know that I have to tell him. Because no matter what games we may play, when you get right down to it, Damien is my husband, and he will always be there for me.

He will always love me.

I take his hand, and slowly stroke the titanium band. Then I look up into his eyes. "Damien," I say, "I really need your help."

Two minutes later, we are hurrying down the staff staircase to reach the service area behind the reception desk. "Why didn't you tell me this before?"

"I only just learned today. And if I'd told you, then I would have been pulling my husband into the mix. And that meant the fantasy would end. I liked the fantasy," I admit softly. "And I thought I could handle it myself. But I was wrong. I don't know why she came back after I sent her away, but she did. And now I think she's in trouble."

"All right," he says in the kind of confident tone that suggests that nothing can go wrong in his world. "I'll take care of it."

And right then, I am certain that no matter what else happens, Marcy will be okay.

Chapter 9

"What are you going to do now?" I ask as we reach the suite of offices behind the reception desk.

On the walk down, Damien had made two calls. The first to the valet stand, letting them know that if they valued their jobs, they would delay bringing up Mr. Jay Monroe's vehicle until Damien said otherwise.

Then he called Ryan, who'd been in the casino gambling with Jamie. "Everything you can find about this guy," he'd said. "I want it in the next fifteen minutes."

But I have absolutely no clue what he intends to do next.

"I'm willing to help this woman because you believe her," he says. "But, Nikki, I don't know her. I've never met her. And she came back to the hotel of her own free will."

I wince at that, because I cannot imagine why she returned, but I cannot deny the truth of what he says.

"So we're going to get her away from Jay. And we're going to hear her say on her own and without prompting that she wants your help. If she does that, then she has whatever she needs. Fair enough?"

I nod. Because I certainly can't ask more than that. "Except she already tried to leave once, and he must know it. He's never going to let her out of his sight."

"Oh, I think we can work something out. Come on."

The hotel has a private reception lounge just past the main entrance where VIP guests can check in and receive concierge services with an elevated amount of pomp, circumstance, and pampering. We go inside, and I pace while Damien issues a series of instructions. Then he takes my arm and we both step behind the counter where one of the clerks is checking in a new guest. Hidden from the guests' view are a series of monitors, including several showing the driveway and valet stand in front of the hotel. It's a customer-service feature that allows VIP guests to rest inside in comfort, confident that one of the clerks will inform them when the valet pulls up with their car or when their limo has arrived.

I have a feeling Damien has something else in mind.

I watch as Marcy stands by her luggage, her shoulders slumped.

A woman rushes by, bumping into her as she tries to roll an overnight case.

Marcy looks up, startled, as the woman grabs hold of her for balance. Then she pulls away and moves on down the drive.

"Wait," I say. "Can you rewind that?"

"No need," Damien says. "She slipped Marcy a note."

"What's it say?"

"When you get inside, use the ladies' room."

I frown—and I understand why Marcy, who is surreptitiously scanning the note, also looks confused.

"Now this," Damien says, and we watch as one of the uniformed valet chiefs approaches Jay. "It turns out that Jay's car has a flat tire. Very unfortunate timing," he says, and I laugh.

"So Jay and his companion will be invited to enjoy the hospitality in this VIP lounge while the tire is being changed."

We watch as Jay and the valet have a heated conversation—well, heated from Jay's side—and then the valet gestures toward the hotel. "That's our cue," Damien says. "Come on."

"Our cue?" I ask, but I follow him to the back of the room and into the ladies' lounge.

I lean against the wall and raise my eyebrows. "Really?"

He shrugs. "Trust me."

I do. And less than two minutes later, Marcy steps through the door, her face flushed, obviously terrified that Jay is going to catch on.

"Nikki!" Her voice is a low, happy whisper, and she gives me a tight hug. "I'm so sorry. Everything you did for me, and I—"

"What happened?" I ask. "Why did you come back?"

She glances at Damien, then at me.

"Marcy, this is my husband, Damien Stark."

"Oh! Well, thank you, too."

"Nikki tells me she put you on the road to Texas. How did you end up back here?"

"He called," she says. "And he said that if I didn't get my fat ass back right that second—that's a direct quote—he'd kill Chester."

"Chester?" I ask.

"My dog," she says. "He's a rescued greyhound. Sweetest disposition, and such a hard life. And Jay just tossed that out there like—" She swallows and blinks back tears. "I had to come back."

"Of course you did," I say, though I'm secretly wishing that she would have called me. Damien could have easily sent someone to get the dog before Jay got home.

"I need to know if you want to leave again," Damien says. "I can have someone go get your dog. Make sure he's safe, and then get him to you in Texas."

"You'd do that?"

"If it's what you want."

"Yes." She nods, then takes a deep breath. "He—he hits me. I don't want to ever see him again."

Damien looks at her, his expression tender. Then he puts a hand on her shoulder. "Done."

When we follow him back out to the lounge, I can see that Marcy is nervous. But Jay is nowhere to be found.

"Did the car get fixed?" I ask. "Did he leave?"

"He's in one of the offices," Damien says. "Having a chat with Ryan."

"Oh." I nod. "Good."

"Come on," he says to Marcy. "Let's try this again."

This time when her SUV disappears into the lights of the Strip, I don't expect to see her again.

I stand for a moment with Damien's arm around my waist, then I lean against his shoulder. "Thank you."

"My pleasure," he says.

He turns me, then kisses my forehead. "Go on back to your room," he says. "Ryan and I will wrap this up."

"What are you going to do?"

"I'm going to make sure he never bothers that girl again."

I think of Damien, who works out so vigorously, and can still send a tennis ball hurtling over the net at incredible speeds.

And Ryan, with his mixed martial arts background that's only been honed and refined during his years in private security.

I remember around Valentine's Day when someone was threatening Jamie with racy photos. Ryan and Damien had tracked him down and put the fear of god in him. And more than a few bruises on him.

Yeah, I think, they'll handle Jay just fine.

I nod. "Okay," I say.

He brushes my cheek, then leans over to kiss me, soft and

sweet. "I'll see you tomorrow," he promises, and though I am looking forward to being home with him, I can't deny the weight of sadness that settles over me when I realize that I will not be seeing him tonight.

Chapter 10

I knock on Jamie's bedroom door because I don't want to be alone, but there is no answer. I wonder if she's with Ryan, and the thought makes me a little jealous. Because right now I am most definitely not with Damien.

I consider calling the front desk to learn what room my husband is in, but I have a feeling that they have been instructed not to tell me. More than that, since he actually said goodbye, I can't help but believe that our fantasy bubble has firmly shattered, and that he has returned to Los Angeles and our real life.

Which is fine. Great, actually. I love my life, and I want to go home.

I'd just been looking forward to tonight.

With a sigh, I decide to pack up my things. I'll text Jamie and tell her to enjoy the limo on her own. Then I'll take a taxi to the airport and grab the next flight back to LA. At least I'll be able to spend the night with Damien in our bed.

I take a quick shower, then slip on the fluffy hotel robe to wear as I pack.

I check one more time to make sure Jamie didn't come back while I was in the shower, but her room is still abandoned, the bed still made from housekeeping's last visit.

I'm actually typing out the text to Jamie when another one comes in.

It's time to finish what we started—D

I smile, a slow burn of pleasure spreading over my skin.

Yes. It is.

Within sixty seconds, there is a knock at the door to the suite.

Within thirty more, I'm right there answering it.

I start to tease him about not just letting himself in—after all, he owns the hotel—but he destroys my plans by grabbing the sash of my robe and pulling me toward him, then pushing me back against the wall even as he kicks the door closed behind him.

"Well," I say. "Hello."

"No," he says. "No more talking." He unties the sash, then spreads my robe open, exposing me. He steps back, then simply looks at me, and my breath shudders as I wait for his eyes to return to my face. "Beautiful," he says, then presses hard against me, the material from his suit rough against my skin, but his mouth even rougher against my lips.

The kiss is wild. Hard. And with such a dangerous edge that I taste blood and it makes me just a little crazy. I'm so wet, so hot, and the damn robe is too constricting. I need to feel the air against my skin before I burn up, and so I start to shrug it off.

Damien helps, pushing it off, his palms stroking my shoulders as he does and sending ripples of heat coursing through me. He catches the tie, pulling it free of the loops as the robe slides off me to pool on the floor.

He steps back, still saying nothing. Then he slowly raises my arms above my head and uses the sash to tie my wrists together. My breath catches, and I feel the tightening in my cunt, a hot, needy feeling, and I want to beg, but I am not allowed to talk. Yet I want him too badly, and since I cannot use my hands I hook my leg around his hips and urge him closer, then tilt my hips to rub against his.

He's hard, and I arch back, feeling the length of him beneath the smooth material of his slacks. He is still dressed for dinner in a suit and jacket, all perfectly pressed and perfectly presentable. And the fact that I am naked in his arms is making me just a little crazy.

Please.

It's a silent plea, but one he seems to understand, and I am weak with relief when I hear the sound of his zipper. He holds my bound wrists above my head with one hand while he teases my cunt with his other. I keep my leg tight against his hip as he thrusts his fingers hard inside me before finally entering me, hard and fast, his cock filling me. He pounds hard into me, still dressed, still silent, and it is wild and crazy and wonderfully exciting. And when he explodes inside me—when his body shudders and he trembles against me—I feel soft and feminine and deliciously used.

He is breathing hard—so am I. And I curl against him, my bound wrists around his neck, when he scoops me up and takes me into the bedroom. He lays me gently on the spread, then he strips, and I watch as the corporate uniform falls away, revealing a man who was surely sculpted by the gods.

This time, he makes love to me slowly. His mouth teasing me, his cock filling me, his hands stroking me until every bit of me is on fire. I am electrically charged, and when I explode, it is as if I am lightning, shooting across the night sky to crackle and burn, bright and wild and hot.

When the tremors of the orgasm fade, I go limp in his arms, then stretch once he unties me, enjoying every sore muscle, every bruise, every ache. And when I curl back up against him and he hooks his arm around my waist, I not only feel well-fucked, I also feel well-loved.

"What are you thinking?" I ask, when I realize that neither one of us has drifted off. I'm breaking the rules, maybe, but I don't care. I want to hear his voice.

"That it's a shame this is a weekend fling," he says. "That if you were mine I would hold you close every day. I would tell you that you are my breath, my life. That you are the thing that gives my life meaning. That makes me whole."

He brushes a kiss over the curve of my ear. "I'd tell you that I love you, and that I feel you in every beat of my heart and in every breath I take. I bless every sunrise because it marks a new day by your side. And that," he says, "is what I would say if you were mine."

My heart skitters with his words, and I roll over to face him. "I don't know how you do it," I say, "but I love you more each day."

His smile is slow and very sexy, and I sigh when he kisses me softly. Then he looks at the clock. "It's midnight."

"Do you turn into a pumpkin?"

"Best not to find out," he says. "Sleep tight, Ms. Fairchild. You are truly a fantasy made real."

Damien slides out of bed. He pulls on his slacks and shirt, then walks back over and kisses my cheek. "Thank you for a lovely weekend."

And then, before I can even process this new twist, he strides to the door, tugs it open, and disappears.

I roll over to his side of the bed, wanting the warmth from his body and the scent of his skin.

Alone.

Except I'm not. And tomorrow I'll be going home.

Tomorrow, everything I've had in play will be mine for real again.

With a sigh, I pull the sheet up higher and snuggle against Damien's lingering warmth. And as I drift off, I can't help but think that I am a very lucky woman.

The next morning, Jamie is back in her bedroom in the suite. Ryan left on an early morning flight to LA, a fact that Jamie shares with me over a huge room service breakfast of omelets and bacon, waffles and hash browns.

As soon as we've devoured enough food to fuel an entire NFL team, we retreat to our bedrooms to pack, a task we both manage in record time. We each have reason to want to get back home as soon as possible. Jamie back to Ryan. And me back to the man who is both my husband and my friend. My fantasy and my reality.

We don't bother calling a bellman since neither Jamie nor I brought more than a rolling bag. But we do have to call the front desk to let them know that we are ready to leave so that someone can bring a limo around.

Edward is no longer in Vegas, having made the drive back to Los Angeles after dropping us off. But there is no shortage of Starfire limos, and one will soon be whisking us home.

"Unless you'd rather go by helicopter," I say to Jamie, who looks at me like I've lost my mind.

"Um, no. Flying freakish death trap. And loud. Besides. We must drink. And recap." She frowns. "Or just recap. I'm not sure my head can stand more alcohol."

I laugh. "A limo it is."

Ten minutes later, we're wheeling our bags through the lobby and then to the valet stand under the portico. I raise my hand to catch the attention of the valet, but he has already seen me and is signaling our limo to pull up. As soon as it does, he opens the back passenger door for Jamie, who climbs in.

I am about to follow suit when I glance over and see Damien approaching. I smile broadly in greeting.

"Checking out, Ms. Fairchild?"

"I am. Time to go back to the real world."

"I hope your weekend was memorable."

My lips twitch. "Oh, it was. Very much so."

"I wanted to give you this before you left." He hands me a business card. *Damien Stark.* That's all it says. And beneath it is the number from which he has been calling me.

I look up, curious, and see the playfulness behind his eyes.

"If you ever feel the need to call. For any reason, any time of the day or night, Ms. Fairchild. Don't hesitate."

"I won't," I promise. "It's been a very interesting weekend, Mr. Stark," I add with a smile. "I'm very glad you bought me that drink."

He takes my hand, then kisses my palm. "Safe journey," he says, then helps me into the limo.

I slide inside and get settled. And as soon as he closes the door, I sigh.

"Okay," Jamie says. "That was seriously fun."

"It really was," I agree.

"We should totally do it again sometime."

I run my finger along the edge of the card I'm still holding and silently agree. But then I slide the card into my purse and pull out my phone. And as the limo turns onto the Las Vegas Strip, I hit the button to speed dial Damien's usual cellphone.

"Mrs. Stark," he says, without missing a beat. "I think it's time for you to come home."

I smile. "So do I," I say. "I'm on my way."

And then I lean back in my seat and shut my eyes, feeling happy, content, and loved.

J. KENNER (aka Julie Kenner) is the *New York Times, USA Today, Publishers Weekly, Wall Street Journal,* and #1 internationally bestselling author of over seventy novels, novellas, and short stories in a variety of genres.

Though known primarily for her award-winning and internationally bestselling erotic romances (including the Stark and Most Wanted series) that have reached as high as #2 on the *New York Times* bestseller list, Kenner has been writing full-time for over a decade in a variety of genres including paranormal and contemporary romance, "chicklit" suspense, urban fantasy, and paranormal mommy lit.

Kenner has been praised by *Publishers Weekly* as an author with a "flair for dialogue and eccentric characterizations" and by *RT Book Reviews* for having "cornered the market on sinfully attractive, dominant antiheroes and the women who swoon for him." A four-time finalist for Romance Writers of America's prestigious RITA award, Kenner took home the first RITA trophy awarded in the category of erotic romance in 2014 for her novel *Claim Me* (book 2 of her Stark Trilogy).

Her books have sold well over a million copies and are published in over twenty countries.

jkenner.com
Facebook.com/jkennerbooks
@juliekenner.com